No Ocean Deep

Cate Swannell

Yellow Rose Books

Nederland, Texas

ISBN 1-932300-36-8

First Printing 2005

9 8 7 6 5 4 3 2 1

Cover design by Donna Pawlowski and Cate Swannell

Published by:

Yellow Rose Books
PMB 210, 8691 9th Avenue
Port Arthur, Texas 77642-8025

Find us on the World Wide Web at
http://www.regalcrest.biz

Printed in the United States of America

Acknowledgments

Without Jennifer Knight, my editor, this book would have been a whole different, saggier, much less readable animal. She was brutal, but brilliant, and I thank her for it. To Beth Shaw, esteemed beta reader and hater of the word 'just', big thanks, as always. To Siggy and Sue - wildly different creatures, but both keeping me sane nonetheless, thank you. To all the folks at Regal Crest, particularly Lori, Cathy, Della and Donna, many thanks for your patience.

To Cris, for lessons learned and love shared.

You've got to jump off cliffs and
build your wings on the way down.

~ Ray Bradbury

Chapter One

MEPHISTO STALKED ALONG the deck of the Seawolf like the stealthy killer he knew himself to be. The big black cat had the scent of prey in his nostrils and he was intent on seeing the hunt through. He padded down the length of the yacht, delicately picking his way around the deck fittings and coiled sheets until he came to the flat transom at the stern. He sat for a few moments, taking long, deep sniffs of sea air. There it was again. Fish. Not the fish swimming around in the dark depths under the boat. That was a background smell he was well familiar with. No, this was much closer, much stronger, much more tempting.

A low purr began in the back of the big feline's throat and his golden eyes blinked in a way that would have looked sleepy if not for the gently twitching tail that signaled another thought process altogether.

Mephisto came from a long line of ships' cats. He recognized the smell of the ocean on the soft, warm breeze that drifted through the boat's rigging. It was a clear night and the boat was anchored in calm waters beneath a wide, black vista sprinkled with stars. There was no illumination on board, save for the yacht's riding lights, but he didn't need any. Cat sight was a wonderful thing. He sniffed again. Wonderful, too, was a cat's sense of smell.

Gracefully, he meandered around to the port side where a low tapping intrigued him. There he found the yacht's dinghy bumping against the hull as it drifted on the ebbing tide, its tethering rope afloat on the glassy surface. Mephisto's purr deepened as the odor strengthened. Whatever was producing the delicious aroma was in the dinghy.

A bobbing dinghy and a proximate ocean were no obstacle to any self-respecting feline and Mephisto didn't give it a second thought, coiling his back legs and springing into the smaller vessel with barely a sound. He tiptoed around the bits and pieces of equipment in the bottom of the boat, following his nose to a large plastic bucket with a conveniently loose lid. From it emanated the smell of heaven, at least for a cat.

Mephisto stood on his hind legs, front paws worrying away at the lid until it slid off with a satisfying thud. He looked over the edge and discovered the source of the happy smell—fish heads. Lots of lovely, odorous, rank fish heads.

"Riiiiiaaaaaaaaaaaaaoww," purred the cat, stretching out with one paw to try to hook himself a head. His weight was too much for the bucket, however, and it tipped, dowsing the feline and the bottom of the dinghy with a wet, rotting load. Delighted, Mephisto hunched down and rubbed his face against a fish head. A moment later, surrendering to his baser instincts, he rolled onto his back and writhed in the putrid mess, purring loudly.

Oh yes, Mephisto was a happy cat.

THE TWO WOMEN slept peacefully in each other's arms in the luxurious but windowless cabin. Outside, the sun was crawling its way over the horizon, but within the cool darkness the lovers were oblivious.

The taller woman lay on her side, long ebony hair splayed across the pillow. Her shorter companion spooned into her lap, blonde head tucked under her chin. They looked like they had slept together for years, belying the short duration of their relationship. Passion had kept them awake much of the night, and now their sleep was deep and dreamless and contented.

When a four-footed visitor padded into the cabin, leaping silently onto the bed and settling onto a spare corner, they slept on...at least for a while.

But something began to irritate the nasal passages of both women. The dark-haired one stirred first. Her nose twitched once, then twice before sleepy eyes blinked open, revealing brilliant blue orbs visible even in the gloom. "Cadie?" she murmured.

Cadie wriggled slightly against her lover and patted the hands clasped around her stomach. She didn't even bother to open her eyes. "I'm asleep," she mumbled.

"Darling, you know I love you, right?" A whispered question.

"Yes I do," Cadie replied, barely awake enough not to slur her words.

"And you know that I love every single part of you too, right?" the dark-haired woman persisted. "Even the nasty bits that make my eyes water."

Cadie's brain finally connected her lover's rambling conversation with the acrid odor burning into her sinuses. Her eyes flicked open.

"And you know I adore you right? Even though that was the nastiest, smelliest, rankest..."

Cadie reached back and slapped her lover lightly on the thigh. "Not nice, Jo-Jo. Don't blame me for your gas, sweetheart." She snuggled in again, closed her eyes and hoped the aroma would dissipate soon so she could fall back asleep.

"But I didn't," Jo said plaintively.

"Didn't what, love?"

"Fart."

Cadie sighed deeply and turned in her lover's arms, entwining herself around the long body that was now in front of her. She burrowed her face gently into Jo's neck, planting a soft kiss. "It's okay," she whispered.

"No, really," Jo insisted, puzzled by the stink. "I didn't." She lifted her head off the pillow, ignoring the grumbles this provoked from the woman in her arms. In the gloom, she could just make out her cat's silhouette as he cleaned himself contentedly on the corner of the bed.

"Mephyyyyyy," she growled, suspicious of the smug look on the feline's face. She untangled herself from Cadie's warm embrace and sat up, leaning closer to the cat. Her nose left her in no further doubt about the source of the stench and, as her eyes adjusted to the dim light, she could make out unmentionably gross globs of...something disgusting stuck to the black cat's fur.

"You malodorous little bugger," she muttered. "What the hell have you been rolling in?" She crawled closer to the smelly feline. "Get out of here, you bastard," she growled, batting the boycat on the rump. He flicked out a claw which she narrowly avoided before she managed to tip him off the bed. Complaining bitterly, Mephisto stalked from the room, the tall, naked woman following him far enough to close the cabin door behind him.

"Come back to bed," murmured a sleepy voice from the double bunk.

"Hang on, love," Jo replied. "Gotta change the sheet, or we're gonna be living with that pong for days."

She pulled open a cabinet near the berth's tiny head and pulled out a fresh top sheet. Quickly she reached over and snagged the corner of the soiled sheet, grimacing as another wave of noxious fumes hit her in the face. She yanked the linen off the bed, a move which revealed a delectably nude figure curled in its center.

It looked like Cadie hadn't moved a muscle and was

probably deeply asleep again. Bundling the dirty sheet into a ball, Jo stuffed it into a plastic bag then dropped it into the laundry basket. After a quick trip to the head to wash her hands, she threw the new sheet over the bed, and the lovely, naked form of her partner.

My partner, she thought as she clambered back into the bunk, snuggling in behind Cadie again. *That's gonna take a bit of getting used to.* She pulled the smaller woman close once more and kissed the back of her head. *But I like it. A lot.*

THE SUN WAS high over the gently rocking yacht when Cadie woke some time later. She blinked at the sight of her partner's angular profile inches away. She and Jo had shifted in each other's arms as they slept and Cadie was now tucked into the crook of Jo's arm, her leg thrown over the Australian's hips.

Cadie chuckled quietly. *Since when did I become a limpet,* she wondered, allowing her fingers to trace lazy circles on Jo's firm, velvety stomach. Her lover slept on, a contented half-smile on her lips, her eyes twitching beneath their lids as she worked her way through some dreamscape. Cadie found herself mesmerized by the sight. *What are you dreaming of, my love?*

It was hard to believe she'd only known Jo Madison for six weeks. *It feels like I've known her forever,* Cadie thought as she continued to caress her lover's belly. She took a deep breath and reviewed the whirlwind of events that had overtaken her life. *Six weeks ago I was in a long-term relationship with a US senator – a woman I can't even imagine being with now.* She laughed in quiet amazement. *And now I'm on a yacht in the middle of the Great Barrier Reef with someone who...* She groaned softly, closing her eyes against the delicious tingle as the woman in question nuzzled her breast. When she opened her eyes again, she gazed down at Jo, flooded with feeling. *Someone I utterly adore.*

As if meeting and turning each other's lives upside down hadn't been enough, Jo and Cadie had endured a series of dramas that had ended with the tall Australian inheriting a thriving yacht charter company. Cadie felt a pang of sorrow at the memory of Jo's boss and mentor who had succumbed to a heart attack three weeks earlier. Since then they'd juggled business meetings with the demands of tourists who already had bookings with the firm.

It's been great fun, Cadie decided. *But, boy, do we need these few days to ourselves. We'd better make the most of them. Things aren't going to get simpler for us any time soon.* She was pleased to see sleep had smoothed out the tension in her lover's face, taking years off her age. Cadie brushed aside a disobedient lock of black hair and planted a tender kiss on the older woman's temple.

We have so many loose ends to tidy up before life settles down for us, she thought and let herself slide slowly back down into the warm nest of Jo's embrace. A vision of her former partner briefly drifted unbidden across her mind's eye, but she squelched the thought quickly and smiled against Jo's soft, black hair. *Everything will work itself out,* she promised herself.

JO GROANED AND stretched, working out the kinks in her long, lean body as she woke up. She was alone in the bed, though she could still feel Cadie's warmth in the sheets next to her. Jo's nose told her what her lover was up to, reacting as tantalizing cooking smells wafted in from the galley. She rolled out of bed and stood up, reaching for the one-piece swimsuit she had left draped over a chair arm the night before.

"Jo-Jo...breakfast is ready," Cadie called out.

"On my way." Jo stepped into the swimsuit and pulled it up, adding a t-shirt over the top.

She wandered out of the cabin and had to smile at the pretty picture her lover made. Cadie had her shoulder-length hair pulled back in a tiny, loose ponytail as she wandered around the yacht's large galley. She was naked except for one of Jo's loud Hawaiian-style shirts she'd neglected to button up. The effect was rather enchanting.

"Good morning, gorgeous," Cadie said cheerfully, not looking up from her task.

Jo walked around the galley's counter and came up behind her partner. She slid her arms around the smaller woman's waist, and rested her chin on her shoulder. "Hello," she said and inhaled deeply. "Damn, that smells good."

"Well, with a little luck, it will taste pretty good too," said Cadie, as she concentrated on flipping the fried eggs without breaking the yolks. Bacon sizzled in the other corner of the fry-pan and there was French toast next to mushrooms and sausage links. "Think I've made enough?"

"For a small army." Jo squeezed Cadie gently. "But I'm starving so I'm sure I'll do it justice."

This was the first time Cadie had cooked her anything, Jo suddenly realized. In the three weeks since Cadie had left her ex-partner Naomi at Sydney International Airport and returned to the Whitsundays, they had been in perpetual motion. Jo had been juggling two jobs—trying to get a grip on running a thriving business, and performing her duties as skipper of the Seawolf, one of the company's two 50-foot yachts. Cadie had been filling in for Jo's regular crewmembers, Paul and Jenny, who were still on their honeymoon. At the same time, she'd also been trying to maintain her own business as a literary agent. With most of her clients based in the US, that was proving to be a logistical challenge.

Thanks to this schedule, most of their meals had been snatch-and-grab affairs eaten on the run. In the evenings they were usually too tired to do anything other than drop into one of the many restaurants dotted around Airlie Beach and the island resorts. It was a treat to eat a home-cooked meal for a change.

Cadie slid their food onto warmed plates and together they wandered over to the cabin's dining area, sitting down opposite each other across the narrow table.

"You do realize this is about the only thing I can cook, don't you?" Cadie said, suddenly self-conscious about her culinary skills, or lack of them. She glanced up at Jo who was tucking enthusiastically into the hot breakfast.

"Tastes great, hon," Jo replied, concentrating on a crispy strip of bacon that was eluding her fork. She finally managed to skewer it and happily popped it into her mouth. Noticing her companion's silence, she remarked, "So Naomi was the cook in the household, huh?" She tried to imagine the arrogant and obnoxious Republican Senator for Illinois making nice with pots and pans. "Somehow I can't see that."

Cadie didn't meet her eyes, preferring to move her food around on its plate with her fork. "Um, no. She didn't do the cooking. She could barely make herself a cup of coffee, actually. We had a housekeeper. Consuela."

"Ah. Makes sense. You were both busy people." Jo continued to watch Cadie playing with her food. "Sweetheart?" She reached out and captured one of Cadie's hands with her own. "What's wrong?"

Cadie dropped her fork and placed her other hand on top of Jo's, lifting her eyes to meet the concerned blue gaze across from her. "I guess I'm a little embarrassed," she muttered.

"About not doing much cooking?" Jo asked, puzzled.

"Yeah, kind of," Cadie replied. She tried to express what was troubling her. "I guess I'm uncomfortable about the privileged life I've led. Mom and Dad were always well off and when I was growing up we had a cook and a maid. And then, when Naomi climbed up the political ranks—well, we never had to struggle financially and we were busy, so having a housekeeper made sense. I never had to learn how to do more than throw a fried breakfast together." She was disconcerted to find herself blushing.

Jo squeezed her hand reassuringly. "And why is that anything to be embarrassed about, darling? You can't help the circumstances you were born into. And having a busy, successful career is a good thing."

"I know...it's just..." She held Jo's gaze for long seconds, finally smiling at the love and acceptance she saw there. "I think it's left me sorely lacking in some of life's more useful skills."

Jo grinned. "Well, if this is as bad as your cooking gets, then I don't think you're lacking at all," she said. "Don't worry about it, love. There's going to be plenty of opportunity for you to experiment, and I make a very good guinea pig." She resumed eating, then paused for a moment. "Honestly, if anyone should be embarrassed about money, it's me. At least you came by yours honestly." *Now who's feeling insecure, Jo-Jo?*

Cadie studied the dark-haired beauty across the table. She knew Jo had plenty of money in the bank—more than plenty, in fact. And most of it was ill-gotten gains, payment for Jo's previous life as a drug dealer's bodyguard in the Sydney underworld. She also knew that, apart from investing the money wisely in the intervening five years, Jo had barely spent any of it. She'd said guilt stopped her from touching the spoils of her criminal past.

"You know what I think?" Cadie asked.

Clear blue eyes indulged her. "What?"

"I think we should let go of all that stuff. The past, I mean." She slid around the semi-circular couch until she was next to Jo, and hooked her hand around the taller woman's elbow. "You and I have led such bizarre lives, Jo-Jo. Have you noticed that?"

Jo laughed. "You only just work that out, my love?" she teased, ducking her head and claiming a gentle kiss.

Cadie returned it, reveling in the tingling connection between them. "No, I didn't just work that out. But I guess it's only starting to sink in now. Everything's happened so quickly. It feels like one minute I was schmoozing with lobbyists at Naomi's last fundraiser and the next I'm head over heels in love with a beautiful yacht skipper in the middle of the Great Barrier Reef. What's more, she's got a dark and mysterious past, a wicked knack with handguns and, as an added bonus..." Cadie slowed down as she saw the serious, slightly unnerved expression on her lover's face. "As an added bonus," she repeated more quietly, "she's in love with me too."

Jo put her knife and fork down. "Yes, she is." She reached out and brushed a finger along Cadie's jaw-line. "Having second thoughts, Arcadia?" she asked, trying to still the butterflies in her own stomach.

Damn Cadie, when are you going to learn that she's terrified of the effect her past might have on how you feel about her? "Not for even a millisecond, Jossandra," she said, capturing Jo's long fingers and tangling them with her own. "You are the best thing that's ever happened to me."

A hesitant grin creased the Australian's face. "I am?"

"You are," Cadie answered simply.

"C'mere," Jo growled as she wrapped her arms around the younger woman's waist and pulled her closer. For several long, pleasant seconds they explored each other, a gentle wash of passion sweeping away any other concerns. Then their kisses grew deeper and lasted longer. Jo slid her hands inside Cadie's shirt, trailing fingertips along her bare skin. She felt her lover's ribs expand as she inhaled sharply at the touch.

"God, Jo." Cadie gasped, suddenly wishing they were somewhere other than the narrow space between the cabin's table and the hull.

Jo smiled against Cadie's neck, loving her partner's responsiveness to touch. "So tell me, Miss Jones, what would you like to spend today doing?"

"Well, you could ravish me," Cadie said, giggling.

Jo chuckled. "Sounds like a full day." Cadie's barely-clothed body was warm and soft against hers and the thought of spending the next few hours in bed was very tempting. *Very.*

Cadie tilted her head and brushed her mouth over Jo's throat, leaving a trail of goose-bumps. "Tell you what," she murmured between kisses. "Why don't we...finish breakfast ...and then...we can figure out...what to do next..." She made her way along the taller woman's collarbone and Jo threw her head back, savoring each and every touch. Cadie backed off, enjoying the look of quiet arousal on her lover's face. "Your breakfast is getting cold, Jo-Jo," she teased.

"It's about the only thing that is," the dark-haired woman murmured.

Cadie laughed. "Come on, skipper. Let's eat, before we completely lose track of what we're doing."

IT DOESN'T GET any more gorgeous than this, thought Cadie as she stretched out on the cowling of the Seawolf's cabin a few hours later. It was another perfect day in tropical far north Queensland. The sun blazed out of a cloudless blue sky and the yacht bobbed gently on a calm jewel-green ocean. They were anchored on the fringe of a small reef close to the outer edge of the Barrier Reef. If Cadie listened really closely she could hear the muffled roar of the open ocean away to the east. She closed her eyes and inhaled deeply, loving the scents of the sea and exposed coral. *This is perfect.*

On an impulse, Jo had decided on this trip after lunch the day before, when it seemed Cheswick Marine could cope without having her around constantly. Cadie had been knee-deep in an online conversation with one of her stable of authors when Jo got home and suggested they escape for a few days. But she was more than ready to take an extended break.

While Cadie wrapped up her business, Jo had collected the boycat and a couple of boxes of supplies and loaded up the Jeep. Together they'd packed enough clothes for a few days on the water and headed to the company's marina, where the Seawolf waited for them. Jo had picked a small lagoon she called Horsehead Reef that wasn't marked on any of the tourist maps and they'd set sail for this little piece of paradise, reaching it by sunset. A romantic dinner on deck had been topped off with slow dancing to soft music under the moonlight.

Lately, every day is a brand new experience, Cadie thought. It had all felt like... *Like heaven,* she sighed, raising her face to the sun, savoring the warmth and peace. After a few minutes she opened her eyes again, pulled herself into a sitting position, and reached for her laptop, flicking it on and waiting for it to boot. She had some research to do and outstanding emails that needed a reply.

"Awwwwww, shit."

Cadie looked up from the screen as a string of distinctly Australian curses floated up from the stern of the Seawolf. One glance at her lover, who was standing on the flat transom at the very rear of the 50-foot yacht, told her Jo was less than impressed.

"What's up, love?" she asked as Jo hauled on the dinghy's tethering line, pulling it towards her.

"I think I found the source of the Stink from Hell," Jo replied. Sure enough, another wave of the all too familiar stench wafted up from the bottom of the dinghy as she drew it closer. Fish heads didn't smell great at the best of times, but after several hours in the late summer sun, the rotting mess was bordering on the unspeakable.

"Geez, that's awful," she grimaced. "M'gonna have to wash this out." She looked up at Cadie, who was grinning back at her, cross-legged, the small computer balanced on her knees. "You laugh now, but I'm going to need your help to get this thing out of the water," she warned.

"Ewww." Cadie put down the laptop and uncurled, pushing herself to her feet. "I guess that means no snorkeling for a while, huh?" She made her way aft and stepped down onto the transom.

Jo nodded. "Probably not a good idea, no. The bities are gonna come from miles away when they smell this stuff in the water."

"It's okay, sweetheart. I'm sure we'll find other things to do." Cadie leaned in to claim a quick kiss.

"Well, yeah," Jo replied, kissing her back. "There's all that paperwork you needed to catch up on and there's that patch I need to put on the spare mainsail, and..." She yelped as Cadie reached around and slapped her backside playfully. Jo grinned down at a pair of twinkling green eyes. "Or we could snuggle some more."

Cadie reached up and brushed Jo's cheek with her fingertips. "You know, only you and I could even contemplate sex with that smell in our nostrils."

"So let's get it cleaned up." Jo unclipped the boat hook from its holders and swung the six-foot pole out over the dinghy. "First off, we need that," she said as she hooked the handle of the upturned fish bucket, lifting it up and out onto the transom.

"Yuck." Cadie wrinkled her nose.

"Oh yeah." Jo gingerly moved close enough to pick up the bucket and tip its rancid contents over the side. Then she crouched down and rinsed it out with seawater. "Now we need to empty out the dinghy without swamping it. If it fills up with water, it'll be too heavy for us."

"Okay," Cadie said uncertainly, eyeing the long length of the aluminum tender as Jo tugged on the rope, pulling it closer. They both crouched down, each gripping one end of the little vessel.

"Ready?" Cadie nodded. "One. Two. Three!" On three they yanked the dinghy up and onto the edge of the transom, dumping the spoiled fish remains into the ocean. "Good thing the yacht's as big as it is or we'd never be able to do this," Jo muttered, grateful that the transom was wider than the length of the dinghy. "You got it?" she asked.

Cadie braced herself and nodded as Jo tentatively let go of the balancing boat long enough to refill the bucket with seawater. She began sluicing out the bottom as Cadie held it steady.

"Okay, that ought to do it." Jo put down the bucket. Together they slid the dinghy back into the water. "Good job."

The tall woman grinned at her lover, who was watching the activity where Jo had dumped the fish.

"Wow, look at that," Cadie said, pointing. As predicted, fish were coming from all directions, including a couple of long-jawed barracuda with impressive rows of razor-sharp teeth. Mephisto appeared from nowhere and crouched on the edge of the transom in a pose of pure feline alertness, his eyes glistening at the feast swimming just out of reach.

"Careful, Mephy," Cadie warned.

"One of these days he's going to find himself part of the food chain," chuckled Jo, leaning against the rail next to Cadie.

A small reef shark joined the scrum and Cadie watched, fascinated. "I've never seen one of those up close before," she said, admiring the sleek creature's aerodynamic lines and dominant presence. "It's beautiful."

"Sharks are so misrepresented," Jo said, settling her elbows on the rail and leaning her shoulder against Cadie's. "When I first came up here, I was as misinformed as everybody else. Any time I was in the water, I figured every shark I saw was out to get me." Cadie nodded. "But they're doing their thing, trying to survive. Most times, when they do bite, it's because they've misidentified you, or, like now, they're in a feeding frenzy."

The shark below them cut through the pack of smaller fish, seemingly not picky about whether it captured live or dead prey.

"I'm guessing that right now would not be a good time to try and pat him on the nose." Cadie grinned.

"Um, no." Jo glanced at Cadie's smiling face, noting that the tension lines that had been normal for Cadie in the last few weeks of her relationship with Naomi were now completely gone. The result was even lovelier. "Do you have any idea how beautiful you are?" she asked quietly, unsurprised to see a very becoming blush rise on her lover's cheeks.

Eyes close to the color of the ocean below turned to Jo. Cadie cleared her throat self-consciously, her blush making her blonde eyebrows stand out even more against her suntanned skin. "Where did that come from?" she asked, bumping Jo with her shoulder.

Her dark-haired companion shrugged nonchalantly. "Just telling you what I see."

Their relationship was still in its infancy, Cadie knew, and they were learning new things about each other every day. One of the most pleasant surprises had been discovering how romantic her new lover could be. Now that Cadie was no longer her client, and they were free of Naomi's presence, Jo thought nothing of saying exactly what was in her heart. It was in stark contrast to the first few weeks they'd known each other and it was impossibly endearing.

Cadie reached up and gently swept the errant lock of black hair off her lover's face. Then she planted the tenderest of kisses on Jo's cheek, provoking a soft smile from the older woman.

"What was that for?" the skipper asked.

"That was for knowing how to melt my heart, Miss Madison," Cadie whispered close to Jo's ear.

The soft words and warm breath on her skin sent tingles down Jo's spine. *Magic,* she thought as she turned to face Cadie. They kissed, a long, slow exploration that left them both gently enervated.

"Unless you want to spend the rest of the day in bed as well as the morning, we'd better find something else to do." Jo grinned.

"Damn, that sounds tempting," replied Cadie. "But you're probably right." She nibbled on Jo's bottom lip teasingly. "Can we go walk the reef?"

"You bet," the skipper answered. "Maybe we'll find a few things to supplement dinner with. It might work off some of this energy too."

"Don't count on it." Cadie laughed. "I'm enjoying being alone with you when we haven't got 17 other things to think about. I'm going to make the most of it."

Jo laughed. "Easy, tiger," she said. "We've got all weekend."

"I know." Cadie looked up into gorgeous blue eyes and suddenly felt herself wanting to explain something. "The last couple of weeks have been kind of strange, Jo-Jo," she said softly. "Everything happened in such a rush for us, and since then it's been go, go, go." She cupped the angular cheek above her with the palm of her hand. "I want to get to know you all over again. My heart knows you, and God knows my body has more than a half-clue." She grinned up at Jo who matched it with one of her own. "But now I feel the need to talk and talk and talk. Does that make sense?"

Jo nodded, taking Cadie's hand and squeezing it. "I'm sorry. I keep forgetting how different all this is for you," she said softly. "You've changed my life, but yours has been changed, turned upside down and flung to the opposite side of the planet. It must feel very weird for you."

Cadie shook her head slowly, giving her lover a reassuring smile. "Actually, one of the ways I know that I've made the right decision is that I feel completely at home here. Everyone's been very welcoming and being with you has been—is—the most perfect feeling I've ever known."

A charmed smile was her answer. "That's mutual, my love," came the murmured response. For a few long, pleasant seconds they swam in each other's gaze before Jo cleared her throat. "How about a walk on the reef, then dinner?"

"Yes, please."

JO COULDN'T REMEMBER the last time she had felt so contented. Her belly was full, the ocean was calm and tranquil, and her lover was snuggled up against her. The late afternoon sun warmed their backs as she and Cadie wound down from an energetic day spent exploring a small coral atoll.

Jo yawned. She was curled on her right side, resting her head on her hand, her back against the deck cowling in the bow of the Seawolf. Cadie sat cross-legged in front of her, propped against her stomach. Computer in her lap, the younger woman trawled through website after website.

Jo found herself fascinated by a long, thin scar that ran the length of the back of Cadie's upper right arm. She trailed a fingertip down the faint, white line, chuckling when it produced the slightest of shivers from her companion.

"Ah, you've found my one blemish," Cadie said wryly.

Jo leaned forward to kiss the scar. "How did you get this?"

"Ice skating on the lagoon at Tenney Park, when I was a kid," Cadie replied. She turned from the computer and brushed her fingers across Jo's cheek. "I'm guessing that ice and snow haven't figured too much in your life."

"I've never seen snow, actually. We don't exactly get a lot of it here," Jo said, looking up into wide green eyes. "When I was living in Sydney, I sometimes thought about going up into the Snowy Mountains for some skiing, but I never seemed to get around to it. Apart from Tasmania, way down south, that's about the only place to see snow. And the only ice I've seen is in my scotch."

Cadie laughed. "I'm really looking forward to showing you Madison. Wisconsin in winter is going to blow your mind." She hesitated, eyes combing Jo's face. "What's wrong, love?"

Jo sighed. "I think the chances of your government letting me into the US with my criminal record are really, really remote," she said. "It's not like I can hide it, or play it down." She lowered her eyes, suddenly ashamed. "I was what I was. And there's no way they're going to shrug their shoulders and say 'okay, come on in, Miss Ex-Assassin.'"

Cadie slid her fingers under the dark-haired woman's jaw and tilted her chin up, demanding Jo meet her steady green gaze.

"Your record was expunged," she said quietly. "That has to count for something."

Jo shook her head slowly. "No," she corrected. "I was given immunity from prosecution for turning those guys in, but nobody's pretending I never did the things I did. I killed people, Cadie. For a living." She could hear the bitterness in her own voice. "There's no getting away from that, and it's there for all to see. And if something happens, and I re-offend—"

"That's not going to happen," Cadie soothed, cupping Jo's cheek. "We'll figure something out, sweetheart. Perhaps Ken can help us."

Detective Superintendent Ken Harding. Jo smiled at the thought of the big Sydney cop she'd surrendered to all those years ago when the killings had become too much. Harding was, in many ways, a complete caricature—overweight, balding, crude and rough around the edges. But he had a soft spot for her, Jo knew. And he'd come to her rescue a few weeks ago when he'd helped take down Marco di Santo, one of her old Sydney cronies who had shown up seeking a little revenge. *Yeah, maybe old Ken can help,* she thought affectionately.

"It certainly can't hurt to ask him," she said, mustering a smile for Cadie. "Tell me more about—what was it?—Tenney Park? Is it in Madison?"

Cadie grinned. "Yes. It's a lagoon with a big island in the middle and seating for outdoor concerts and picnics and stuff. In winter the lagoon freezes over and the kids go wild."

"And you went a little too wild, huh?"

Color swept Cadie's cheeks. "I was a pretty decent athlete back then." She put the laptop down on the deck and turned towards Jo, leaning her elbow on the supine woman's hip. "Part of that was because of Sebastian."

"Your brother?"

Cadie nodded. "After he died ...well, he had been into everything, y'know? Football, hockey, track..."

"All-American boy, huh?" Jo said, watching the memories of childhood and a now-distant grief cross her partner's face.

"Oh yeah," Cadie answered softly. "Anyway...I kind of took up where he left off, I guess. So playing pick-up games of hockey on Tenney Park lagoon was pretty much my preferred winter activity."

Jo returned her attention to the scar. "Somebody get a little rough with you?"

Cadie snorted. "Nope. I zigged when I should have zagged and slid into a tree branch. Broke my arm in two places."

"Ouch."

"Big time."

Mephisto sauntered across the deck and draped himself over Jo's shoulder and arm. "Don't mind me, boycat," the skipper said dryly. "Feel free to use me as your personal cushion."

"Riaaaaaaaooooooooow."

"Oh, shut up."

Watching her lover stroke the big-boned feline, Cadie felt a peaceful sense of happiness settle over her. However quickly their relationship had snuck up on them both, however drastically their lives had changed, she felt completely blessed to be here with this beautiful woman. *On a yacht. With a cat.* She laughed and scratched Mephisto between his ears, an action which produced one of the most blissful expressions she had ever seen.

She glanced down at her lover, whose half-lidded eyes watched her avidly, a tiny smile gracing the full lips. *Except perhaps for that blissful expression.* "Penny for your thoughts," Cadie said softly.

The tiny smile grew wider. "I love you."

Oh my. Cadie felt a warm ball of...*It's mush, that's what it is,* she thought happily. *When did I start to crave her? The idea of her has always been in my mind, I know that now. Naomi never did fill that need.*

"I love you too," she answered.

They basked in each other for a few more seconds before Jo laughed a low rumble of amusement that sent Mephisto scurrying away. With a glance at the laptop, she remarked, "I thought you said you couldn't connect to the Internet out here."

"I can't," Cadie confirmed. "I downloaded these sites to my hard drive yesterday before we left."

"Ahhh, okay." Jo flicked through a series of hyperlinks, noting that Cadie had been surfing the Australian government's Department of Immigration website. "So what have you been able to figure out about your visa?"

Cadie sighed. She wished she had good news to tell her lover, but so far her research had yielded some pretty depressing results. She changed position to sit cross-legged. "Well," she began, "you know I'm here on a standard, three-month visa, right?"

"Right. And you've got about six weeks to run on that."

"Yes. Turns out I can apply for a three-month extension."

"Okay," Jo said cautiously. "That's a good thing, right?" She pushed herself up off the deck and turned around, sitting with her back against the cowling.

Cadie slid between Jo's knees and leaned back against her

lover's solid frame. "It's a good thing." She sighed contentedly as strong arms encircled her waist and held her close. Warm breath tickled her ear.

"Yes, you are." Jo captured Cadie's lobe gently between her teeth and nibbled it playfully.

Cadie groaned and dropped her head back onto the taller woman's shoulder. "You are so wicked," she murmured, pressing even closer.

"And I'm beginning to think you quite enjoy that," Jo whispered, loving the way Cadie's body responded to her touch.

Cadie's answer was to turn her head slightly so she could claim Jo's wandering lips in a soul-deep kiss that left them both breathless.

"What were we talking about?" Jo asked a few minutes later.

"I have no idea."

The skipper pressed her lips against Cadie's hair and gazed out across the gold-flecked sea. "I want you here permanently," she said quietly. "You can't shuttle between here and the States every few months. It's not fair on you." She smiled as Cadie snuggled closer. "So, as long as you want to be here with me, we should do everything we can to avoid all that hassle. Permanent residency can't be all that hard to get. Immigrants from all over the world settle here every day."

Cadie took a few seconds to let the words sink in. *It's so different from being with Naomi,* she reflected. *I can't remember if she ever told me she loved me just because that's what she was feeling. There was always an ulterior motive with her.* She looked up at her new lover's profile. The setting sun had thrown her face into shadows. There was still enough light to catch the pale blue of her irises, though. *With Jo it's real,* Cadie thought. *There's no pretence, no artifice. She says what's in her heart, not what she thinks I want to hear.*

"I do want to be here with you, Jo-Jo," she said softly. "More than anything in the world. I don't think it's going to be as easy as we want it to be."

A dark brow quirked at her. "I thought I just had to sponsor you," Jo said seriously. "You know, I guarantee to cover whatever debts you might incur in the first couple of years, that sort of thing."

Cadie shook her head. "Not that simple, I'm afraid." She detached herself from Jo's cradling arms and pulled the computer towards her, flicking through the pages she had downloaded until she came to the relevant information. "See, according to this, there's two ways of immigrating to Australia." She lifted the laptop onto her knees, making it easier for Jo to see. "There's a skilled program and there's a family program."

Jo's brow furrowed. "Meaning what?"

"Well, the skilled program means if you are in an occupation that's listed as being crucial to Australia's economy then you have an excellent chance of being accepted."

Jo looked at her. "And is literary agent on the list?"

Cadie shook her head. "Not even anything close, as far as I can see."

"So what about the family program?"

"That's a little more hopeful, but it's still not simple." She clicked through a couple more pages. "Here we go. A spouse or fiancée or de facto can sponsor someone as an immigrant. It doesn't specifically include same-sex couples." She thought about that a moment. "Of course, it doesn't specifically exclude them either. But there are other conditions."

"Like what?"

"For a start, we have to have been together for a minimum of 12 months."

"Ah."

They smiled wistfully at each other.

"Sometimes I have a hard time believing we've only been together a few weeks," Cadie whispered. She reached for Jo, brushing her cheek with the pad of her thumb. "But somehow I don't think the immigration officials are going to buy the 'but we've been together forever in our hearts' line."

Jo sighed. She didn't think she could trust her voice, so she took a moment to rest her forehead against Cadie's.

"There are exceptions," Cadie continued after a few seconds. "We don't have to actually live together for 12 months, but we do have to prove we've been in a committed, sharing relationship for at least that time."

Jo blinked at her from close range. "So that means..." She thought about it some more. "That means, even if you have to keep going back to the States every few months for a while, as long as we can prove that we're still in contact and still together...then, after a year, we will meet the criteria?"

Cadie leaned closer and kissed the soft lips in front of her. "Yes, I think so."

She was rewarded with a stellar grin that transformed the somber mood of the moment. "So what the hell are we worried about?"

JO BALANCED HERSELF on the Seawolf's bowsprit. The narrow railing encompassed the big yacht's pointed nose and, if she shuffled herself out far enough, she could hang out over the cool, clear ocean. She wrapped her legs around the snub end of the rail and let the slightly chilled pre-dawn air settle around her. Away to the east the horizon was beginning to be tinged by pink and a haze of mist from the breakers that crashed against the outer reef diffused the rising sun's rays.

Jo let herself relax into her deep breathing exercises as she watched the slowly spreading colors. It had been quite a while since she had practiced her early morning meditation routine, she realized. What with one thing and another, every minute of sleep had been precious.

She grinned. *And of course there is the fact that Cadie and I can't keep our hands off each other. Can't say I mind too much about that.*

But this morning she had woken before dawn and her body had shown every sign of wanting to be up and about. Cadie had been deeply asleep against her side. Somehow Jo had managed to untangle herself from Cadie's unconscious grasp without waking her and had tiptoed out of the cabin.

Slowly she inhaled and exhaled, listening to each breath. She closed her eyes, reaching out with her other senses to experience the sunrise—the gentle slap of water against the Seawolf's hull, the distant roar of the breakers, the clinking of the rigging against the mast as the breeze disturbed them. She took another deep breath, this time concentrating on the smells of the ocean, tangy and full of life.

She started the meditation techniques, imagining the breeze blowing through her rather than around her. Bit by bit she felt herself relaxing, her consciousness spreading outwards as if her molecules were scattering with the wind. She let herself drift with it, sensing the growing warmth of the sun.

CADIE ROLLED TOWARDS her lover's side of the bed, disappointed to find an empty space in the sheets where Jo's lanky frame should have been.

"Jo-Jo?" she mumbled, pushing herself up and blinking sleepily at the obviously empty cabin. "Where did you go?" The door to the head was open and Jo was clearly not in there. Cadie slumped back into the bedclothes. *She's probably getting a drink of water, or something.* Contented with that solution for the time being, she allowed herself to hover between wakefulness and slumber.

Minutes later, with no sign of her bedmate, Cadie came awake again. This time a little worm of anxiety gnawed in her gut as she let her eyes adjust to the cabin's lack of illumination. She couldn't see much and could hear even less. There was no movement either in the main cabin or up on deck.

Well, it's a boat. It's not like she could go far, she chastised herself. *Unless she fell overboard.* She thought about that for a few seconds and dismissed it. *For God's sake, Arcadia, would you relax?* Impatient with herself she punched her pillow, fluffing it up and thumping back down into it. Then a thought occurred to her. *Maybe she needed some time to herself.*

"In the middle of the night?" she wondered aloud. The small clock on the bedside table mocked her. "Okay, so it's not the middle of the night," she muttered. "But near enough to it, damn it."

Cadie clutched the pillow to her and curled up on her side in the middle of the bed, suddenly feeling irrationally insecure. *Am I crowding her? She's been alone so long, perhaps having me around has been a little too much, too soon.* She gnawed at her bottom lip, giving it some more thought. *She hasn't given any sign that she's unhappy. And I've never yet seen her manage to keep anything like that hidden, so...*

Resolving to get over the insecurity, she rolled out of the bed, reaching for her cutoff denim shorts and a t-shirt. A couple of minutes later she stepped up into the Seawolf's cockpit.

"Oh wow," she murmured, taking in the gentle pinks and oranges that suffused the dawn sky. A warm, furry body bumped around Cadie's calves, weaving back and forth between her legs. "Hello boycat," she said. "How about we find your mom, hey?"

One good thing about staying on a yacht, she reflected. *You don't have to go too far to find somebody.* She quickly spotted Jo and smiled at the precarious position she'd picked to watch the sunrise. As Cadie walked closer she could hear her lover humming in a low monotone. *Meditating,* she realized, surprised. *I swear I learn something new about her every day.*

Rather than disturbing Jo, Cadie soundlessly dropped to the deck and rested her back against the mast. *Might as well enjoy the sunrise as well,* she thought, her eyes firmly on Jo, who was silhouetted against the golden background of the sky.

JO REACHED THE end of her meditation routine and let herself return to consciousness slowly. She blinked a few times, smiling at the sun as it climbed a few degrees up off the horizon.

Mmmmmm, that felt good. I needed that, she thought contentedly as she stretched. Her spine popped and crackled.

She twisted around, swinging her legs over the bowsprit rail and sliding back onto the deck in one smooth movement. The sight that greeted her brought her up short.

Cadie was sound asleep, slumped against the mast, her face turned to the sun, blonde hair framing a blissful expression. Mephisto was draped bonelessly across the woman's lap, also dead to the world.

Jo chuckled, totally enchanted by the scenario. "Well, isn't that the prettiest picture of the morning so far," she murmured, tiptoeing closer. Slowly she lowered herself to the deck, stretching out on her side next to Cadie, resting her head on her hand. With her other hand she reached out and tickled Mephy's belly, making his tail twitch. The fluffy tip brushed across Cadie's thigh and she woke up abruptly.

A pair of blue eyes twinkled at her. "And good morning to you too, sweetheart," Jo said.

Cadie groaned and rubbed the back of her neck, where she'd developed a crick. "I didn't mean to fall asleep," she grumbled.

Jo pushed herself up, placing one hand on either side of Cadie's lap, and ducking her head for a kiss. "Don't worry about it," she said after they had thoroughly greeted each other. "You looked so peaceful, I didn't want to disturb you."

"S'funny," Cadie murmured. "That's exactly what I was thinking when I first came up to find you." She ran her thumb over Jo's lips, tracing the gentle smile she found there. "I missed you. I started to wonder if I was crowding you, and you'd gone off to find some space for yourself." That produced a raised eyebrow. "And then I gave myself a hard time for that, because I know you would have said something if that was the case." She waited for the nod before she continued. "And then I decided to get up and come find you," she concluded.

Jo wrapped her arm around Cadie's waist then rolled onto her back, pulling the smaller woman down on top of her as Mephisto scurried off to find a new place to snooze. "I'm not feeling the least bit crowded, actually," she said as Cadie's compact frame settled against her.

"Does that surprise you?" Cadie asked.

"A little," Jo admitted. "I've never lived with anyone before, so I guess I was expecting it would be something I'd have to get used to. But it really has been easy." She beamed up at her lover.

"So it doesn't drive you nuts that I'm not as tidy as you are?"

Jo laughed. "You're not *un*tidy, love," she reassured. "I'm a bit of a neat freak, is all."

It was Cadie's turn to chuckle. "Have you always been like

that, or is it because you spend so much time on boats?"

Jo thought about that. "I think I've always been like that," she decided. "I can remember, back home, my mother used to joke that my bedroom was 'unnatural.'" She grinned. "I always had to have everything in its place, y'know?" Cadie nodded and smiled back at her. "I like being organized, I think. It's the way my mind works."

Cadie kissed her softly. "I love the way your mind works."

"This is a good thing."

They occupied themselves for a few minutes kissing and nibbling, hands touching and exploring in a slow and gentle reawakening.

"Do you miss them?" Cadie asked finally.

Jo looked where her hands were resting, and squeezed the perfect handfuls gently. "Constantly." She grinned.

"Not *them*, silly." Cadie giggled.

Jo watched the faint blush making its way up her neck. *Gorgeous.* "You are so beautiful," she murmured, smiling as her words deepened the color.

"You are so biased," Cadie demurred.

"Yes I am," the dark-haired woman agreed. "But that doesn't make you any less beautiful."

Cadie's heart melted. "You didn't answer the question," she whispered.

"What question? Oh. Do I miss my parents, you mean?" Jo's gaze drifted from Cadie's face to somewhere over her shoulder.

Cadie watched the emotions flicking across her partner's face. Jo hadn't seen her parents in about 15 years, she knew. Not since she had sneaked away from their farm in the west of New South Wales as a troubled teenager and headed for the temptations of Sydney. They had talked over the phone a few times, but Cadie knew it had been at least a year since their last contact.

Jo sighed. "I guess I do, kind of, yeah. I don't...it's been so long. I don't know who they are any more, and for sure I'm a completely different person from the kid they knew." Her eyes flicked back to Cadie's. "And I guess I feel guilty as well. The longer it goes on, the easier it is to stay away."

Cadie absorbed that, wondering how true that was, or if Jo was avoiding the issue. *I'd like to meet her parents*, she thought. *But unless she's comfortable with the concept, I'm not going to push it.*

Jo had her hands behind her head, eyes closed. "I'd like them to meet you, though," she said suddenly. Cadie smiled quietly, watching the older woman's face carefully. "Maybe with you around, they'll see that I'm not such a waste of time."

Awwwww, Jo-Jo, don't do that to yourself. Cadie pushed Jo's bangs away from her eyes. "Why do you think that's how they see you?" she asked gently.

She watched Jo swallow. Blue eyes blinked repeatedly.

"Because they've never asked me to come home," came the bleak response.

"Oh, Jo-Jo." Cadie leaned closer, wrapping her arms around her soulmate's waist. She felt Jo bury her face against her neck and she planted a soft kiss against the black hair. "I don't think it's about them thinking you're a waste of time, sweetheart," she whispered. "I think, when you ran away, they were hurt and scared and angry because they didn't understand. But I also think they wanted you to have what *you* wanted—which was to be anywhere but the farm."

She felt Jo go very still in her arms. *Softly, softly, Arcadia.* "Maybe staying silent was their way of letting you go. And as time went on, like you said, it got more and more difficult to ask for what *they* really wanted. To see you. To ask you to come home."

Jo sniffled slightly, and wiped her face on Cadie's t-shirt, provoking a smile from her lover. "D-do you want to meet them?" Very quiet.

"I'd like to very much, yes," Cadie answered honestly. "But I understand how difficult that will be for you, sweetheart. And I'm in no hurry."

Jo pulled back a little and Cadie kissed a stray tear from her cheek.

"I, uh...maybe we could start with a phone call?" she asked uncertainly.

Cadie laughed softly, kissing Jo's lips. "Yes, hon. We can do that."

Chapter Two

IT WAS SILENT in the darkened office. A shadowed form slumped in the mahogany leather chair, looking down on the organized chaos of a Washington, DC, winter's evening. Bustling traffic around Union Station was evidence of rush hour; the imposing building glistened against the night sky as cars and people swirled around it. Naomi Silverberg's mind was a long way from the city, though; her mood was dark and uncertain.

The junior Republican Senator for Illinois was deeply depressed, and that was always a dangerous state for her. But she had good cause. Thanks to an ill-thought-out, drunken evening on the tiles at an Australian island resort she had been visiting, Silverberg had been detained and her face splashed all over the Australian media. It hadn't taken long for the good news to filter across the Pacific and she had been recalled to Washington. She had arrived in the States to be greeted by a hostile press, and had soon found herself in a chilly meeting with the GOP's higher echelons.

It was no secret that many Republicans had been waiting for any opportunity to take her down a few notches. Most were slightly to the right of Genghis Khan to begin with and had grudgingly supported her career only when the power of the gay dollar had been pointed out to them. After the Australian debacle, Naomi had been carpeted, keelhauled, and hung out to dry by her masters. It would be a long climb back.

To make matters worse, she had returned without her partner, and that had set tongues wagging. Her long-term relationship with Arcadia had been one of the cornerstones on which her successful political career was built. Naomi had concocted a cover story to explain Cadie's absence to the press, but the time was rapidly approaching for her partner to stop this nonsense and come home.

On Naomi's wall, below the clock, a series of lights blinked into life, and bells began ringing through the building. Behind her, a door opened, admitting a member of her staff. In his early

30s, neat, bespectacled and earnest, Jason Samuels was one half of the senator's public relations team. He and his partner, Toby McIntyre, had been with Naomi in Australia. They had watched her relationship with her partner unravel. It hadn't been that great before the trip, but in the face of the powerful chemistry between Cadie and the yacht skipper they'd come to know, it had been doomed. And since their return to the US they had witnessed the steady splintering of the senator's personality.

Naomi Silverberg had always been an abrasive character, but despite her flaws she had never failed to do her job as a politician. That wasn't the truth any more. She had skipped important meetings and brushed off lobbyists she wouldn't have dreamed of ignoring a few months ago. And lately...well, lately she'd had a gleam in her eye that didn't look quite sane.

Jason shook that last thought away as nonsensical. *She's tired and angry and defensive,* he decided and approached cautiously, casting a glance up at the lights. These indicated a vote in the Senate Chamber, and showed how much time Naomi had to make the quick trip over to the Capitol to cast her vote. The silhouette in the chair hadn't moved.

"Vote's on, Senator," Jason said quietly. "You've got about 10 minutes."

There was no movement from over by the window and he waited. Lately his boss had been hard to predict and he no longer knew when he could push her and when it was best to leave her be. After almost 10 years' working for her, that was unnerving. *She's never been the most affable of people, but since we came back from Australia...* He let that thought go unfinished as he stepped forward and placed a file of documents on the large oak desk.

"Get me the phone number of Cheswick Marine," came a husky voice from behind the high back of the leather chair.

"I'll have it for you when you come back from the Chamber," Jason answered, attempting to steer her toward her obligations.

"Get it now," she growled.

"You don't have time to call now, Senator," he said patiently.

"Get it *now*!" The senator spun her chair around to face him. Sparking brown eyes brooked no argument.

"Yes, ma'am." Jason turned on his heel and walked back out to the aides' room. He closed the door behind him and caught the eye of his partner, who was tucked behind a plain wooden desk in the far corner of the cluttered room. The two men looked disconcertingly alike, though Toby was the slightly taller of the two.

"Problem?" he asked, noting Jason's harried expression.

"She wants the phone number of Jo's yacht charter company," Jason answered, dropping his voice so they couldn't be overheard by the receptionist and the other aides in the room.

"Shit. Now?" Toby glanced down at his watch. "She's never gonna make that goddamn vote, and we'll have the Sergeant-at-Arms on our ass. Again."

"I know," Jason said, quickly flicking through the Rolodex on Toby's desk. "Here it is." He yanked the card from the file as the office door behind them burst open and their stocky boss stalked out.

As she drew level with the two men, she reached out a hand and Jason wordlessly placed the card against her palm. "What am I voting on?" she asked gruffly, tucking the card in her pocket.

"Child Protection Bill," Toby replied.

"Yea or nay?" She straightened her jacket and twisted her skirt slightly, realigning it.

The two men looked at each other.

"You're in favor of it," Jason said dryly.

"Fine," Naomi muttered. Without another word she stepped out into the hallway, joining the steady stream of politicians and aides making for the Capitol.

JO BROKE THE surface and spat the snorkel's mouthpiece out as she trod water between the Seawolf and the small coral reef to her left. Cadie was in front of her, about 20 feet away, face down as she took in the colorful vista below. Jo wasn't sure what had made her stick her head up, but she reached up and flipped the mask off her face as she looked around. There it was again—a distant rumbling that had her blinking up at the unblemished blue sky.

Thunder? She swiveled around to the southwest, where the mainland was just over the horizon. Sure enough, a line of thick black thunderheads was gathering, and if the weather patterns followed their usual course, the storm would soon be rolling towards them. *Oh yeah.*

"Seawolf, Seawolf, this is Shute Harbor Coastguard. Come in." The radio crackled and spat in reaction to a distant bolt of lightning before the voice returned. "Seawolf, Seawolf, this is Shute Harbor. Please respond."

Jo cursed softly and struck out for the short metal ladder hanging over the port side of the yacht. She tossed the snorkel and mask on board before she climbed up, ignoring the large puddles of water she splattered over the deck. Quickly, she ducked down the companionway, flipping the radio handset off its clip.

"Shute Harbor, Shute Harbor, this is Seawolf. Come in."

"That you, Jo-Jo? You had me worried there for a bit."

Jo smiled as she recognized the man's voice. "Yeah, Mike, it's me. Sorry, mate, I was in the water. I bet you're about to tell me there's a storm coming."

"You got it," came the static-distorted response. "And it's supposed to be a beauty, too. They're predicting hail with high winds."

Shit. "Okay, thanks Mike. Is it moving northeast?"

"Yeah. Let us know what you decide to do, eh?"

Jo held down the transmitter button again. "Will do, Shute Harbor. Seawolf out." She replaced the handset and stood, hands on hips for a few seconds, contemplating her options. "Bugger," she muttered as she climbed the steps up to the cockpit.

A glance over her shoulder told her the line of storms had already advanced noticeably. Jo walked to the side, looking for her partner. Cadie had moved closer to the reef, oblivious to the approaching weather.

The skipper cupped her hands around her mouth and called out. "Cadie!"

Immediately the blonde head lifted, turning towards the sound. "Hey!" Cadie answered. "What are you doing up there?" Jo pointed towards the storm front. Cadie followed the line of her hand, eyes widening at the sight of the threatening sky. Straight away, she began swimming back to the yacht. Jo walked over to the ladder and reached down to help her lover up.

"I guess we've got to get moving, huh?" Cadie asked as Jo handed her a towel.

They stood together, drying off in the last of the sunlight.

"Well, we've got a few options," Jo replied. "We could stay put and ride it out. Or we can head out to sea and try to outflank it on the open water. Or we could head for the nearest port."

"Which would be?"

"Hayman." Jo named the northernmost island resort in the Whitsunday group.

"Can we get there in time?" Cadie asked, pulling a pair of cutoff denim shorts up over her swimsuit.

"Probably not, no," Jo said bluntly. "It's still our best plan, though, I think."

Truth be told, the Seawolf was a little too big for two crew members, especially when one of them was as inexperienced as Cadie. Not that Jo doubted the younger woman's abilities.

Cadie had learned a lot in the short weeks since she had first come onboard, plus she was fit and strong for her size. But taking on the open ocean in the middle of a storm in a large, under-crewed yacht was something even Jo thought twice about.

"If we're going to get caught in a storm, I'd rather do it in the Passage than out at sea," she said, watching Cadie's face for her reaction.

"Sounds good to me, skipper," Cadie answered confidently, utterly sure of her partner's judgment. "Hayman it is. And maybe," her green eyes sparkled, "maybe we could even coax dinner out of Mama Rosa."

Jo grinned. Rosa Palmieri was an old friend. She and her family lived and worked at the Hayman Island resort and they had swiftly adopted Cadie as one of their own. Mama Rosa was a traditional Italian cook, prone to producing gargantuan meals that were truly legendary.

"Now that does sound like a plan," Jo said. "God, my mouth is already watering."

Cadie stepped closer, using her towel to brush the last of the water from the taller woman's shoulders.

"Hello, Miss Jones," Jo burred, amazed as always by her visceral response to her partner's proximity.

"Hello," Cadie answered with a quiet smile. She stood up on tiptoe and softly kissed the corner of Jo's mouth. "Oh captain, my captain."

"Oh, shut up," Jo murmured, and for several long, leisurely seconds she put the thought of the oncoming thunderstorm firmly in the back of her mind, preferring to concentrate on the luscious feel of the soft lips on hers. Cadie had wrapped her arms around her neck and Jo lifted her closer as the kiss deepened.

When they broke apart, it was with a mutual sigh.

"Ready to do some sailing?" Jo murmured.

"You bet. What do you need me to do?" Cadie answered as Jo kissed her forehead gently.

"Find the boycat and shut him below decks," the skipper replied. "Last thing we need is him wet and miserable. Then give Shute Harbor a call. And let them know we're heading to Hayman."

Cadie nodded and moved away. "I'll dig out the wet-weather gear as well," she said. "I have a feeling we're going to need it."

"Oh yeah," Jo muttered.

TWENTY MINUTES LATER they were under sail, tacking into a hefty breeze coming off the front of the storm's wall cloud. They had picked their way through the maze of small reefs using the yacht's motor, but once in deep water Jo had hoisted the large mainsail and the smaller foresail and they had pointed towards Hayman Island, due west from them.

Cadie was at the helm, the wind whipping her hair back from her face as they raced towards the oncoming storm front. Jo finished trimming the mainsail, winding hard on the geared winch until she had the rigging taut. There was no rain yet, but she grabbed one of the yellow slickers Cadie had brought up from below and pulled it on, grimacing at the clammy feel of the plastic against her sweaty skin. She picked her way aft to the helm and handed Cadie the other waterproof jacket.

"Thanks," said Cadie, stepping back so Jo could take the wheel. "How long do you think it's going to take us?" she asked, donning the slicker.

Jo glanced down at the gauge that clocked the boat's speed. They were nudging 10 knots, about as fast as they could go without risking the rigging. They listed to starboard by about 20 degrees and so far the yacht was cutting nicely through the moderate chop.

"Probably about another hour," she calculated. "We're lucky we weren't further north or we'd be beating right into the wind. At least we've got a bit of a favorable angle this way." She handed the helm back to Cadie, sliding in behind and wrapping her arms around the smaller woman's waist.

"I know this isn't the best weather in the world," Cadie said. "But I'm really enjoying this." She looked over her shoulder and caught the feral grin on her lover's face. "You are too, aren't you, skipper?"

"Oh yeah," Jo answered happily. "I'm glad you love doing this. I find it pretty hard to imagine not being able to get out here every now and then."

"Well, you don't need to worry about that," Cadie replied. She adjusted their heading a little, pointing them more directly at Hayman, which was now visible on the horizon. They were almost under the lip of the dark wall cloud and the atmosphere was rich with ozone.

"Wow," said Cadie. The clouds were low enough that she felt she could almost reach out and touch them. Behind the leading edge lightning crackled sporadically, illuminating an impenetrable blanket of rain that was fast approaching. But it was the cloud formation immediately overhead that gave Cadie goose-bumps. Ragged tendrils hung down and she could see that there was a slow rotation to their movements. Unconsciously, she gripped the wheel even tighter, grateful for the long arms around her waist and the solid frame behind her.

"You okay?" Jo asked, her breath a welcome warmth against Cadie's ear.

"Yeah, she's bucking a little," Cadie grunted, wrestling the helm as the yacht labored through a bigger than average wave. "Jo, you know I was raised in the Midwest, right?" Cadie flicked her gaze to their course and then back up to the swirling cloud.

"Yeah," the skipper replied, also transfixed by the menacing formation above them.

"You ever heard of Tornado Alley?"

Jo tore her eyes away and looked down at her partner's anxious face. "Sure," she answered.

"Well, in my part of the world, if you see clouds doing that," Cadie pointed at a rotating mass hanging from the bottom of the advancing front, "you move the hell away in the opposite direction."

Jo nodded, understanding her partner's anxiety. "Tornados are a pretty rare thing in this part of the world, love," she explained. "Besides which, we're so far under it now, any direction we go is away from it."

"Oh, thanks," Cadie snorted. "That's reassuring."

Large drops of rain began to splosh onto the deck and both women flipped up the hoods on their wet-weather gear.

"Keep your fingers crossed that we don't get hit by hail," Jo muttered close to Cadie's ear.

"Wonderful."

Jo spotted a bullet of faster-moving air rippling across the water and she scooted past Cadie. "Bear away!" she yelled as she dove for the winches, trying to bleed some air out of the taut sails.

Cadie didn't ask questions, but swung the yacht starboard until the wind was coming from directly behind her. She held the Seawolf steady while Jo reefed the mainsail, reducing the big boat's sail area and lessening the risk of damage to the rigging in the blustery winds.

"Okay!" the skipper shouted, waving.

Cadie leaned her weight against the wheel, fighting the inertia. Slowly the nose turned to port again and the sails refilled. Now the yacht felt more manageable, less inclined to fight Cadie's control as the rain started coming down in sheets.

"How's that?" Jo returned to the helm, wiping water from her face.

"Better," Cadie acknowledged. Focusing firmly on their

final destination, the safe haven of Hayman Island's sheltered marina, she shook the rain out of her eyes.

"We're gonna make it, love," Jo said, blinking happily at her through the downpour.

Cadie couldn't help grinning back. "You're loving every minute of this, aren't you?" she yelled.

"Oh yeah! Woooohooooo!"

NAOMI SLAMMED THE phone down, the sound reverberating around the empty office. It was late and she was alone, the rest of her staff having left for the night. She had tried calling Cheswick Marine but had gotten nothing but a busy signal, a frustrating beginning to her quest to contact her ex-partner.

No. Not my ex-anything, she thought grimly, feeling the burning anger gnawing at her gut. *My partner. My goddamn, lying, cheating, slut of a partner.* For the first few weeks after she'd returned without Cadie, it had been easy for the senator to carry on as usual. But as the time approached for Cadie to come home and the press started to ask difficult questions, Naomi had found it harder and harder to contain her anger.

She pressed her head back against the leather of the chair and stared at the ceiling. *She's not going to get away with humiliating me like this,* Naomi vowed. *Nobody jeopardizes my career and my happiness this way. All I need to do is get her back here, then I can make her see that this is where she belongs. There isn't anything that woman can give her that I can't. She has a nice house, she has her little job...she's the partner of a US senator, for Christ's sake.*

"And there isn't going to be anything that tall bitch can do about it," she muttered. *But first we try the easy way.* She dropped her head again and reached for the phone.

This time, when she redialed, she heard the double ring tones of the Australian phone system, then someone picked up.

"Cheswick Marine," said a cheery female voice with a broad accent.

"This is Senator Naomi Silverberg," Naomi answered. "Please give me a phone number for Arcadia Jones."

There was a pause as the woman on the other end of the phone processed the abrupt request. "I'm sorry, Senator," she finally replied. "Cadie is out on the water at the moment and out of contact."

"Don't give me that crap," Naomi growled. "I've been on that boat. I know that they're never out of contact. They have a cell phone. They have a radio. Now give me the goddamned number."

But Doris Simmons, faithful office manager of Cheswick Marine, was not going to budge—not when it came to company policy, and certainly not when it came to the well-being and happiness of her boss and her boss' partner. "There's nothing I can do, Senator," she insisted, her voice firm and unyielding. "It's not company policy to give out cell phone numbers of our employees. The best I can do is take your number and pass the message on."

Naomi closed her eyes against the rising frustration and fury building in her head. "Fine," she grunted through clenched teeth. "You tell Arcadia to contact me, urgently, in Washington, DC. I'm sure if she thinks hard enough, she will remember the numbers." She crashed the receiver into the cradle, jamming her finger in the process. "Fuck." She sucked the offended digit. "Fuck, fuck, *fuck*!"

Beyond furious, she swept her arm across the desktop, knocking phone, rolodex, diary and pens flying onto the floor.

CADIE PEELED OFF her rain slicker and slumped onto the sofa in the main cabin. Jo took the wet-weather gear from her as she passed into their berth and hung the damp garments in the head to dry out. When she re-emerged, her partner's eyes were closed, her head resting against the back of the sofa.

"You okay, sweetheart?" Jo asked, settling into the seat opposite.

Cadie grinned and lifted her head. "I'm great," she said. "Just pooped. My arms are killing me."

Jo reached out with a long leg, bumping Cadie's knee with her bare foot. "I'm not surprised. You did a whole lot of hard, physical work, my love. This is a big yacht, and you're..."

"I'm what?" Cadie asked sharply, raising a challenging eyebrow. "So small?"

"No," Jo retorted. She dropped onto the floor and slid between Cadie's legs, wrapping her arms around Cadie's waist. "If you'd let me finish, brat, you would've heard me say that you're not used to manhandling something as big as a 50-foot yacht in a thunderstorm." She kissed the tip of Cadie's nose. "The first time I had to do it I strained my rib cartilage. Couldn't lift my arms above my shoulders for a month."

"Wow, really?" Cadie smirked. "I'm impressed with myself." She leaned down and kissed Jo softly. "That was fun. Can we do it again?"

Jo groaned.

"Seawolf, Seawolf, this is Cheswick Marine," crackled the radio.

Jo pushed herself up, surprised to hear Doris' voice on the two-way. "Did we switch off the cell phone?" she asked.

"Yeah, but the storm knocked out the network anyway," Cadie replied.

"Cheswick, this is Seawolf," Jo said into the handset. "What's up, Doris?"

"Trouble, I think, skipper." Cadie walked over and leaned against the taller woman, listening to the conversation. "Senator Silverberg called in wanting to talk to Cadie."

Ah shit, thought Jo, feeling Cadie stiffen against her. She wrapped an arm protectively around her partner's shoulders.

Cadie reached up and took the handset from her. "Did she say what she wanted, Doris?" she asked, her voice quiet and uncertain.

"Hi, Cadie. No, not really. She said it was urgent and that you should call her in Washington."

Cadie didn't seem to know what to say to that, so Jo took the handset back and keyed the transmitter. "Thanks, Doris. You did the right thing. How did you guys survive the storm?" Cadie burrowed deeper into her embrace.

"Oh, no problems. Bit of wind and water, that was about it. How about you?"

"We're fine. Do me a favor and call Mike at the Coastguard? Let him know we made it to Hayman okay."

"Will do. You'll be back here tomorrow, yes?"

"Yeah, some time in the afternoon. Thanks for letting us know, Doris. Seawolf out."

The contact broke and Jo freed up her other hand, wrapping it around Cadie.

"This sucks, Jo-Jo," came a muffled voice.

"I know, love, but it was bound to happen sometime. She was never going to let you go without a fight."

Cadie nodded against her chest. "I know, but why did it have to be this weekend?"

"Do you want to call her back?" Jo asked.

"No, I don't want to call her back, but I guess I don't really have much choice. She said it was urgent."

Jo was supremely skeptical about that. Her brief experience with the obnoxious politician had taught her that Naomi did nothing that wasn't guaranteed to benefit herself. But she also knew Cadie had a lot of loose ends left in the US.

"What time is it in Washington, right now?" she asked.

Cadie glanced at her watch. It was almost five in the afternoon. "Um." She ran a quick mental calculation of time differences. "Coming up to two in the morning."

"So let it go for now," Jo said, smiling as she looked down into a pair of anxious green eyes. "Let's go enjoy an evening with Rosa and the family and then maybe tomorrow morning we can kill two birds with one stone. You can call the senator and I'll call my parents." She blew out a ragged breath at the thought.

"Oh boy," Cadie murmured. "Sounds like the morning from hell." She managed a weak smile.

"All the more reason to keep our strength up with Rosa's cooking," Jo answered, mustering a grin from somewhere.

"God, that sounds wonderful," Cadie groaned. "Let's go."

MAGGIE MADISON STRAIGHTENED up and pushed her hands into the small of her back, wincing as she stretched out locked muscles. She'd been hunched over the flowerbed for the past hour. She adored working in the garden, but her beloved plot was a shadow of its former self, thanks to the drought. The truth was they couldn't spare the water for the flowers, not when there were cattle and sheep dying out on the property. She sighed and brushed a strand of long gray-shot hair away from her face with a gloved hand.

These days she only really had time to spend an hour or so in the garden at the end of the day, and even that wasn't enough to save a lot of her favorites from withering in the dust. Maggie poked at one forlorn specimen with her trowel, loosening up the crumbling soil before adding a handful of fertilizer and a cup of precious water.

It was late in the day, and thankfully the sting of the heat was less now as the sun dipped lower over the modest homestead. She had dinner on the go and was waiting for her husband and the two jackaroos they employed to come home from whatever far-flung paddock they had worked today.

She put the finishing touches on the last of the struggling plants, then pushed herself up off her knees with a groan. "I'm getting too old for this," she murmured, wincing as the arthritis in her left knee made its presence known. Away to the west she could see a dust cloud trailing up from a gap in the trees she knew to be the main track up to the house. "That'll be them," she decided, pulling her gardening gloves off and stuffing them in the back pocket of her jeans.

She walked through the homestead's back door and on into the large, airy kitchen. Before too long she was assembling the evening meal, laying the food out on the wide wooden table in the center of the room. The sound of the truck pulling up out front, followed by boots on the floorboards, told her the men were home.

"Wash up before you come in my kitchen," she called out, hearing the footsteps immediately divert to the two bathrooms in the house. A couple of minutes later her husband walked into the kitchen.

"G'day, darl," said the familiar voice.

Maggie smiled as she turned from the stovetop and accepted his light kiss on the cheek.

"H'lo, love," she replied as she spooned vegetables onto a plate. "How was your day?"

"Pretty bloody grim," he said wearily. He tossed his wide-brimmed felt hat onto the hook on the door and sat down on the nearest chair. "We went out to the No.2 bore up in the back paddock. Had to pull three carcasses out of the trough."

Maggie walked over and slid a plateful of food in front of him. "Ewes?" she asked quietly, noting the dark circles under her husband's gray eyes.

He nodded. "Two lambs orphaned. Damn near dead themselves. But we brought them back. Hughie's gonna hand-rear them 'til they're weaned."

As he spoke, two other men walked into the room. The first was Hughie, a young Aboriginal man in his early 20s. He'd been working for the Madisons since he'd left school at 15 and Maggie was very fond of him. Maybe it was because he was quiet and reliable, or maybe it was that he worked hard and had stuck by her and David even when the drought had bitten deep and they'd had to pay him less. She smiled at the young man and got a shy grin back.

Maggie hadn't made her mind up about the other man yet. Jack Collingwood was lean, tall, and carried a constant scowl. He'd only been with them a few months and her husband seemed to think he was a good worker, but there was something about him that made Maggie's skin crawl. And she suspected that, away from the big house, Jack was less than gentle with his younger coworker.

And if I ever catch him at that, he'll hear about it, she thought as she prepared plates of food for the two men.

"Evening, missus," Jack muttered as he followed Hughie into the room.

"Jack," she acknowledged. "Are you two going to eat with

us tonight?"

"No thanks," he replied. "We want to get those two lambs settled and fed, don't we, Hughie, mate?" He roughly clipped the younger man's shoulder in a playful gesture but Maggie didn't miss the slight wince on Hughie's face.

"All right," she said quietly. She placed covers over the two plates she'd made up for them and handed them over along with two sets of cutlery. "There you go, fellas. Have a good evening."

"Thanks, missus," Jack said gruffly, taking his plate and walking out the back door towards the worker's cottage 50 yards away from the main house.

"Thanks, Miz Maggie," Hughie said quietly, smiling at her as he took the plate from her hands.

"Hang on, Hugh." Maggie touched his arm to stop him leaving. She reached over to the fruit bowl on the table and took out an apple and an orange, placing them in his other hand. "For afters," she said.

A big grin creased his face, and she brushed his cheek gently with her knuckles. "Go on," she said. "Make sure those lambs get enough milk, okay?"

"Yes, missus. No worries." He beamed at her then followed Jack out the back door into the rapidly descending darkness.

"You spoil that boy," growled her husband from his seat at the dining table.

She put together her own dinner and then sat down opposite him. "He works hard, David, and we're his only family. He deserves to be spoiled every now and then. I wish we could do more for him."

David grunted his response, concentrating instead on his food.

Maggie watched him, noting his stooped posture, and the bone weariness that colored every movement and gesture. *He's aged so much over the last couple of years*, she realized. His large, weather-beaten hands still fascinated her, as they always had, and she smiled as an incongruous memory of his hands touching her floated through her consciousness. *Where did that come from?*

"David," she said tentatively.

"Yes?" he responded, not looking up from his dinner plate.

"Next week is Jossandra's birthday." His hands stilled for a couple of seconds and then resumed cutting up his steak. "I was thinking maybe we could send her a card this year."

He swallowed a mouthful of food and glanced up at her. "You do what you want," he muttered, stabbing a baby potato with his fork and shoving it in his mouth.

Maggie sighed. It was always the same with him when it

came to their daughter. He'd never gotten over her abrupt departure, and although he might have forgiven her for leaving them in the dark for so long, the pain of it had cut deep and left many scars. And after the heart attack debilitated him to the point of not being able to run the farm the way he wanted to, she'd found it hard to forgive Jossandra herself.

But she had found a way. *Mothers always do,* she thought. *She's my daughter, and whatever she's become – and God knows, I only have a fleeting idea of what that is and that only because of...well, never mind – I love her, and always will.*

She watched her husband for a while longer.

He loves her too. If he didn't it wouldn't still bother him like it does, 15 years on. I wish there was a way of getting them both to see that there's love there. She chewed on a mouthful, wondering what her wayward daughter was up to these days. *I haven't spoken to her since the Christmas before last,* she realized sadly.

"We could even call her for her birthday," she said wistfully, pushing her food around on the plate.

David dropped his knife and fork noisily onto the now-empty plate and stood slowly. He took the dishes over to the sink and silently began washing them. Maggie watched the hunched shoulders of the man she had loved all her life, aching for him.

"Why would she want to hear from us?" he said so quietly she almost didn't hear it.

Slowly Maggie stood up and carried her plate over to the sink, dropping it into the warm, soapy water and wrapping her arms around her husband's slim waist. She rested her cheek on his shoulder blade, breathing in the dusty, familiar scent of him. "I think we should do it for us, Dave," she replied softly. "She's an adult." At his slight snort, she conceded, "All right, she's always been an adult, even when she was a kid. My point is, if we want to talk to her, we should call her. I'm tired of treading on eggshells around her, wondering if she wants to hear from us or not. *I* want her to hear from us."

The man continued washing the dishes, letting the soapsuds drain off a plate before carefully slotting it into the holder next to the sink. "I need to run into town tomorrow morning," he said gruffly. "Best give me a list of things you want. Won't get a chance to get back in there for a few weeks. Too much to do around here."

Maggie closed her eyes. She knew him well enough to know that he was talking around the conversation because it hurt too much to do anything else. "All right, love," she said, giving him one last squeeze before she moved away. A soapy hand stopped her and she turned back to a pair of gray eyes that gentled as she met them.

"Call her for her birthday," he said. "If I'm here, I'll say g'day too."

She kissed him, loving him all over again.

JO AND CADIE planted goodnight kisses on Rosa, each taking a cheek, before waving and setting off down the hill towards the marina.

"Nice night," Jo murmured as they wandered along, arms wrapped round each other.

"It was wonderful. They're good people. Rosa gave me her recipe for those cannelloni you love so much." Cadie smiled up at the taller woman. "I guess now I *have* to learn to cook."

"Wow." Jo looked surprised and pleased. "Those recipes are like state secrets. She must really like you, sweetheart."

"I really like her," said Cadie. "You know that I don't have a problem being on the other side of the planet from my parents, because I'm with you, but having Rosa and the family be so welcoming has made it a lot easier." She felt Jo's grip tighten slightly.

"I'm asking a lot of you, aren't I?" the skipper asked quietly, as they walked through the resort grounds.

"It's nothing that I don't want to give, Jo-Jo," Cadie replied. "There isn't anywhere I'd rather be."

Wow, thought Jo. *How did I get this lucky?* "You know, there's only one thing that could make this evening even better than it already is," she said.

"Let's see," Cadie pondered. "Would it be chocolate?"

"Nooooo," Jo teased.

"Would it be...a long, cold glass of beer?"

"No, it would not."

Cadie laughed low and knowing, sure of where her lover's mind was at, but enjoying the long and meandering road they were taking to get there. "Well, perhaps you'd rather show me than tell me about it," she said as they stepped onto the wooden jetty that included the Seawolf's berth.

"I could do that," Jo mused. "Of course, there would need to be some audience participation, or it's not going to be the same."

Jo let her go long enough to allow Cadie to walk out onto the yacht's gangplank first, then followed close behind.

"Audience participation, huh?" Cadie said as she stepped down into the cockpit. "Does this mean I get to watch, and then join in?" She backed down the companionway, her eyes naturally sliding down the long length of Jo's body as the taller woman followed her below decks. Cadie took her lover's hand and pulled her into the cabin.

"Looks to me like you'd rather start first," Jo said, grinning as a look of lusty determination settled on Cadie's face, and she began undoing the skipper's shirt buttons.

"Are you complaining?" Cadie slid her hands inside the now open shirt and leaned forward, kissing the soft skin she found between Jo's breasts.

Jo gasped and caught her breath at the explosion of sensation from such a small gesture. "Uh, no, no, I'm not complaining." She reached for Cadie, cupping her cheek and tilting the fair head back. Ducking down, Jo parted her lover's lips with her own, probing gently with the tip of her tongue. The response was immediate and they deepened the kiss, opening each other with tender ease.

Mid-kiss, Jo bent her knees, wrapped her arms around Cadie and lifted her, walking them to the bed and lowering her down into the soft sheets.

"Mmmmmm, is this the audience participation bit?" Cadie sighed as she pulled Jo closer.

"I think it might be," Jo whispered. She pushed Cadie's t-shirt up and, with her mouth, began a sensual assault upon the velvety skin of her stomach, drawing a low, growling response. Cadie raised her hips and Jo took the hint, hooking her fingers under the waistband of her partner's shorts and pulling them down.

Cadie felt a sense of urgency, sudden and overwhelming. She wanted—no, needed—to feel Jo against her skin, intimately, deeply. She groaned again as Jo's tongue trailed lower. *And quickly. Quickly would be good, too.*

It was the end of conscious thought. Jo's touch was unendingly relentless, in the best possible way. The teasing and the wash of sensations became Cadie's total focus and she gave herself up to it.

I want to spend the rest of my life doing this, Jo thought, letting her own body get caught up in the rhythms of the connection between them. *There is nothing better than this.*

"LET'S GET THIS over with," Jo muttered.

She and Cadie were snuggled together in the Seawolf's main cabin's bed and they had woken after... *After a wonderful night,* the skipper thought as they lay tangled in their warm nest. *But now we have to face our respective demons.*

Cadie reached over to the small table on her side of the double bunk and picked up Jo's cell phone. They both looked at the small handset glumly while Cadie turned it over and over in her hand.

"You want to go first?" Cadie murmured.

"Hell, no," Jo snorted. "Do you?"

"Hell, no."

More turning. More staring.

"We could wait until we get home," said Jo hopefully. "We'd save money using the land line."

Cadie looked at her skeptically. "Weak, Jo-Jo." She had a bright idea. "We could make love instead."

Jo laughed. "Oh, you're good. And as tempting as that sounds..." She kissed Cadie softly. Then did it again because it felt so good. "As tempting as that most definitely is, my love, I don't think it's going to do either of us any good to keep putting this off."

Cadie nibbled at the dark-haired woman's neck teasingly. "Damn. I thought I had you there for a minute."

Jo smiled. "You've always got me," she replied, tickling fingertips lightly against Cadie's ribcage, chuckling as the smaller woman squirmed. "Ah-hah, a sensitive spot, huh?" She reached out again to continue the torture but Cadie was too quick for her.

"Oh, no you don't." She wriggled away and then flipped Jo over, straddling her hips and effectively pinning her to the bed. She grabbed the older woman's wrists and pressed them into the pillows. "Tickle me, will ya?" She grinned down at her lover, rubbing noses with Jo.

"I think I like this," Jo said, arching her back and pressing her hips up to meet Cadie's warmth. The sensation tore a gasp from Cadie's lips and Jo laughed wickedly. "Just when you think you're in control," she murmured, then bucked, throwing Cadie off and quickly reversing their position. "You're not."

"Oooooo," purred Cadie, not at all sorry to find herself in a vulnerable position. Jo leaned over her and Cadie liked what she saw in the sparkling blue eyes that were now at very close quarters. There was just one problem. Cadie winced at the sharp pain in her lower back. "Jo-Jo."

"Yes?" Gentle teeth nibbled at her collarbone.

"I'm lying on the phone."

Jo sighed. She had the distinct feeling this particular bout of distraction wasn't going to get them anywhere other than right back looking at that damn phone. She fished around under Cadie's backside until she came up with the offending gadget.

"No getting away from it, is there?" Cadie said quietly.

"I don't think so, love, no." Jo rolled away from her and sat up, resting back against the wall of the cabin.

"Damn." Cadie crawled between the taller woman's legs, taking the phone Jo offered. Nestling against her lover's bulk, she muttered, "Here goes," and punched in the number for Naomi's Washington apartment.

IT WAS 4 O'CLOCK on Sunday afternoon in DC, and the Wizards were taking their usual beating. This time, though, it was at the hands of the Chicago Bulls, a situation that, for once, gave the Senator from Illinois a modicum of pleasure. The Bulls were 11 points up with a quarter to play and Naomi was lounging in her recliner, a bowl of peanuts balanced on one side, a lukewarm beer in her hand.

The luxurious apartment was a mess. Old newspapers, clothes and dirty dishes were dotted about and the senator's chair was surrounded by litter. The maid usually came once a week, but she'd quit over some ridiculous excuse. None of these people knew the meaning of work, Naomi had told her staff.

"Pass the ball, you goddamn moron," she growled, pinging a peanut at the large-screen television on the wall. "Jesus Christ, pass it!"

Naomi was edgy. She had muttered and ranted to herself for most of her waking moments since she had tried to contact Cadie. Most of her day had been spent sitting near the phone, getting ready for her conversation with her wayward partner, going over and over in her mind what she would say. She was disheveled; the casual clothes she wore weren't particularly clean, and there were dark circles under her eyes.

Cadie's going to come back to me, she brooded as the Bulls turned the ball over and gave up an easy lay-up. She drained the last of the warm beer, crumpled the can and dropped it on the floor to the side of the chair. *She's going to come back to me, or, or...*

The truth was, the senator didn't yet have a plan for what she would do if words couldn't persuade her partner to come back home.

But I will come up with something, she thought grimly. *Because nobody walks out on me. And as for that goddamned Australian – nobody takes my property before I'm well and truly finished with it.*

The phone rang.

CADIE BIT HER lip as she waited for the line to connect. Jo had her wrapped up safe and warm and she burrowed in closer, unwilling to brave this phone call alone. Electronic beeps echoed the numbers she had dialed and then there was one ring before the line was picked up.

"Hello?"

Damn, she must have been sitting on the phone, Cadie thought, recoiling from the senator's deep voice. "Hello Naomi," she answered.

"Arcadia." There was an awkward silence while both women waited for the other to start the conversation.

"You asked me to call, urgently," Cadie eventually said, wanting to get this little chat over and done with. "Are you okay?"

The senator snorted. "Of course I'm all right. I just want to know when you're coming home."

Well, straight to the point then, Cadie thought wryly. She knew Jo was close enough to hear Naomi's half of the conversation and she looked up into concerned blue eyes. "I'll be flying back into Madison in about five weeks' time," she said cautiously. "I need to sort out some loose ends. And I still have to go through all that stuff you sent from the Chicago house to Mom and Dad's place."

Stony silence from the other end of the connection.

"Don't let her freak you out," Jo whispered against her right ear, and Cadie snuggled even closer.

"When are you going to stop this nonsense?" came the low growl from Washington. "You can't honestly believe that you have a future with that Australian bitch."

Cadie decided to ignore the insult to her lover, instead opting to push to the heart of the matter. "Leave Jo out of this, Naomi. This has nothing to do with her and everything to do with you and me."

"Bullshit," was the quick-fire response. "We were fine until she interfered."

Cadie sighed. If Naomi was ever going to understand why she had left, it would mean taking some responsibility for the failure of their relationship. But she knew how pig-headed the senator could be. "Naomi, listen to me," she said quietly. "This didn't happen in a vacuum. I was thinking about it before we came to Australia, and the fact is, it was only a matter of time." She let the statement hang out there, giving it a chance to sink into her ex-partner's brain.

"That's not true," Naomi finally said.

"It is true. There was a lot wrong with our relationship

before Jo came along. And you need to understand that I am *not* your partner any more. I'm sorry if that hurts, and I'm sorry if it damages your career. But I can't squeeze myself back into that box you made for me. And I can't change how I feel about Jo, and how I don't feel about you anymore."

Jo felt her lover shaking. It was the first time Cadie had managed to articulate her exact feelings to Naomi and Jo knew it was taking a lot of effort for her to keep herself together. *Hang in there, love,* she projected, squeezing Cadie a little tighter.

Cadie waited for Naomi's response, wondering if any of this was sinking in. What she got was a complete surprise.

"Come home. Please. I need you." The voice was raw and tired and contained a touch of something that Cadie didn't think she'd ever heard before from her former partner.

Jo winced and held her breath. *There's truth buried in there somewhere,* she thought. *But Naomi's just playing the pity card. Let's hope Cadie sees that for what it is.* She closed her eyes and rested her cheek against the fair head.

Helena Jones hadn't raised a fool for a daughter, but she had raised a tender heart. For several long seconds Cadie absorbed the shock of hearing Naomi beg, then her brain kicked back into gear and she took a deep breath. "I'm sorry, Naomi, but I don't believe you. For a long time, you haven't needed me for anything a maid or secretary couldn't do just as well." She paused, wondering at the anger that was welling up in her. "It took me far too long to see that."

She could almost hear Naomi's teeth grinding. "Is that your last word?"

Cadie exhaled a long, slow breath. "Yes, it is."

There was a click, and then a disconnected signal. Cadie dropped the phone from her ear and tilted her head back to look up at Jo. "She hung up on me."

Jo kissed her softly, comfortingly. "Blessing in disguise, sweetheart," she said quietly. "She didn't seem any more reasonable than the last time I saw her."

Cadie was silent. She preferred not to speculate too much on her ex-partner's state of mind. It made her feel distinctly uneasy.

NAOMI REPLACED THE phone's handset slowly and let her gaze wander back to the television, where the Bulls had surrendered their lead and were in the process of folding, like a cheap accordion, in the dying minutes of the game. For some reason it was that, rather than the final words of her partner, which drove a wedge into the widening crack in Naomi's temper.

She picked the phone up and hurled it at the screen, snarling as it bounced impotently off the glass. "How could you lose it, you incompetent *morons*!" she yelled. "How could you..." Frustration clenched and unclenched her fists, rage wanting to escape, but not knowing how. "How could you...how could *she leave me*!" she screamed at the ceiling.

Her throat hurt. Absently soothing it with her hand, she fell into brooding silence, the germ of an idea beginning to form in her mind. She slid out of the chair and dropped to her knees, picking up the scattered pieces of the phone. Once they were reassembled, she dialed Toby and Jason's number. It rang repeatedly. "Come on, come on, goddamn it."

"This is Toby," came a breathless response.

"It's me," Naomi said bluntly. "Who do we know in Immigration?"

Chapter Three

"SO I GUESS it's my turn, huh?" Jo said, reluctant to lay claim to the cell phone lying on the bed between them. For a few seconds, both women let the gentle rocking of the boat soothe them.

"Well, it's still pretty early," Cadie replied, snuggling close. "Maybe you should wait a little while yet."

Jo chuckled. "Honey, for one thing they're an hour ahead of us, so it's after 8 a.m. down there. And Dad will have been out in the paddock for about three hours already." She glanced down at Cadie and kissed her softly. "They'll be up and about, don't worry."

"Okay," Cadie replied. She let her eyes drift closed, and floated in the warm nest created by Jo's arms. Then a thought occurred to her and she was very much awake again. "Jo-Jo? They do know you're gay, right?"

Good question, Jo thought glumly. "We've only ever talked about it once," she replied. "And that wasn't so much a talk as a shouting match." She felt Cadie's arms tighten around her. "I told them after Phil died."

Cadie remembered Jo telling her about the childhood friend who had killed himself when his father found out he was gay.

"Mum fell apart and Dad yelled an awful lot," Jo continued. "And a month later I left home. So...they know I thought I was gay when I was 17. We haven't discussed it since, so who knows what they think now."

Cadie felt the tension in the long body next to hers and slid her hand under Jo's t-shirt. With gentle fingertips she began a soothing pattern of caresses across the firm stomach. The effect was almost immediate. Her lover's eyes closed and the tautness began to bleed away. "So I'm going to come as a bit of a shock, then," she said.

Jo's eyes flew open and focused intently on her. "They take us together or not at all, love."

Cadie smiled, recognizing that stubborn set of the jaw.

"Thank you. But, sweetheart, it might not come to that. My guess is, they're going to be so glad to hear from you that you could show up with a one-legged sewer rat called Ralph and they wouldn't care."

A fierce blue gaze held hers. "I want them to care, Cadie. You're my partner. They're going to accept you and treat you with respect or we're going to be out of there." Growing anxiety and belligerence washed off Jo in waves.

Can't let her call them when she's feeling this uptight, Cadie thought. Quickly, she straddled her lover's hips, placing her hands on the taller woman's shoulders and leaning forward until they were inches apart. "Jo, breathe," she said. "Think about this from their perspective for a moment. How many times have they heard from you in the last 15 years?"

Jo swallowed and tried to concentrate on the calm green eyes in front of her. "Five, maybe six times," she muttered.

"So, basically, they don't really know you at all, right? All they remember is the 17-year-old you were. So, you're starting with a clean slate in many ways. They haven't got a clue what to expect, so take things gently with them. If you call them anticipating a confrontation, chances are you'll get one."

That brought a wry smile from her lover. "Honey and vinegar, huh?"

"Exactly." Cadie kissed the corner of Jo's mouth teasingly. "And the bottom line is, you don't know them any better than they know you. You could be in for a pleasant surprise."

Jo shrugged. "I doubt that, but I guess you're right." She sighed and picked the cell phone up, nervously nibbling at her bottom lip.

"Want me to leave you alone for a bit?" Cadie asked.

"No way," Jo insisted as she keyed through the cell phone's directory listing until she came to the entry for her parents' home number. "I'm going to need cuddling, one way or another."

Moments later, a breathless voice came on the other end of the line. "Hello?"

Jo's throat caught at the familiar tone. "Um, hi, Mum," she said.

There was a pause. "J-Jossandra? Oh, Josie, is that really you?"

"Yeah, Mum, it's me. Did I catch you away from the house?"

"I was down at the cottage changing the bed linen." Her mother's breathing was still rapid. "Your father put up one of those bells on the outside of the house, though, so I can hear the phone."

Cadie watched, fascinated at the play of emotions across her lover's face. Suddenly she could see the teenager in Jo's angular features. *If she was standing up, she'd be shuffling her feet,* she thought with a smile. *I'm glad she got up the courage to do this. She needs more family around her.* She snuggled closer still, happy that Jo trusted her enough to have her present for this difficult conversation.

"So how are things down on the farm, Mum?" Jo asked.

"Oh not so bad, love. Not so bad." Jo could hear her mother dragging one of the wooden kitchen chairs across the floor and her exhalation as she sat down. *I can see that kitchen,* she thought wistfully. *I bet it hasn't changed a bit.*

"The drought's been pretty bad, and money's a bit of worry, but there's nothing new in that."

Jo frowned. *Maybe now I can start helping them with that,* she thought. "How's Dad?" she asked.

Maggie sighed. "He's all right. We're all getting older, though, Josie." She laughed, obviously trying to make light of things. "He hired a new jackaroo a few months ago, and that's taken some of the load off him a bit." She paused, then side-stepped the topic. "Tell me about you. It's been forever since we talked. Are you still up in the islands?"

"Yeah," Jo answered. "Quite a lot's happened lately, actually." She looked down into sparkling green eyes and grinned.

"Oh really? Good things, I hope."

"Some of them very good, yes. Do you remember Ron Cheswick, the guy who owned the charter company?" A murmured assent. "Well, he died about a month ago."

"I'm sorry to hear that, love."

"Yeah, he was a top bloke," Jo said. "Um, the positive news is that he left me the company."

There was a gasp as her mother absorbed that news. "Josie, that's fantastic," she finally responded. "What a great opportunity for you. That must be a dream come true."

"So far, so good," Jo said. "Um, there's something else, too," she ventured. "I've...um, met someone."

In her farmhouse kitchen, Maggie fell silent for a moment, trying to take in everything she had heard during the last few minutes. A phone call from her wandering daughter hard on the heels of her conversation with David the night before was shock enough. But then to get more momentous news out of Jossandra in five minutes than she'd heard from her in five years was making her head reel.

She pushed a silver strand of hair off her face and tried to focus on what her daughter was saying. "You met someone?" *Someone? What does that mean?* Memories of arguments with the rebellious teenage Jo resurfaced and Maggie's heart started pounding. *She's not that kid anymore. Don't let those memories influence your response to her now. She's an adult. Treat her like one, and accept what's coming.* "Someone special, love?"

There was a pause and it occurred to Maggie that the 'someone special' might be in fairly close proximity. "Yes, someone very special." Another pause. "She's right here, actually."

She. Maggie closed her eyes and tried to still the doubts and fears that welled up. *So it wasn't a phase.* She spent half a second wrestling a generation's worth of prejudice. *I don't care,* she decided. She recognized the phone call for what it was—a real chance to get to know her daughter again, in person. Maggie tried to imagine her independent offspring in love with someone. *And she's happy, by the sound of it.*

"That's wonderful, Josie," she finally responded, fighting back the tears. "I'm so happy for you."

"W-would you like to say hello?"

Oh my goodness. "Um...of course, yes, all right," Maggie stammered, wondering if her brain was going to explode from the influx of information.

Cadie's eyes widened and she backed away a little. "You don't think it's a little soon, Jo-Jo? She didn't know I existed until a minute ago."

Jo grinned at her mischievously. "Come on, you'll be fine. She doesn't bite."

Cadie raised a skeptical eyebrow. "And you know this, how?" Taking the phone, she settled back against Jo, hissing, "You are so going to make this up to me." She took a deep breath and summoned up her best campaign manner. "Hello, Mrs. Madison, this is Cadie."

Maggie gasped. "Oh, you're American. I wasn't expecting that," she said, wondering at the gentle, cultured accent of her daughter's—*goodness, what do I call her... friend?,* so different from Jo's rich, low tones. "Heavens, that wasn't very polite of me, was it?"

Cadie laughed, already liking the older woman's open approach. "That's all right, I don't think any of us were expecting this conversation to go quite the way it has," she replied.

"Well, that's certainly true. It's amazing, really. Jo's father and I were saying last night that we were going to call her on her birthday...you do know it's her birthday on Wednesday?"

"I sure do, though she keeps insisting it's no big deal and we should forget about it."

Maggie snorted. "Don't you believe that for a minute. Why, when she was a girl..." Her voice trailed away as she remembered how long ago that was. She cleared her throat. "Anyway. It's good to know that Josie has found someone nice. You sound lovely."

This time it was Cadie's turn to be embarrassed. "Uh, thank you. Please finish what you were going to say. I'd love to hear about Josie's childhood."

Hearing a yelp, Maggie remarked, "Giving you a hard time, is she?"

Cadie giggled. "I don't think I'm supposed to hear her baby stories."

Charmed by the young woman's easy laughter, Maggie said, "Well, suffice to say, she very much anticipated her birthdays when she was little. I'm sure there's a bit of that still inside her. Give her a hug for me on the day, won't you?"

"Oh, I will certainly do that," Cadie answered. "It was so nice to finally say hello to someone I've heard so much about. I'm going to hand you back to Josie. Yow! To Jo. Bye, Mrs. Madison."

"Bye, dear," Maggie said. She felt somewhat dazed and rubbed her hand over her face. She could hear rustling and subdued whispers on the other end of the line.

"Hi, Mum," said Jo a few seconds later.

"Hello, love," Maggie replied. "It sounds like you've found yourself someone very special."

"Oh yes," Jo breathed. "Very special." In a rush, she added, "Look, Mum, we were kind of thinking of coming for a visit. Cadie wants to meet you, and I..." Maggie waited, hearing the catch in her daughter's voice. "I'd like to come home, Mum."

Oh my. She's not sure if she's welcome, Maggie suddenly realized. *As if there was any question of that.* "Yes Josie. You come home any time you want, love, and stay as long as you want. And bring whoever you want." Tears streamed unnoticed down her cheeks. "You're always welcome here. If we haven't made that clear before, let me make it clear now. Come home. Please."

Cadie watched as the emotion of the moment swamped Jo and she struggled to regain her composure. The dark-haired woman's throat was working hard but no sound was coming out. Jo rubbed at her eyes with the back of her hand before Cadie took pity on her and took the phone back again.

With one arm, she held Jo close as she juggled the phone in

the other. "Mrs. Madison? It's me again," she said calmly.

"Did Josie hear what I said?" Maggie replied anxiously.

"Yes, ma'am, she sure did. I think it's overwhelmed her a little bit right now." Cadie gently kissed the dark head. "Um, listen...we were thinking of coming to see you this weekend, maybe for a couple of weeks or so," she continued. "Would that be okay?"

"More than okay," came the quick response. "Wonderful. Josie's father is going to be so pleased."

Finally, Jo got herself back together, wiping her eyes as she gestured for the phone. She had been totally disconcerted by her emotional reaction to her mother's invitation, but it wasn't fair to leave the details to Cadie. She took the phone once more. "Mum? If we can get ourselves to the air strip at Pemble, can someone pick us up?" she asked, aware that her voice sounded raw.

Her mother was silent for a moment. Jo could almost picture her stiffening her shoulders and calming herself the way she always had, by counting slowly. "Of course," she said warmly. "Let us know when, exactly, and one or other of us will be there."

Jo closed her eyes, feeling almost giddy. "Is Dad going to be okay with all this?"

"Don't you worry about your father, Jossandra," Maggie replied firmly. "I'll sort him out right enough. And to be honest, I think he's going to be really chuffed to see you."

"Okay, Mum." Now was not the time to challenge that opinion. *She knows him a lot better than I do,* Jo reminded herself. "I'll give you a call when we have more idea about when we'll get there."

"Rightio, love. Talk to you then." Jo heard her mother clear her throat. "It's been so good to hear your voice, Josie. Thank you for calling."

"I figured it was about time," Jo answered, suddenly very sober. "Look, Mum, I..."

"Shhhhhh, love, don't worry about it now. We're going to have plenty of time to talk, I'm sure. And I can't wait to meet your girl."

Jo caught herself grinning. *My girl. Yeah.*

"Okay, Mum. Bye for now."

Jo hung up the call and dropped her head back against the wall of the cabin in sheer relief. "Wow," she murmured.

Cadie took the opportunity to climb on top of Jo, settling her legs on either side of her lover's long thighs. She sat back on her heels and smiled. "I think I like your mother already. She's got your voice...only with about 20 more years' hard work in it."

Jo thought about that. "She and Dad do the hardest work there is, I reckon. Trying to make a living on the land has never been easy, but this drought makes it a million times harder." She frowned, and Cadie knew there were all kinds of plans and schemes swirling in the dark head.

She gets the cutest little furrow on her brow when she's trying to work out how to get something done.

"You want to help them out, don't you?" she deduced, smiling as Jo raised an eyebrow at her.

"Yeah, I do. We can afford to, I think. Is that okay with you?" Jo reached out and slid her hands around Cadie's hips, pulling the shorter woman down until she was resting on her chest again.

Cadie felt a warm glow spreading through her. *She said 'we'*, she thought giddily. *I don't care about the money—there could be a buck-50 in that account and I could care less. In 12 years, Naomi never once considered asking me what I thought about decisions like this.* She wrapped her arms around her lover's waist and squeezed possessively. "I'm more than okay with that," she replied happily. "Thank you for asking. I'm not used to being included in those sorts of decisions."

"Cadie." Jo tilted her partner's head up with a gentle fingertip under her chin. "I'm not Naomi."

"Thank God," Cadie murmured, provoking a broad grin from her lover.

"Agreed. My point was that you and I are nothing like you and her. I don't ever want us to get to that place where you and Naomi were—not talking, not sharing, not trying anymore. If it ever looks like I'm neglecting you—neglecting us—the way she did, I want you to hit me with something large and blunt."

Cadie looked at her solemnly. "I can do that."

She nuzzled Jo's neck, loving the feel of the taller woman's pulse against her lips. She nibbled a teasing line up to her jaw then trailed the tip of her tongue across the soft skin to Jo's ear.

"God, I love the feel of you," Jo whispered hoarsely. Their faces were barely touching, cheeks brushing together in the finest of contacts. She could feel the rising heat between them, and her hands moved restlessly across the soft skin of Cadie's back. Cadie licked at her earlobe with the delicate tip of her tongue, drawing the sensitive flesh into her mouth. Jo groaned as Cadie bit down gently. "You're making me ache, Arcadia."

"Mmmmmm," Cadie growled. "I like the sound of that."

"I like the sound of you." Jo knew they were in danger of spending yet another morning lazing around in bed, indulging themselves in each other's bodies. *And loving it,* she thought, happily letting the sensations wash through her. It never failed to amaze her that her body reacted so powerfully to Cadie's touch and closeness. "I don't ever want to stop touching you," she murmured. "Or stop being touched by you."

Cadie responded by moving even closer. They were belly to belly, breast to breast, soul to soul. "Josie, huh?" she teased, her mouth against Jo's ear. "Does that make me your pussycat?"

Jo smiled, burying her face in the soft, fair hair. "You're certainly purring loudly enough." She felt rather than heard Cadie's laughter, and found a way to slide her right hand between their bodies. Her fingertips found the soft, wet spot they were searching for and Cadie gasped, shuddering against her.

"Oh God, Jo," Cadie groaned. "If I wasn't purring before, I certainly...am...n-now."

Any ability Cadie had to form coherent sentences drifted away on a current of pure sensuality as Jo's fingers teased and circled, flicked and stroked. She pressed down with her hips, undulating against Jo's hand and wrist. Passion had risen fast, its speed and strength leaving her speechless.

Jo avidly watched the look of utter skin-hunger on her lover's flushed face. Cadie was almost in her own world, moving as her body demanded, using Jo. *In the best possible meaning of the word,* Jo thought. She felt liquidly lustful herself, desire sitting low in her belly. The combination of Cadie's heat and wetness, the pressure of her own hand wedged between them both, and her lover's movements and sounds was delicious. Not enough to push her over the edge but...she was surprised to hear a groan that wasn't Cadie's, and recognized her own voice, ragged with craving.

She wrapped her free arm around Cadie's hips, pulling her closer as she arched up, counter-pointing the smaller woman's movements. "Tell me what you want, darling," she urged.

Cadie responded by pressing herself upright, back arched, hands splayed across Jo's chest. "You...know...what I want."

Jo smiled. "Yes I do." She waited, watching Cadie's rhythms, feeling her desire's ebb and flow. And then, as anticipation hovered on the brink of frustration, she gave Cadie what she needed, pressing deep, filling and stroking.

Cadie threw her head back, Jo's name spilling from her lips, over and over. Movements once smooth and purposeful were suddenly mindless and reactive. Jo thrust and coaxed, nuzzled and soothed, continuing to touch and tease Cadie's trigger points.

So beautiful, so sexy, she thought when the younger woman finally slumped forward, fair hair spilling across Jo's breasts as the energy drained out of her.

"Oh. My. God."

Jo chuckled. She left her right hand where it was, relishing the aftershocks and quivers that surrounded her fingers. She brought her left hand to Cadie's head, tenderly pushing perspiration-dampened locks away from her face. "You okay, angel?" she whispered.

"Oh. My. God." Cadie felt like butter. Soft, pliable butter. She couldn't have moved if her life depended on it. "I wonder if anyone will notice if we spend the rest of our lives in this position," she muttered, kissing the damp skin above Jo's heart.

"You're going to make a hell of a lump under my shirt," Jo mused. "Sailing's going to be interesting. I'll have to remember which hand to grind with, and which hand to, um..." She wiggled the fingers of her right hand playfully, grinning when Cadie twitched spasmodically. "Wouldn't want to get them the wrong way round."

Cadie laughed weakly, her fingers scratching lightly across Jo's sides. "You are the most awesome lover, Jossandra," she murmured. *I feel like I've been turned inside out.*

"You are the most awesome inspiration," Jo replied, kissing the top of the fair head.

Cadie mustered the strength to lift her head and she gazed up into hooded, blue eyes. "Are *you* okay?" she asked, reading barely held back arousal in her lover's expression.

Jo exhaled slowly. "I'm about seven steps beyond okay and one step short of nuclear fission," she explained, just failing to stop the broad, sensual grin. "I think if you touched me right now, I'd probably explode."

"Oooo, I think I'm intrigued," Cadie drawled. "I guess this means I have to let you go, huh?" She squeezed Jo's fingers.

The movement sent tingles through Jo she couldn't even begin to describe. "Keep doing that, woman, and neither of us will have to move a muscle," she growled.

"Well, maybe one or two, sweetheart."

Chapter Four

JO WALKED THE length of Seawolf's huge boom, pulling the sail cover tight around the furled mainsail and clipping it shut buckle by buckle. They were anchored at one of Cheswick Marine's buoys in Shute Harbor, having just arrived from Hayman Island. Cadie was below decks cleaning out the main cabin and galley while Jo made sure everything was shipshape up here. Seawolf was due out again the next morning with a boatload of tourists and it wouldn't do to have the big boat looking less than pristine.

It was mid-afternoon. Jo had meant to be back here a little earlier than this but somehow the morning had drifted away on a tide of lovemaking and pillow talk. She grinned to herself. *Can't think of a better reason to be late.*

She took in the arresting scenery of the deep-water harbor and sighed contentedly. Shute was surrounded by high, lush green hills that came right down to the water, which was a dark, rich blue. Yachts and motor cruisers were dotted across the expanse of the port, leaving only the main channel out to the islands free of anchorages. Summer, traditionally the off-season in oppressively hot far north Queensland, was coming to a close and the place was starting to prepare itself for the main thrust of the tourist season, when the number of boats in the harbor would close to double.

It had been a good off-season for Cheswick Marine. Both boats, the Seawolf and the Beowulf, had operated almost constantly across the summer, with only a few quiet weeks. *And they'd come at convenient moments,* Jo thought. The company was in relatively good shape, for which she silently thanked Ron Cheswick. But in another month or so, things would start to get interesting. *If we're going to get away for a break, now's the time.* She neatly coiled a rope around itself as she contemplated the next couple of months. *It's going to get busy here just at the time when Cadie has to go back to the States,* she realized, and frowned. *Damn it.*

She was shaken out of her reverie by sounds of movement from below. She glanced aft in time to see Cadie emerge from the companionway with a large plastic bag in tow.

"How did we manage to collect so much garbage in three days?" Cadie griped as she tugged at the bag.

Jo wandered back to give her a hand, dropping casually down into the cockpit. "Beats me, sweetheart," she said with a shrug. "I didn't think we'd done anything except swim, eat and f—" She was silenced by Cadie's hand across her mouth and a pair of sparkling green eyes that widened in mock outrage. Jo grinned against the warm skin pressed to her lips. But the hand soon withdrew when she flicked her tongue out and licked it.

"Ewww, gross," Cadie yelped. She wiped the hand on her shorts and then leaned in for a kiss. "You gonna give me a hand with this?"

"You bet." Together they hefted the bag into the dinghy, ready for the short trip to the Cheswick Marine jetty and office. "Any more down there?" Jo asked.

"Nope," Cadie replied. "Just our bags and the boycat."

Jo raised an eyebrow. "How'd you go getting him in the cage?"

Cadie put her hands on her hips and grinned up at Jo. "Funnily enough, he let me pick him up and put him in. Purring like a fool." She laughed at the look of astonishment on the tall skipper's face. Jo had suffered many a wound trying to get the boycat to do what he didn't want to do. "Face it, Jo-Jo, he prefers blondes."

Her dark-haired lover snorted. "Can't blame him for that. God knows, I can't say no to you either."

"Oh, hush."

They smiled happily at one another for a few long seconds, each knowing exactly what the other was thinking. Their mutual absorption was broken by a shout from the jetty.

"Hey, skipper!"

They turned towards the sound and saw a familiar tall man waving at them from outside the Cheswick office.

"They're back!" Cadie said with delight, recognizing the man as Seawolf's regular crewman, Paul. A moment later Paul's new wife, Jenny, stepped out of the office and waved at them.

Jo grinned and waved back. "Come on, let's go say hello," she said, and they both scooted down the companionway into the main cabin, making a beeline for the double berth where their bags were waiting for them.

"Does Paul know yet?" Cadie asked, as she stuffed clothes into her bag. Paul had taken the exam for his Master's ticket a couple of days after the wedding, before he and Jenny had disappeared on their honeymoon. He'd passed with flying colors and Jo had the official piece of paper sitting on her desk.

"Nope," the skipper smirked. "I can't wait to tell him. It's gonna make it much easier for us to get away, too, knowing I can leave him with the Seawolf."

Cadie nodded. "Little does he know he's gonna be skippering that bunch of Japanese around from tomorrow morning." She chuckled. "Are you going to go out with them for a couple of days?"

"Probably," Jo answered. She double-checked the cabin, making sure they'd picked up all their personal belongings. "Just until Josh is settled in and Paul's ready to go it alone." Josh was Jo's young next-door neighbor who had come on board as an employee of Cheswick Marine. She was hoping the teenager would bond with Paul and Jenny to form a good, working crew.

"I'm glad he's part of the family now," Cadie said.

"Me too," Jo muttered. "We ready to go?"

Cadie zipped up the sports bag and patted it. "You bet."

Jo picked up the cat cage, trying to ignore the plaintive meowing from the big black cat inside. She was stopped by a hand on her elbow and turned to face her smiling partner.

"Thank you for a lovely few days, Jo-Jo," Cadie said quietly, letting her eyes convey the depth of her feeling for the tall skipper.

Jo felt herself melting from the inside. "We needed it, huh?" she answered, brushing Cadie's cheek with tender fingertips.

"Riaaaaaaowwwwwwwwwwwwwww."

They both laughed.

"Come on, gorgeous," Jo chuckled. "Let's get the monster home."

CADIE WAS BEGINNING to think this was the longest week in history. *Though perhaps it's running a close second to the week after Naomi got arrested on Hamilton Island,* she thought grimly as she tossed a sheaf of papers on to the desk. It was Friday afternoon, they'd arranged for Paul and Jenny to house-sit, and she and Jo were supposed to be leaving for Jo's parents' place the next morning. But they were nowhere near ready.

The week had started out wonderfully, with those three peaceful days to themselves, but it had been all downhill since then. Jo had gone out with Paul and Jenny on the Seawolf but she'd ended up skippering the Beowulf for the last few days of its tour when Frank, Cheswick's third skipper, went down with the flu. Cadie hadn't seen her since Tuesday morning, and though they had talked every night by phone, they were both beyond grumpy thanks to the enforced separation.

How the hell are we gonna survive when I have to go back to Madison, if we can't handle three days apart? Cadie wondered glumly.

To cap off the lousy week, one of Cadie's stable of authors was enmeshed in a contract dispute with her publisher and had been sending plaintive emails to Cadie all week. Normally Cadie would have been acting as a buffer between the two parties, but being half a world away was making it almost impossible for her to work effectively. It was fast becoming obvious to her that, in the long term, she would not be able to serve her clients' interests living Down Under. Cadie sighed and pulled her reading glasses off, rubbing the bridge of her nose. She had a headache she wouldn't wish on her worst enemy and her neck and shoulders were stiff from a day spent hunched over her laptop. She kept meaning to transfer all her stuff over to Jo's desktop, but so far she hadn't had a chance.

She tossed her glasses onto the desk and uncurled herself, twisting and stretching in her chair. From where she sat, she had a panoramic view of Whitsunday Passage. *She's out there somewhere. Probably having a bunch more fun than me.*

Cadie started when Mephisto leapt up onto the desk in front of her. The big black cat settled his haunches between her and the laptop's keyboard, his head at eye level. Looking like a sleepy-eyed sphinx, he gazed at her implacably, purring gently. She smiled at him wanly.

"Hello, boycat," she murmured, reaching up to scratch under his chin. He stretched his neck, giving her more access, and closed his eyes blissfully, the purr intensifying. Cadie chuckled. "You like that, don't you, huh? When do you think your mom is gonna be home?" She leaned in to the cat and he reciprocated, bumping her nose with his forehead.

Jo had thought she'd be home for lunch, but obviously something had slowed the Beowulf down. Cadie glanced at her watch. *Just after five.*

"You want some food, Mephy?" she asked. In reply, the cat meeped at her, stood up then stepped forward, placing his front paws on her chest. "Oh I see. You want a cuddle and then some food, huh?" She pulled him forward and he settled on her shoulder, curling and uncurling his claws into the fabric of her shirt. For a few minutes, Cadie enjoyed the contact, burying her face in the soft fur at his neck while the feline purred on.

God, what is up with me? she wondered. "What do you think,

Mephy, am I going nuts?" she said aloud. The cat nudged her with his nose. "Maybe it's because this is the longest we've been apart since I came back." She shuffled the papers on the desk with her left hand. "Or maybe it's that everything I've touched this week has turned to horse poop." She frowned, turning her mind back to the logistical nightmare her agency was becoming.

Troublesome authors weren't the only problem Cadie was having as she tried to operate her business from a distance. Cash was an issue.

She had redirected all her payments to her parents' address in Madison and her mother was doing a good job of getting that money into the business' account, but it wasn't easy to transfer it to Australia without Cadie being there to sign the necessary bank forms. For the time being, Jo was supporting them both, and although the skipper had absolutely no problem with that, Cadie most certainly did.

"That's it, Mephy," she muttered. "That's another thing that's bugging me." Starting her own business hadn't been about financial independence in the beginning. It had been a way to establish and maintain her own identity separate from the very public persona of her then-partner. But as the business had grown and become successful, Cadie had come to appreciate being able to have complete control of her own money. It gave her the chance to crawl out from under Naomi's imposing shadow once in a while. And now...

She scratched Mephisto's back absentmindedly. She had a decision to make and its consequences weighed on her. Closing the agency and placing her clients elsewhere was almost certainly the right thing to do. But where would that leave her? Dependent on Jo? *I know she can more than afford to support me, and she keeps saying what's hers is mine but... But that's easy to say from her position.* She sighed again. "I hate not being able to pay my share, and it's as simple as that," she told the cat. She felt a twinge of cramp low in her belly and grimaced. "Yeah, and that's not helping either." Mephisto stuck a wet nose in her ear and snuffled, almost provoking a smile. "Thank you. Come on, let's get you fed."

The cat picked up on the magic word and pushed himself up and off Cadie's shoulder, making her wince as his back claws dug in a little. She stood and followed him into the kitchen, where she found him circling his empty dish, meowing.

"Okay, okay." She plucked the bag of kibble from the top of the fridge and poured a good-sized handful into the bowl, watching as the feline tucked in with relish. "Go slow, boycat. You're gonna give yourself indigestion." Cadie lifted the bag back into its spot and wandered back to the desk just as the phone rang.

It was Naomi, she knew. Not that her ex-partner ever said anything, but the cold, heavy silence on the other end of the line was very, very familiar. Several times a day since their conversation on Monday, Cadie had answered the phone only to find a chilling presence and not much else.

So far, she hadn't told Jo about the calls, preferring to have that conversation face to face. *And changing the number isn't going to help. If Naomi found this one, she'll find the new one. Damn her.*

Cadie lifted her head at the sound of car tires on gravel. *Finally!* As the front door opened, revealing a tall, dark and very welcome figure, the phone rang again. *Damn it, Naomi, not now.*

Cadie snatched the phone from the cradle. "What the hell is it you want, Naomi?" she yelled into the mouthpiece.

"Uh, Miss Jones, it's John Jacobs," came the hesitant reply.

Cadie slapped her hand over her mouth in consternation. "God, I'm sorry, John. I thought you were someone else." She felt herself flush with embarrassment as she caught stormy blue eyes looking at her. "Jo's just walked in. Hang on. I'll get her for you."

Naomi's been calling here? Why the hell didn't she tell me? Jo took the phone from Cadie, trying not to let her irritation show. "Hello, John," she said. "What can I do for you?"

Cadie covered her eyes with her palms, feeling the heat from her blush. *Damn it. Damn you, Naomi.* She rubbed her face distractedly and moved into the kitchen, deciding to make a start on dinner while Jo talked with her attorney. Forcefully, she diced a couple of tomatoes, taking out some of her frustration on the fruit.

It wasn't long before Jo joined her. Placing her hands casually on top of the counter, she remarked, "Naomi's been calling, huh?"

"And hello to you, too," Cadie said testily. She tossed the tortured tomatoes into a salad bowl and reached for the small lettuce she'd pulled out of the fridge. "I don't know for sure if it's her," she conceded. "A few times a day since Monday, I've picked it up but there's been silence."

"Maybe it's just a wrong number," Jo said, her temper frayed from the mechanical hassles and ungrateful tourists she'd been dealing with all day. "Or maybe it's aimed at me."

"Oh, please," Cadie retorted, chopping the lettuce viciously, an action not lost on her partner.

"Given my history? I can think of about 20 people who'd

make scare calls," said Jo sarcastically. "Why didn't you tell me?"

"I didn't tell you because you were in the middle of the ocean and could do precisely nothing about it. Believe it or not, I thought you might appreciate not being bugged about something like that." Slice, dice, hack.

Jo watched the massacre of the salad continue. *What's got her so fired up? She looks like she's had as bad a week as I have. And I bet I'm not helping.* "Um, what say we go out for dinner?" she suggested tentatively.

Cadie groaned and dropped the knife onto the chopping board. *More money she'd be spending on me.* Part of her knew she was making more of it than she should, but her foul mood was in full swing now. Besides, she had already made a perfectly decent salad.

"Now you tell me," she replied, shoving the chopping board aside.

Jo rubbed her eyes tiredly. "I don't have the energy to cook tonight," she muttered, wishing Cadie would quit arguing so they could get on with it.

"I'll cook, all right?" Cadie retorted, exasperated. "Believe it or not, I can throw a meal together."

Jo put her hands on her hips and glared at her partner, her last nerve in danger of being worn away. "I never suggested you couldn't, Cadie. I thought it might be easier for both of us if we went out."

"Well, it wouldn't be easier for me."

"Fine." Jo backed away, hands up, palms outward in surrender. "You do what you like, okay? I'm taking a shower."

For the first time Cadie noticed the grimy blue bandanna wrapped around Jo's knuckles. "What did you do to your hand?" she asked.

"Nothing." Jo turned away and stalked into the main bathroom, slamming the door behind her.

Cadie picked the knife up again, jamming the point into the wooden chopping board and resting her hand on the hilt. "Well, that's great, Arcadia. Well done," she muttered to herself. "She's your one ally on this side of the planet, you love her to death, and you just treated her like a kicking post."

JO STOOD UNDER the hot water, forearm against the shower wall, forehead resting on her arm, eyes closed. She hadn't even bothered to strip off the makeshift bandage on her hand and now the deep graze was stinging like a son of a bitch.

What the hell are you doing? she berated herself. *Take the jealous, knee-jerk reaction about Naomi and shove it somewhere deep and dark, Jossandra.* She pressed her fingers against the bridge of her nose. *Clearly Cadie doesn't want to hear from the senator. That's got to be part of her bad mood. So can it, will ya? Don't take out your bad mood on her, damn it. She doesn't deserve that. Even if she is in a foul temper.*

The water felt so good against her skin. Jo let the heat begin to bleed away her tension, feeling the muscles in her back start to unwind. She started when she heard a shuffling sound. A glance over the shower door revealed a blonde head and a pair of sheepish green eyes.

"Can I come in?" Cadie asked.

"Of course," Jo replied. "You don't have to ask."

"Well, the door was shut, so I figured you wanted some privacy. And I don't blame you, frankly." Cadie sat down on the toilet lid, despondently surveying her feet.

For a while they were both silent. As Jo soaped herself up, Cadie breathed in the steamy atmosphere of the bathroom. She wished she could rewind the last half-hour or so and start again.

"I'm sorry, Jo-Jo," she said finally.

"I'm sorry too, sweetheart." Jo finished rinsing the shampoo from her long hair and stepped out of the glass cubicle. Without waiting for her to dry off, Cadie got up and wrapped her arms around the tall, wet woman. Grinning, Jo reciprocated, pulling her close. "You're gonna be soaked, darling."

"Don't care," Cadie muttered, relishing the solid, damp warmth she pressed against. "Can we start again, please?" She lifted her head and looked up into tear-filled blue eyes.

"That would be wonderful," Jo agreed, placing a kiss on her lover's forehead.

"Let me look at that hand?" Cadie pulled Jo towards the sink. The taller woman sat down on the edge of the bathtub and held out the offended appendage. Cadie eased the wet bandana off and winced at the sight of the ugly gouges on the backs of Jo's knuckles. "You've been battling engine parts again, haven't you?"

"Yeah. Damn wrench slipped," Jo mumbled. She watched as Cadie opened the bathroom's medicine cabinet behind the mirror and extracted a bottle of Mercurochrome and some cotton buds. "This is gonna hurt, huh?"

"It's probably gonna sting some, yeah. Sorry, love." Cadie dipped a cotton bud into the bottle. Carefully, she began dabbing the antiseptic onto each wound, making sure she got every piece of dirt and grease out. Jo sat stoically still, not even the glimmer of a wince touching her face.

"Tough girl, huh?" Cadie teased.

"Well," Jo drawled, "I have my image to think about." Her eyes rested on the blonde head bent low and she felt a rush of affection for her lover. "Can I ask you something?" A pale eyebrow lifted in answer. "It's not just Naomi that's bugging you, is it? There's something on your mind. I can tell."

Cadie finished her cleaning task and dropped the cotton bud into the small rubbish bin under the sink. Resuming her seat on the toilet lid, she leaned her elbows on her thighs and clasped her hands in front of her. Drying herself, Jo watched a range of emotions cross the face she loved. Most evident was frustration.

"I'm having a bit of trouble with the whole money situation," Cadie finally confessed, not meeting Jo's somewhat surprised gaze. "I can't see how I can work here and I'm not used to feeling dependent...expecting you to take care of me..."

Jo finished toweling off and unhooked the bathrobe hanging on the door, sliding into its warm softness. Then she crouched down in front of Cadie and cupped her hands around her lover's. "Please don't worry about that. I've plenty for—"

"I know," Cadie said. "That's not the point. Listen, before I started the agency I never thought about money and the power it has. I had a trust fund and Naomi was in much the same boat. Plus, she was earning good money. While I was working as part of her campaign team, we lived on what she was making. If I wanted anything else, I used my trust. That was how I started the agency. I used the rest of the capital." She looked up into attentive blue eyes. "When the business started bringing in money, I felt like I could look Naomi in the eye. As an equal." She focused on Jo's long fingers, which were chafing against hers. "That sounds pretty pathetic, doesn't it?" she whispered. "Needing money to feel like an equal."

Jo bent down and kissed Cadie's thumbs softly. "We all have our pride, sweetheart," she answered. "That certain something that gives us self-confidence, or at least the appearance of self-confidence, until we can find it in ourselves." She lowered her eyes briefly, then found Cadie's again. "With me, it was a gun. Took me a long time to figure out I could be who I wanted to be without that little friend strapped to my hip."

"Talk about perspective," Cadie said wryly. "Here I am worried about a few dollars."

Jo shook her head and squeezed Cadie's hands. "No. Don't do that. Don't minimize what you're feeling, okay? You can't access your money, and having me pay for everything is pushing your buttons, right?"

Cadie nodded. "I keep telling myself it's only temporary. And I know you don't mind." She met Jo's grin with one of her own. "Okay, that you actually quite enjoy it," she conceded. "But the thing is, I don't know when this will change. I don't see how I can run the business properly from here."

Jo thought about that for a bit. "Okay. I understand that. But the bottom line is there's not much we can do about it now except do our best to get through the next few weeks. This will work itself out. Meantime, try and relax. I'm on your side."

Cadie smiled softly at her lover. "I know. And talking about it has helped."

"Good." Jo patted her knee and pushed herself upright, pulling Cadie up with her. "So, apart from money and Senator Stalker, is there anything I can actually help with?"

Cadie stood on tiptoe and kissed Jo lightly. "You help by being here. Now, tell me about your bad mood."

Jo shrugged. "Seasick Germans, noisy engine, sore knuckles, and I hate being away from you." She dropped a gentle kiss into the fair hair. "I've got an idea. How about we cook dinner together?"

A brilliant grin greeted that suggestion. "That's the best idea I've heard all week," Cadie said.

JO LEANED BACK against the soft leather of the sofa and sipped at her glass of red wine, thinking through what had been their first real argument. She wished Cadie wouldn't be so hard on herself. So much had happened in such a short period of time, there was bound to be some fallout. She held some of the warm, fruity liquid in her mouth before swallowing. *I was worried. I don't like not being on the same wavelength with her.* She glanced around, wondering what was keeping her lover, who'd disappeared on some pretext a few moments earlier.

"Cadie?" she called, just as her partner returned. She was holding something behind her back and came to a halt near the coffee table.

"You know how Wednesday was your birthday, but because we were both having such a busy, crappy week and you were out on the boat, you decided we'd forget about it?"

"Mhmmmm."

"And you know how I agreed with you?"

"Mhmmmm."

Cadie stepped around the table and sat down next to her lover. Slowly, she brought her hands around and handed Jo a long, thin package. "I lied."

Jo's face was a picture. "Y'know, you weren't supposed to do this," she admonished.

Cadie shrugged. "I know. And I know we've just had a whole argument based around money, but, um...Well, I still had a little of the prize money that we won during Hamilton Island Race Week, so I thought I would spend it on my favorite girl."

Jo raised an elegant brow at that. She could count the number of birthdays she had celebrated after she left home on the fingers of one hand. Most of her friends here in the islands didn't even know when it was. And apart from a few phone calls from her parents over the last five years, she really had never marked the day. Somehow, this was a lot different. Jo carefully lifted the corners of the paper, painstakingly peeling back the Scotch tape.

"You haven't done a lot of this, have you?" Cadie asked quietly, suddenly putting together what she knew about Jo's past and the grin of delight on her partner's face.

Jo looked up as she slid a finger along the longest edge of the paper. "No," she said quietly. "Not since I was pretty small." Finally, she slid the gray velvet jewelry case out of the paper and eased it open. "Oh, Cadie," she breathed. Delicately, she picked up the fine gold chain. Hanging from it was a small filigreed locket. "Sweetheart, it's beautiful."

Cadie beamed. "I didn't put anything in it," she said, showing Jo how to open it. "I thought you could choose the photo you wanted."

Jo leaned across and placed a gentle kiss on her cheek. "Thank you, darling," she whispered. "I know which picture I'm going to put in there." She nuzzled Cadie's neck.

Cadie tilted her head, giving her lover more access, totally unable to say no to the languid sensuality washing over her. "Which one?" she murmured.

"Which one what?" Jo replied as she nibbled the soft skin so close.

Cadie giggled. "Photograph, Jo-Jo, photograph." She grinned as Jo pulled back.

"The one Frank took of you at the wedding," the dark-haired woman said softly.

"Ah. You liked that one."

For long seconds they gazed at each other, blue eyes and green sparking off each other. Jo held the locket up. "Help me put this on?"

Cadie took the chain and reached behind Jo's neck, manipulating the clasp until it closed securely. The locket hung perfectly, nestled at the base of Jo's throat. She nodded in satisfaction. "It suits your coloring," she said.

"It's gorgeous, Arcadia. Just like you."

Cadie quirked an eyebrow at the singular expression on Jo's face. *I think I like what's on her mind,* she thought, tingling at the prospect.

"Happy birthday, sweetheart," she whispered as Jo wrapped arms around her waist and bore her gently backwards until they were lying full-length along the sofa. Very blue eyes twinkled at her at close proximity. "I'm in so much trouble, aren't I?"

"Oh yeah," Jo burred, silencing any further conversation by brushing her lips lightly over Cadie's.

"Oh yeah," Cadie breathed, slipping a hand into the dark locks and pulling her beloved closer.

Chapter Five

"YOU'VE NEVER ROASTED marshmallows over an open fire?" Cadie stared incredulously at the dark-haired figure sitting across the campfire from her. "You, my Outdoor Queen, have never stuck a marshmallow on a stick?"

"Um, no," Jo admitted with a wry smile.

"Well, then you're in for an education," said Cadie as she gleefully produced a packet of the sweet treats from under her sweatshirt.

Jo watched, amused, as her partner set about the business of raising her blood sugar by several notches. They'd changed their minds about flying out to the Madisons' station, opting instead to fly into Brisbane and drive from there, camping along the way. The idea of showing her lover the Australian countryside up close and personal had excited Jo. *And for someone who admitted she wasn't a big fan of camping, Cadie's really getting into the swing of things.*

"Here you go." Cadie handed Jo a long, straight stick she'd cleaned of dirt and debris, and a handful of marshmallows. "Stick it on the point and hold it close to the flames. Not right in it, though, or you'll be chewing charcoal." Cadie grinned, her nose wrinkling endearingly.

That's guaranteed to turn me into...well, a marshmallow, Jo thought, taking the stick. "Rightio, then, here we go," she said, more than happy to indulge Cadie's infectious, upbeat mood. She skewered a marshmallow and dangled it briefly over the fire, watching as the sugary surface of the sweet began to bubble and caramelize.

Cadie popped a melty morsel into her mouth and rolled her eyes in exaggerated ecstasy.

"Good?" Jo asked, not really needing an answer to know her lover was in heaven.

"Mphmghmm," came the muffled reply, followed by a happy sigh. "Yours is probably about done, sweetheart."

Jo plucked the marshmallow gingerly from the end of the

stick and dropped it onto her tongue. *Wow,* she thought. *That's really, really...sweet.* "I think I like it," she said around the mouthful.

"I thought you might," Cadie laughed, her eyes sparkling.

A timely phone call from an old friend had prompted the change in travel plans earlier in the week. Rita, a gorgeous brunette who shared Jo's sense of humor and taste for red wine, had been a Cheswick employee when Jo had joined the company over five years ago. She and her husband, Brian, had more or less adopted Jo in those early days when she was trying find her feet and rebuild her life, and they'd done it without asking too many questions or expecting too much of her. They lived in Brisbane, the Queensland capital, these days, and had urged Jo to come visit.

She and Cadie had set off early on Saturday, and had been sitting on Rita and Brian's back patio, cold glasses of wine in hand, by mid-afternoon.

It was great to see them, Jo reflected as she stuck another marshmallow on the end of her stick and placed it in the fire. All the more so because they'd offered to lend Jo and Cadie their truck, loaded up with more camping gear than they'd probably need. It was typical of their generosity. *Good people.*

After a very pleasant afternoon and evening in their excellent company, Jo and Cadie had hit the road late on Sunday morning, driving west from Brisbane before heading south and crossing the border into New South Wales. They'd driven most of the day, covering about 310 miles before arriving in Moree late in the day. Cadie had shared the driving with her, Jo confident in her ability to handle the unfamiliar conditions. *Not to mention driving on the wrong side of the road.* It had been fun to watch Cadie's eyes growing wider as the countryside became harsher and drier. *And flatter.*

They'd had an easier day today, putting another 260 miles behind them before they hit the small mining and agricultural town of Bourke, known as the Gateway to the Outback. They'd arrived by early afternoon and had done some shopping at the local RM Williams outlet.

Jo grinned at Cadie, resplendent in her new cream-colored moleskins and elastic-sided tan boots. She'd only just been persuaded to take off her Akubra stockman's hat and Driza-bone oilskin riding coat to eat dinner. Jo chuckled. It had been great fun outfitting Cadie like a fair dinkum Aussie bushman, and she had been relieved that Cadie seemed more relaxed about their financial arrangements.

Shopping completed, they had wound their way through the

small town until they'd reached a campground on the banks of the Darling River. After setting up the tent and getting a fire started, Jo had fashioned a tasty meal from the steaks and vegetables they'd bought earlier. It had been a very pleasant evening.

"I am having fun," Cadie declared. "This is one big country, Jo-Jo. I never really realized that before now. It's hard to believe that there can be the islands and the reef and all that, and a couple of days' drive away it's like this." She swept her arm around, taking in the flat, dry landscape beyond the ring of their campfire's light.

"Yeah, it's big," Jo agreed. "But this is where it really starts to get different. There's an Aussie saying—going out the back of Bourke—it means going out where there's nothing and nobody." She popped another marshmallow into her mouth.

"So we're really on the edge of the desert here?" Cadie asked.

Jo waggled a hand at her. "Not desert in the sense of dunes and oases, and camels and all that," she replied after she finished her mouthful. "But in terms of arable land—stuff that can actually be farmed in some way—we're heading into country that's as hard as it gets. There's nothing too glamorous about working the land out here."

"So I shouldn't expect much in the way of green grass and contented cows, then," Cadie said, thinking of the rich dairy farms of her home state of Wisconsin.

"Er, no." Jo smiled across the fire at her. "From what Mum was saying on the phone, they're in the middle of a drought, too, so things are tougher than normal." It occurred to her that Cadie deserved a bit of a warning. "Um, sweetheart?" A blonde eyebrow lifted, waiting. "Things can get a bit harsh out here," Jo continued, hesitantly. "Especially in a drought. Animals die, and sometimes the farmers are the ones that have to do the killing." She looked steadily at Cadie, not wanting to sugarcoat reality.

"Okay," her lover said. "I'm not sure how I feel about that, but I understand it's the way things are."

"It's been a very, very long time since I was here. I hope I'm exaggerating how bad it could be." Jo mustered a smile for her partner. "Whatever happens, it's going to be different, and there's always an element of fun in that, right?"

Cadie moved around to Jo's side of the fire, dropping down and winding her arm through her lover's. "I'm having a ball, honey," she insisted. "And whatever happens, happens. As long as we're together, I'm happy."

Jo leaned in and kissed her forehead softly. "Ditto," she replied. "Here, have a marshmallow." She dropped a sticky finger-full onto Cadie's bottom lip.

Cadie drew the morsel into her mouth with sensual abandon. "Tastes almost as good as you."

"Tease."

"Yeah, and you love it."

"Yes, I do."

JO CAME AWAKE slowly, the unfamiliar sounds of their surroundings prodding her out of a rather pleasant dream involving chocolate-covered strawberries and a certain blonde American. The real thing was tucked under her chin, warm and limpet-like. Jo smiled into the lightening dark, charmed by the small sounds of protest Cadie made when she half-sensed Jo's wakefulness. Jo wondered briefly what it was that had woken her, when a magpie resumed its morning song, warbling high above the tent.

It was colder than she had expected and she sent out a silent thank you to Rita and Brian, who had insisted she and Cadie borrow their alpine-rated double sleeping bag as well.

Cadie snuggled closer and Jo took a few minutes to revel in the sleepy sense of contentment she felt whenever the younger woman was close by. She cast her mind back to her previous lovers, and wondered at herself. She'd always hated actually sleeping with other people. That skin on skin thing, all night long, drove her nuts. *So why can't I seem to get enough of this?* Jo glanced down at the woman whose warm breath was tickling the skin of her throat. *Well, love, obviously*, she answered herself. *But I've seen plenty of people in love who don't do this night after night.* Unconscious fingertips began a gentle movement across her ribs and Jo smiled into the gloom.

"Good morning, sleepyhead," she said, squeezing Cadie gently. "How do you feel about breakfast?"

"Orgasmic. Want me to call room service?"

Jo chuckled. As much fun as Cadie was having discovering the joys of camping, she was missing her creature comforts a little. "No room service, darl, but I can promise you hot food and a cup of tea. How does that sound?"

Cadie clutched at Jo's t-shirt. "Zat mean I have to let you go?"

"Yes. But the good news is, you get to stay snuggled in here 'til it's ready. How about that?"

Green eyes flickered open, their expression one of pathetic

gratitude. "I adore you."

"You adore food," Jo teased and extracted herself from Cadie's grasp, unzipping the front of the sleeping bag and crawling out before Cadie gathered the warm material around herself again.

The tent was a standard two-person model, wide enough only for the double air mattress and not much in the way of head room. Even sitting on the ground sheet to pull on her sweatpants, the top of Jo's dark head brushed against the roof. A thick pair of socks was next, followed by a sweatshirt, then her unlaced hiking boots. A quick search in her overnight bag revealed a towel, soap, shampoo and toothbrush. Jo unzipped the tent's fly screen and pushed aside the flaps before crawling out into the cool morning air.

Lovely morning, she reflected as she walked to the ablutions block. The campground was pretty much deserted and she had the spartan concrete building to herself. *Always a bonus when it comes to public bathrooms,* she mused. She entered one of the shower cubicles and turned on the hot water, letting the steam warm her while she stripped off her clothes. After tempering it with some cold, she stepped under the high-pressure jet.

IT WAS THE smell of gently frying bacon that finally drew Cadie out of the warm nest of their sleeping bag.

How do vegetarians resist that? She sat up and blinked at her surroundings. It was still quite cool and she grabbed the sweatshirt Jo had discarded after her shower, pulling it over her head. It smelled wonderfully of her partner's unique scent, combined with clean cotton and soap. *Yum.*

Cadie finished dressing, grabbed her toiletries bag and towel, and crawled outside the tent. The view brought her up short.

"Oh," she gasped. They were camped on a gentle curve of the Darling River. The early morning mist still hung over the gray-green water and a flock of large white birds swooped lazily over the river's course, the air crisp and clean. On the opposite bank, tall, ghostly gum trees emerged from the light fog, but there wasn't a breath of wind to disturb their olive-green leaves. It was a tableau out of a watercolor painting. "Gosh, Jo, this is gorgeous," she breathed.

Jo looked up from where she was crouched in front of the small fire, glancing around at what had Cadie so entranced. "Yep, it sure is," she murmured. "Did you sleep okay?" She turned back to the fire and poked at the sausages and bacon sizzling away in the frying pan she'd balanced on the coals.

Cadie tore her eyes from the landscape and studied her lover. Jo's dark hair draped over her shoulders as she cooked. Cadie watched as a long-fingered hand absently pushed an errant lock back behind her ear. The t-shirt showed off Jo's finely-muscled arms to good effect and the sweatpants were stretched over firm thighs.

Cadie sighed happily. *It's 6 a.m., I'm not awake yet and I have crusty crud in the corners of my eyes, but looking at her still makes me twittery.* An inquiring brow quirked in her direction as Jo's question went unanswered. *Wakie, wakie, Arcadia.* "Uh, sorry. Did you ask me something? I was all distracted."

Jo snorted but smiled up at her lover. "I asked if you slept okay."

Cadie walked over and sat on the large log that lay on one side of the fireplace. "Actually, I did, thanks," she answered. Green eyes met blue across the column of smoke. "As long as I have you for a pillow, darling, I'm pretty sure I could sleep anywhere." *Interesting how even something as simple as that can make her blush,* Cadie thought as a tinge of color touched Jo's cheeks.

"Well, that's good to know," her lover answered huskily.

"Have I got time for a shower?"

"Yep. I'll eat this lot." Jo indicated the bacon and eggs that were about done to perfection. "And I'll have yours hot and ready for you when you get back."

Cadie grinned. "I like this kind of room service," she said cheekily as she swung her legs over the log and headed for the ablutions block.

"Damn, I love watching you leave," Jo called out, provoking a laugh and a jaunty addition to Cadie's natural gait. "Tease," she muttered, happily tipping her breakfast onto a waiting plate.

"SHOW ME AGAIN where we are and where we're going?" Cadie said an hour later. She had finished washing the breakfast dishes while Jo packed up their gear and loaded it into the back of the truck.

"Sure." Jo pulled out the map from a pocket on the spare wheel cover and spread it out on the picnic table next to their campsite. She pinned down the edges with a ketchup bottle and her Swiss Army knife. Cadie came up beside her, tucking herself under Jo's left arm. "Okay, we're here." Jo jabbed a finger on Bourke. "See this triangle?" A long finger traced the blue spidery line of the Darling River, southwest to Wilcannia, then east to Cobar and north again to Bourke.

"Yep," Cadie replied.

"Well, Coonyabby is about in the middle of it," Jo said, pointing at a bare patch in the center of the triangle.

Cadie peered at the map. "Um, sweetheart? There are no roads leading to the station."

Jo chuckled. "None marked on the map, that's for sure," she agreed. "No more bitumen for us, kiddo."

Cadie blinked at her quizzically. "Bitumen?"

"Um..." Jo searched her limited lexicon of American phrases for the appropriate equivalent. "Asphalt?"

"Ah, thank you."

Jo pointed at the faint unfilled-in lines following the course of the Darling. "That's an unsealed road from Bourke to Wilcannia. But we're gonna stop at Louth." She flicked a fingertip at the tiny town about 60 miles southwest of where they were. "We turn left and there's another unsealed road that runs to Cobar. But we're only going about halfway along it. Hopefully we should find Mum and Dad's mailbox somewhere along there. They've got a dirt track running from the road to the homestead."

Cadie stepped back and put her hands on her hips. "The words 'somewhere' and 'hopefully' are not generating a lot of confidence in me, Miss Madison," she mock scolded, provoking a laugh from her partner, who started refolding the map.

"Well, it's been a while since I had to find the place, Miss Jones. But we've got my cell phone, so we'll be fine." She tossed the map in Cadie's direction. "If we have trouble finding the track to the homestead, I'll call Mum and she'll come and get us." A small flicker of something crossed Jo's face, catching Cadie's eye.

She's nervous, Cadie realized. "I'm looking forward to meeting her, Jo-Jo," she said carefully.

"So am I."

"Is that how it feels?" Cadie asked. "Like you're meeting her for the first time?"

Jo sat down on the picnic table, her feet resting on the bench. She fiddled with her Swiss Army knife, opening and closing each tool as she thought about her reply. The silence was long enough to make Cadie believe she wasn't going to answer, but then Jo cleared her throat.

"Kind of, I guess," she murmured, not meeting Cadie's eyes. "To be honest, I'm more worried about Dad than Mum."

Cadie watched as the emotions passed across Jo's face, tugging at the corners of her mouth and eyes. She walked over and stood in front of Jo, resting her hands on the taller woman's denim-clad knees. She didn't say anything, but offered comfort through the small strokes of her fingers as Jo continued to wrestle with her thoughts.

"I feel really guilty," she eventually said, so quietly that Cadie almost didn't catch what she was saying.

"For leaving the way you did?"

Jo nodded. "Yes, but not just for that," she replied hoarsely. Now she lifted her eyes and met Cadie's. "The farm's been in the family for 130 years. Passed down from father to child. Dad wants so much to be able to continue that tradition. Or at least," she corrected herself, "that's what he wanted when I was a teenager. He was always trying to teach me everything he could about running the place. But that wasn't what I wanted."

"You were a kid, Jo-Jo," Cadie said. "That was a lot of pressure to put on you."

Cadie saw the baby blues flood with tears. "But I still don't want to run the farm. Which means when Dad stops being able to run the place, that'll be the end of the tradition. They'll have to sell up. All that blood, sweat and toil for nothing." Her voice cracked on the last word and Cadie stepped forward, wrapping the tall, dark streak of misery up in a hug.

"Jo-Jo, sweetheart," she soothed, rocking them both gently back and forth. "I think you're beating yourself up a little prematurely. Who knows what either one of them is thinking? When was the last time you had a significant conversation with your father?"

Jo pulled back enough to be able to wipe her eyes with the back of her hand. "It's not just that, though," she muttered. "There's the whole..." She indicated the two of them. "*Us* thing." She looked up quizzically at Cadie. "Why aren't you more nervous about meeting them?"

Cadie smiled softly at her older, but in this sense, infinitely less experienced, lover. "Probably because I've done it before. Remember, I met Naomi's parents, and trust me, after that I can survive anything." She grinned wryly at Jo, relieved to see a spark of humor return to her face.

"Tough, huh?"

Cadie rolled her eyes. "You have no idea. Once you've met her mother, you know exactly where Naomi got that mean streak."

Jo chuckled, somehow vaguely satisfied to know that no matter how bad she thought her relationship with her parents might be, Naomi probably had it tougher.

"Besides," Cadie continued, "I've yet to see anything in you that would suggest your parents are anything but good people."

Jo's eyes narrowed. "How can you say that, knowing my history like you do?" she asked incredulously.

Cadie leaned forward slightly and brushed her lips across her lover's. "Sweetheart, there's a dark streak in you, no question." She put a finger against the soft lips inches from her own. "But you have it so tightly under control, you're so wary of it, that I end up feeling totally protected by it." She smiled at the look of wonder on Jo's face. "You don't believe that, do you?"

Jo shook her head silently.

Cadie thought about how to explain herself a little better. "The only time I've ever seen your dark side has been when you've been defending me, or someone else you care about." She looked at Jo adoringly. "Do you have any idea how safe that makes me feel?" The dark head shook again.

"When you were living that life in Sydney, did you feel like you had any choice about what you were doing?" Cadie asked gently.

Jo bowed her head again, and Cadie could feel the shame radiating from her lover.

"I killed people, Arcadia. It shouldn't have mattered how I felt about my circumstances. I should have made the choice not to do something like that." Jo felt a wave of self-hatred wash through her.

Gentle fingers gripped her chin, forcing her to look into fierce green eyes at close proximity. "You did the right thing in the end," Cadie said. "And you've been working your ass off to do the right thing ever since, including what you did to save Josh not so long ago. Maybe it's time to start forgiving yourself."

Blue eyes blinked at her helplessly. "I can't, Cadie. There isn't anything I can do to make up for taking those lives. Maybe that's what's scaring me the most about seeing Mum and Dad again. Maybe it's *their* forgiveness I need." Jo made a defeated gesture. "But I'm not sure they'll be able to give me that, once they know the truth."

Oh my love, Cadie thought. "I understand," she whispered close to Jo's ear. "You really feel like you have to tell them everything?"

Jo sighed. "I don't see any way it can be avoided, do you? I've never told them anything significant about my life, and they have to be curious. I don't want to lie."

Cadie rested her chin on top of the dark head as she gazed out over the river. "Maybe you won't have to tell them the details. Just saying you made mistakes and you want to put them behind you might be enough."

"Cadie?"

"Yes, love?"

"Do...do you forgive me?"

It was like someone slid a long, thin dagger into her heart, hearing the level of pain in her lover's question. Cadie placed a kiss into the soft, black hair. "From the second I saw you I didn't give a damn what you'd done, Jo-Jo." She cast her mind back to their early conversations on the Seawolf—the reluctance of the tall skipper to reveal anything of her mysterious past. "I never saw you as anything other than what you are. A good person. So yes, I forgave you. Long ago."

Jo held on to her even tighter and Cadie realized that the adult in her arms was feeling very much like a child at the moment. She couldn't help smiling at the concept and was unsurprised by the sudden sense of protectiveness she felt. "Whatever happens, Jo-Jo, we'll get through it together, I promise," she said. "Whatever you want to do, or tell them, I'll back you up."

Jo pulled back again, managing to find a smile from somewhere. "Have I mentioned today that I love you?"

"Nope," Cadie replied, using the bottom of her shirt to wipe the tears from Jo's cheeks.

"Well, I do."

Cadie kissed her again, this time applying the full force of her feelings for the skipper as she sought to soothe away the rough edges. Jo responded in kind, drawing Cadie closer. Their tongues met in a tender, but intense exploration that made them both forget where they were.

But not for long.

"Well, well, well and what do we have here?"

Cadie stepped back from Jo's embrace with a startled gasp. The man had come from nowhere, it seemed, walking out from behind their truck. He was short and stocky with a beer gut that hung over the grimy pair of work shorts he wore. His blue singlet was sweat-stained. Jo recognized him as a truck driver who'd parked his rig further down the river late the night before.

"Don't let me stop you, ladies," he said with a gap-toothed grin. He sauntered closer and sat down on the end of the log near their fireplace. "There's nothing revs my engine more than the sight of two good-looking sheilas going at it." He reached down and adjusted himself lewdly. "Tell you what, how about fifty bucks for you to continue the show?"

Cadie moved closer to Jo, who stood slightly in front of her, putting herself between Cadie and the repugnant stranger.

"Toto, I don't think we're in Kansas anymore," Cadie muttered under her breath, just loud enough for Jo to hear. The tall woman snorted quietly.

"Why don't you get lost, mate," Jo said to the truckie.

"Now, now, gorgeous, no need to be like that," he chastised her. "You two looked like you were enjoying yourselves. Don't be selfish about it. Share it around a little." He leered at them and Cadie felt a jolt of nausea as his eyes raked up and down her body. "Play your cards right, girls, and you could get yourselves some cash and a taste of the best dick in the central west." He advanced a few feet, one hand still gripping his crotch.

"Cadie," Jo growled, her voice low and dangerous. "Get in the truck."

Cadie felt, rather than saw, Jo's fingers manipulating the Swiss Army knife, flicking its longest blade out. "I'm not leaving you out here alone," she muttered.

Jo thought about arguing, but the implacable presence at her back didn't waver. Instead she accepted the fact that from now on she had a sidekick. Somehow the concept made her smile, and she closed the knife and slid it back into her pocket.

I don't need a weapon to deal with this moron, she told herself. "Back off, mate," she warned him.

"Or what?" He was close enough that Jo could see the sweat-matted black hair on his shoulders. Worse, she could smell him, and he was no bed of roses.

"Look, you're barking up the wrong tree, all right?" *Why am I even trying to reason with this guy? He's got the IQ of a cowpat and the stench to match.* "If you were the last dick on the planet neither of us would be interested, so why not be on your way and we'll be on ours." She felt Cadie's hand on the small of her back and together they turned to walk away from the man.

But ego or rank stupidity nudged the man on. He reached out and grabbed Jo's left elbow, yanking her back around to face him.

Oh, you shouldn't have done that, buddy, Cadie thought, resigning herself to a non-diplomatic solution. She felt the heightened tension in Jo's body under her hand, a faint vibration that thrummed. Cadie almost thought she could hear it.

"Where d'ya think you're going?" Mr. Smelly said.

Jo went very still, her eyes narrowing to ice-blue slivers. "Let go of me." Her voice was almost a purr now, deep and threatening.

Mr. Smelly, oblivious to all but his twitching testosterone levels, persisted. "All right, look, 75 bucks each. You won't regret it." He yanked on Jo's arm one more time.

Enough, Jo decided, and felt the darkness inside slither up from the depths of her personality. She clenched her right fist and snapped her arm through in a short-arm jab that was so fast the bastard never saw it coming. He certainly felt it, though. The jolt rocked him backwards, his nose splattering with a squelching sound that was deeply satisfying. He was on his backside in the dust before Jo had uncurled her fingers.

"You fucking dyke bitch!" he yelped, both hands reaching for his blood-spattered face. "You'll fucking pay for that!"

Jo dipped a hand in her pocket and came up with a half-dollar piece, which she flipped with her thumb in the direction of the man writhing in the dirt. It hit him on the forehead. "There's 50 cents, mate. Call someone who gives a rat's arse." She turned to Cadie, who was standing calmly behind her, the tiniest smile on her face. "Let's get out of here," she said, stalking off to pick up the last of their gear.

"Right behind you." Cadie turned back to the picnic table, scooped up her Akubra and jammed it on her head.

The man scrambled on to his hands and knees, blood dripping onto the dirt from his shattered nose. "You haven't seen the last of me, bitch!" he whimpered.

In two strides, Cadie was standing next to him. "You're the one who hassled us, mister. Not the other way around," she said pleasantly. She lifted her left boot and placed it on the point of his shoulder. With one gentle nudge he fell over again, sprawling in the dust. *He looks like a bug trying to get back on its legs after it's been tipped over,* she thought dispassionately. *A stink bug.*

"Cades!" Jo shouted, opening the driver's side door. "Let's go!"

Cadie clambered into the front passenger seat of the truck as Jo started the engine. Glancing back as they pulled out of the campsite, she saw Mr. Smelly drag himself to his feet. He picked up a nearby rock and hurled it at the retreating vehicle.

"Fucking bitches!"

The rock made a sharp metallic sound as it ricocheted off the truck and both women rolled their eyes. Cadie leaned against the door, resting her arm along the back of the bench seat as her partner concentrated on getting them onto the main road through Bourke.

"See what I mean?" Cadie said.

"Huh?" Jo let a cattle truck pass before turning right onto the road to Louth and Wilcannia.

"Protected," Cadie explained, waiting for blue eyes to turn to her before beaming at her partner.

Jo snorted. "You could have handled him perfectly well without me, sweetheart. I happened to be closest to him."

Cadie raised an eyebrow. "Not to start with, Jo-Jo. You moved between us." A blush rose on Jo's angular cheeks. "Face it. You're naturally heroic."

"Awww, quit it, will ya?" Jo squirmed in her seat.

Cadie chuckled. "Think he'll come after us?" she asked, looking around at the stores and pubs they were passing on the outskirts of town.

Jo shrugged. "Who knows? Depends if he's traveling our way, I guess." She glanced at Cadie, who seemed completely absorbed by their surroundings. "By the way, there's a metal box behind our seats here." She reached back and tapped the box in question. "Something Brian lent us."

"Do I want to know what's in there?" Cadie shifted 'round to take a look.

"It's his two hunting rifles and some ammo," Jo said, catching Cadie's eye and shrugging. "I know. But I wasn't going to argue with him, and I guess they're insurance."

"Don't you need a license to have a gun here?"

"Yep. But I don't plan on either using 'em or advertising the fact that we've got 'em." They caught up to the cattle truck and Jo hung back, trying to avoid the cloud of dust that trailed behind the huge vehicle. "Do you know how to use one?"

Cadie took off her hat and ran a hand through her hair. "My dad does a lot of hunting," she said. "Because there were guns in the house he made sure we knew how to use them properly, how to load them and handle them safely. But I've never fired one."

"Okay."

They left the last of Bourke behind them and Cadie glanced around at the landscape. It was breathtaking. The unsealed road stretched straight in front of them away to a shimmering horizon. Yellows and reds dominated, even the olive-green of the low scrubby bushes giving way to the ever-present dust. The sky was the most brilliant shade of blue Cadie had ever seen, rivaling even the tint of her favorite pair of eyes.

"Wow, Jo, this is amazing," she murmured. "Just beautiful."

Jo blinked. Even though it had been 15 years since she'd walked away from this kind of countryside, it was starkly familiar to her. She'd always thought of her home territory as nothing but flat, boring, harsh land. Seeing it through Cadie's eyes was illuminating. "I guess it is," she replied. "It's looking way drier than usual, though. Mum wasn't kidding about the drought."

Thankfully, the cattle truck had taken another route once

they'd left Bourke and Jo kicked the truck into high gear. Even though the road was essentially a well-made dirt track, the going was smooth. If there had been any significant recent rainfall it would have been a mess of ruts and rough edges, but the dry weather had compacted the surface into dusty concrete. The road was wide enough for two lanes, but only just.

"How long 'til we get to Louth?" Cadie asked.

"Just over an hour, probably," Jo answered. "Goddess willing and the creeks don't rise." She smiled at her partner.

"Not much chance of that," Cadie said, looking up at the cloudless sky.

Chapter
Six

"JO! PULL OVER! Please."

Jo chuckled at the delighted note in her partner's voice. Massaging the brake, she pulled the big four-wheel drive over onto the soft edge of the track. They came to a halt in a cloud of red dust. Cadie was enchanted by a flock of emus that had been running alongside them for half a mile or so, nearly giving Jo a nervous breakdown for fear they would try to cross the road.

"I need my camera," Cadie said excitedly. "I guess it's buried in my bag somewhere, huh?" She looked over her shoulder at the camping equipment piled high in the back of the truck.

"Yeah," Jo said. "But dig it out. It doesn't look like these guys are going anywhere in a hurry."

They both climbed out, Cadie rushing to the back of the truck and opening the tailgate. She clambered up and ducked under the roof line, disappearing amongst the bags and boxes. Jo leaned back against the vehicle, one leg bent, the foot against the tire, her hands jammed in her pockets.

They were north of Louth, a small cluster of buildings laughingly called a town, where they would turn off to head for Coonyabby. The emus were on the other side of a light wire fence that ran along the road, marking the boundary of someone's property. Jo dug back into her memory, trying to remember the geography of the area and who lived where.

"This might even be the edge of Phil's parents' place," she muttered, remembering riding the boundaries on horseback with her childhood friend. "Then again, I might be wrong." All the properties around here looked pretty much like the others. It bothered her a little that she couldn't remember exactly.

"Did you say something, sweetheart?" Cadie was still scrabbling around deep in the inner recesses of their luggage.

"Nah," Jo said, lifting her voice a little. "I was talking to these silly birds out here." She flicked a glance at the milling emus. The biggest of them probably topped her six-foot frame by a good half a foot or so, but what they boasted in height, the big flightless dumb idiots lacked in brain. Emus were known to try and run through an obstacle rather than figure out a way to walk around. "Not more than one brain cell between the whole flock," Jo murmured. Discerning grunts of frustration from the back of the truck, she asked, "Any luck?"

"No, damn it. Maybe I put it in your bag?" Renewed activity ensued and Jo laughed at the whirlwind of destruction that was her determined partner.

Her smile faded as she caught sight of a trail of dust coming from the north. They hadn't seen another vehicle in either direction since they'd left Bourke and Jo suddenly had a bad feeling she wasn't going to be too happy to see this one. She walked slowly to the rear of the truck, automatically putting herself between Cadie, who was still rooting around in the gear, and whatever was coming. The dust cloud drew closer and she could hear the rumble of a big semi-trailer.

"Great. Just great," Jo grumbled, recognizing the rig as belonging to the creep from the campsite. "This guy's too dumb to know when he's had his arse kicked." She glanced over her shoulder, making sure Cadie was still buried in the back of the truck. "Cadie?"

"Yeah?"

"Stay where you are, okay?"

"Huh?"

"Stay where you are."

The warning note in Jo's voice was unmistakable, and Cadie didn't argue, though she did squirm around so she could see what was going on. She didn't need more than a glance past Jo's shoulder to fathom what was happening. "Wonderful," she grumbled and tucked herself back out of sight.

Jo tipped her battered black Akubra low over her eyes and assumed her best bad-ass attitude, her hands on her denim-clad hips. "You are such a poser, Madison," she muttered to herself, but grinned anyway. She was fully aware that the sleeveless checked work-shirt showed off her tan and her lithe, muscled arms, and it gave her a rush to know how intimidating she looked. It felt good. Very, very good.

The rig eased to a halt, dust settling around it as the air brakes squealed and hissed. Jo held herself still, waiting to see what the congenital idiot behind the wheel would do next. She didn't have to wait long. His door swung open and he jumped to the ground. He'd come prepared, hefting a large crowbar in his right hand. He walked towards Jo, slapping the end of the iron bar rhythmically into his left hand. The damage she had already inflicted on him was painfully obvious. There were bloodstains on his grubby singlet and his broken nose was bent between two rapidly blackening eyes.

"Fancy meeting you here," Jo said, keeping any hint of interest out of her voice.

"Shut up, bitch." He stopped about 15 feet away from her.

She let a slow, dangerous, sexy smile touch her lips. "Nice. Do you kiss your mother with that mouth?"

The hairy freak took a step forward, brandishing the crowbar like it was a baseball bat. "Is that a crack about my mother?"

Jo rolled her eyes and sighed. "My God, you really are from the shallow end of the gene pool, aren't you, mate?"

"Huh?"

"Get lost, ya buffoon."

Enraged, the man charged her, lifting the crowbar above his head and letting out a wild yell. Unfortunately for him, he hadn't allowed for Jo's greater height, not to mention the gulf between their IQs, mobility and strength. She saw the blow coming when it was little more than a spark between the man's ears. She blocked the attack with one simple movement, grabbing the crowbar as it swung towards her shoulder. Then she shoved back, catching the man in the midriff with his end of the iron rod and knocking him on his backside for the second time that morning.

Her hand stung from the crowbar, but there was no way she was going to let him know that. Her assailant scrambled to his feet, still grasping the makeshift weapon.

"Isn't getting beaten up by a woman once a day enough for you?" Jo enquired. She knew she was goading this bag of shit, but she was taking a perverse pleasure in watching him make a complete fool of himself.

Once more he came at her, this time swinging the crowbar from side to side. But before Jo could do anything about it, she heard the unmistakable sound of a bolt action behind her right shoulder.

The truckie stopped in his tracks, his bloodshot eyes widening at the sight of the diminutive blonde standing on the tailgate of the truck, a large Winchester tucked up against her right shoulder. Its muzzle looked big and black and menacing. *Oh boy,* Jo thought. *I wonder if she's loaded it.*

"Why don't you take your ugly, fat butt back to your rig, mister, and be on your way?" Somehow the words and Cadie's cultured Midwest accent didn't go together. Jo had to smile.

"You bitches are insane!" the man yelled. "You can't pull a

gun on a bloke."

"This from the imbecile who tried to take my head off with a crowbar," Jo answered, one eyebrow raised as she folded her arms casually across her chest.

He lurched forward again. This time Cadie shifted her aim and fired. The bullet kicked up the dust to the right of the man's feet. She winced at the thump of the recoil, surprised by its force. *Not gonna let him know that,* she decided, resetting her feet determinedly.

Guess she loaded it, Jo thought, impressed by her partner's accuracy. *Not bad for someone who's never fired a gun before. God knows what she'll hit next time.* She chuckled internally.

"You bitches! You goddamn, motherfucking, dyke bitches!" The truckie was dancing around like some kind of enraged lunatic. "Who do you think you are?"

"We're the motherfucking dyke bitches kicking your ass for the second time today," Cadie called out. Jo hadn't turned to look at her lover, but she knew the rifle was still trained on the man. "Go on. Get out of here, before your luck with my aim runs out."

Jo hitched a thumb in her partner's direction. "Did I mention that she's actually the one with the hair-trigger temper?" she said cheerfully.

Finally, the message seemed to get through. Mr. Smelly dropped the crowbar and backed up towards his rig, his hands raised above his head. He stumbled when he encountered the massive bull-bar in front of the radiator grill, but he was soon clambering up into the cab. Cadie kept the gun on him the whole way, even as he fired up the big semi-trailer, pulled out onto the road, and passed them, heading south.

Jo swiveled on her heel to watch him leave, then completed the turn, gazing up at her partner. *Damn if that's not the sexiest thing I've seen in ... well since the last time she looked sexy.*

Shouldering the heavy rifle, Cadie picked up the cue, green eyes sparkling. She jumped down and sauntered over to Jo. "Y'know, I know it's crazy, but I feel like I've got a knack for this shit."

"I believe you do," Jo murmured. She slid a hand into Cadie's silky fair hair and around to the back of her neck, pulling her closer. Ducking her head, she brushed her lips against Cadie's.

Cadie lowered the rifle, keeping it well clear of their bodies as she melted against Jo's tall frame. Jo's long fingers in her hair set her scalp tingling and the strong arm around her waist laid unmistakable claim. The kiss deepened, their tongues exploring and teasing as they gave in to knee-weakening passion. For a few seconds, they lost themselves, drinking in each other's warmth, then Cadie wriggled a little.

"Um, Jo-Jo? I have a loaded, deadly weapon in my hand and it's..."

"Making you uncomfortable? Scaring you?"

"Getting heavy." Cadie grinned.

A fine, dark brow lifted. "Well, I think I can do something about that," Jo drawled. She placed a hand on the rifle's stock and took it out of Cadie's grip. Quickly she unloaded it, her expert handling of the piece not lost on Cadie.

"You've done that before," she stated, looking up into hooded eyes.

"Many times," Jo said bluntly. She flashed Cadie a quick smile. "But not where you think. Out here, guns are part of life on the farm. I was shooting cans off the old stump in the back garden when I was four." She took a long look at the Winchester. "This one's a bit flashier than the ones I shot back then, though." Carefully she placed it on the truck's tailgate. "I'm afraid you scared off the emus."

Cadie looked around, disappointed to find no trace of the flock. "Damn," she said. "Guess they recognized a lucky shot when they saw one, huh?"

Jo laughed. "I guess so." She vaulted up onto the tailgate and replaced the rifle and bullets in their metal box. "Come on, let's hit the road."

"SO, CAN I expect that kind of behavior from all the males of the species out here?" Cadie asked once they were settled back into the drive and their adrenalin levels had flattened out.

Jo clasped her hands on top of the steering wheel, the big truck not needing much help to stay on the straight and narrow track. She considered her reply. "Well, on the one hand, I think our friend there was from the lower end of the evolutionary ladder." Cadie snorted her agreement. "On the other hand, we are smack bang in the middle of Ocker Central."

Cadie turned to look at her. "Ocker?"

"Uh, yeah. Um, ocker is Australian for redneck," Jo replied.

"Ah. No more public make-out sessions, huh?"

"The good news is, we're not exactly going to be out in public from now on, sweetheart," Jo said. "We're gonna be on 60,000 acres of private land in a couple of hours."

"Cool. What's the bad news?"

Jo smiled, a little grimly. "The bad news is I have no idea

how my parents, and whoever else is working on Coonyabby these days, are going to react to us. For all I know we're walking into a den of homophobes. Hell, I don't even know if we're gonna get to sleep in the same bed."

Cadie swung her head around quickly. "Jo, I'm not sleeping away from you."

Jo raised her hand in a placating gesture. "I know, I know. And I'm not going to let them pull any *while you're sleeping under our roof you'll live by our rules* bullshit. We've got the camping gear. If they can't deal with us sleeping together then we'll go camp under the stars." Apprehension welled and she tempered it with a little anger. "Screw 'em."

"Easy, skipper," Cadie soothed. "You know your mother better than I do..."

"You would think so, wouldn't you?" Jo replied.

"You know what I mean. Anyway, all I meant was that so far she hasn't struck me as the type to get uptight about that." Cadie thought about it a little more. "Of course, she might think twice when she hears us in the middle of the night."

Jo's head whipped round, her blue eyes wide with shock. Cadie was alarmed to see the color draining from her lover's face even as she gripped the steering wheel tighter.

"Honey, I was kidding. Relax." Jo didn't say anything, just gazed ahead up the long, straight road. *Oh boy.* Cadie unclipped her seatbelt and sidled across the bench seat until she was up against Jo's side. She could feel the tension thrumming through Jo's body. "Sweetheart, it's okay."

"I-I never even thought about that," Jo whispered, trying to concentrate on driving even as her brain was flying in a million different directions. "Cadie, I don't think I can...I mean, not with them..."

Cadie smiled. Parts of her more-than-capable lover were still so adolescent it was like watching a kid grow up before her very eyes. She patted Jo's belly. "Pull over, love, before you drive us into the desert," she said calmly.

Jo sighed and did as Cadie requested, bringing them to a halt in a convenient byway. "Sorry, I had a bit of a moment there," she muttered.

Cadie kissed her on the cheek softly. "It's okay. You're running headfirst into a bunch of issues you've never had to think about before, huh?"

"I guess so. It never occurred to me."

"What? That we'd be sleeping together in close proximity to your parents?" Cadie rested her cheek against Jo's shoulder and slid her hand under her lover's shirt, trailing fingertips over tense stomach muscles. "Sweetheart, sex is not a requirement. We don't have to do anything you're not comfortable with. And believe it or not, I can go a couple of weeks without it."

Jo could feel Cadie's grin and it flicked a switch in her head. *Get over it, Jo-Jo, ya big coward. You're 33, not 13.* She unclipped her seatbelt and turned slightly so she could capture Cadie's lips in a soft, sensual kiss. Cadie moaned faintly into her mouth and Jo met the sound with one of her own. Playfully she nibbled Cadie's bottom lip, then gasped as Cadie turned the tables, entwining her fingers in Jo's dark locks to pull her closer and intensify the contact.

Jo gently nudged her backwards until they were stretched along the narrow bench seat. She ignored the discomfort of the steering wheel digging into her thigh, concentrating instead on the entirely too sexy movements of the woman under her.

Cadie wriggled blissfully under the weight of her heavier lover. Jo's lips trailed along her jaw, wreaking havoc on her composure. She nuzzled the long neck close by, finding Jo's earlobe and gently biting down on it.

"You can't be comfortable," she murmured, knowing Jo's lanky form was tangled around the wheel and the gear stick.

"I'm perfect," Jo burred.

The next several minutes were spent in a happy reconnaissance of each other's bodies, neither woman pushing the moment past the point of low burn.

"Jo-Jo?" It was a gasp more than a question, as Jo's fingers found a particularly sensitive spot.

"Yes?"

"I think the logistics of this are going to get the better of us."

"I know, but God, I'm having fun trying."

The words rumbled down Cadie's spine like a hum of electricity. "You are driving me crazy. You know that, right?"

In answer, Jo nuzzled the curve of her breast one last time before pushing herself upright. "Are you sure?" she asked, drawing Cadie up as well.

"Am I sure about what?"

"Are you sure you can go a couple of weeks without sex?"

Cadie laughed as she rearranged her fetchingly mussed hair. "No sex I can live with, darling," she said. "No love-making with you is another question altogether."

They giggled their way around another kiss as Jo fumbled for the ignition key. Before long she had the truck fired up and they were on their way again.

"We're taking a lot of detours on this trip," Cadie observed, happily settling her hormones into an undercurrent of tingles.

"Only way to travel," her lover purred around a feral, wildcat grin.

Chapter Seven

MAGGIE STOOD, HANDS on hips, at the threshold of what used to be her daughter's bedroom. For several years, they'd kept it exactly as Jo had left it. But as time had gone by and they'd needed it, the room had gradually become a storage space. Over the past few days, Maggie had been emptying it out and restoring Jo's belongings to their proper place. As she stood at the door a flood of memories washed over her and she sighed, wondering if she would ever be able to think of that time without the hurt.

Posters of pop stars and athletes covered the walls, faces from 15 years ago lined up like a museum display. Teenage knick-knacks were scattered around—models her detail-driven daughter had put together from kits—planes mostly, but some yachts. There were schoolbooks and, in one corner, an old portable record player and an enormous pile of albums and singles, all on vinyl. Books packed the shelves along the walls.

Maggie had to smile. When Jo hadn't been helping her father out in one of the far-flung paddocks, she was most often to be found in here, playing music, reading or tinkering with whatever gadget had caught her attention.

"She always did live inside her head," she muttered to herself as she walked into the room for one last look before Jo's arrival. She glanced at the bed. It was a double, Jo's tall frame having outgrown the confines of a single bed before she was 15. "I hope there's enough room for the two of them in here." Maggie placed her fingers against her right temple in a bid to chase away the headache that was gnawing away at her last nerve. *Don't want to think about that too much, do you, girl?*

She'd spent most of the last week in the dual task of placating her husband and trying to get her head around the reappearance of her daughter with her special someone in tow. David Madison had been shocked into silence by the confirmation that Jo was gay, involved and about to land on their doorstep. Maggie knew it had stirred up a lot of long-buried hurts for her husband, but there had been no way around telling him the news. She wasn't going to let this chance to reconnect with Josie go by.

David had spent the last few days as far away from the house as he could get, starting his days early and not coming home until after dark. *Doing his own thinking, I expect. Living in his head, like his daughter.* Maggie smiled quietly to herself. *I wonder if they realize how alike they are. I wish he would talk more.*

She'd tried to persuade her husband to stay close by the house this morning, but he was determined to carry on as if there was nothing special about today.

Our daughter's coming home. The thought still brought Maggie up short. Slowly, she eased herself down onto the edge of the bed. The butterflies in her stomach were more like hummingbirds. *Why am I nervous?* she wondered. *She's my own flesh and blood.* She flicked at a speck of fluff on the cover. *The truth is, it's not me or her I'm worried about. It's David.*

The first year after Jo's disappearance had been a terrifying mix of uncertainty and stress that had taken a tremendous toll on them both. With no word from their daughter, their lives had become an endless stream of phone calls to police, hospitals and government officials. Not knowing if Jossandra was alive or dead had been a nightmare neither of them could escape.

Maggie stood up and walked out into her kitchen. Three steps took her to the sink and its big window overlooking the garden and the track up to the house from the road. *We dealt with it so differently,* she remembered. *I threw myself into finding Josie, and David...* She swallowed. *David didn't seem to change much on the outside, but inside the stress ate him alive.* The heart attack had hit him while he was out on the far north boundary of the property. Pure luck and blind cussedness had kept him alive until the Royal Flying Doctors Service had been able to reach him.

Everything had changed after that. Maggie eyed the dirt road that would soon bring her daughter home. David had needed bypass surgery and a long recuperation. They'd had to employ more men and a temporary station manager until he was back on his feet and ready to work again. It had almost cost them the farm. Only an understanding bank manager, a rare member of his species, had stood between them and going under.

Just as things had started to improve, Josie had called them out of the blue one Sunday afternoon. Relief and shock had quickly been followed by anger, at least from David. Maggie had never seen him so pale and shaky. It had crossed her mind that he was close to another coronary.

A lot of years have passed since then, she reflected. *We've all changed, no doubt Josie most of all.* She turned away from the window and leaned back against the counter. *I hope everyone can handle the consequences.*

"THAT'S THE ONE," Jo said quietly as they approached the next mailbox.

Cadie pulled the truck over, sliding to a halt about 10 feet from the battered green receptacle. "No offence, sweetheart, but how do you know? It looks like all the others we've passed."

Jo didn't answer. Instead she opened the passenger side door and dropped to the ground, her boots kicking up a puff of dust. Walking slowly over to the mailbox, she placed one hand on top of its metallic surface and gazed up the track to the unseen homestead.

Cadie wasn't surprised by her lover's silence. Jo had been quiet since they'd turned off the main road to Wilcannia onto the dirt track that had brought them to this point. They'd passed three or four other mailboxes without a word from the tall skipper, but this one had brought her up short. Cadie switched off the engine and climbed down. Slowly, she walked over to Jo and placed a comforting hand on her back.

"That's how I know," Jo murmured, nodding at the side of the mailbox. 'Madison' was neatly printed in uniform white letters. But underneath, in a sprawling, childish hand was written "and Jo."

"Oh," Cadie gasped, noticing the words for the first time. She grinned up at her lover. "I'm guessing you were about 10 when you did that."

"Eight and a half," Jo replied, mustering a small smile of her own. "Phil was with me. We were out for a ride and I brought a little pot of whitewash with me. I think I was trying to tell the world I existed."

"Ride—as in horses?"

"Yep. We've got quarter horses. Or at least we did then." She glanced up the track leading to the homestead. "I can't believe how dry it is," she muttered. "I don't ever remember it being as bad as this." They gazed around at the landscape. Its harsh lines and dry colors shimmered in the oppressive heat.

"I don't know how anyone can make a living out of this land," Cadie said, awed by the stark beauty of it all.

"You don't make a living out of this land," Jo replied grimly. "You survive off it. And wait for the next rain and the wool prices to go up."

Cadie watched the tensions and anxiety flicker across the uniquely angular features of Jo's face. "Come on, skipper," she said. "Let's go get the most nerve-wracking bit over and done with, eh?"

Jo was suddenly immeasurably glad to have Cadie along for the ride. "I would never have had the guts to do this without you," she said. "You know that, right?"

"I'm glad I can help," Cadie replied as they eased apart.

Jo began to walk to the truck but hesitated when the memory of another family ritual resurfaced. She turned back to the mailbox and gingerly lifted the lid. Visions of close encounters with redback spiders tickled her senses and she looked inside before carefully reaching in. As expected, there were at least two of the nasty bities in residence. Some things, at least, hadn't changed. Smiling, she plucked out the small pile of letters and closed the lid again, leaving the spiders to their dark, hot little world.

As she settled back in the truck, Cadie gave her a quizzical look from the driver's seat.

"Family rule," Jo explained. "If anyone's close to the mailbox, bring in the mail. Otherwise it can sit in there for days."

Cadie turned over the ignition, directing the truck onto the rough dirt track. "How far from the homestead are we?" she asked as she carefully negotiated her way around a fallen log.

"About 15 minutes." Jo drummed her fingers on the bench seat between them. "Wish it was about 15 years."

"I'm betting you won't think that in about 16 minutes, sweetheart."

DAVID MADISON SAT back on his haunches and wiped the sweat from his tanned forehead with the back of his hand, the rough work glove scraping against his skin. He looked up into the cloudless sky and tried to judge the position of the sun.

Just after noon, he decided. Scattered around him were the pieces of the bore pump he'd spent the morning disassembling. So far, he'd found not a damn thing wrong with it, but that was all right. He'd come out here because it was about as far as he could get from the homestead and still be home just after dark. He'd sent Jack and Hughie in the other direction, knowing there were some boundary fences that needed four hands to fix.

David's mouth was parched and he could feel his sweat-soaked work shirt sticking to his back. Slowly he pushed himself up off his knees and walked to his four-wheeled ATV. Clipped onto its tray were a large water cooler and a thermos bag full of cold roast lamb sandwiches. David pulled his gloves off and stuffed them in the pocket of his jeans, then dropped his Akubra onto the tray.

Coward. He poured himself a cupful of ice-cold water, downing it in three big gulps before filling the cup again. *Stubborn, useless coward.* David drank deeply again. *Leaving Maggie to do the meeting and greeting on her own.* He pulled a handful of sandwiches out of the bag and sat down on the ground, leaning against the ATV's big grooved wheel. The bread was fresh and the cold meat tender and juicy. *She's a good old girl. I don't deserve her, honest to God I don't.*

All week long he'd been dreading this day. And when push came to shove he preferred to put off the inevitable for as long as possible. So he'd come out here on the pretext of needing to do some repairs.

It wasn't that he didn't want to see Josie. *God knows, I've been dreaming of this day for 15 years,* he admitted to himself, picking up another sandwich. *My baby's coming home.* He bit down on the sandwich, viciously ripping away a mouthful. *Except she's not my baby anymore. She's...* He chewed thoughtfully for a few minutes. *I don't know what she is. Not anybody I know anymore. Not normal, that's for sure.*

He and Maggie had argued last night about it. The sleeping arrangements. David could not for the life of him see how they could allow Josie and her... "Jesus, I don't even know the word for it," he muttered aloud. *Anyway.* He wasn't happy about them sleeping together in his home. But Maggie had insisted.

"We're going to make them both welcome, David," she'd argued. "And I don't care what you have to say about it. Josie is what she is, and I don't care what that is anymore. This other woman seems very nice. If she's a part of Josie's life, and makes her happy, then so be it."

So be it. Maggie had spoken and that was that. David stretched his legs out and crossed them at the ankles. He gazed at the mess he'd made of the water pump. *Whole thing's a shambles,* he thought morosely. *I guess I should be like Maggie. But I can't get my head around any of it.*

He'd long ago let go of the anger in his life. The drawn-out recuperation from the heart attack had taken care of that. Anger at Jossandra for the way she'd left. Anger at the banks. Anger at the Americans for their lamb tariff. Anger at the goddamned weather. None of it mattered anymore, he knew that. *All that matters is putting food on the table and paying the bills,* he thought.

It had become his mantra.

What did we do wrong? he wondered. *Jo couldn't wait to get away from us. She had no problem staying away from us. And now she's...* Impatiently he pushed himself up off the ground, tired of the circular debate going on in his head. *Fix the damn pump. Just fix the damn pump.*

THE OBJECT OF David's frustration felt like her stomach had turned itself inside out and switched places with a lung. She fidgeted in her seat while Cadie drove and almost insisted they turn back when a white dwelling came into view. "There it is," she pointed out, her voice at an odd pitch.

Cadie lifted an eyebrow. It was rather difficult to miss the homestead, it being the only manmade object around. She didn't comment, however, recognizing that her partner was wound tighter than the wire fence that ran alongside the track. Instead, she patted Jo's thigh and turned the truck into the gap in the fence. They rattled over an iron cattle grid and across a bare patch of dusty ground toward the neat, white, one-story home. Cadie pulled up and applied the parking brake. She looked around, taking in her lover's childhood home.

Apart from the main house, set 50 yards to the left, near a stand of forlorn gum trees, was a smaller cottage that Cadie guessed was for the workers. Behind that was a collection of ramshackle buildings, including a large shed and what looked like stables. Around the main house was a white fence and beyond it a garden.

Cadie shifted her gaze to her lover. Wide blue eyes blinked at the scenery, focused on the dark and open doorway in the middle of the homestead's wall. "You okay, sweetheart?" she asked, squeezing the dark-haired woman's knee.

"Scared shitless," came the curt reply.

MAGGIE MADISON GRIPPED the edge of the kitchen sink so hard her knuckles turned white. She had watched the four-wheel drive approach from the northeast and now she knew the moment had arrived. A blonde woman sat behind the wheel and the tall figure next to her could only be...

My daughter.

"Get out there, Maggie," she told herself. She dropped the tea towel onto the draining board and smoothed her hands down over her denim-covered thighs. *Damn, I'm nervous,* she realized, looking down at hands that were visibly shaking. With a deep breath, she steadied herself and stepped out into the brilliant sunshine.

Inside the stationary vehicle, Jo fidgeted.

"It's going to be fine," Cadie said soothingly. "Whatever happens, we'll get through it together. Be yourself. That's all they're going to want from you."

Jo's eyes softened. "How did you get to be so wise, kid?" she asked, managing to find a grin from somewhere.

"About 15 years' more experience with parents than you, Grandma," Cadie replied. "I'd kiss you now, but I think that might truly freak your mother out at this point." She nodded in the direction of the house.

Jo's head whipped around. "Oh God," she said as a tall, familiar female figure approached.

Cadie gave her one last pat before Jo opened the door and climbed out of the truck. Her palms were damp as she clenched and unclenched her hands. Tentatively, she stepped forward, disconcerted to find her legs unsteady. Her only consolation was that the woman coming towards her looked equally unsure of herself. *Please God, don't let me throw up on her.*

Maggie drank in the sight of the lovely woman approaching her. *She grew up beautiful,* she thought. *My gangly, clumsy teenager grew up into a beauty.* They came to a halt outside arm's reach of each other and for a few endless seconds neither knew what to say.

Jo tried to match the elegant, gray-haired woman who shared her facial features with the memories of her youth. The face was the same—more tanned and more lined, but unquestionably it was her mother. A surge of something very familiar and warm caught Jo by surprise.

"H-hello, Mum," she said hesitantly, a smile playing across her lips. Just as quickly, it was chased away by uncertainty.

Maggie's hands flew to her mouth as the emotions rose up and engulfed her. She caught her daughter's fleeting smile, the youthful insecurity that swept over her face. She couldn't form coherent words, the ache in her throat too tight and jagged.

Jo raised a hand, half-reaching for her mother, seeing that the older woman was close to tears. But she felt awkward, unsure of what her parent wanted or needed.

"Mum, it's okay," she said, startled to find her own voice strangled.

"Oh, Josie." Maggie stepped forward quickly, wrapping her arms around her daughter's shoulders and pulling her close. Tears came hot and fast as she held the warm body to her own. "Oh, Josie, baby, welcome home."

The words curled around Jo's heart like a soothing balm. She hadn't been held by her mother in...so long. Gradually she relaxed into the hug, absorbing her mother's scent—clean and sun-warmed, with a trace of the lavender soap she'd always used. Tears drifted down her cheeks.

"M-mum, I'm s-so s-sorry," she managed around hitching breaths. Immediately she felt her mother's hands changing to a soothing movement on her hair.

"Sshhh, baby girl. None of that matters now. You're home, that's all I care about. You're home."

Home. Jo closed her eyes and let the warmth of her mother's welcome wash over her. *I'm home.*

WAITING DISCREETLY IN the truck, Cadie felt tears sting her eyes and quickly wiped them away. *Come on, Jones,* she urged herself. *Time to meet the in-laws.*

Jo had left the small pile of mail on the seat next to her and Cadie scooped it up as she opened the driver's door. She walked around to the front of the truck and leaned against the bull-bar, trying to pick her moment.

Maggie pulled back a little from the hug and took her daughter's tear-streaked face between her hands. With long thumbs she brushed the tears away. Over Josie's shoulder she could see the pretty blonde standing quietly, head bowed.

"Are you going to introduce me to your girl, Josie?" she asked, warmed by the joy that flickered in her offspring's brilliant blue eyes.

"I-I was worried that...that you..." Jo was silenced by her mother's fingers against her lips. Maggie's eyes, paler than her own, but just as intense, held nothing but acceptance and curiosity.

"Don't you worry about that," her mother reassured. "If you're happy, that's all I care about. Now, come on, introduce us."

She was treated to Jo's trademark killer grin before the younger woman turned to look at her partner, extending a hand.

Relieved, Cadie took the proffered hand and moved to Jo's side. To her surprise, Jo pulled her close to place a kiss in her hair. Cadie wasn't about to argue though and slid her arm around her partner's waist.

Well, now I know what Jo will look like in 20 years or so, she thought. Maggie was every bit as beautiful as her daughter, though a lifetime spent working in a harsh landscape had added weather-beaten lines of experience to the familiar features.

Something to look forward to, Cadie decided, smiling tentatively at her future mother-in-law.

"Mum, this is Cadie," Jo said simply.

Cadie reached out with a hand. "It's great to finally meet you, Mrs. Madison."

Green eyes gazed candidly at Maggie from beneath an unruly fringe. Their quiet intelligence impressed her. *This one has depths,* she decided. *I thought this would be hard, but I was wrong; they seem good for each other.* Maggie took Cadie's hand and firmly pulled her closer, wrapping her in a warm, welcoming hug. "You must call me Maggie," she insisted, letting Cadie go, although she kept hold of her hands. "Welcome to Coonyabby."

"Thank you, Maggie." Cadie warmed to the older woman immediately. "Jo's told me so much about it, I'm really looking forward to exploring."

Maggie glanced around at the countryside she was so familiar with. "I'm afraid it's not as pretty as it can be, right now. This drought's been hard on the grass and flowers."

"It's still beautiful country," Cadie murmured. She was aware of Jo's warmth at her back, of an edginess in her demeanor. Cadie remembered the mail and handed it to Maggie. "Jo-Jo picked this up on our way in," she said with a smile.

"Ah, thank you." Maggie glanced cursorily at the stack of letters. "Bills, mostly, I'm sure." She looked up, sensitive to her daughter's jitters. *I think we all need to relax a little,* she thought. "Well, I don't know about you two, but I could certainly go a cup of tea. Josie, blossom, why don't you bring the truck around to the side of the house and bring your bags inside?"

Cadie turned to Jo. "Blossom?" she mouthed, tossing her the keys to the truck. Jo flushed despite the twinkle in Cadie's eye.

"Oh great. Thanks, Mum. Give her teasing material, why don't you?" *Some things never change.*

Maggie dismissed it with a poo-pooing wave of her hand. "Something tells me this one doesn't need much encouragement on that score. Now, go do." She took Cadie's hand again and pulled her in the direction of the homestead. "We'll see to that tea."

Cadie looked back over her shoulder at Jo, flinging her a helplessly apologetic look. Jo snorted and flashed her a happy grin, letting her know it was more than all right.

"I'm beginning to feel like John F. Kennedy," she muttered to herself as she watched her mother dragging her girlfriend away. "I'm the woman who accompanied Arcadia Jones to Coonyabby." The thought made her giggle and she felt almost light-headed with relief as she climbed up into the truck and turned the key in the ignition. *Now all we have to do is convince Dad.*

Chapter Eight

THE KITCHEN WAS cool, a blessed relief from the relentless sun and airless heat outside. Cadie sank gratefully down onto one of the wooden chairs that surrounded the central table. Maggie bustled around her, putting together cups and saucers while the kettle heated on top of the stove. The room had a vaguely 1970s feel about it and although the fittings and appliances were elderly, all were sparkling, obviously well-cared for. It was kind of comforting, Cadie decided, looking around. *It feels like home.*

Being left alone with Jo's mom this early on in their visit was slightly awkward, but it only took one look at the older woman's all-consuming interest in the bottom of a tea cup to tell Cadie that she wasn't alone in her discomfort. "This is a lovely room, Maggie," she said, hoping to find a way of putting them both more at ease. It won her a slightly distracted smile in reply.

"Thank you," Maggie replied. "It hasn't changed much over the years, but it's always served us pretty well." They lapsed into silence again before the kettle began to whistle and steam. Maggie quickly lifted it off the heat, trickling the boiling water over the leaves. "How do you take your tea, Cadie?"

"Black with one sugar, thanks."

Both women listened to the sounds of Jo pulling the truck up to the side of the house then slamming doors as she extracted their luggage from the back. Maggie placed Cadie's tea in front of her and sat down at the table.

"So," the older woman said tentatively. "How did you and Josie meet?"

Cadie smiled. It was the obvious question and did at least put them on fairly safe ground.

"I was with a group that chartered a yacht from her company for three weeks. She was our skipper." Cadie beamed, the happy memories of their first hesitant steps towards romance obvious on her face.

"Ah, and you couldn't resist each other?" Maggie found

herself reacting to Cadie's happiness. She decided to ignore the incredulous little voice inside her head that couldn't quite believe she was having this conversation.

Cadie blushed under the inquisitive blue gaze that was so like her partner's. "Something like that," she replied. "It was a little more complicated." She felt her color increase even further as Maggie's look intensified. "I was, um, with someone, when we first met." Cadie held her breath, waiting to see what the response was to that.

Maggie absorbed the news, stirring a spoonful of sugar slowly into her tea, her eyes on the swirling liquid. Finally, she looked up, catching the faint hint of anxiety in Cadie's green eyes. She smiled gently. "Love's a complicated thing," she said, reaching across to pat Cadie's forearm.

Cadie nodded and breathed again. "Yes, it can be," she agreed. *Okay, that's one little hurdle out of the way,* she thought with relief.

They were interrupted by the arrival of Jo at the back door. The tall woman had Cadie's large sports bag in one hand and her own backpack slung over her left shoulder. She turned sideways to negotiate the narrow doorway and then came to a sharp halt just inside the room. Cadie smiled at the look of shocked wonder on her lover's face.

Jo felt like she had stepped into a time warp. Apart from the very familiar appearance of the kitchen—she swept her eyes around the room she had grown up in—it was the smells that brought memories flooding back.

"You've been baking," she murmured as her mother handed her a cup of tea.

Maggie raised an eyebrow and patted her cheek softly. "I'm always baking, love." She chuckled as Jo sniffed the air speculatively.

"Bread," Jo guessed. "And..." she inhaled again. "Chocolate cake?" Cadie giggled at the look of childish hopefulness that lit up Jo's face. Maggie nodded and her daughter grinned triumphantly. "Oh, Cadie, you haven't eaten until you've tasted Mum's chocolate cake," she stated.

"Good?" Cadie asked, playing along.

Jo dropped the bags long enough to take a sip of her tea. *Dead milky and two sugars,* she thought. *Just the way I like it. Trust Mum to remember that.*

"Not just good. Heavenly."

"Tch, you're exaggerating, Josie," Maggie demurred. She moved over to the sink and began washing out her teacup.

"I'm not," Jo disagreed. She put her mug down on the table

and picked up the bags again, exchanging a meaningful look with Cadie as she did so. "Where am I taking these bags, Mum?" she asked.

Maggie turned around and leaned back against the sink as she dried her hands on a tea towel. "I've put you both in your old room," she said quietly. "I hope the bed's big enough."

Brownie points for you, Mrs. M, Cadie thought .

"Um, okay then." Jo winked at Cadie as she hefted the bags again and headed out of the kitchen.

Maggie watched her go, a tiny smile playing across her lips. Her eyes drifted away and caught the pale green gaze of the petite American leaning on her kitchen table.

"Thank you," Cadie said softly. "That was worrying her."

Maggie fiddled with the tea towel, tying the cloth into a knot in front of her. "I'm not going to pretend that it's not taking some getting used to. But it's more important to me to see her happy." She gave Cadie a frank look. "And it seems you make her happy."

"The feeling is mutual." Cadie was about to expand on that when she heard Jo call her name. "Excuse me," she apologized, and scurried down the hallway that bisected the house. Her partner was standing in the doorway to a small bedroom.

Cadie peeked around her into the room. "Wow," she murmured.

Jo's bedroom was almost like a museum piece—an exhibit on childhood. Cadie entered the room, wandering the edges to take in the minutiae of her soulmate's youth. A wooden shelf held a collection of crystal and porcelain animals. Some were exquisite, but most bore the telltale signs of a child's handling. A china cow balanced on three legs, a horse was missing a tail. At the other end of the shelf were a large number of Matchbox model cars of all varieties. Cadie grinned at them, picking up a sports model with opening doors. *My girl the tomboy,* she thought.

A higher shelf was piled with books—Cynthia Harnett, Rosemary Sutcliffe and a wide range of science fiction and fantasy—Asimov, Heinlein, and Donaldson. A battered, well-thumbed copy of *Lord of the Rings* held prized position.

Cadie continued to pick up items, learning something new about Jo from each one: stuffed toys, a crystal radio set. Posters of Bjorn Borg, Martina Navratilova and television cops Cagney and Lacey lined the walls.

From the edge of the bed, Jo watched Cadie explore. Her emotions were rubbed raw and close to the surface. *I can't believe they kept all this stuff,* she thought. *How could they have stood to look at it all after I left the way I did?* She must have had the most bemused expression on her face because when Cadie finally turned around to look at her, she promptly walked over and crouched between Jo's feet, placing her hands on her partner's knees.

"How are you doing?" she asked, smiling up into uncertain eyes.

"Um, I think my brain is dribbling out my ears," Jo muttered, provoking a gentle laugh.

"I think I like who you were when you lived in this room, Jo-Jo," she said.

Blue eyes finally focused on her. "You can tell that from the things in here?"

"I can." Cadie dropped a kiss on the top of Jo's head.

"That feels good," Jo said and wrapped Cadie up tighter.

Maggie found them like that, the sight stopping her in her tracks at the entrance to the bedroom. Neither woman had heard her approach and she spent a few seconds absorbing the reality of a type of relationship with which she'd had utterly no experience. *How can people think of this as a bad thing?* she pondered. *Look at the love and support they give each other. Everybody should be so lucky.*

She leaned against the doorjamb and cleared her throat quietly, unsurprised, and perhaps a little relieved, to see the two young women move apart quickly. "You don't have to do that, you know," she said matter-of-factly.

Jo rubbed her face, trying to dispel the blush she knew was coloring her cheeks. "Sorry, Mum. This takes a bit of getting used to." She glanced up at her partner, who had moved over to the large stack of vinyl music albums and singles in one corner. "At least it does for me. Cadie is an old hand at the parental thing."

Maggie stepped into the room and sat down next to her daughter. "Your parents know about...um, you?" she asked Cadie, who sat down next to the pile and began sifting through the treasure trove of 1980s music.

"Oh yes," she replied. "They've known since I was in college. I think I was 20 when I told them."

Maggie leaned back on her hands, unconsciously mirroring Jo's posture. *Two peas in a pod,* Cadie thought, smiling quietly to herself. *The apple certainly didn't fall too far from the tree in this family.*

"How did they take it?" Maggie asked tentatively.

Cadie braced herself against the wall and crossed her legs at the ankles. She thought about it before answering. "Bear in mind that my home town has a large, and pretty vocal, gay and lesbian community and my parents were both born and bred there," she explained. "So they certainly weren't unaware. Even so, I guess you're never prepared for it to be one of your own children." She sought Maggie's eyes and found candid interest there. "By the time I came out, Mom and Dad had already figured out that having me alive and healthy was the most important thing."

Maggie sensed there was more to that story than she was getting. But this wasn't the time to dig deeper. "You're going to find us awfully backward out here, then," she said. "I'm embarrassed to say that you're the first...gay person...I've ever known."

Jo nudged her mother's shoulder. "You've known me for over 30 years, Mum," she reminded her. "And there was Phil."

Maggie blushed. "I'm sorry. I think it's still a little hard for me to think of you...that way." She shrugged apologetically.

There was an awkward silence, as if each woman had a lot to say but couldn't quite see a way to start the conversation. Observing mother and daughter, Cadie decided it was time to let them work it out for themselves. She pushed herself up from the floor, dropping the handful of 45s she'd been looking at back onto the pile. "I'm going to do a little exploring," she announced.

As she walked to the door, Jo grabbed her hand and squeezed it gently. "Don't go out of sight of the house for now? It's easy to get disoriented out there if you don't know your way around."

Cadie leaned down and brushed a light kiss across her partner's lips. "Aye, aye skipper," she agreed.

"Oh, shut up," Jo retorted, laughing at the retreating back.

"Skipper?" Maggie raised a surprised eyebrow at her daughter who blushed under the scrutiny.

"S'a nickname my crew uses when we're working," Jo explained.

Maggie shook her head wonderingly. "This is a lot to absorb, Josie. Last time I saw you, you were a kid. And now you've got all this responsibility, your own business." She nodded her head in the direction Cadie had disappeared. "A partner."

Jo grinned, happy to latch on to a subject she was comfortable discussing, even if her mother wasn't. "She's great, isn't she?"

Maggie took in the sparkle in Jo's eyes and the undisguised happiness in her smile. "She's lovely." Hesitantly, she reached up and cupped the beautiful, and familiar, face in her hands. "I feel like I've missed so much of your life, Josie."

Jo nodded. Maggie's hands dropped away and Jo's gaze dropped with them. She suddenly found the fading pattern in the worn rug fascinating. "You have, Mum. And that's my fault. I did the wrong thing by you and Dad leaving the way I did, and I wouldn't blame either of you if couldn't forgive me for that."

"Now you cut that out, young lady," her mother said sternly. "You were a baby. And this is a hard life for kids out here. You got impatient and wanted to get on with your life. We always understood that."

Jo looked at her incredulously. "You can't honestly believe that what I did was acceptable, Mum," she exclaimed.

"I never said we thought you did the right thing," Maggie corrected. "But we always understood why you did what you did."

Jo still looked skeptical. "I hurt you both."

Maggie nodded slowly, wondering how far she should push. "Yes, you did. You scared us and hurt us and angered us." She bit her lip as Jo winced visibly. *Don't stop now, Maggie,* she thought. *This is a chance to start over with her. Clear the air.* "But if you think that means we don't forgive you, then you need to think again."

Jo blinked, not quite comprehending what she was hearing. In her wildest dreams she couldn't have imagined her mother would be calmly sitting next to her, forgiving her within an hour of seeing her again. She felt tears sting her eyes once more and tried to squelch them.

Maggie smiled at her dumbstruck offspring. "Is that so hard to believe, bloss?" she asked, brushing an errant tear from Jo's cheek with the pad of her thumb. "Josie, you're my daughter. I can forgive you anything."

God, I wish that were really true, Jo thought, repressing the urge to tell her mother every terrible crime she'd ever committed. She felt fingertips brush against her cheek. *For now, it's enough – a blessing – that she forgives my leaving.* Searching her mother's face, she asked, "Does Dad feel the same way?"

Maggie sighed. "That's a very complicated question to answer, love." Regret swept across Jo's face and she hastily put her arm around her daughter's shoulders, pulling her close. "No, no, I don't mean he doesn't forgive you. Of course he does. He adores you, Josie. He always has, always will."

Jo breathed in the memory-laden scent of her mother and felt a sudden childish urge to bury herself in Maggie's embrace. The older woman sensed the hesitation and made the decision for her, wrapping her up in an all-encompassing hug, her cheek resting on the top of the dark head.

"You have to understand that everything your father is—everything he values—is wrapped up in this place," Maggie continued. "Of course he hoped you would want to take over running the property when he retired, but he also knew there was every chance you wouldn't want to. And he knew that before you left."

Jo listened quietly, the rumble of her mother's rich alto vibrating against her cheek. She could also feel Maggie's heartbeat, slow and steady, calming.

"When you left, and Dad had his heart attack, we nearly lost this place. Your father had a lot of anger, but it wasn't all about you, Josie. It was a lot of things...frustration with the banks, wool prices, the weather...all of it. But it all got focused on you because you were the one thing Dad felt he could have some influence over. But you proved him wrong on that when you left the way you did."

"God, I am so sorry," Jo whispered hoarsely.

"Shhh. We all made mistakes, love. Your father blamed himself a lot, and probably I blamed myself. But there were some positives to come out of it, especially once we'd heard from you and knew you were okay."

"Positives?"

Maggie kissed the top of her daughter's head. "Oh yes. For a start, your father learned to delegate some of the work around here. That's something I'd been nagging him about for years. More importantly, it made him realize that there might be a life beyond this station."

Jo lifted her head and looked at her mother. "Beyond...you mean—"

"—I mean we're not getting any younger, Josie. And this place isn't getting any easier, or, God knows, any more profitable. Your father was born here, was brought up to believe this farm was everything. When you left, he found out there are more important things than working day in, day out, for not much reward." She smiled wearily. "Believe it or not, that's probably going to be a good thing in the long run."

Jo pulled away and flopped backwards down onto the bed. She couldn't help smiling as she found herself gazing up at the fluorescent stars and planets stickers she'd attached to the ceiling sometime in her dim, dark, past. *And now for the 64 million dollar question.*

"And how does he feel about me being gay, Mum?" she asked quietly.

Maggie sighed. *I wish I knew. From the time I told him to this moment, he's barely been able to say a word about it.* "Well, you know your father, Josie. He doesn't exactly talk a lot about what he's thinking or feeling. And it's only been a week." She didn't know what else to say, so instead she rested a hand on her daughter's thigh, listening to the wheels in Jo's brain spinning.

"In other words, he's not too keen on the concept and doesn't know how to say so without getting pissed off about it," Jo theorized.

"I'm not going to lie to you, bloss," Maggie replied. "I don't know how he's going to react. You're both probably going to have to be very patient with him. He's an old-fashioned man."

Jo snorted, memories of beating her teenage head against her father's intractability suddenly very fresh in her mind. "Where is he?"

"The north-west back paddock, fixing a bore pump," Maggie replied.

Jo grinned rakishly at her mother. "Did it really need fixing?"

Maggie just laughed. "It's good to have you home, kiddo."

CADIE SCOOPED HER Akubra off the kitchen table and jammed it on her head as she stepped out of the homestead's back door. The heat hit her full on as she walked into the sunlight. To her left was a large water tank nestled against the wall, its sides covered in ivy. Skirting it, she headed for the gate in the white fence that surrounded the garden, her booted feet scuffing through the orange dust that covered the hard-packed earth.

To the west of the homestead lay a couple of worker's cottages, and beyond them again, other buildings that included a stable and a wire pen that looked to be currently uninhabited. Cadie decided the lure of saying hello to some animals had the most appeal.

She tried not to be too anxious about the conversation going on in the house. *Somehow I don't think Maggie is going to be biggest problem,* she mused as her footsteps took her along the well-worn path past the cottages. *I wonder when Mr. Madison will be home.*

The stables were dilapidated, but serviceable. Cadie guessed they'd have to be close to collapse before any precious resources were spent on fixing them. As she approached, three horses meandered towards her from different parts of the stable corral. Two were chestnuts and one, the mare, a palomino. Cadie climbed up onto the top rail of the metal fence and swung her legs over as the two chestnuts approached. Both wuffled against her legs, the young colt reaching higher to nudge against Cadie's shoulder.

"Hello there," she said softly, rubbing the back of her hand against the soft sensitive end of the colt's nose. "Aren't you a handsome boy?" The other chestnut, an older male, picked at her shoelaces. "Yes, hello, so are you." Cadie chuckled as the pair vied for her attention, while the mare—she guessed the pale golden beauty was mother to the two boys—hung back cautiously. The horses looked well-fed and cared for despite the hard times Cadie knew the Madisons were living through. Somehow, that made her feel less anxious about Jo's father. *He treats animals well, that has to be a good thing.*

"I'm sorry, guys, I didn't think to bring you any treats," she said as the two young horses nudged and nuzzled her in a quest for food. "Tomorrow, I promise." She reached out and stroked both animals between the eyes. Reluctantly, the pair moved away and Cadie found herself eye-to-eye with the gorgeous palomino.

"Hello, beautiful," she murmured. The mare whickered softly and cautiously walked forward until she was within arm's reach. Cadie resisted the urge to touch, though, preferring to let the mare get comfortable with her first. Large, caramel eyes blinked at her, sizing her up. "Are you going to say hello?" Cadie kept her voice low and gentle.

The mare snuffled tentatively against her thigh, then, seemingly satisfied, moved one step closer and gently head butted Cadie's shoulder.

"Well, hello to you too, madam," she answered, offering an upturned palm for the horse to mouth. Cadie grinned, loving the smell and feel of the large animal. "I wonder if you were around when Jo-Jo was a kid." The mare was definitely old enough, she thought, taking in the mature lines and experienced twinkle in the brown eyes. "Bet you could tell me a story or two."

The mare huffed against her shirt in response and Cadie laughed gently. "Yeah, I'm sure." She rested her cheek against the big horse's muzzle, breathing in the unmistakable smells. The mare tolerated her touch patiently and Cadie closed her eyes for a few moments. *It's been a long day. And still a way to go.*

Cadie jumped down into the corral and walked towards the stable, her new-found friends meandering after her hopefully. The interior of the building was clean, if a little rough and each stall had fresh feed and water, confirming her feeling that the animals had high priority.

She found a curry-comb hanging on a nail and pulled it

down, immediately attracting the mare who whickered softly and nudged at her, lipping the comb in her hand. Cadie laughed. "Okay, okay, I can take a hint."

Slowly, she began working the comb over the pale, smooth coat, the action bringing back a lot of memories. Her childhood had been filled with days spent doing exactly this. The private boarding school in which she had spent her teenage years had a stable of five horses, and Cadie had clocked many happy hours in equine company. She hadn't ridden in a long time, but the prospect of going out with Jo some time in the next few days was definitely something to be relished.

When Cadie was done, she walked back outside, the mare happily following. The two geldings fell into step behind their mother as Cadie wandered down the middle of the dusty corral.

"What do you think, guys?" she asked, turning and stopping in front of the horses. "Think I've given Jo-Jo enough time to thrash things out with her mom?"

The four-footed trio was predictably silent on the matter and Cadie tucked her hands into her back pockets and dragged a foot casually through the red dust. With a quick shake of her head, she headed for the metal fence and clambered back up and over. "Don't worry, I'll be back," she called to her new friends. "And I'll bring treats next time, I promise."

Cadie walked towards the workers' cottages, past a small stand of tall, gnarled gum trees that provided a meager amount of shade. This time she noticed a dog curled up in the cool gloom at the base of the largest tree. Curious, and always a sucker for an animal, Cadie turned her footsteps towards the dog. She was brought up short when the blue kelpie uncurled himself in a flash and came charging out at her, barking loudly with teeth bared.

"Whoa!" yelped Cadie. She knew enough not to run, but found herself backpedaling anyway in the face of the small bundle of ferocity. The dog barreled to a halt, front legs stiff, hackles raised. He growled loudly enough for a dog twice his size and Cadie held her hands out in front of her, palms up.

Cadie was beginning to wonder how she was going to retreat without being savaged when a gravelly voice came from behind her right shoulder. "That's a workin' dog, girlie, not for pettin'."

Cadie glanced quickly toward the source of the remark, not wanting to take her eyes off the angry dog for too long. A wiry, bowlegged man sauntered over, wiping his hands on an oily rag, which he proceeded to tuck into the back pocket of his soiled jeans.

Is this David Madison? Cadie wondered, not seeing any resemblance to Jo in the hard-bitten man coming her way.

"Do you think you could call him off?" Cadie asked. The dog hadn't moved from his aggressive stance and every time Cadie tried to step one way or the other, he shifted to block her path.

"He's a big coward, nothin' to worry about," the man said bluntly. "Give 'im a kick and he'll bugger off."

Cadie shook her head, hoping like hell this abrupt man wasn't her father-in-law.

"I'd rather not, actually," she muttered, disconcerted by the dog's behavior. Usually she had the best of relationships with animals, but she'd never encountered a dog as tense as this one. *But that doesn't mean I'm going to kick him to get my way.*

"Bloody hell, what's the matter with you, girl?" the man muttered. He stepped between Cadie and the dog and swung out viciously with a booted foot before she could protest. The point of his toe caught the dog on the shoulder and the canine crumpled into a yelping heap. "G'on, get out of here, ya bastard!" the man shouted. He pulled his leg back for another swing at the whimpering, cowering dog, but he hadn't counted on a certain feisty blonde.

"You asshole!" Cadie yelled as she grabbed the man's drawn-back foot and twisted hard. She caught him with all his momentum moving forward and the maneuver flipped him over into the dirt where he sprawled awkwardly.

"What the bloody hell do you think you're doing, woman?"

JO AND HER mother emerged arm in arm from her bedroom and headed back to the kitchen.

"Want to help me get dinner on?" Maggie asked, smiling at her daughter.

"Sure," Jo replied amiably. "What do you need me to do?"

Her mother unhooked her arm from Jo's elbow and headed for one of the drawers set into the counter near the sink. She opened it and pulled out a potato peeler. With a grin, she tossed it at Jo. "Spuds," she said.

Jo caught the peeler and laughed. "Some things never change. You keeping them in the same place as usual?"

"In the pantry, yes," Maggie confirmed.

"How many for dinner?"

"Six. We four, plus Jack and Hughie."

Jo pulled potatoes out from a sack under the bottom shelf of the pantry. "Hughie?" She cast her mind back, trying to figure out why that name sounded so familiar. "You don't mean that little Aboriginal kid who used to come out on the weekends with his dad?"

Maggie chuckled. "That little kid is 23 now, Josie," she said, extracting pots and pans from one of the cupboards. "You remember his mum died when he was a baby?" Jo nodded. "Well, his father finally drank himself to death when Hughie was about 15. Your dad ran into Hughie in town one day and the kid looked half-starved. He's worked out here with us ever since."

"Wow." Jo scooped more potatoes out. "My brain is spinning out a bit," she admitted. "Everything seems the same—I mean, look." She pointed at a large, gaily colored metal tin, sitting on the pantry shelf. "You're still using the same tin I used to raid for biscuits when I was a kid." She ran her fingers over the horses and dogs that covered the cool surface, then pried the lid off. Jo laughed when she saw the contents. *Tim Tams. She still keeps the Tim Tams in here.* She fished out one of the chocolate-covered treats.

"Same biscuits," her mother laughed from across the room as she watched Jo happily crunching.

"That's what I'm talking about," Jo said around a sweet mouthful. "So much has happened to all of us. But it looks like nothing has changed." She used her shirt to carry the potatoes over to the sink and tipped them out onto the draining board.

"Except for my gray hairs," Maggie said.

Jo looked over at the familiar long ponytail, which was indeed streaked more gray than ebony. She smiled. "It suits you."

Maggie snorted. "Looking old suits me? Thanks," she said dryly.

"You don't look old," Jo protested as she started to wash the dirt off the potatoes. "You look..." The hairs on the back of Jo's neck stood up suddenly and she was moving towards the back door, even before Maggie could open her mouth to ask what was wrong.

"What the...?" Maggie dried her hands off on a tea-towel before following her running daughter out the door.

Jo emerged into the sunlight at a sprint. One part of her brain told her that she'd heard Cadie yell, but her legs told her that she'd started moving before that. *What's up with that?* she wondered, even as she vaulted the garden fence and headed for the two figures near the cottages. *Uh-oh.*

"What the bloody hell do you think you're doing, woman?" the man on the ground was yelling as Cadie stood over him. She was balling and unballing her fists in barely controlled fury as Jo came to a skidding halt next to her.

"What happened?" Jo asked breathlessly, taking in the angry man and the whimpering dog.

"This asshole—" *please God, don't make it be her father* "—kicked the dog to get him out of the way," Cadie shouted, adrenaline still coursing through her body and making her shake with anger. "How would you like it, you piece of..." She felt a strong arm slide around her waist and pull her back a little.

"Easy, Tonto," a deep, rich voice murmured in her ear. "He's not gonna do any more damage today."

Cadie let out a long ragged breath, realizing Jo was right and she was in danger of acting as big an ass as the man had. "Okay," she breathed. "You can let me go now."

As Jo's hand withdrew, Cadie swept a look around, seeking out the dog. It had taken the opportunity to crawl painfully back into the shade of the tree. Ignoring the man glaring at her from the ground, she approached the animal, murmuring quiet words of reassurance. This time the dog showed no signs of aggression, whimpering as the woman came within reaching distance.

"It's okay, sweetie, I want to make sure you're okay," she said quietly, extending a hand, palm up, for the dog to sniff. He did, eventually, giving her fingers a tentative lick of acceptance. Gently, she probed the dog's shoulder, carefully stretching out the leg and moving it through the full range of motion. "Nothing broken, boy," she reassured him, looking into big brown eyes that were now all trust and doggy faith. "Friends, huh?" She scratched his ears and gave him one last pat before she pushed herself up and turned away.

Jo watched her lover's gentle ministrations with a soft smile. *She is such a tenderheart,* she thought affectionately. Her smile faded as she turned her gaze back on the man. He scrambled to his feet and brushed the dust off his jeans. Jo felt her mother come up behind her. "Who are you?" she asked the man.

He ignored the question, looking instead from daughter to mother and back again. "No need for me to ask you that," he muttered.

"Josie, this is Jack Collingwood, our foreman," Maggie said, her hackles yet again on edge thanks to the rat-faced man she'd long ago decided she didn't like. "Jack, this is my daughter, Jossandra."

"I'd say nice to meet you, but I'm not so sure," Jo said bluntly. "Do you usually go around kicking animals, Mr. Collingwood?"

The man's face reddened again, flushed with anger and humiliation. "The bastard was having a go at the young lady, there," he objected. "Someone had to do something."

Cadie stepped back into the conversation. "He was protecting his territory from a stranger. That's only natural. All you had to do was call him off."

"That beast don't listen to me, girl. A swift kick's all he understands."

Jo leaned forward to make a point. "Then you don't have him too well trained, do you?" she said. "Perhaps you need to rethink your methods."

Collingwood stepped forward one pace, getting up in Jo's face. "Who do you think you are?"

"That's enough!" Maggie intervened, letting the rarely-used authority she held over Jack show in her tone. "Jack, where's Hughie?"

Collingwood flicked a glance in Maggie's direction, taking in her glowering look and hands on hips posture. *Damn her, she'll be telling the boss all about this,* he realized. He backed off a step from the tall young woman in front of him. *You haven't heard the last from me, bitch.* "He's feeding the orphaned lambs," he growled.

"Perhaps you'd better go help him," Maggie suggested pointedly. "Dinner will be in a couple of hours."

Without another word, Collingwood stepped away, holding Jo's steely gaze for long seconds before he turned his back on them and headed towards the sheep pen.

"Charming," Jo remarked.

Maggie snorted. "I've never liked that man, but your father says he's a good worker and he can rely on him." She shrugged her shoulders. "It's hard to find men willing to work these days."

"I'm sorry, Maggie," Cadie said quietly. "I didn't mean to cause any trouble."

Jo's mother smiled and stepped forward, hooking her arm through Cadie's as they started to walk back toward the homestead. "Don't you worry about it, dearie," she said breezily. "I like a woman who stands up for herself, and for animals. To be honest, I've been wanting to knock that idiot on his backside from the moment I met him."

They all laughed and Jo fell in behind her mother and her partner, raising an eyebrow at the rapport the two women had already developed. *I'm in trouble here,* she though wryly. *The best kind of trouble.*

Chapter Nine

DAVID MADISON SWUNG the ATV into the shed and killed the engine. It was late afternoon, and he knew he was a few minutes away from being face to face with his daughter again. His stomach was in knots—butterflies didn't even come close to describing the sensation.

I have no idea what's going to happen when I see her, he acknowledged. *I don't want a scene, that's all. Not in front of strangers. Not in front of the men. Jesus, not in front of anyone.*

He climbed off the four-wheeler and lifted his knapsack over his shoulder. He was sweaty and covered in dust, not to mention the scraped knuckles that were par for the course when he was working around the machines. He hung the ATV's keys on a nail near the door of the shed and stepped out into the late afternoon sun. As always, the sight of the homestead touched something deep in him. The impending sunset cast a golden glow over the white house, and lent the farm buildings and red earth an oil painting quality that never ceased to intrigue him. For a few seconds, David stood and took it all in. The deep crow's feet at the corners of his gray eyes crinkled as he smiled slightly.

This is home, he told himself. *Always has been. Always will be.* He scuffed his boots against a wooden fence paling, knocking the excess dust off his trousers. *Even if I can't be here, this'll always be home.* His father, his grandfather and his great-grandfather had worked this land. *It's never made us rich,* he thought. *But it's never broken us, either.*

Until now, maybe.

He sighed deeply, consigning the never-ending problem of how to squeeze money from his land into the darker recesses of his mind. *More immediate things to worry about right now,* he realized. Wearily he trudged towards the homestead, steeling himself for...*for God only knows what.*

JO COULD FEEL the tension winding tighter and tighter inside her gut as the afternoon began to slip into evening. The time since Cadie's confrontation with Jack Collingwood had passed very pleasantly. They had been helping her mother, laughing and chatting as they prepared the last meal of the day.

Mum's been great, Jo thought as she ran a tea towel over the pan she had washed. *I didn't give her enough credit.* She lowered the pan rack that was suspended from the ceiling and hung the pot back on its hook. *This trip was definitely a good idea,* she thought. *Why did I wait so long?* She looked across the kitchen to where her mother and Cadie were laughing over some reminiscence of Jo's childhood. Cadie looked happy and comfortable. *That's why,* Jo acknowledged, affection for her partner warming her nervous stomach as she hoisted the rack back up to the ceiling. *I needed that support behind me.*

Cadie laughed at something Maggie told her and caught Jo's eye, bringing her back to the moment. "You rode an emu?" she demanded, her eyes wide and incredulous.

Jo felt herself flushing. "Well, I mean...um, yes," she admitted, grinning sheepishly. "The really hard part was catching him in the first place."

"How did you manage that, Josie?" Maggie wondered. "You never did explain it to me."

Jo's eyes narrowed. "You're enjoying this, aren't you, Mother?"

"Thoroughly," Maggie confirmed, crossing her arms and leaning back against the counter as she waited for her squirming daughter's reply. She smiled, knowing that despite the blush, Jo was becoming more and more comfortable with being home. *And that's a very good thing.*

"I don't remember how we caught it," Jo dissembled. "Phil was with me," she explained to Cadie.

"You had Phil wave his arms in front of it, and you lassoed it with a bit of old rope," came a deep voice from the hallway.

Jo's heart stopped, then tripped over itself to catch up, sucking the breath out of her in a rush. She turned her head and was met by a cool gray gaze that faltered and flicked away after a couple of seconds.

Maggie held her breath. Beside her, Cadie did the same.

Jo was experiencing a weird sense of disorientation. She knew the man standing in the doorway was her father. Those eyes couldn't belong to anyone else. But he was a far cry from the tall, strong man who had dominated her childhood memories. *He's gotten so old,* she thought sadly, taking in the stooped set of the shoulders, the almost-white at the temples and the deep sun-bronzed wrinkles that lined his face. *Did I do that?*

My God, she's the image of her mother at the same age, David realized. *Beautiful.* A pang of something like regret made him wince. *All those years I could've known her, gone.*

"Hello, Dad," Jo managed.

"Hello, Josie." His eyes glanced by her before taking in Cadie's presence.

Hesitantly, Jo stepped towards him, but stopped when he quickly moved away.

"I'm, uh, going to get washed up for supper," he muttered. With a brief nod, he disappeared down the corridor.

Jo turned anxious eyes on her mother.

Maggie raised her hands in a calming gesture. "It's okay, love," she said. "You've got to give him a bit of time."

Jo nodded, then hung her head, disconcerted to find tears filling her eyes. She buried her hands in her pockets, at a loss to know how to feel or what to do.

Cadie let out the breath she had been holding and walked over to her partner. "C'mon, baby," she murmured, coaxing Jo into relaxing a little in her arms. Gradually, Jo did, until her cheek rested against Cadie's temple. "That wasn't so bad. You took each other by surprise, that's all. Your mom's right. It's gonna be okay."

Jo sniffled slightly. "You think?"

"Yes. Now, come on. He'll be back soon." Cadie was vaguely aware of Maggie walking out of the kitchen in the general direction of the bathroom. "And I think you freaked him out as much as he did you."

Jo chuckled tearily. "Yeah, I guess I did, huh?"

MAGGIE CLOSED THE bathroom door, and leaned back against it. The room was filled with steam from David's shower and she could see his wiry form behind the glass door of the cubicle. Her husband was leaning forward, hands on the wall, letting the hot water pound on the back of his neck.

"You all right, love?" she asked.

David snorted and turned off the water, rubbing his face with one hand. "Yeah, darl, I'm fine," he muttered. "Glad that was you coming in. Anybody else and it would've killed me."

With a chuckle, Maggie took a large fluffy towel from the rail and unfolded it. David opened the door and stepped towards her, letting his wife wrap the soft material around his waist. Maggie kissed him lightly on the cheek.

"You should be used to me walking in on you by now," she

said, her fingers grazing the long, thin scar that ran the length of his breastbone.

"Uh-huh." David watched his wife gather her thoughts. He knew that if he kept quiet and let her think, she'd soon enough tell him what was what.

"You know your daughter is terrified, don't you?" she eventually said. David stopped drying his hair and stared at Maggie. "And don't stand there and tell me you're not a little scared as well, David Madison."

"I can't pretend everything is okay, Maggie," he replied gruffly and pointed in the general direction of the kitchen. "If you haven't noticed, wife, there's another person out there. Another woman. Our daughter is...she's..."

Maggie silenced his frustration with a touch of her hand. "Is that really what's bothering you, David?" she asked, gazing into steady gray eyes that had never changed in all the years she'd known him.

"It doesn't help," he replied.

She smiled at him. "Be around them for a while, love. You'll find out what I've found out in one afternoon."

"And what's that?"

"You'll see, if you let yourself look. Anyway, believe it or not, that's not actually why I came in to see you." His eyebrow lifted inquiringly. Maggie stepped away, allowing him to finish drying off. With a sigh, she said, "It's Jack."

"Ah." David didn't really want to hear this. Maggie had been negative about the foreman from the moment he'd stepped onto the property. But the man was a good worker and they were few and far between.

"Cadie caught him kicking one of the dogs today," Maggie went on. "And Hughie's got a mouse the size of an egg under his eye."

That brought David up short. "I'll deal with it," he said bluntly.

Maggie knew that was all the discussion she was going to get on the subject. She also knew when her husband said he would deal with something, it would be dealt with.

"Thank you." She watched him pulling on clean clothes. "Don't forget your tablets, love," she reminded him as she headed out the door.

MUCH TO JO'S relief, Maggie and Cadie kept up an almost endless stream of cheerful conversation through dinner. Her mother was full of eager questions for Cadie, curious about her family background and home town. Maggie had decided to keep dinner to the four of them, taking out covered plates to Hughie and Jack in the cottage. Jo kept one ear on the chatter while she watched her father.

The taciturn man concentrated hard on his plate of roast beef and vegetables. She found her eyes drawn, as they always had been, to his hands. They were large, weather-beaten mitts, with broad, flat fingers and gnarled knuckles that sported a few fresh grazes. Jo looked down at her own hands and the slowly-healing scrapes from her brush with the Beowulf's engine days ago. She flexed her right hand, curling and uncurling a fist.

Guess we have some things in common, she thought.

There was a pause in the talk while Maggie and Cadie stopped swapping family history long enough to eat.

"Got your own business going, eh?" David said out of the blue. He held his knife and fork casually, forearms resting on the table. His eyes locked on to hers briefly.

"Um, yeah," Jo replied. "Got a couple of yachts running charters pretty much all year round these days."

He nodded. "Making money for you?"

Jo looked at him. He'd gone back to sawing at his meat. "So far, so good," she answered, unconsciously matching his blunt tone. "I've only been the owner a month or so, so it's a case of suck it and see." She felt Cadie's hand squeeze her thigh in gentle reassurance.

"Jo's got some ideas for expanding, though, don't you?" Cadie said proudly.

"Yeah, I do—maybe another boat."

David flicked a look at her again. "Tricky thing, expansion," he said gruffly. "Can't do it too soon."

"Well, I don't have any immediate plans to go spending a lot of money," Jo said, in full agreement. "We've got a pretty busy winter season coming up. We'll get through that and then see what the off-season looks like before we make any decisions."

David chewed thoughtfully. "Good business to be in these days," he said. "Tourism."

Jo caught her mother's eye, not missing the gleam. *Guess she's pleased we're actually having a conversation,* Jo thought. "Yeah it's certainly taking off up there," she replied. "And as long as we can keep giving better service than our competitors, we should do all right."

Cadie gave her partner's leg another squeeze before withdrawing her hand and continuing with her meal. "This beef is delicious, Maggie," she said.

"Thank you," Jo's mother replied. "It was one of our own

beasts."

Of course it was, Cadie thought wryly, suddenly reminded that she was at the sharp end of the food chain. *It's not like they were going to trot down to the supermarket and buy a frozen roast. Why do that when you can go out and slaughter your own?* For some reason the mouthful she'd bitten off became a little harder to swallow at the thought.

Maggie read Cadie's mind and she smiled kindly. "Don't worry, I promise I won't subject you to anything too bloodthirsty," she said, the twinkle in her eye bringing a grin to Cadie's face.

"Thanks," Cadie replied. "I'm not used to my food having a face."

David snorted. "You're out in the real world now."

"You're right," Cadie agreed, not really knowing whether the older man was criticizing her or not. So far, she hadn't been able to get much of a sense of how he felt about her. He'd barely given her a glance.

Jo came to the rescue. "What are your plans tomorrow, Dad?" she asked. "And whatever they are, can we tag along?"

David cleaned off his plate with a slice of bread, resting his knife and fork down while he munched at the gravy-soaked morsel. "One of the bores at the top end is blocked," he said. "Thought I'd head up there with Hughie and clean out whatever's causing the trouble."

Jo shot a quick smile at Cadie. "You up for that?"

Cadie grinned. "You bet," she replied enthusiastically.

"Means getting up before dawn," David muttered.

"No problem," Cadie said. "We're usually up pretty early most mornings anyway."

Maggie raised an eyebrow in disbelief. "My daughter makes a habit of waking up early? My daughter, who could barely be rousted out of bed before midday on the weekends?" She laughed. "The times really have changed."

"You'd be surprised," Cadie said, trying not to sound like she was rushing to her partner's defense. "She's out there most mornings, meditating with the sunrise."

That caught David's attention, she noticed, even as she was aware of the fetching blush coloring Jo's cheeks.

"Cadie ..." Jo began to hush her.

"Meditating?" David exclaimed, for once holding his daughter's gaze for more than a passing second. "Don't tell me you've turned into one of those hairy-legs-and-sandals types all concerned about saving whales and kangaroos?"

Oooo, guess I hit a raw nerve, Cadie thought.

Jo was silent for a few seconds, unsurprised at her father's vehement response to any suggestion of anything approaching the spiritual or intangible. "It's not that, Dad," she answered quietly. "Don't worry, I'm not about to start telling you that you should be putting pink ribbons on the 'roos instead of shooting them. Meditating's what I do to relax myself before the day starts." She decided not to try and explain the Buddhist philosophies that had found a place in her spiritual values lately. "It's great." She grinned cheekily at her parent. "You should try it one day." *As if.*

David snorted and noisily pushed his chair back from the table. He stood up and carried his utensils over to the sink, where he dropped them in to the water with a splash. "No thanks," he muttered. "Is there any pudding, love?" he asked his wife.

Grateful for a chance to ease a little of the steadily growing tension, Maggie jumped to her feet and headed for the refrigerator. "There sure is," she answered. "Complete with birthday candles, what's more."

Jo groaned. "Aw, Mum, you didn't have to do that."

"Oh, hush." Maggie lifted an enormous chocolate cake off the fridge shelf and placed it in the middle of the table. She fished a box of matches from her pocket and struck one, lighting the six candles with it.

"Six?" asked Cadie.

"Yes," Jo murmured. "Three long ones for each decade, and three short ones for each extra year." She looked up at her mother and caught Maggie with the glimmer of a tear in her eye. "I remember."

David returned to his seat. "Sorry we couldn't actually say it on the day, Josie," he said, using his daughter's pet name for the first time since they had arrived. "Happy birthday."

"Thanks, Dad." Jo was disconcerted to hear her voice cracking, but then it had been a very long time since she'd heard her father speak to her affectionately. *Wow.*

CADIE PULLED OFF her t-shirt and extended the movement into a long, luxurious stretch that popped her spine back into place and tugged at muscles that felt like they hadn't rested in days.

"Ugh," she winced, relaxing back into her normal posture. Cadie half-expected a teasing zinger from her partner, but Jo was silently pensive, lying on her back on her childhood bed. Cadie dropped her t-shirt on the chair and rubbed her face wearily.

It's been a very long day, she thought. She watched Jo cover her eyes with her right arm, the exhaustion evident in every angle of her body.

Cadie pulled on the old baseball shirt she wore on the rare occasions she and Jo didn't sleep nude. She slowly walked to the bedside and leaned one knee on the edge of the narrow mattress. *It's gonna be a tight squeeze,* she thought, barely concealing a small smile. *Pity it's so hot, but I'm sure we'll survive.* The air was still and full of dry heat even now, four hours after sunset.

Cadie slid onto the bed, lying on her side with her head propped on her hand, watching Jo. "It's been a day, huh?" she murmured.

Jo snorted quietly. "Oh yeah," she whispered hoarsely.

"You okay, sweetheart?" Cadie reached out and slid her hand under Jo's t-shirt. *She's wound up tight, still,* she realized, feeling the abs twitch and contract at her touch.

"I'm whipped," Jo replied. "Inside and out." She stared up at the ceiling for a moment, lost in her own thoughts. "Don't take Dad's grumpiness personally. He's like that with everyone when he first meets them. I used to think he was rude, but I think I've figured out he's shy."

Cadie cocked an eyebrow at her lover. "How did you know I was thinking about that?"

Jo smiled wearily. "You looked like you were fretting on something, and given how well you're already getting on with Mum, I figured it had to be Dad who was bothering you."

Cadie bent and kissed her lover. "He's bothering you, too, I think."

Jo nodded slowly. "To be honest, they both are. Did you notice? Not one question about my life before I moved to the Whitsundays. They're either both pathologically non-curious, or that shit-scared of what they might find out."

Cadie thought about that. Both options were possible, she supposed. Though what she had already seen of Maggie told her the woman was as curious about the world as her daughter. But there was a third option Jo hadn't considered, she was sure.

"Could be they don't need to know, love," she suggested. She let go of her partner long enough to reach up to the wall control for the ceiling fan, turning the rickety old appliance up a notch. Then she slid under the thin top sheet.

Jo turned onto her side, gazing down at her lover. "You really think that's possible?" she asked quietly. "I mean, if I was them, I'd be desperate to know."

Cadie brushed fingertips across Jo's cheek, marveling at the high planes and angles that somehow combined to create a beautiful face. "Would you really? I mean, think about it. If your daughter had gone away a child and come back a woman who was, to all intents and purposes, happy and successful, would it really matter to you how she'd gotten there?"

"It would matter if I thought she'd got there by being a criminal, by doing wrong things," Jo persisted stubbornly.

"Honey, that's your conscience talking." Cadie smiled at Jo's confused expression. "You know those things about yourself and so it colors your perception of how you would react in their position."

Jo rolled over on to her back again. "I'm too tired for such deep and convoluted thoughts," she grumbled.

Cadie chuckled, knowing that was as close to a concession as she was likely to get. "It's only day one, sweetheart," she said, snuggling into the crook of Jo's arm and throwing her leg over the taller woman's hip. "I'm sure they'll come up with a few curly questions over the next couple of weeks."

Jo didn't reply and Cadie glanced up into a face that was already relaxed into deep sleep. "Well, goodnight to you too, darlin'," she whispered.

Chapter Ten

"JACK!" DAVID MADISON walked towards the machinery shed, where his foreman and Hughie were readying the ute and two ATVs for the day's work in the top paddock. It wasn't yet dawn and the air was crisply cool with a light dew. It was far and away David's favorite time of the day.

Collingwood and Hughie looked up as their boss stalked towards them with the rolling gait characteristic of a man who had spent the greater part of his life in the saddle. Coonyabby had all the modern conveniences of a 21st century farm, but given a choice, David would much rather be on horseback. As stations got bigger in an effort to stay economically viable, motorized transport was the only real option.

"Mornin', boss," Collingwood said with mock cheerfulness. It didn't take a genius to interpret the look on Madison's face. *Those bitches have been yappin' in his ear, that's for certain,* he thought sourly.

"Hughie, do me a favor, mate, and go pick up the packed lunches from Maggie. She's in the kitchen. Give me and Jack a minute." David smiled tightly at the young man, who tugged the brim of his Akubra in acknowledgement.

Once Hughie had slipped out of the barn, David turned back to Collingwood who was shuffling from foot to foot. "Not gonna beat around the bush, Jack. You're a good worker and I appreciate that. But I don't like you as a man." He pinned the foreman with a steely gray gaze until Collingwood's muddy brown eyes dropped to his boots. "I hear, or see, one more sign that you've raised a hand, or a boot, to Hughie or any of the animals, I'll sack your arse and kick it from here to Wilcannia. You hearing me?"

Jack scowled at him, the flush of anger starkly evident on his otherwise pale and pinched face. "Someone's been telling you tales, boss."

"Are you calling my wife and my daughter liars?" David barked, his patience about worn thin even after this briefest of confrontations. Jack had the good sense to say nothing. "I think you should shut your mouth, keep your fists and feet to yourself and consider yourself warned." David cocked his head to one side, challenging the man to take him on again. "You hearing me now, Jack?"

Collingwood spared him one more filthy look before bowing his head again. "I hear you, boss."

"Good."

MAGGIE APPROACHED THE closed door to her daughter's bedroom with considerable trepidation. The sun wasn't up yet, but she knew David would be champing at the bit to get moving and would have little patience if Jo and Cadie dallied. She balanced a tray loaded with two plates piled high with bacon, fried eggs and toast in one hand as she raised her fist to knock on the door. Biting her lip, she hesitated before disturbing the occupants.

What if they're ...? she pondered. "Tch, come on Maggie, it's 4.30 in the morning," she chastised herself quietly. After the day they'd had yesterday it would be a miracle if they were awake, let alone doing anything else. Still the persistent voice in her head nagged away at her. *It's a small bed. They're still going to be...in close contact.*

"What are you? A mother or a mouse?" With one deep breath, she took her courage in both hands and knocked softly. Leaning forward she strained to hear any response but there was only silence. She slowly turned the doorknob and stepped into the darkened room.

As she had expected from the silence that greeted her knock, both women were deeply asleep, wrapped around each like contented puppies. Maggie slid the tray of hot food on to the desk that ran along one wall of the crowded room, then turned back to the sleeping women. It seemed almost wrong to wake them.

Cadie was on her side, facing Maggie, and Jo was spooned up behind her, arms thrown around the smaller woman, one leg hooked over Cadie's thigh. They had kicked off the thin top sheet at some point during the night. Maggie had expected the sight of the two lovers to bother her on some level. Instead, she found herself smiling at them, warmed by the deep connection between them, obvious even in slumber.

Maybe I should get David in here to have a look before they wake up, she thought. *If he can't see the innate goodness in this love by looking at it, then he's more blind than I think.* She swept her eyes down the long length of her daughter's bare legs, and the slightly suggestive way Cadie's t-shirt had twisted and ridden up during the night. *Then again, why give him another heart attack?*

Her eyes ranged back up the two bodies lying in front of her until her gaze was met by a sleepy pair of blinking green eyes. "I'm sorry, Cadie, I didn't mean to startle you," Maggie said. "I did knock, but you were both out to it. Anyway, good morning."

"G'morning." Cadie lifted a hand and rubbed her face blearily. "I guess it's time to get up, huh?"

"If you want to catch David before he heads out into the great brown yonder, yes. I've put some breakfast together for you both."

"I can smell it. Thanks." Cadie smiled up at Maggie, wondering how she was dealing with the sight of her daughter wrapped half-naked around another woman. "I guess that means rousting Miss Coma, huh?"

"I'm awake," came the muffled rumble behind Cadie's right shoulder, where Jo's face was snuggled. "I'm just too embarrassed to open my eyes and face a parental unit in this position."

Cadie raised an eyebrow, meeting Maggie's amused look. She could feel the heat of Jo's blush between her shoulder blades and she gently patted her partner's hands.

"If I can deal with it, Josie-love, so can you," Maggie pointed out. "I'll leave you two to your breakfast," she said diplomatically, heading back to the door. "But don't be too long about it or your father will be away without you." With that she exited, leaving the two scantily-clad women blinking at each other in the dim light of pre-dawn.

"Your mom is so cool," Cadie finally decided. A muffled groan was all the response she got as Jo slumped back onto the pillow. Cadie laughed. "Come on, Stretch," she said, patting her lover's long, naked thigh. "Let's get the day started or we'll never live it down."

HALF AN HOUR and several rashers of bacon later, the pair walked out of the house and into the cool dawn air, beating a path to the machinery shed. Jo could see Jack Collingwood and another man working on the engine of one of the ATVs. Something about the lean figure struck her as familiar. *And then again...*

"Wow, that must be Hughie," she marveled.

"Who's Hughie?" Cadie asked, adjusting the straps of the

small backpack she carried. Maggie had loaded it up with sandwiches, drinks and sunscreen for the day ahead.

"This little Aboriginal kid who used to hang around a lot," Jo replied. They walked closer and she could now see that the young man was probably going to best her own six-foot height by at least a couple of inches once he stood upright. "I guess he grew up." They drew closer and she called out. "Hughie!"

The dark-skinned man looked up and broke into a wide grin. He raised a hand in greeting and then began walking towards them, ignoring the scowl he was getting from Collingwood.

"Damn, Hughie, look at you," Jo exclaimed, opening her arms wide and pulling the bashful man into an all-encompassing hug. "If it wasn't for the dopey way you wear that hat, I wouldn't have recognized you."

"'lo, Miss Josie," Hughie replied, pulling away from the hug and dipping his head shyly.

"Hey, didn't we have a conversation a long time ago about you dropping the 'Miss'?" Jo chided him gently, grinning all the way. "Just because you haven't seen me for 15 years, there's no need to go formal on me."

Even with his coloring, it was possible to see the blush reaching all the way to the tips of Hughie's ears. "Yes, Mi—uh, yes, Josie," he mumbled happily.

"That's the way, mate," Jo laughed. She turned to Cadie who had been watching the scene from a step or two back. "Hughie, I want you to meet my partner, Cadie."

Cadie stepped forward and extended a hand, surprised to find the large, brown one that wrapped around it more soft and gentle than she'd expected from a man who worked with his hands all day.

"Hello, Hughie. It's nice to meet you."

If it was possible for the young man to blush harder, he did, Cadie's sparkling green eyes and sunny smile charming him utterly.

"N-nice m-meetin' you, M-miss C-Cadie," he stuttered.

Cadie chuckled kindly. "Same rule applies for me, Hughie," she said. "Call me Cadie. I also answer to 'hey, you.'" She grinned up at him, an action guaranteed to scramble his already besotted senses.

"Oh, I'd n-never do th-that, Mi—uh, Cadie," he said hastily, even as he continued to hang on to her hand and avert his eyes.

Smitten, Jo thought, rolling her eyes good-humoredly. "Is there anybody on this farm you haven't charmed instantly?" she teased her partner aloud, contributing even further to the man's flustered state.

"Hughie!" He startled at the sharp yell, dropping Cadie's hand immediately before he turned back to its source. Jack Collingwood beckoned to him. "Come and help me finish this, boy, or we won't be going anywhere today."

"Oh, I think I can come up with one I haven't charmed," Cadie muttered darkly as she watched Hughie hurrying back to his task. She wondered briefly if calling a black man 'boy' had the same unpleasant connotations here as it did back in the US, making a mental note to ask Jo later, when they had more time to themselves. "I don't think I like that man, Jo-Jo," she said out loud.

Her partner grunted her agreement, watching the way the two men interacted. Collingwood was as dismissive of the Aborigine as he would have been of a dog. The thought made Jo's blood boil.

"And I bet I can guess where Hughie got that lump under his eye, too," she murmured. "I wonder if Dad knows."

"He knows," came a growl from behind her.

Jo swung round. "Uh, hi, Dad," she said.

"Morning," her father said gruffly. "Don't you be concerning yourself with Jack, all right? I've already put him on notice. I'll not have him kicking dogs, or mistreating Hughie. But he's a good worker, and I need him."

Jo raised her hands in concession. "It's your call, Dad. No argument from me." She wished she could break through her parent's standoffishness for a moment or two.

"Come on, then. We're wasting the best part of the day." David stumped off towards the vehicles. To the men, he said, "You two take the ATVs and when we hit Ingham Creek, one of you head to the north boundary, and the other one go to the east fence. We'll meet you at the top corner. All right?" David turned to the two women, trying not to let his discomfort with their easy affection show on his face. "You two come with me in the ute."

Jo and Cadie exchanged a look. "Okay," Jo said, unsure about being in close quarters with her father for the next hour or so. *What the hell are we gonna talk about?*

THEY BOUNCED ALONG a dirt trail between stands of low scrubby bushes. Ahead of them the two men on the ATVs flanked either side of the trail, staying out of the ruts made by the larger vehicle on innumerable earlier trips. The ute's air-conditioning unit was working overtime keeping the interior cool. The dust trails from the ATVs meant opening a window was not an option. David sat silently behind the wheel, negotiating the rough track at full speed thanks to years of practice and an intimate knowledge of the pitfalls of the dirt thoroughfare.

Cadie, as the smallest, sat between David and Jo, who was pressed against the left-hand door. Cadie wasn't exactly comfortable in the confined space, well aware that her thigh was up against David's, but there hadn't been a lot of choice.

Maybe we should have sat in the back, she pondered. *But then, that wouldn't have gotten these two any closer to having a conversation, would it? Not that they've been exactly talkative anyway.*

She glanced left at her lover's profile, noting the tense ripple of muscles at the corner of Jo's jaw. *Grinding her teeth*, Cadie realized. *Oh yeah, she's calm.* A glance right revealed something that made her grin in reflex. David's jaw was working as hard as his daughter's. *Great, it's genetic.* She stifled a giggle.

Jo was aware that her partner was amused by something and turned to raise an enquiring eyebrow. Cadie tapped her thigh and smiled quietly as she shook her head.

Fine, Jo thought grumpily. *Don't tell me.* She sighed. *God, I wish I knew what to say to make everything all right with him,* she thought, glancing over Cadie's head to her father. *I can't even work out what it is that's bugging him so much. Is it the past?* She felt Cadie's fingers slowly, and unconsciously, tracing a pattern on her thigh. *Or is it the present?* As no answer popped magically into existence, she turned her eyes back to their path through the trees and tried to figure out where they were exactly. Hazy, 15-year-old memories started to coalesce. *Coming up on Ingham Creek*, she realized.

"Hughie and Jack going boundary riding once we hit the creek?" she asked her father.

"Yep," he said succinctly. "We'll cover a lot more ground if we split up and we haven't looked at the fences at this end for a while."

As he finished talking, Cadie could see they were approaching an intersection of sorts. Jack looked back over his shoulder at them and waved his right hand before splitting off and taking another track that led away to the left of them. A few seconds later, Hughie did the same before steering his ATV to the right. David raised a hand in acknowledgement before gunning the ute forward along the original track.

Jo saw the slightly confused look on her partner's face. "We're heading for the northeast corner of the property," she explained. "Hughie and Jack are going to the fence lines north and east of us and they'll meet us in the middle at the Top End Bore."

"Ah, okay, thanks," Cadie said, smiling at Jo. "They'll fix any holes in the fence on the way, right?"

"That's the theory," David muttered. "If they come across anything too big for one bloke to fix, we'll get to it on the way back."

"Is there a problem at the bore that needs fixing?" Cadie asked.

"Yeah. I think the bore's blocked," David replied. "Even if it's not, we haven't been up here in a bit, and it'll need a good clean out and a bit of maintenance, no doubt."

"Good thing I brought my Swiss Army knife, then," Cadie said dryly. Both Madisons stared at her. "Kidding, kidding."

THEY PULLED INTO a wide, barren stretch of red earth where the two fence lines converged. David swung the ute around in a wide arc, pulling to a halt in a cloud of dust. After an hour of being bumped and jostled at high speed, Cadie was grateful to be in one piece as she and Jo tumbled out of the truck. Jo stretched her long frame skywards, working the kinks out from being folded into the cramped quarters of the ute's cabin.

Cadie turned in a slow circle, taking in the harsh environment. To her right was a strange metallic contraption that seemed to be a jerry-rigged collection of pipes and motors. Water spurted intermittently from one rust-colored pipe into a long metal trough that ran for 30 feet along the line of the northern fence. Except things weren't quite going to plan. Something was blocking the trough and water was backed up towards the pump, spilling over the side and puddling uselessly on the brown, hard-packed earth.

"Ah, bugger," muttered David as he walked around from the driver's side of the ute. "Wonder how long it's been like this."

Jo had walked over to the trough and she stood grimly, looking down at whatever was blocking the flow of water. "Yeah, you're not going to like this either, Dad," she said.

He stalked over to join her, cursing as he caught sight of the sheep carcass sprawled in the trough. "Can you two clear that out, and I'll get to work on stripping back the pump," David said. "It'll need recalibrating after that. God knows how long it's been choking on itself."

Jo grunted her assent to the task and took a quick glance at her partner, who was standing uncertainly a few paces away and had yet to see the none-too-pleasant sight. *Let's see if I can pull it out myself,* she decided as she stepped up on to the edge of the trough.

A fully-grown sheep is a hefty beast at the best of times; water-logged and semi-bloated, the animal was a considerable weight to move. *Thank God it was shorn not so long ago,* Jo thought as she wrapped her hands around the sheep's back legs. With a grunt, she tried to straighten her back, yanking the dead weight slightly in the right direction.

"Jo, wait," Cadie exclaimed as she watched her partner straining. Carefully, she stepped up onto the side of the trough, wincing as a sickly sweet smell wafted up from the disturbed carcass.

"It's okay, I can do this," Jo protested.

"Don't be crazy. I can see how heavy that is. If you go hurting yourself on day one, the rest of the vacation isn't going to be much fun, is it?" Cadie smiled thinly at her partner as she put her hands on her hips. "And besides, Jo Madison, I'm no shrinking flower to be protected. I can handle it, okay? Remember the fish guts?"

Jo grinned at her, feeling an interesting sense of pride welling up. "I remember. Okay, then. If you grab the front end, maybe together we can swing it up and out," she said.

They stood at opposite ends of the dead sheep, one foot on each rail of the trough. Together they bent down and grabbed a leg in each hand. Cadie tried to ignore the way her stomach flip-flopped at the greasy feel of the water.

"Here we go...one, two, *three*!"

The two women hauled the sheep up, dripping water all over their feet and jeans. Then, with one combined grunt, they swung the carcass over the edge of the trough and dropped it with a squelch.

David sat on his haunches behind the pump, surreptitiously watching the women deal with their nasty chore. Despite himself, he was quietly impressed by the little American. She hadn't flinched at handling the carcass, even though Jo had been prepared to do the job herself. *Cadie's got a bit of ticker,* he decided as he began the laborious task of shutting the pump down.

"You want us to bury it, Dad?" Jo asked, looking back over her shoulder at the older man.

"Better," he replied. "None of the animals will come for a drink if we leave it to rot."

"Rightio," his daughter agreed.

She's not doing too badly either, David conceded. *You can take the girl out of the bush, but you can't take the bush out of the girl.*

For the first time since Josie had come home, he allowed a little pride in his wayward daughter to surface as he watched her dragging the carcass over to a nearby tree. *She's remembered the soil'll be softer over there,* he realized. Cadie was pulling shovels out of the back of the ute.

Not sure I'll ever be comfortable with this, he thought as he refocused on dismantling the bore head in front of him. *But I've got to find a way to get past it.*

Jo let the sheep's back legs drop with a grunt once she'd yanked it into the shade under the tree. Something about the carcass didn't look right to her. *Not that any dead animal looks right,* she conceded. Jo's brow furrowed as she tried to figure out what was bugging her about it. It certainly wasn't the first time she'd seen one of her family's livestock dead in a paddock. *Although it has been a while,* she conceded.

The sheep had been in the trough a couple of days, she figured. Tentatively, she reached out and rubbed her fingers through the animal's short regrowth of wool. Nothing unusual, apart from the stark reality of a half-starved beast, evident in the ribs she could easily feel through the cold skin. She tried not to think about it too much.

Finding nothing, she stood again and turned the sheep over. Frowning, she crouched down and began another search.

"What are you doing?" Cadie asked. There was something unnerving about watching her partner probing and prodding the carcass. *Guess she's used to dead bodies.* Cadie mentally slapped herself. *Get off that.* But a part of her brain couldn't help going to that dark place Jo had once inhabited.

"Something's not right," Jo muttered. And then her fingers found what they were looking for, near the beast's temple. Immersion in the water had removed all traces of blood, but what Jo was feeling was unmistakable, and something she was all too familiar with. "Dad!"

David looked up from his task. "Yeah?"

"This sheep's been shot."

"What?" David dropped his spanner and stalked over to where Jo was crouched over the carcass.

"Take a look for yourself," she said, shuffling out of his way. "Just behind the left eye."

David grabbed the sheep's head unceremoniously, poking about with hands that were long used to dealing with the unpleasant realities of life on a farm. "Bugger me," he cursed as his senses confirmed Jo's theory.

"Why would anyone do that?" Cadie asked, stealing a closer look. "Was it injured in some way, or nearly dead from starvation?"

David looked up sharply. "Haven't had to shoot any of my animals so far, young lady, and I don't ever intend things to get that bad."

Cadie was taken aback by the man's vehemence. *Guess I hit a nerve. Again.* "I didn't mean any offence," she said quickly. "I thought that was what happened when the animals got too sick to eat and drink properly."

"It is. But not around here," David reiterated. "And not without me giving the say-so."

"Ease up, Dad," Jo said quietly but firmly, frowning at her father.

Wearily, David said, "Sorry about that, Cadie. I'm pretty pissed off. Bloody sheep are worth too much, even in this weather, to go shooting them for no apparent reason. I want to know who did this, so I can kick his arse from here to Coober Pedy." He took his hat off and ran his hand through his thick, graying hair in frustration.

"How far are we from the road?" Jo asked, her memories of the lay of the land still vague.

David pursed his lips and shrugged his shoulders. "Five miles, maybe, as the crow flies. But there's no track. If anyone came from that direction, they'd have to be pretty determined."

Jo dusted off her jeans. "What's the alternative?" she asked. "Either someone came off the road to do it, or your neighbors got the urge to destroy your property." She nodded in the direction of the northern fence, which separated the Madison land from their immediate neighbors. With a jolt she realized that farm belonged to Phil's parents. *Or, at least, it did.* And knowing Phil's parents like she did – *or had done* – that theory was out.

David looked up at his daughter, knowing her logic made sense.

"Alternatively, Hughie or Jack did it," Jo continued.

"Not Hughie," David said emphatically. "Boy doesn't have a malicious bone in his body. Last time we lost a lamb, I found him in tears over it."

Cadie and Jo exchanged a look. *We know exactly who is inclined to that kind of maliciousness,* Cadie thought, seeing her partner's startling blue eyes narrow as she reached the same conclusion.

David looked at the two women, finding it easy to read their minds. "Why would Jack want to kill sheep?" he asked. "This was done a few days ago, so it certainly can't be anything to do with that barney he had with you yesterday."

Cadie could see his point. It was too soon to jump to any

conclusions, but she had a bad feeling about Jack Collingwood.

"Well, nothing we can do about it now, except bury it where it won't stink and keep our eyes open for anything else," David said.

"HAVE YOU EVER ridden one of these things?" Jo asked Cadie, indicating one of the ATVs. After burying the dead sheep, they'd eaten lunch as they'd waited for Hughie, and then Jack, to arrive in the clearing. Now they were helping the men load the equipment back into the ute.

"No," Cadie replied, assessing the sturdy little vehicle's controls. "But I've ridden a motorbike a couple of times. Is it much different from that?"

Jo shook her head. "Easier, actually. These have an automatic transmission, so there's none of that fiddly gear-changing to do." She looked over at her father. David was talking with Hughie and Jack about some repairs that needed doing along the northern fence line which required more than one pair of hands. "Dad," she called out. "Do you need Cadie and me to come with you?"

The older man shook his head. "Don't think so," he said. "You want to take the ATVs and head back home, love?" The endearment provoked a raised eyebrow from his daughter.

That's a first, Jo thought. Somehow, as much as she wanted her father's acceptance and affection, it kept surprising her when she caught glimpses of it. "Yeah, that's what I was thinking," she said.

"S'fine with me," he replied. "You got a cell phone with you?"

Jo felt for the instrument clipped to her hip. "Yep," she replied.

"Okay," he said, closing the back of the ute and clipping it in place. "Call and let your mother know what we're doing, eh?"

"No worries."

"Um, Jo," Cadie said uncertainly. "I'm not sure I can learn to handle this thing that quickly."

Jo flashed her a broad grin that was full of confidence and love. "Sure you can," she disagreed happily. "Piece of cake. Hop on."

Cadie smiled up at her lover, feeling Jo's faith in her settle around her like a favorite old jacket. Impulsively, she reached up and cupped the taller woman's cheek with a gentle palm. "Have I told you lately that I adore you?"

"Yes. But don't let that stop you from telling me again," Jo teased. She let Cadie's hand draw her closer and then tenderly brushed her lips over hers. "We're scandalizing the men," she whispered, aware of three pairs of eyes burning into her back. It didn't stop her from enjoying the feel of Cadie's soft cheek against hers, though.

"Too bad," Cadie murmured. "If they don't like it they can kiss my a—" She was silenced by her lover's mouth kissing her soundly. When they parted they were both grinning wildly. "You are so bad," Cadie chuckled.

"Me?" Jo protested innocently. "You started it."

Cadie let her eyes flick over to the three men who were hurriedly moving around the ute in a flurry of activity. For an instant, she caught her father-in-law's eye but his glance slid away almost immediately. *He's so cagey,* she thought. *Wish I knew what he was thinking.*

"Did Dad throw up on his boots?" Jo asked quietly, watching the frown crease Cadie's brow. She preferred not to look back at her father, unwilling to see the disgust on her parent's face, if that was indeed his reaction.

"No, love," Cadie reassured her. "I'm not really sure what he's thinking, actually. But maybe he is opening up a little." Blue eyes met hers, hope and doubt vying in their depths. "Could be as good a time as any to have a real conversation with him."

Jo flashed a quick smile. "Could be."

Cadie threw a leg over the ATV's saddle and lowered herself down on the wide, comfortable seat. Settling her feet on the rests, she said, "Come on, Stretch. Teach me how to use this thing."

"Okay," Jo said, moving to show Cadie the controls. "Throttle is like a bike—twist the handgrip here." She demonstrated. "Brakes, front and back, squeeze both hands. Take a tip from me; don't hit the front ones too hard on their own." She grinned, remembering a childhood accident that had sent her flying over the handlebars.

"There's a story behind that smile, I'm thinking," Cadie said.

Jo sniggered. "Oh yeah. I missed the roo with the bike, but found the tree with my head."

Cadie winced. "Ouch. Is that how you got this?" She gently fingered the tiny scar at the corner of Jo's left eyebrow.

"Uh, no, actually," Jo muttered, her mood suddenly darkening at the memory of that particular hurt. A flick knife and soon-to-be-dead drug addict had done that.

Uh-oh, Cadie thought. *One of these days I'm going to remember the life she's led.* "Come back, sweetheart," she soothed, placing a calming hand on Jo's belly. Blue eyes gone cold flicked to hers and warmed perceptibly. "I'm sorry," Cadie said. "I didn't mean to dredge that up."

Jo smiled thinly. "Not your fault, love. I wish all my scars were childhood accidents. It's one of the consequences of the life I chose to live."

"Stop it, Jo," Cadie urged. "That life is gone now. It's over."

Jo looked down into green eyes that loved her totally, openly. Not for the first time, she felt the wonder of that warming her belly, like Cadie's hand was warming the skin of her stomach through the thin cotton shirt she was wearing. "I don't deserve you," she whispered.

Cadie looked up into a face full of vulnerability and honesty. "Bullshit," she said bluntly. Then she broke into a crooked grin. "Now, come on. Show me how to start this thing and let's get going."

"Bossy little thing, aren't ya?" Jo ruffled her companion's hair, grateful both for Cadie's faith and her willingness to leave Jo's insecurities alone for the time being. *I wonder if Mum would help me do something special for Cadie tonight,* she pondered.

"And you love it," Cadie said, gunning the ATV and taking off with a roar and a cloud of dust.

"MUM, IS THE Swinging Tree waterhole still running?" Jo asked Maggie later in the afternoon while Cadie was taking a shower.

Maggie looked up from the kitchen table where she had been working on the station's books. "I think so, love." She tried to remember the last time she had been out to the waterhole, one of Jo's favorite childhood haunts. "That's always one of the last places to dry up. I'm sure there's still some water in it."

Jo hummed pensively. "I hope there's still some flow through it," she said. "Not much fun to swim in it if it's gone stagnant."

Maggie smiled at her freshly showered daughter. She looked younger somehow with her wet fringe plastered against her forehead, and her bare feet slapping against the cool tile of the kitchen floor as she moved around, getting herself a drink.

"Only one way to find out," she said. "Unless you want to give your father a call. But I don't think he's been out there in the last couple of weeks or so. What have you got in mind, bloss?" *There's definitely something going on in that head, and I'm betting it's got something to do with the full moon, and that pretty young woman in the bathroom.*

Drink in hand, Jo sat down opposite her mother. Casually, she lifted a long leg and draped it over the corner of the kitchen table, leaning back until the chair rocked on one leg. Maggie had to fight to contain the chuckle the very familiar posture provoked.

"It's a full moon tonight," Jo said.

Bingo, thought her mother smugly. "Yes," she drawled.

"What?" Jo answered with a drawl of her own.

"And, don't tell me, you want to take Cadie out to the waterhole and have yourselves a romantic, moonlit picnic?" Maggie grinned at the look of undisguised surprise on her daughter's face.

"I can't be that predictable," Jo complained. "And I know I didn't make a habit of it when I was 17."

Maggie put on her most innocent face. "Let's say it's genetic." Jo thought about that for a few seconds before the realization dawned on her. She blushed furiously, and her mother laughed out loud at her discomfort. "Relax, Josie. I swear, sometimes your generation thinks it invented sex." She pushed herself up and walked into the kitchen's large, well-stocked pantry. "Now then, let's see what we can come up with for your picnic."

Chapter Eleven

THE HORSES PICKED their way through the trees and bushes as the sun dropped low towards the shimmering horizon. The moon, full and silver, was already beginning its climb as Jo and Cadie let the horses find their path towards the waterhole.

Earlier, Jo and the palomino mare, Tilly, had enjoyed a happy reunion at the stables, though there was an element of wistfulness to the tall woman's mood. Cadie could have sworn the gentle old mare had a twinkle in her caramel eyes as Jo had crooned softly to the horse, forehead to forehead with her four-legged friend. In the end, on Maggie's advice, they'd left Tilly to pick at her fresh basket of hay and saddled the two younger horses. The colts had proven to be placid and sure-footed, a relief to Cadie, who didn't like to think about how many years it had been since she'd tested her ability to stay in the saddle.

Now they were following a barely-visible track that wound through scrubby trees and low brush. The light was eerie, the golden sunset and pastel hues gradually giving way to the silvery glow of moonlight.

The two women hadn't spoken much since they'd saddled the horses and set off, content to absorb the peaceful surroundings. Both had backpacks, filled with a picnic dinner Maggie had somehow magicked from nowhere. A cold bottle of wine and two glasses were buried in Jo's.

Watching her lover ride slightly ahead, Cadie was fascinated by Jo's ability to adapt to the environment in which she found herself, seamlessly blending in. *A few weeks ago, I was thinking I'd never seen anyone more at home on the ocean than she looked onboard Seawolf,* Cadie thought. *And now look at her.* She watched Jo's easy posture in the saddle and the happy smile touching the corners of her mouth. *You'd never know she hadn't been here for the past 15 years.*

"Penny for your thoughts," Jo said, curious about the expression on her partner's face, an interesting mixture of query and delight.

Cadie laughed gently. "I was thinking about that day out on Seawolf, during Hamilton Island Race Week, when you were standing on the edge of the cockpit, looking like Captain Ahab."

Jo's eyebrow almost disappeared up into her hairline. "What made you think of that?"

"Looking at you then, I couldn't imagine you anywhere else but out on the ocean," she replied.

Jo kneed the colt gently, sidestepping him around until they were facing Cadie and her mount. "And now?"

Cadie grinned. "And now, I can't imagine you anywhere but on a horse in the middle of the outback. How do you do that?"

Jo's pearly white teeth glistened in the moonlight. "Beats me, sweetheart. If anything, this is where I should feel most at home, but I've never really thought about it. I've always made my home wherever I was."

Their eyes locked, and Cadie already knew where this conversation was going.

"And now?" she asked as Jo brought the colt alongside.

"And now you're my home," Jo said, acknowledging the truth of that for the first time.

"And you're mine."

For the next few minutes they rode side by side, hands clasped across the space between the two horses.

As the sun dropped below the horizon, they came upon a picturesque oasis in the middle of the dustbowl through which they had been traveling. Two of the three creeks that crisscrossed the Madisons' land came together here, forming a small waterhole. Jo was pleased to see there was still water flowing through the little billabong despite the ravages of the drought around them.

"You beauty," she exclaimed as she slid off her horse's back and walked to the top of the small rise that formed the bank of the waterhole. "This place always was the last to dry up." She looked back over her shoulder and grinned at Cadie, who had dismounted and was leading both horses by the reins.

"Oh, sweetheart, it's gorgeous," Cadie gasped as she reached the top of the bank. Surprisingly, the water flowing through the waterhole looked crystal clear and deep. *Maybe it's the moonlight*, she thought. The billabong was ringed by gums, their bark silver-gray and fluorescent. Thick, green grass had managed to eke out an existence close to the water.

It was there that Jo began to unload the bags and backpacks. She unsaddled her horse and stripped off the blanket underneath, spreading it on a level patch of grass overlooking the waterhole.

"Do we need to hobble the horses?" Cadie asked as she handed Jo her backpack.

"Nope. They won't go far away from the water. Tie their reins up so they don't get tangled, and they should be right."

A few minutes later they were sprawled on the blanket, tantalizing packages of food laid out between them. Cadie handed Jo a paper plate and a knife and fork before she started to pull the lids off the various containers. Soon, potato salad, cold roast beef, ham, freshly baked crusty bread, and homemade pate were served.

"Have I mentioned lately how much I love your mom?" Cadie said, her mouth watering even as her stomach rumbled ominously.

Jo laughed. "You love anyone who feeds you, sweetheart."

Mock outrage sent Cadie's eyebrows on a trip north. "I think you have me confused with your cat, Miss Madison," she said haughtily. Delicately, she spooned a few mouthfuls of potato salad on to her plate, not an easy task, given that her nose was high in the air. Eventually, she too burst into giggles as one spoonful missed the plate altogether.

"Klutz," Jo teased.

Cadie carefully maneuvered her half-laden spoon around until she had it poised to launch its load in Jo's direction. Again she raised her eyebrows, this time in challenge.

"You wouldn't," Jo growled. Cadie said nothing, but pulled the bowl of the spoon back even further. "In this light, your aim's going to suck anyway," Jo warned. "So it's going to be a complete waste of good potato salad."

Cadie stayed silent but let a slow, slightly feral smile spread across her lips. She raised the laden spoon higher and then let fly. The glob of creamy potato sailed through the air, seemingly in slow motion, splattering across Jo's cheek with a very satisfying squelch. She waited for the inevitable reaction from her partner, but for several seconds there was a heavily pregnant pause. *Uh-oh,* she thought. *There's no way she's gonna let me get away with that. Better get my running shoes on.*

Jo's eyes had closed automatically as the incoming missile approached and now she slowly opened them. With the tip of her tongue, she licked the mess from her lips then took a deep breath. Two could play at this game.

"You know, that's not bad," she said, tasting the tangy dressing her mother always used on the potato salad. "And, in any other circumstances, I'd let bygones be bygones so we don't waste any more of this delicious food." She deliberately kept her voice low and calm, knowing she was giving Cadie chills.

Slowly, she reached out for the container of potato salad. For the first time she met Cadie's eyes, and she chuckled internally at the look of wide-eyed apprehension she saw there. "However, on this occasion," she grinned wickedly, a glob of potato salad dripping from her chin, "I don't think I can let it go."

"Jo-Jo," Cadie said, raising a warning hand. "Don't do anything I might regret, okay?" She started to backpedal, pushing herself away from Jo, towards the far edge of the blanket.

"Oh, I think it's a little late for that, don't you?" Jo drawled, even as she let her long fingers dip into the salad bowl. Quickly she grabbed a handful and lunged across the other dishes towards Cadie.

Cadie squealed and scrabbled backwards, but she wasn't quick enough to move out of range of her partner's long limbs. Jo launched herself, leading with the handful of potato salad, laughing wildly as she managed to grab Cadie, mashing the sloppy mess into her lover's face.

Cadie howled in outrage and twisted under Jo's oncoming weight, trying to get a purchase on the long body that would give her some kind of advantage. Before long the women were rolling and wrestling in the soft grass on the verge of the waterhole, giggling and squealing and tickling.

Breathless, they finally exhausted themselves and they lay on their backs, side by side, gazing up at the stars. Cadie laughed. "Oh, I needed that, thank you," she said, panting.

"You started it," Jo pointed out, turning her head and grinning.

"I couldn't resist." Cadie rolled on to her side and slid her leg over Jo's hips. She snuggled in close, resting her cheek on the dark hair splashed across Jo's chest. Jo's arm curled around her shoulders and pulled her in. Cadie tilted her face up and extended her tongue to lick the remnants of potato salad off Jo's chin. "Tasty," she murmured.

"Yes, you are," Jo growled in response and rolled them both over in the grass until she was holding herself above Cadie.

"Oh my," Cadie breathed, gazing up into silvered blue eyes that glinted in the moonlight. Jo's face was etched against the star-laden night sky and she exuded barely restrained energy that made Cadie shiver with anticipation. "Good thing we didn't bring any hot food," she murmured as Jo leant down and nuzzled her neck.

"I want you, Arcadia," Jo burred against her skin.

Cadie groaned, low and throaty. "What is it with you and the outdoors, Jossandra?" she murmured back, sliding her hands around until she could tuck her fingers inside the back pockets of Jo's jeans.

"It's the fresh air," came the breathy, deep response close to her ear and Cadie felt the goose bumps rise on her arms.

Jo's lips caressed along the line of her jaw and Cadie tipped her chin up in reflex, giving her lover access to her neck. Jo obliged, sliding the silky tip of her tongue down, before nibbling sensually in the hollow at the base of Cadie's throat. Long, sure fingers slid under the cotton of Cadie's shirt, brushing teasingly against the skin of her stomach.

"Oh, Jo," she gasped. "I want you too." She felt Jo smile against the curve of her breast.

"I know." Fingers brushed against the telltale response of Cadie's nipple.

Cadie laughed throatily. "Dead giveaway, huh?"

Jo cupped Cadie's breast, the pad of her thumb teasing and encouraging. "Hardly dead, my love," she said softly. "Very much alive and well."

Cadie closed her eyes against the sensation, absorbing the jolting tingle that followed every movement of Jo's fingers. "God, sometimes I think all I need is the sound of your voice," she muttered.

"Oh really?" Jo drawled. "Want me to stop touching?" She stilled her fingers, grinning as she saw Cadie's eyes fly open.

"God, no!" she exclaimed. Jo laughed out loud, a rumbling that sent vibrations through them both. Those fingers resumed their roaming exploration. "I meant your voice does things to me I can't even begin to describe," Cadie explained, distracted by the sensation of a thumb barely brushing her nipples.

To be contrary, Jo didn't reply, electing to use her mouth for other things.

"Oh my," Cadie gasped, feeling the warm wetness around her breast as Jo suckled her through the thin fabric of her t-shirt. "Very good thing," she breathed, "about the hot," she swallowed, "food..."

"Uh huh." Jo lifted herself off Cadie's breast and found Cadie's willing mouth with her own. The world contracted around them, and the two women lost themselves in the easy sensuality of their love under the full moon and watching stars.

WE NEED TO do this kind of thing more often, Jo thought drowsily as she watched Cadie crouch at the edge of the water to rinse out the plastic food containers. The moonlight was strong and bright, illuminating the curves and hollows of Cadie's body like a painter's brush. Jo enjoyed the view of her lover's silhouette through half-lidded eyes. *Gorgeous, inside and out. How did I get so lucky?*

Cadie stood and shook the excess water off the containers before she walked back to where Jo lay sprawled on the horse blanket.

"You look very languid, sweetheart," Cadie said with a smile. She dropped down onto her knees next to the backpacks and stored the containers inside.

Jo leant on one elbow. "I feel pretty good," she observed. "Funny, that."

Cadie laughed softly. "Me too. Must be the company, huh?"

"I guess."

They smiled at each other for a few seconds.

"This light is so eerie," Cadie said as she broke Jo's gaze to look around at the silvery scenery. Unconsciously she rubbed her arms, the cool night air raising goose bumps on her bare skin.

"Cold, darling?" Jo asked.

Cadie turned back to her. "A little. It's a pity we can't light a fire."

"I know, but it's too risky. The way the wind is blowing, it would carry sparks back into the trees and that would be that. This place is a tinderbox at the moment."

Cadie looked around at the idyllic scene the waterhole and its surrounds presented. "Hard to believe from this little patch. But I guess you're right." Her attention shifted to the smoldering mosquito coils Jo had set up around their picnic area. "Are these safe?"

"Yeah, I think so." Jo smiled at her naked partner, who was hugging herself against the chill. "Why don't you come snuggle?" she suggested. "That'll keep us both warm."

Cadie chuckled. "Y'know, for an old ex-assassin, you sure are a cuddlehound," she teased, even as she crawled closer and happily curled up in the crook of Jo's arm.

Something old and rotten in Jo almost bit back at the reference to the dark past she would much rather forget, but she had learned that with Arcadia Jones she was safe from judgment. The soft puff of Cadie's breath warmed her skin and she looked down at the fair head resting on her shoulder. "I love you," she whispered against the silky hair.

Cadie tipped her head back and blinked curiously at her partner. "I love you, too, Jo-Jo. What brought that on?"

Jo shrugged. "Felt it, so I said it." Her standard response to that inquiry, Cadie had learned.

"Somehow I don't think so, Jossandra. Something else triggered that one." She reached under Jo's shirt and playfully tickled her ribcage, making the taller woman squirm. "Spill it, skipper."

"Okay, okay," Jo laughed. "It was what you said about me being an old assassin."

Cadie sat up quickly, apology written all over her face. "Oh, honey, I—"

"Shhh." Jo placed a gentle finger against Cadie's lips, silencing her. "I know you didn't, and that's my point. If anyone else had said that to me, especially a few years ago...well, I don't know what I would have done, exactly, but it wouldn't have been pretty." Cadie looked at her with gentle understanding, a look so intense it made Jo lower her eyes. "But there isn't any part of me that I don't want to share with you. You make me feel safe to be myself." She lifted her eyes and met Cadie's gaze again. "That's new for me."

Cadie nodded. "I know. And I'm glad I can give you that. You deserve it." She opened her mouth to say more, but the sharp retort of a gunshot cracked the air.

Cadie ducked down instinctively as the horses, startled from their grass-picking further down the watercourse, whinnied and shied away into the scrub behind them. Jo was on her feet before Cadie had a chance to draw breath.

"Was that what I think it was?" Cadie asked as she scrambled up to stand next to her.

"Shhh," Jo urged, then nodded wordlessly. She leaned close to Cadie's ear and whispered. "Hunting rifle, and close by. Stay here. I'm going to go see what I can find." She made to move away but was pulled up short by Cadie's hand on her elbow.

"First of all, you need some clothes on," Cadie reminded her. "And second, there's no way you're leaving without me. I'm staying with you, Jo-Jo."

"I can move faster and quieter without you," Jo snapped, her mind already tracking the shooter.

"Hey!" Cadie yanked on the tall woman's arm again, forcing Jo to look down at her. Cadie summoned her fiercest frown and waited until Jo's eyes acknowledged her. "I'm going with you. I'm not staying here alone with some gun-toting idiot stumbling around in the dark."

"All right," Jo muttered. "But stay close." Cadie let go of her elbow, her expression still showing signs of hurt and annoyance. *Fix this, Madison,* Jo thought as they both scrambled into their clothes. *She didn't deserve to be snarled at.* Jo reached out and touched Cadie's cheek gently. "I'm sorry."

Cadie smiled at her, her forgiveness instant. "Come on, let's go find out who's shooting."

"And at what," Jo murmured.

The two women skirted the edge of the waterhole, Jo deliberately leading them through the longer grass in the hopes of keeping their footsteps as silent as possible. Another gunshot rang out, and both women dropped to their haunches, Cadie wrapping a hand around Jo's elbow.

"This way," Jo hissed.

Together, they picked their way through the scrub, Cadie instinctively making sure her feet followed in Jo's footsteps almost exactly. The tall woman was bristling with...*something,* Cadie thought, *but I can't put my finger on the right word for it.* One look at her lover told her that something ingrained was guiding Jo's responses. Ice-chip blue eyes were narrowed and sweeping left and right for signs of trouble. Jo moved silently and swiftly, trusting that Cadie would keep up. She did, but Cadie was breathing hard by the time they came to a sudden halt at the edge of a small clearing. Jo waved her hand, telling Cadie to get down.

Crawling forward on her elbows until she was side-by-side with Jo, Cadie whispered, "Who is it?"

Jo sighed. "Collingwood. How predictable."

Cadie wriggled until she could see through the tiny gap in the foliage that Jo was looking through. What she saw sickened her. A lean figure, silhouetted in the moonlight, stood over what could only be the carcass of a sheep. Another lay close by. Cadie swallowed back the nausea. "We've got to do something, Jo." She turned to look at her lover's grim profile. "What's the plan?"

"I'm working on it," Jo murmured, her eyes flicking around the clearing, absorbing the lay of the land.

For long seconds they watched as Collingwood nudged the corpses with his foot.

"Hey, Jo?" Cadie whispered, an idea forming in her brain.

"What?"

"Remember the snake?"

Jo looked at her, puzzled. "What snake?"

Cadie crawled closer so she could put her mouth close to Jo's ear. "The snake up in the islands, remember? The taipan?"

Jo did remember, suddenly. She had been with Cadie and two other members of the group of Americans she had been chaperoning around the islands. They had been on a hike up one of the islands when they had come across the taipan in the middle of the track. Jo had moved around the venomous nasty, coming up behind it while Cadie and the men kept its attention focused on them, and she'd been able to trap it with a stick, while the Americans had got past. She chuckled quietly. "Honey, that's not gonna work here."

"Why not?"

Jo shifted slightly, pulling Cadie against her and brushing her lips against her earlobe. "Gun-toting idiot, remember?" she whispered. "Unlike that snake, this guy is stupid, and can't see what he's shooting at. That's a dangerous mixture. But part of it's a good idea though, love," she conceded. "We do need to split his focus."

"So, what are we waiting for?"

Jo chuckled at her partner's bizarre taste for this kind of adventure. "I created a monster, showing you where that rifle was the other day, didn't I?" she teased.

Cadie leaned in, the smirk evident on her face even as she kept her voice low. "You've awakened my dark side."

"Yeah, well, keep Arcadia the Conqueror in check for a bit, will ya, while I try and figure out what to do with this idiot." She softened her words with a friendly tickle of Cadie's ribs and gazed out into the clearing. Collingwood was circling the two sheep carcasses slowly, almost as if he didn't believe the animals were dead.

Pretty hard to miss a standing target like a poor, dumb sheep, Jo thought grimly. A slow, burning anger smoldered in her guts at the actions of the man her father trusted to help him run the station. *What the hell is going on here?* She listened as Collingwood cocked the gun again, and she wondered if perhaps the man wasn't half-aware of their presence.

"Does he know we're here?" Cadie whispered close to Jo's ear.

"Not us specifically, but he might think there's something else worth shooting. Stay here," she instructed. "I'm going to circle around until I'm opposite this position."

"And then what?"

Jo's brow furrowed. "By the time I'm round there, I'll have figured that out."

"Yeah, but—"

"Follow my lead, okay?" With that, Jo was gone, slinking away into the shadows before Cadie could raise any further objections.

"Right. Follow your lead. I can do that," Cadie muttered. She bit her lip as she lost track of her elusive lover. Through the small break in the foliage she could see Collingwood crouched near one of the sheep, his rifle resting across his thighs as he smoked a cigarette, its red tip glowing. Cadie waited, knowing that once Jo was in position, something was going to happen. *God knows what,* she pondered. *But it isn't going to be dull.*

Some yards away, Jo moved through the dry underbrush with a stealth that came to her automatically. While her body took care of business, avoiding sticks underfoot and tree branches overhead, her brain went into overdrive, finding a way to deal with Collingwood without getting herself, Cadie, or any more animals shot in the process. She tried to picture a scenario in which the man wouldn't react first and think second, but no matter which plan formulated the outcome was always a risky one. By the time Jo had reached the place she'd pinpointed earlier as being opposite Cadie's position, she was quite frustrated by her lack of any idea.

Collingwood seemed totally unconcerned, smoking in the moonlight like he had all night to accomplish his task. *Whatever the hell that is,* Jo thought. *Okay, now what, Madison? Cadie's sitting there waiting for some grand plan to unfold, and if you don't come up with something shortly, she's likely to go all gung-ho on you and take matters into her own hands.* She couldn't help grinning. There was something surprising, but downright sexy, about her diminutive lover's newfound taste for excitement. *Concentrate, would you?* Jo berated herself. *This isn't a game. That idiot out there's got a gun.*

She growled under her breath and shifted slightly as she tried to get a bead on the man sitting in a pool of moonlight in the middle of the clearing. As she moved, her foot kicked against a baseball-sized rock. Jo looked down at the stone and laughed softly. *It can't be that simple, can it?*

She dug her fingers under the rock and pulled it out of the dirt, hefting it in the palm of her hand. *Well, if nothing else, it'll certainly get his attention.* Slowly, she stood up and moved to a patch of relatively clear ground, where she could move her arms freely. Collingwood had his back to her and had thoughtfully removed his Akubra, making the back of his skull a tempting target.

Jo sized up the distance between them, allowing for some depth perception errors due to the moonlight, and then slowly drew her arm back. She unleashed the throw and held her breath as the rock whizzed through the still air. With a sickening thud, it smacked into Collingwood's skull. He slid bonelessly to the ground without a sound and Jo stepped out into the clearing.

"That's it?" came a plaintive shout from the other side of the clearing. Cadie emerged into the moonlight, her hands on her hips. "That was the grand plan?"

Jo stood over the unconscious man and shrugged nonchalantly. "I thought it had a certain simple elegance."

"Uh-huh. Nothing to do with the fact that you couldn't come up with anything better, I'm sure."

"I didn't need anything better. Look." Jo gestured at the unconscious man, whose cigarette still dangled from his lips. "Mission accomplished." She flicked the cigarette out of Collingwood's mouth with the toe of her boot and then ground it into the dirt, making sure it was extinguished. No one who had grown up in the fire-prone Australian bush was careless with a cigarette butt.

Cadie found it hard to resist the confident grin on her partner's face, but pouted anyway. "I didn't get to do anything," she complained.

"Sure you did. You were my inspiration, darling." Jo beamed at her shorter lover.

"Oh, you are so full of shit, Jo Madison," Cadie replied. She glanced down at Collingwood. "Sure he's only unconscious?"

Jo knelt down behind the man and felt for his neck pulse point. "Alive and well," she concluded. "Relatively speaking." Carefully she slid the rifle out of Collingwood's grasp and stood again as she unloaded the weapon. She almost tossed the bullets into the bush, but a realization that they would be useful evidence made her tuck them into her pocket.

"So what now?" Cadie asked. "How are we going to get him home?"

"I am so tempted to tie his feet together and drag him behind the horses." Jo sighed. "But I guess we can't do that."

Cadie smirked. "Tempting. Um, do we even have any rope?"

Jo nodded. "We do, if we can find the horses. I'm beginning to wish we had hobbled them after all." She raised her fingers to her mouth and blew, a sharp piercing whistle echoing around the clearing. "That always used to work for Tilly, but I don't know if these two have been trained the same way."

She needn't have worried. Half a minute later, both colts trotted into the clearing, trailing their reins and wuffling breathily.

"Pretty cool," Cadie murmured, capturing her horse's reins while Jo pulled a coiled-up length of rope from where it hung around her saddle horn.

The skipper knelt down by Collingwood and proceeded to tie his hands behind his back, leaving a long section of rope free. "Give me a hand?" she asked as she moved to shift the dead weight of the man's body.

Between the two of them, they managed to sling Collingwood over the saddle of Jo's horse, his head hanging down one side, and his feet down the other.

"Not the most dignified position in the world," Cadie said.

"Who cares?" Jo muttered. "This guy's an arsehole." She grabbed her colt's reins and reached out with her free hand to take Cadie's in a firm grip. "Come on, love, we've got a picnic to finish before he wakes up."

Cadie grinned up at her. "Now, *that* sounds like a plan."

IT WAS CLOSE to midnight when they finally made it back into the homestead compound. Collingwood had come to eventually and after listening to him whingeing and moaning as he hung over the back of the horse, Jo had finally relented and let the roped man walk in front of them as they sauntered home. Collingwood had remained stubbornly and sullenly silent throughout, and neither woman had pushed it.

As they came in range of the homestead, Cadie was surprised to see the lights on. "I thought they'd be in bed by now," she said as both women slid down from their saddles.

"Well, we're about three hours later than we said we'd be and they may well have heard the gunfire," Jo reasoned, unsurprised to see her mother bustling out of the kitchen door.

She busied herself with the saddlebags, finding herself unaccountably grumpy and out of sorts. *Maybe it's this damn headache,* she decided. *Or maybe I'm really pissed off with Collingwood.* She glanced at the stone-faced man, who looked close to exhausted, and felt the low burn of anger deep in her chest. *Ya think?*

Maggie peered through the gloom. "Where on earth have you two been? We heard shots."

Jo and Cadie exchanged a look, the taller woman's face saying: *See, I told you so.*

"We ran into a little trouble, Maggie," Cadie explained.

"I'm beginning to think you attract trouble almost as much as my daughter does." Maggie surveyed them, hands on her hips. "Well, you both look like you're in one piece and the horses are fine. So what kind of trouble was it?"

Jo hauled on the rope and dragged Collingwood into the pool of yellow light spilling from the kitchen. He stumbled and fell to his knees in front of the family matriarch.

"Why does this not surprise me?" Maggie muttered, scowling at their employee. She looked up at her daughter.

"What happened?"

David Madison walked out of the house and Jo waited until her father had absorbed the scene before launching into the sorry tale. "Caught him shooting sheep away to the north of the billabong," she replied succinctly. "They weren't hurt or dying, so we figure he's doing it for fun. Didn't seem acceptable to me." She shrugged.

"You were right," David growled. He reached down and pulled Collingwood's head back with a rough hand, ignoring the copious amounts of slowly drying blood in the man's thin hair.

Jo couldn't remember ever seeing her father being so physical with another human being.

He bent over, getting right up into Collingwood's face. "What's the story, Jack?" he demanded. "Wasn't it enough that I trusted you with this place? Why are you killing my stock?"

"I'm not saying a word," Collingwood spat back. "So you can shove it, Madison. You and your bitch wife and bitch spawn."

Cadie leaned forward and put her mouth close to the man's ear. "What about me, Jack? Don't forget how much you and I enjoy each other's company."

"Fuck you, you Seppo bitch!" Collingwood shouted.

Cadie straightened up and looked at Jo. "Doesn't have an extensive vocabulary does he? Not much imagination."

David shoved Collingwood away in disgust. "If you haven't already figured it out, Jack, you're fired. Not only that, but I'm calling the police out here, right now. So you can tell it to them."

"Fuck you."

David pulled his hand back to strike his former employee, but Maggie put a restraining hand on his arm.

"Don't, love," she murmured. "It doesn't do anyone any good, least of all you."

For long seconds her husband looked at her, cool gray eyes sparking. Then he relaxed noticeably.

Maggie patted his arm. "I'll call the police," she said and walked back into the house.

Chapter Twelve

"ARGH!" CADIE COVERED her eyes and groaned in frustration. "I just don't get this game. You guys are killing me!" She tossed her cards on the table.

Maggie and Jo laughed.

"What you don't know, Cadie, is that canasta is a Madison family tradition," Maggie said.

Jo bumped Cadie with her shoulder. "My grandmother was a demon card player. She taught me the game and I never could beat her."

Maggie gathered the cards together and began shuffling them. "That woman was a walking superhero. She could brand a steer, shear a sheep, break a horse, service the tractor, cook a three-course meal and still whip me at canasta, bridge and a few hands of poker before bed." She shook her head in wonderment. "Bulletproof, she was."

Cadie grinned. "She sounds amazing."

Jo snorted. "Gran was an old battleaxe. Scaring small children was a relaxation technique for her."

Maggie slapped her daughter's wrist lightly before she started dealing the cards. "Don't you let your father hear you talking that way," she warned.

"Talking what way?" David asked as he strode into the room. He carried a pair of dress shoes in one hand, and a small plastic box filled with boot polish and brushes in the other. "Don't tell me," he said, taking in the pointed, if amused, silence of the three women. "Someone taking my mother's name in vain? Again."

"I was just explaining to Cadie what a card shark she was," Maggie said, smiling at her husband.

David sat down on the couch and began arranging his shoe-polishing equipment on the coffee table in front of him.

"My mother," he began. "Was an honest-to-goodness..."

"Pioneer," Maggie and Jo said together, rolling their eyes in unison. Cadie broke into giggles at the look of outrage on

David's face.

"We know, Dad, we know," Jo said. She tossed her cards on the table and got up.

"Well, she was," David said. "She and my dad started this farm." Cadie got up too and joined Jo on the sofa opposite him. He picked up a shoe and began applying black polish to its toe. "The land had been in our family for a while, but nobody had ever been able to make a go of it. She and Dad built this house and cleared the land themselves."

Jo slid down until she could rest her head on Cadie's shoulder. She had been feeling rough around the edges since they'd packed Jack Collingwood off to Louth police station. Nothing too grim, just the general feeling that she was brewing some annoying little bug deep in her lungs. But she didn't want to make a fuss, especially as the next day was...

"Anzac Day tomorrow," David said as he continued to polish his shoes to within an inch of their lives. "You going to come into town with me, Josie?" He looked across the coffee table at her. "Thought we might drop in at the cop shop, too. See what's happening about Collingwood."

Jo smiled. Spending Anzac Day with her father was a childhood tradition she had never thought she would get the chance to relive. There was no way she was going to say no, brewing bug be damned. "You bet, Dad. Wouldn't miss it."

"What's Anzac Day?" Cadie asked.

"It's a holiday for commemorating Australia and New Zealand's war dead and those who survived their times in battle," Maggie said quietly from the card table. "It's the day all the war veterans get together and walk in parades, and sit around in pubs reminiscing."

"Ah." Cadie nodded in understanding. "Like our Veterans Day."

Before there could be any further talk about Anzac Day, David stood up abruptly. "Well, these are done," he said gruffly, making a show of inspecting his shoes. "I'm going to go press my suit." And with that he was gone, down the corridor.

"Um, did I say something wrong?" Cadie asked anxiously.

Maggie smiled at her from across the room. "Don't you worry about him, sweetie. Anzac Day is just a sore point for men like David. He'll tell you all about it some time, I'm sure."

Jo patted Cadie's thigh reassuringly and shifted position, resting her head more squarely against her lover's shoulder. "And if he doesn't, I will," she whispered.

Cadie looked down at her. "You okay, love? You look a little pale."

Jo lifted her head and smiled. "Yeah, m'okay," she answered. "Just a bit tired, I think."

CADIE WOKE TO the sound of groaning from the warm lump curled up next to her.

"Jo-Jo?" she mumbled blearily as she rolled over to seek out the source of the noise. "What's wrong, sweetheart?"

Jo moaned piteously again. "Did someone get the number of that buffalo herd?" she grumbled. "I feel like I was caught underfoot."

Cadie pulled back the covers, which, she realized, were damp and cool. "Honey, you're soaking." Quickly, she placed the back of her hand against Jo's forehead. "And you're burning up." She looked more closely at the pale, clammy face. "I knew you were feeling less than great last night. Why didn't you say something?" *Why didn't I make her say something, damn it.*

Bloodshot blue eyes blinked at her. "It was the middle of the damn night before I really started feeling bad." Jo coughed dryly. "Started sweating like a horse and I couldn't breathe properly."

"Well, you should have woken me up," Cadie chastised.

"Why? So you could say exactly what you're saying now, only three hours earlier?" Jo complained. "I decided to let at least one of us get some sleep." She sniffed pathetically. "I feel like poo."

Cadie smiled down at her suffering lover. "Yeah, you pretty much look like it too." She leaned down and touched her lips to Jo's forehead. "You're running a fever."

Jo shivered and hunkered down further into the bedclothes. "No shit, Sherlock. What was your first clue?"

"Oooo, and grumpy with it," Cadie said, forgiving Jo her bad temper. "If you'd said something last night perhaps we could have gotten some aspirin and vitamin C inside you. But no, you had to play the strong, silent type." Jo started to object, but a series of wracking coughs reduced her to a shuddering mess.

"Okay, stay there. I'm going for some maternal aid." Cadie slipped out of the bed. "And some dry bedclothes."

Some time later, huddled in a blanket while Cadie changed the sheets, Jo muttered, "Guess I'm not going in to town with Dad, then."

"Nope," Cadie said bluntly. "You're not going anywhere, my love. Not until your fever's broken, at least."

Jo scowled. "I wanted to watch that arsehole get his just desserts."

"I know, love, but I'm sure his butt is gonna get kicked whether we're there or not," Cadie said, shaking the pillows into fresh cases.

"I think you should go," Jo said.

Cadie thought about that. *A few hours alone with David Madison.* She smiled to herself. *I can do that.* "Okay, sweetheart. I'll try and remember all the details so you feel like you were there."

Jo managed a weak smile. "Thank you."

Cadie patted the mattress in satisfaction. "Okay, that's done." She walked over to the chest of drawers where she and Jo had stored their clothes and pulled out a fresh t-shirt and cotton boxers. "Come on, let's get you into something clean."

Jo stuck her bottom lip out in a child-like pout that almost made Cadie giggle, it was so cute. "Vicks first?"

"Vicks second, clothes first," Cadie insisted. She helped Jo stand and together they got her out of her drenched nightclothes and into the cool, clean cotton. "Better?"

"Much," Jo agreed as she crawled back into the fresh sheets. Cadie picked up the small jar of salve Jo's mother had given her and sat down next to Jo. She unscrewed the lid and dipped her fingers in, coating them with the slippery, aromatic cream. Jo lifted the edge of the t-shirt and Cadie slid her hands underneath, rubbing the ointment over Jo's upper chest.

"I think you're enjoying this," Jo observed, a tiny smile touching the corners of her mouth.

"Looking after you, or rubbing your chest?" Cadie asked mischievously.

"Yes," Jo replied.

Cadie grinned. "You're so good at looking after yourself that I don't often get the chance to pamper you." She withdrew her hands reluctantly. "How does that feel?"

Jo closed her eyes and let the warmth from the menthol and eucalyptus oil soak in. The sharp aroma immediately cleared her head a little. "Better," she said hoarsely. "Thanks."

"No thanks necessary, love," Cadie replied. She leaned down and kissed Jo's fevered brow. *Still hot as hell,* she realized. There was a light tapping on the door. *Good timing.* "Come on in."

Maggie pushed open the door and stepped inside. In one hand she held a large bottle of spring water, and in the other she carried a bowl of steaming soup. "Luckily, I keep a few tubs of my legendary chicken soup frozen for just such an emergency." She placed the bottle of water on the bedside table and looked down at her suffering daughter. "Well, Josie, looks like you're not going anywhere for a while."

Jo groaned. "I'm dying."

"You'll stay alive for some soup, won't you, sunshine?"

"Not hungry."

Maggie sighed and looked at Cadie, who shrugged.

"She's been a really good patient so far," Cadie said.

"That won't last," mother and daughter said together, provoking a laugh from Cadie.

"Here you go," Maggie said as she handed the soup bowl and spoon to Cadie. "Maybe you can persuade her to get a few mouthfuls down." She smiled knowingly at her daughter's partner. "I have a feeling you can get her to do almost anything."

Cadie felt the flush of a blush across her skin. "Oh, Maggie. How do you do that?" she complained.

"It's a mother thing," came a croaky retort from the bed. "Get used to it."

Maggie leaned down and kissed her daughter's cheek. "Be good, Josie." She straightened. "I've got some baking to do." To Cadie she said, "David should be back by about 9 o'clock if you're interested in going in to town with him."

Cadie nodded. "Tall, dark and diseased here wants me to go watch Jack Collingwood's rear end get a kicking."

"Hey!" Jo grumbled. "I'm still in the room, y'know."

Cadie and her mother-in-law exchanged amused glances. "I'll leave you to it," Maggie said cheerily. "Yell if you need something."

MAGGIE WITHDREW THE metal skewer, satisfied that the freshly-baked loaf of bread was done to perfection. She wrapped it in greaseproof paper and slid the loaf into the bread bin sitting on the counter. She looked up when she heard the familiar sound of David's truck pulling into the yard.

He looks pretty fresh, considering he's been up since before dawn and has already driven an hour each way, Maggie decided. David walked slowly towards the house, his suit jacket slung over his shoulder and his other hand buried in his trouser pocket. She smiled quietly. *He still scrubs up pretty well for an old fella.*

"Hello, love," she greeted him as he walked in the kitchen door. He dropped his jacket over the back of a convenient chair and kissed her. "How was the service?"

David sighed. April 25 was always a day of mixed emotions for him. As a Vietnam veteran, he had always participated in the services and marches whenever he could, even through the awful times in the 70s when he was more likely to have been spat upon than cheered. Anzac Day was a more pleasant affair now. Even as the numbers thinned among the ranks, it was heartening to see the large groups of young people who joined in the activities these days.

That morning, he had made the long drive down to Cobar to take part in the dawn service at the small town's War Memorial. It was an annual pilgrimage for him, a chance to catch up with other veterans who were normally scattered widely around the region.

"Not too many of us left," he said in response to Maggie's query. "Remember Scoby Jackson?" A member of David's platoon in Vietnam. Maggie nodded. "He's gone," David said sadly. "His wife was there. Said the cancer came back about six months ago."

Maggie reached out and took her husband's hand, squeezing it gently. "I'm sorry, love."

He shrugged fatalistically. "That's the way it goes."

Maggie watched as he eased himself into the chair and reached for an apple from the fruit bowl on the table in front of him. She knew Anzac Day was something David needed, a connection to friends and comrades and memories she would never be able to share. But she had never enjoyed it. She could see the sadness draping itself around her husband's shoulders as he sat munching the apple, his eyes far away in some memory of Scoby Jackson. *Sometimes,* Maggie thought, *I wish he could let all that go.*

"You're back earlier than I thought you would be," she said.

David nodded. "Thought I'd come back and pick up Josie, and then we could go to the two-up game at the Louth pub," he said, smiling up at her. "Y'know, like we used to do when she was a kid."

Maggie smiled back, hating the fact that she was about to disappoint him. "It's a lovely thought, sweetheart, but unfortunately, Jo's sick."

He frowned, concern warring with disappointment on his face. "Sick? What's wrong? Is she okay?"

"She's got a bad cold and is running a temperature, but she's getting some sleep and Cadie is looking after her."

David relaxed again and loosened his tie. "Not like Josie to get sick like that," he muttered, wondering now if he could be bothered going back up the road to Louth, though he did want to drop in at the police station to see what the news was about that bastard Collingwood. *And I suppose I'll have to start looking for a new foreman,* he thought glumly.

"Well, the poor baby's all wrung out and feverish so she's not going anywhere today." One glance at her husband's face told her he was now in two minds about going to the game. "Here's an idea," she said. "Why don't you take Cadie?"

David scowled. "She's American."

Maggie put her hands on her hips. "And your point is what, exactly? It's not like they don't have days like Anzac Day as well. They've fought in wars too."

David grunted. "Yeah, when it suited them."

"Oh, stop that. You know better," Maggie said, wondering if this wasn't part of the reason David was so uncomfortable around Cadie.

Her husband squirmed in his seat. "Yes, I do, but some of the older blokes might not be too friendly around a Yank, Maggie. You know they're all pretty set in their ways. I don't want to spend all my time looking out for her."

Maggie sat down in the chair next to him. "I think you're underestimating Cadie, love. She's not helpless, y'know. She can look after herself, and from what I can gather, she's more than capable of holding up her end of the conversation." She held her husband's gaze. "And taking her will make her feel like part of the family," she said pointedly.

David scowled again. "All right, all right. I'll take her." He stabbed a finger at his wife. "But don't expect me to be telling anyone that she and Jo are..." He hesitated. "...what they are."

Maggie rolled her eyes at him. "Do you usually go around discussing your daughter's sleeping arrangements, David?" she said. "It's not even going to come up."

"All right, all right."

MAGGIE LET HERSELF into the bedroom after her knock brought no response. One glance at the scenario in the bed told her why and brought a gentle smile to her face. Cadie had climbed back into bed and her arms were wrapped securely around Jo's shoulders in a protective embrace. Maggie chuckled softly and sat down on the edge of the bed. She reached out and patted Cadie's forearm.

"Cadie. Wake up, sweetie."

Green eyes blinked open immediately. "Oh, hi." Cadie grinned sheepishly. "Guess I needed some more sleep too, huh?"

"I guess so. If you still want to go in to town with David, though, you'd better get up now."

Cadie nodded. "Yep, I do." She glanced down at the still sleeping woman in her arms. "Do you mind keeping an eye on her, for me? She's still really hot."

"Don't you worry about that, now," Maggie said. "I'm not going far from the house today. We'll be right."

Jo stirred, mumbling softly in her sleep, and Cadie took the opportunity to slide out from underneath. "Where you going?" Jo muttered without opening her eyes.

"Shhh, sweetheart, go back to sleep. Your mom's going to be around while I go with your dad, okay?"

"'k," Jo replied, barely waking at all.

Cadie clambered off the bed and moved around, gathering clothes together.

"Listen, this trip into town's more than a visit to the police station," Maggie said as the young American pulled on her moleskins and zipped them up.

Cadie hesitated over the shirt she'd chosen, wondering if she should be finding something less casual to wear. "Are these clothes going to be okay, then?" she asked.

"They're fine," Maggie confirmed. "David's already been to the dawn service, and now he wants to go to the Louth pub and catch up with some old mates, play some two-up."

"Two-up?

Maggie grinned. "You'll see."

Cadie nodded, accepting that. A sudden flash of insight made her look up at Maggie sharply. "Jo always used to spend the day with him, didn't she?"

"Yes," Maggie replied, impressed with Cadie's ability to cut to the chase.

"So I'm daughter-by-proxy for the day." Cadie met Maggie's steady gaze again. "Oh boy."

Her mother-in-law laughed. "Don't worry. He really is a teddy bear. And he likes you." Cadie raised a surprised eyebrow. "Trust me, I can tell."

Chapter Thirteen

IT TOOK ABOUT 15 minutes for Cadie to screw up the courage to start a conversation with the silent man behind the wheel. David had given her a brusque nod in greeting before pulling on his suit jacket and waiting for her to climb in the passenger side, but his utterances had been few and far between.

"So," she said eventually. "Tell me more about Anzac Day."

Gray eyes flicked over her then away again. "What do you want to know?" David asked gruffly.

"Well..." Cadie shifted slightly so she was turned more towards him. "Why is it today? April 25, I mean."

David took a deep breath and bit back a retort. *Figures. World history doesn't make much of an impact in America,* he thought. *Not her fault, though, and at least she's interested.*

"April 25, 1915," he said. "That's the day Australian and New Zealand forces landed on the beach at Gallipoli." He looked quickly at Cadie, who kept her face impassive. "That's on the Turkish peninsula at the entrance to the Black Sea." She nodded understanding. "Trouble is, the British commanders got it wrong and the landing took place too far north. The Turks were sitting at the top of the cliffs, waiting for our blokes. We were pretty much cut down the moment we landed. Eventually we managed to dig in at the foot of the cliffs. Nine months later, forces were withdrawn. It was all for nothing. Twenty-six thousand Aussie casualties, seven thousand-five hundred Kiwis."

Cadie let the hot, dry wind from the open window wash over her for a moment. "Sounds like it was a terrible, pointless war," she said quietly.

"It was," David said bluntly. "But a lot of people think it was the making of us."

"How do you mean?"

David rested his elbow on the edge of the window, his fingers pressed against his temple. "Up until then, we'd pretty much followed around after England, doing whatever they wanted, whenever they wanted. I mean, that's why we were fighting in World War I in the first place, after all," he explained. "But after Gallipoli we were a lot more skeptical about being at their beck and call. It was the start of our independence as a nation, I guess."

Cadie did a quick sum in her head. "I guess there aren't too many Gallipoli veterans left," she said.

"None," David replied. "Last one died last year. There's only a handful of Great War vets left as well." He looked at her again. "You're going to meet one this morning."

Cadie grinned. "Cool." She fell silent then, studying the scenery. She was desperately curious about David Madison's own military history, but she knew better than to blunder in with a bunch of clueless questions. She had been a politician's wife long enough to know that Vietnam vets were not always happy to talk about their war service.

She cast a darting glance at the man next to her and saw a tiny smile crease the corner of his mouth. "It's okay, Cadie, you can ask," he said wryly.

She grinned. "Thanks. You were in Vietnam?"

"Yep. Shot at and shat upon," he said quietly. "I was with 6RAR." He glanced at her. "That's a regiment."

"I figured." Cadie smiled.

"Served in Phuoc Toy province in '66 and '67. You ever heard of the Battle of Long Tan?" he asked, not expecting any answer other than a negative.

Cadie thought about it for a moment. Naomi had served on a couple of House Committees for veterans' affairs and Cadie had gone along with her ex-partner to several functions. Naomi had never been interested in the details, but for Cadie it was different. Talking to the veterans and hearing their individual stories had been something she'd greatly treasured. More than one of those functions had featured visiting Australians. Cadie dug around in her memory banks, and smiled when she realized she did know what David was talking about.

"Didn't President Johnson..." She paused, suddenly unsure. "Or Nixon...give out some honor to the Aussies for that?" she said, ridiculously pleased with herself when she saw David's double-take.

Maggie was right, David thought, impressed despite himself. *She can handle herself.* "Yeah, he did," he confirmed. "A Presidential Unit Citation from Lyndon Johnson to Delta Company of 6RAR." He looked at Cadie thoughtfully, even as he continued to steer the truck along the road. They were nearing the outskirts of Louth and his attention was divided as he dodged a rheumy old cattle dog that was meandering across the highway. "That was my company," he said.

"So you were right in the middle of that battle, huh?"

David shrugged and swung the truck onto the main street of Louth. "There were three platoons involved. It was 11 Platoon that made contact with the Vietcong first, and they got hit hard. Then 10 Platoon went in from one side and tried to help them out. I was in 12 Platoon. We were held back in reserve and then sent in from the other direction. We were the ones who eventually extracted what was left of 11." He went silent, and Cadie could see his throat working hard.

"This all happened in one night, didn't it?" she recalled.

He nodded wordlessly, and then took a deep breath. "Yeah. The 11 Platoon survivors stayed with us, but we had to leave the dead and wounded out in the field overnight. Then the next morning we went in and pulled them out. Seventeen dead, and some twenty-odd wounded. All good mates. All young—twenty or twenty-one. A couple were nineteen or so."

Cadie shook her head in disbelief. "I can't even begin to imagine what that must have been like."

"You don't want to know," David muttered.

She watched as a whole range of emotions swept across his lean, lined face. The telltale rippling at the corner of his jaw told her he was grinding his teeth. "Do you still dream about it?" she asked. His head snapped round and she felt the full blast of his cool, gray gaze. *Oooo, may have pushed a little too hard on that one, Jones.* But it didn't take long for his eyes to soften.

"Yeah, I do," he muttered. "But don't tell Maggie." He grinned suddenly. "She'll have me taking those damn herbal concoctions again, and I can't stand the taste of those buggers."

Cadie chuckled. "My lips are sealed," she promised. "But I think it's a fair bet she already knows."

"Yeah, probably. But as long as I don't say anything she won't push it."

"Well, now I know where Jo gets it," Cadie said.

"Gets what?" David asked, eyebrows raised.

"Damn-fool stubborn nothing-hurts-so-don't-expect-me-to-say-ow stoicism," Cadie shot back. "Jo about has to be bleeding on the floor before she'll admit she's hurting."

"So I guess she's pretty crook if she's laid up in bed this morning, then?" David asked.

Cadie smiled, her brain now automatically flipping through its growing lexicon of Australian phrases. *Crook is sick.* "Yeah. I'll give her credit, though. She's been a good patient so far." She folded her arms and looked pensively out the windscreen.

David snorted. "That won't last," he said. "Wait 'til she gets bored."

MAGGIE STARTED SLIGHTLY as the phone jangled next to her. "I've got to figure out how to turn that bloody thing down," she muttered, turning away from the computer screen. She'd been working on the station's accounts and, despite her grumbling about the discordant sound, she was grateful for any excuse not to keep looking at the grim figures. She picked up and said, "Hello?"

"Mrs. Madison? Uh, g'day. It's Ken Harding here." The gruff voice of the Sydney-based policeman surprised Maggie.

"Oh, Detective Harding," she said. "Hello to you, too. How are you?"

"Fair to middling, thanks," replied Harding. He was sitting at his desk in a seedy corner of NSW police headquarters on Charles Street. It was a public holiday, but Harding, himself a Vietnam veteran, preferred to avoid the Anzac Day rituals. It was a chance to catch up on some paperwork. "Thanks for the Christmas card, by the way. Sorry I didn't get around to sending one back."

Maggie swiveled her chair around to face out onto her back garden. "That's all right, Ken. We know how busy you get, especially at that time of year." Aware of her daughter's presence in the bedroom, a short walk away, she lowered her voice. "What can we do for you today?"

"Just checking in really, Maggie," the cop said. "Haven't talked to you in a while so I thought I'd see how things are going."

Maggie grinned. "Well, actually, I've got some news for you, for once," she said, a little smugly. "Jo is here."

There was a silence on the other end of the phone as Harding absorbed that totally unexpected piece of information. *Bugger me,* he thought. *Madison finally got up the nerve to go home.* "That's great news," he said.

"We're pretty happy about it. Cadie is here, too."

Harding wrapped his pudgy, nicotine-stained fingers around his coffee cup and spun the mug idly in his hand. "Yeah?" *Jesus, one surprise after another. She went home* and *she told 'em she's a dyke. Gutsy.* "She's a feisty one, that young lady. She beaten anyone up yet?"

Maggie laughed. "Yes, actually," she replied, thinking of Cadie's run-in with Jack Collingwood. "She's lovely."

Harding smiled, his memories of the fierce little blonde fond ones. "Yeah, she's not bad," he understated. He cleared his throat awkwardly, suddenly feeling like he didn't quite know what he was doing in this conversation. "Does Jo know yet...well, you know." He hesitated to spell out the extent of his relationship with Jo's parents.

"Not yet," Maggie replied, hearing a quiet note in the policeman's voice that she hadn't heard before.

"Fair enough," Harding murmured. He felt vaguely disoriented, as if the natural order of things in his world had been tilted strangely. He had been so used to Jo Madison's self-imposed isolation and the sense of duty he felt towards her parents, that now... *Well, if she's back in the family fold, then I guess they won't need me hanging around,* he thought glumly.

"I hope this doesn't mean we won't be hearing from you any more, Ken," Maggie said, as if she could read his mind. "You know David and I will always consider you a friend of the family. I don't know what we would have done without knowing you were there to help when we needed it."

Harding swallowed around the lump that had suddenly developed in his throat. "Awww, you know I was just doing my job, Maggie," he said huskily.

"Rubbish," Maggie retorted. "You know damn well you went above and beyond what you needed to do for the job."

Five years ago, when Jo had turned herself in, Ken Harding had been the Madisons' contact with the police. He had planned on offering protection for her parents as part of the package in exchange for Jo's testimony. But when Jo had turned down any form of police help, Harding had taken it upon himself to contact the Madisons and put them out of their misery as to her safety and whereabouts. Over the years, since he was keeping tabs on Jo anyway, Harding had become the Madisons' only link to their wayward daughter.

Along the way, he had also been the one to tell them what Jo's "job" in Sydney had been. He knew it was something for which Jo would probably never forgive him, but at the time, it had seemed the right thing to do. He'd also made sure to point out the good Jo had done by turning on her former cohorts. The lives she'd saved. The Madisons had rewarded him with friendship and gratitude.

"Did you decide to let her tell you herself?" the detective asked tentatively.

Maggie studied the line of ants marching along the sun-warmed windowsill. "Not necessarily," she answered. "It's been difficult to know how to bring it up, and, to be honest, there hasn't been much chance yet. Now," she went on briskly, "when are you going to come out and visit?"

Harding tried to imagine himself out in the bush without ready access to a McDonald's and fresh packs of Winnie Blues and couldn't see it. All the same, there was something deeply appealing about getting away from the city and spending time with the Madisons. It touched something in him that had never gotten a lot of attention over the years—a sense of family.

"I'd like that," he heard himself say. "Not sure when I can get away, though."

Maggie wouldn't hear anything of it. "Well then, it's time you looked into it, Ken. There's a side of beef walking around my back paddock that's got your name on it."

JO PADDED OUT into the kitchen. She had pulled on a pair of sweatpants and yet another fresh t-shirt and was wrapped in a blanket. Waking up about 20 minutes earlier, she'd felt a little better, although disappointed to be alone, so she had gathered herself up to search for company.

The kitchen was empty, and Jo figured her mother was probably somewhere in the flower garden. Barefoot, she shuffled out the back door, trailing a corner of the blanket in the dust behind her.

"Hi, Mum," she croaked, spotting her mother on her knees in a corner of the flower bed.

"Tch, Josie, what are you doing out of bed?" Maggie pushed herself to her feet and strolled over. Her daughter was swaying slightly, as if unsure of her balance. "You should be horizontal, love. You've gone all pale."

"Yeah, I'm deciding that you're probably right," Jo replied. Her bottom lip slipped out in a fair imitation of a pout. "I got lonely."

Maggie took her daughter's arm and led her to a folding deckchair that sat in the middle of the lawn. "Here, sit down before you fall down." She helped Jo lower herself into the comfortable hammock-like seat, tucking the blanket in around her shoulders.

"Cadie went with Dad, huh?" Jo asked. It was a nice feeling, the sunlight on her face and her mother looking after her. *Warm and fuzzy.*

"You don't remember her leaving?"

Jo frowned, trying to think. She had a vague memory of Cadie saying she wouldn't be long, but other than that, the morning was a bit of a blur. "Not really." She snuggled down further into the blanket, lassitude fast overtaking her. "Cadie okay with spending the day with Dad?" She knew how much Anzac Day meant to her father, and she hoped Cadie wasn't going to be overwhelmed by the experience.

"I think she'll be fine." Maggie smiled as her daughter's eyelids began to droop. *I give her about 10 more seconds and she'll be fast asleep again,* she thought. *Such a life you've led, my girl. I hope you can tell us about it yourself one day.* Sure enough, Jo's eyes closed and Maggie backed away slowly before returning to her task in the rose bushes. She turned the soil over with her trowel, mulling through all she knew about the young woman's history. Some of it still hurt to think about, even though her gut told her Jo was no longer that person. *I'll bet my last dollar you're scared to tell us because you think we're going to reject you.* She glanced over, smiling again at the figure sleeping soundly in the sunlight. *Going to have to convince you otherwise, kiddo.*

CADIE STEPPED INSIDE the circle of men and felt butterflies in her stomach. She was half-aware of her father-in-law beyond the perimeter of faces, watching her from where he leant against the bar, cold beer in hand. They had been at the pub a couple of hours, and Cadie had met all the old-timers of the town, including one World War I veteran and a handful of David's Vietnam *compadres*. He'd introduced her as a friend of Jo's, and she hadn't seen any reason to elaborate on that. One or two of the men had baulked at her accent, but she'd shown plenty of interest in their history and medals, and as a result had managed to charm everyone in the smoke-filled bar.

The two-up game, illegal on every day of the year except Anzac Day, had been in full swing for about an hour. Cadie had watched long enough to get a handle on the rules, such as they were, and it hadn't been long before her new friends had urged her into the middle of the pit.

"Place your bets, gentlemen," yelled the pit boss. Cadie pulled out her wallet and extracted a five-dollar bill, handing it to him as he passed. He gave her a short, flat, wooden stick on which lay two large pennies, one head-side up, the other tail-side up. All she had to do was toss the coins in the air, using the paddle. As the tosser, she automatically bet on two heads coming up. Everyone else in the circle could either bet with her, banking on two heads, or against her, banking on two tails. If the coins landed different sides up, she got to throw again.

Cadie waited while all the bets and side bets were negotiated and laid. A nod from the pit boss gave her the all-clear and she stepped into the center of the circle and flipped the coins up into the air. Whoops and calls came from the ring of men, urging the coins to fall their way. As they clinked metallically to the floor, silence descended. The pit boss stepped forward.

"Heads it is!" he shouted and a roar went up from the majority of the surrounding men, most of whom had backed Cadie's hand.

"Good on ya, lass," said one old-timer close to Cadie's shoulder. "I'll be riding on your coat-tails, never you mind." Cadie grinned at him as the pit boss gave her a handful of cash and the paddle for another toss, before making his way around the ring again. Winnings were doled out and further bets laid as a crowd began to gather beyond the inner ring of participants.

Well, it's not the most complicated game in the world, Cadie thought happily. *But it's a lot of fun.* Her next throw ended in a split result, which served to raise the tension levels and heighten the chatter and banter around her. A quick glance over in David's direction told her that she was doing all right, as her father-in-law raised his beer glass in acknowledgement. Twenty minutes later Cadie was the toast of Louth. Happy punters pocketed fistfuls of cash while the losers consoled themselves with another round of cold beer.

Cadie sauntered over to David, feeling somewhat impressed with herself. "I did okay, for an American, huh?" she said smugly, and was not surprised to see the patented Madison expression of skepticism on the older man's face.

"It's a game of chance, ya know," he said gruffly, taking another mouthful of ale. "It's not like there's any real skill involved."

Cadie opened her mouth to retort when the man who had been acting as the pit boss tapped David on the shoulder. "Here ya go, Dave," he said, handing David a wad of cash. He grinned in Cadie's direction. "You want to hang on to this one, mate. She's a dab hand. I reckon she's got a bit of a lucky streak about her." He tipped his hat at Cadie. "Come back and visit us again, lass. You're good for business." And with that he walked away.

Cadie raised a sardonic eyebrow at David, who cleared his throat and tucked the money into his back pocket. Neither said a word as he caught her clear green-eyed gaze and held it. Finally, as if admitting defeat, he let his face relax into a grin that dropped years off his lined features. Cadie chuckled, relieved that a barrier seemed to have disappeared between them. *It's about time,* she decided.

"Come on, girl," David said, downing the last of his beer. "They're expecting us at the police station."

"YOU ARE KIDDING me?" Jo's mouth dropped open in astonishment. She was trying to figure out if this whole conversation was part of some weird fever-driven delusion because she couldn't quite fathom what it was her father was telling her.

"Nope. Fair dinkum," David confirmed.

All four of them were in the Madisons' living room. Cadie and David had arrived home after spending the afternoon watching the police grill the Madisons' sheep-killing ex-foreman, Jack Collingwood.

Jo was curled in a corner of the couch, wrapped in a blanket and surrounded by a ring of used tissues and various packets of medication. After her nap in the garden she had moved in here, where at least the satellite television helped distract her from the misery of her sneezing jags. Stuffed in the head and still with a high temperature, she felt crappy, but at least she'd managed to stay awake to hear the news from Cadie and her father.

"Let me see if I've got this right," she muttered stuffily. "Collingwood was working for a loans officer from the bank?" Jo looked at Cadie for confirmation.

"Apparently," Cadie nodded. "The idea was to try and put your parents out of business, so they'd default on their mortgage." She shrugged. "Brownie points for the loans officer, I guess."

"That, and the bank'd make more money, in the short term, by selling off the defaulted property than by waiting for me to pay off the damn mortgage," David growled.

Jo snorted derisively, or tried to. All she really managed was to make herself go deaf in her left ear. "Well, if that isn't the stupidest damn scheme I've ever heard," she said, shaking her head. "One sheep at a time? With something as obvious as a shotgun? Did he think you wouldn't notice?"

Maggie moved from her spot near the door and came and sat on the arm of the sofa by Jo's shoulder. "I always suspected Jack wasn't just a slimy character. Now I know he's a complete idiot as well," she said.

"So what now, Dad?" Jo asked, looking over at where her father lounged wearily in his armchair. "You're not gonna let them get away with it, are you?"

"No fear of that, Josie," he mused. "They'll both be charged, and I'll make sure it goes through to the right conclusion. And what's more, there'll be an investigation at the bank. I dare say this isn't the first time this kind of thing has been tried, and they'll want to see how far up the ladder it goes."

"You've got a great case if you ever wanted to sue them,"

Cadie pointed out. Everyone looked at her, and she shrugged. "Hey, I'm American. We understand lawsuits."

"It's something to think about, that's for sure," David agreed, giving Cadie a small smile. She felt a warm glow in the pit of her belly.

Something nudged at Cadie's thigh and she looked down to see Jo's foot begging for attention. "You should be wearing socks," she murmured, feeling the cool of Jo's skin against the palm of her hand when she wrapped her fingers around the foot.

"My feet are the least of my worries right now, love." Jo reached for yet another tissue. "So, are you going to be compensated for the sheep you've lost?" she asked her father.

"Yeah," he grunted. "Not that it will make much difference." He turned away from his daughter's intense, if bloodshot, gaze. "If it doesn't rain soon, I'll have to start shooting the buggers myself." He pushed himself up and stalked out of the room, leaving a pregnant silence behind him.

"Is that true, Mum?" Jo asked quietly, looking up and over her left shoulder into her mother's face.

Maggie's answering look didn't waver. "Pretty much," she replied. "But not to worry, love. Rain has to come some time, and it takes more than a bit of sunshine to beat your father. We'll survive."

Cadie could feel the tension in Jo. "At least we can help out for the next few weeks, until you guys find a new foreman," she said hopefully.

"That you can." Maggie smiled back at her kindly. "But first we'd better get this one healthy." She touched Jo's shoulder before standing up and moving towards the door. "And we can start that by getting some food inside her. Time to get dinner on."

Cadie waited until they were alone before she locked eyes with her partner. "You want to help them out with some money, don't you?" she asked softly.

"Yeah, I do," Jo admitted. "But that means..." She let the sentence hang.

"That means pretty much telling them everything," Cadie finished for her.

"Yes, God help me," Jo muttered, and they held each other's gaze for long, telling seconds.

Chapter Fourteen

"TELL ME AGAIN why we're still working for Naomi Silverberg?" Toby McIntyre asked, gazing across his wide desk.

Jason peered out from behind his laptop, his round rimless glasses endearingly crooked. "I think you're asking the wrong guy. I don't have a clue. All I know is, this week's been way too long."

Toby sighed and removed his own tortoiseshell glasses. Wearily, he rubbed the bridge of his nose. "This whole damn year's been too long."

Even now, deep on a Saturday night, in the privacy of their own DC home, the two PR men couldn't escape the idiosyncrasies of their boss. Today's challenge was how to put a positive spin on Senator Silverberg's latest Senate Chamber indiscretion—a none-too-sober rant on gay rights that had done little to further the cause. They weren't having a lot of luck.

Jason shut down his laptop and closed it. "Well, I don't think we're going to get much more accomplished tonight. Let's give it a rest, eh?"

Toby blinked at him through bloodshot eyes. "No argument from me." There was a minute or so of pensive silence as both men sat, lost in their own thoughts.

"You think it's time to get out, don't you?" Jason finally asked, looking his partner in the eye.

Toby gnawed on his bottom lip for a while before answering. "I know we always said we were in this for the long haul, but I think Naomi's lost it. And I don't mean her usual rant-and-recover cycle. I mean I think she's having some kind of breakdown. Who knows if she'll get herself together or not. Either way, her career's in the toilet." He paused and got up from his stool, taking his empty coffee cup over to the sink and washing it out. "To be honest, I'm not sure I've got it in me to save Naomi Silverberg from herself yet again."

Jason sighed. The disappointment in his partner's voice was obvious. Toby had been the one to get them involved with

Naomi in the first place, convinced by her charisma and commitment that they were onto a winner. He had been a true believer, and Jason knew how much this must be hurting him.

"She's not the person we once knew," he said. "Maybe it's time we started thinking about our own reputations for a change." He met Toby's eyes, knowing that it wasn't anything his partner particularly wanted to hear. Then again, he *had* started this conversation.

Toby nodded slowly. "Yeah, that's pretty much what I've been thinking." He returned to the workstation and wrapped Jason up in a hug from behind. "You think she's gone too far this time?"

Jason placed his hands over his lover's forearms. "Oh yeah. She was drunk when she gave that speech yesterday, Tobes. And everyone knew it. Did you see the look on the Leader's face? I thought he was going to stroke out. Forget about the contents of the speech—it was drivel, but that's not the point. She was slurring and swaying. Being drunk and disorderly 9000 miles away is one thing. Doing it right here...and in the Senate Chamber to boot, is another thing altogether."

Toby rested his chin on Jason's head. "I know. I think I'm in denial."

"The bottom line is, our reputation is going down the crapper with hers," Jason said, more harshly than he had intended. He felt Toby flinch and adopted a more positive tone. "It's salvageable. But I think we need to cut our losses now."

There was silence for a moment, then Toby released him and paced restlessly. "She's going to go ballistic when we tell her."

Good, we've made the decision to go, then, Jason thought with relief. "Well, that won't be our problem any more."

"I know whose problem it *will* be." They locked eyes. Both knew who their boss's kicking post was.

Jason's brow furrowed. "You don't honestly think she'd do anything to hurt Cadie, do you? Physically, I mean."

Toby shrugged. "Well, she has to come back here some time. Even if she's going to stay with Jo long-term, and live in Australia eventually, she can't start that process over there. She'll need to come back and get a different visa. Naomi's already got her buddies in Immigration keeping an eye out. I'm not sure that's a good thing, are you? All I know is, she hates Jo enough to do anything. No, I can't imagine her physically hurting Cadie." He folded his arms across his chest. "But if she could hurt Jo? You bet."

"And the quickest, surest way to hurt Jo..." Jason left the thought unfinished. "So what do we do?"

Toby made a decision and stood upright. "Quit. Then we'll track Cadie down and warn her."

"STICK A FORK in me, I'm done," Jo purred, rolling onto her back in the cool grass of her parents' back garden. She dropped her now-denuded paper plate beside her and tucked her hands contentedly behind her head. Her belly was full, her unhappy brush with influenza was now just a bad memory, the stars were out and her family was all around her. *Never thought I'd ever experience this again,* she reflected as she gazed up into the clear black sky. *And it's all down to Cadie.* Jo glanced over to her partner, unsurprised to see the compact American making her way through an enormous bowl of Maggie Madison's homemade apple crumble doused in hot custard. Jo chuckled, catching Cadie's attention.

"Yeah, you look like you're done, Jo-Jo," Cadie mumbled around a mouthful of the sweet treat. "It's a good thing we've been working hard these past few weeks or I'd be the size of a house by now." She grinned at her mother-in-law who was lounging in the deckchair. "There's no way I'm leaving without a whole book full of your recipes, Maggie. This is sensational." She took another spoonful of crumble.

"Thank you." Maggie smiled fondly back at Cadie, whose appetite seemed to be outstripped only by her metabolism. "When do you think you'll have to go back?"

It was a question they'd been avoiding. The three weeks since Jack Collingwood's arrest had been busy and enjoyable ones for them all. Cadie and Jo had mucked in around the property, more than making up for Jack's departure and giving David time to advertise and interview prospective new station managers.

Without a lot of success, Maggie thought glumly. *And Jo and Cadie can't stay forever.*

The question hung in the air for a few seconds before Jo cleared her throat. "Well, I can't really stay away from Cheswick Marine much longer," she said. "We're about to get into the really busy season. And Cadie's visa runs out in..." She looked across at Cadie. "When is it? Soon?"

Cadie did a quick calculation in her head, the result taking her by surprise. "Thirteen days," she said, feeling unprepared for the sudden sense of impending separation.

Jo did a double-take, startled by Cadie's answer. *Where the hell did that time go?* "Really?" Their eyes met in a quiet acknowledgement of the situation. "Damn."

Maggie watched the interplay between her daughter and daughter-in-law. For the first time she realized that, despite the seemingly perfect match of their two personalities, the couple had serious obstacles to overcome. "How long will it be before you can come back, Cadie?" she asked.

Cadie held Jo's gaze for a few more seconds before she turned and smiled gently at Maggie. "A few weeks, at least," she said. "I have some work I have to do to wind my business up, including making some changes to bank accounts and things like that. Then, of course, there are still some loose ends to be tied up with my ex." She dropped her eyes, wishing she never had to deal with Naomi Silverberg again.

"Do you really have to see her?" Jo asked. She regretted the question immediately. *A conversation better had in private, Jo-Jo, you idiot,* she chastised herself. "Forget I asked that," she said.

"No, it's okay," Cadie insisted. It hadn't taken her long to figure out that Maggie was the last person on the planet to make judgments, and she didn't have a problem talking about Naomi in front of her. *Even if Jo does,* she acknowledged. *And it won't do her any harm to let her parents in a little more.* "I'm not even sure I will have to see her, Jo," she said. "First I have to figure out what she pulled out of the Chicago house and sent to Mom and Dad. If there's anything still there that I need, I'll have to go retrieve it. With any luck, she'll be in DC."

There was a pause as David entered the circle of conversation. He'd been scraping down the barbecue plate after cooking them all a lavish main course of steak, sausages, and lamb chops. Now he wandered over to his chair, a plate of apple crumble in one hand and a cold glass of white wine in the other.

"Who might be in DC?" he asked as he sat down.

"Cadie's ex-girlfriend," Maggie said. "If you're going to wander away, love, you're going to miss half the conversation."

"Ah well, someone has to do the tidying up around here," he replied in a mellow tone. He glanced at Cadie. "Your ex is the politician, right?"

Cadie nodded, ignoring the snort of derision coming from the long body next to her on the grass. "That's right," she said. "A senator."

David looked almost impressed. Almost. "Pretty important person, huh," he said between mouthfuls of crumble.

"She thinks so." Cadie felt Jo's hand against the small of her back, circling in slow, reassuring movements against her skin.

"Josie, are you going to go back with Cadie?" Maggie asked. She thought she knew the answer to that already, but for three weeks she had been waiting for an opportunity to finally talk to her daughter—really talk to her—and so far, this looked like the best chance.

"Um, I can't really, Mum," Jo muttered. "Bad time to leave the business."

David and Maggie looked at each other. Unspoken between them was a conversation they'd had many times since Jo and Cadie had arrived. How to broach the subject of Jo's past—how to tell her that they already knew, and that it was okay. David sensed his wife was burning to keep this conversation going and signaled his support with a nod.

"It's survived all right without you for the last three weeks, Josie-love. I'm sure it could manage a few more," Maggie said, taking her cue from her husband and pressing on. "You've obviously got good people looking after things for you."

Jo cleared her throat, and felt the knot in her stomach tighten and twist. She knew this moment had been coming. For three weeks she had ducked and weaved around it, even though a large part of her wanted very much to get this conversation over and done with. But now that the moment had come, she found herself trembling. Cadie's fingers wrapped warmly around her own and squeezed gently. Jo took one last look into loving green eyes and breathed in deeply.

"Mum, I can't go to the United States because I have a criminal record," she said. Two sets of parental eyes regarded her steadily. "And I'm not talking about petty stuff. There are things on my record that would make any Immigration officer stop me at the gate. And rightly so." She dropped her eyes, a flush of shame warming her cheeks.

Jo's parents seemed calm, Cadie noted. Maggie even smiled slightly as Jo struggled. *I'm missing something here,* Cadie thought. *They're reacting almost as if they...* She gasped, realization hitting her like a baseball bat between the eyes. *They already know. Son of a—*

"Do you want to tell us more about it, Josie?" Maggie asked cautiously. Fear and shame had held her daughter back from them for too long. They'd come too far in the past few weeks to let ancient history keep them apart now. But a firm hand on her arm stopped her from pushing further.

David wasn't sure what to do. He could see that his daughter was suffering, even though she still seemed relatively contained. "Enough, Maggie," he said softly. He turned back to Jo and reached out with his left hand, waiting until she hesitantly took it, her fingers almost shy in his larger, callused palm.

Jo couldn't remember the last time her father had held her

hand. His skin was rough, but familiar, and she felt a wash of safety rush over her with a warmth that was almost startling. She blinked up into gray eyes that were steady and calm.

"Josie, we know," her father said simply.

Confused, she tilted her head, trying to figure out what he was saying. "You know what?" she finally asked.

"Everything," Maggie replied.

"We know about your record, and the things you did in Sydney," her father continued. "Terrible things you did," he conceded, gripping his daughter's hand tighter when his words prompted her to try and withdraw. "But you made good, Josie. Tried your best to make up for what you did."

"I can't ever do that," Jo half-sobbed. Cadie, whose silent support had kept her feeling strong so far, held her other hand fiercely. "Not ever. No matter what I do the rest of my life." Tears made her voice ragged, its harshness making them all wince.

Maggie couldn't stand it any longer. She slipped down out of her chair onto her knees in the grass in front of Jo. With both hands she cupped her daughter's tortured face. "Josie, stop. Don't do this to yourself. Please."

Jo looked stunned. Her eyes widened, as if her father's words were only just sinking in. "I don't understand. How can you possibly know?"

"When you turned yourself in to the police...well, Ken Harding made it his business to tell us what was going on," Maggie explained, knowing that on some level Jo would find the policeman's actions a betrayal.

"Harding?" It was all getting a bit much for Jo.

"Yes, love." Maggie smiled softly at the younger woman's confusion. "He's become quite a good friend to us."

Cadie shook her head in wonder. "He never let on," she murmured.

Jo had no idea what to think or what to feel. On the one hand, she was angry with Harding for going where he had had no business going. On the other hand, it appeared he'd done her a favor. *They've had time to absorb this and come to some kind of peace about it. How, I have no idea.*

Maggie kept her hands around Jo's face, gently stroking at the trail of tears with the pads of her thumbs. "It's okay, sweetheart," she whispered. "I promise you, it's okay."

Over her mother's shoulder, Jo saw David nod and it was like someone broke open the dam of fear and uncertainty that had blocked her emotions for a long time. A strangled sob forced its way out of her and soon the cries came bubbling up.

Maggie gathered her in, wrapping long arms around Jo until finally her daughter gave in and collapsed into her embrace.

Releasing Jo's hand, Cadie felt her own tears well up and she covered her mouth, trying to stay quiet. She watched as David reached over his wife's shoulder and gently ran his fingers through Jo's unruly fringe. *Thank God,* she thought. *Thank God.*

Maggie closed her eyes as she held her child close against her chest. Sobs wracked Jo's body, her breath coming in long, hitching gasps as she cried. Maggie heard herself making the soothing sounds of comfort only a mother seems to know. Memories flooded her consciousness, other times when a much younger Jossandra had needed her this way. A lost puppy when she was four, a broken arm when she eight. Maggie's eyes opened again. *And when Phil killed himself. That was the beginning of the end.* She felt Jo's arms squeeze tighter around her waist. *And this is the end of the new beginning,* she realized. *Now we can really start to be a family again.*

"I'm sorry," Jo kept saying, over and over. "I'm so sorry."

"What are you sorry for, love?" Maggie asked quietly. She could feel David behind her shoulder, his calm presence rock steady even as his fingers continued to lightly stroke Jo's head.

"I never meant for all that to happen," Jo moaned. "I never meant to become that person. I, I just..."

"Shhh. It's all right. It's all done and over with now," her mother soothed.

"But that's it. It's not done with," Jo insisted. "Not in my head. Not ever."

"And maybe that's something you're meant to live with, Josie," Maggie argued. "But that's not a reason to shut people out or isolate yourself. And it's no reason to be afraid of your father and me."

"We're not going to lose you again," David said firmly. "I don't like what you did, Josie, not one bit of it. I'll admit to that and it's something you and I are going to have to learn to deal with. But we're going to do that together. And nothing you can tell me, nothing you can do, will ever separate me from my love for you. Do you understand that?"

Jo blinked at her father, her eyes moist with tears that threatened to spill over again. "I didn't," she admitted. "But I'm trying to understand it now."

David nodded. "I know. And perhaps the only thing that will make it clear for you is time. But we've got plenty of that now." He cupped her cheek with his rough palm. "Thank you for coming home again."

Jo turned her head slightly, tilting it in Cadie's direction. "I can't take credit for that, Dad," she said hoarsely. "Without Cadie's encouragement, I can't say that I would have."

David nodded and looked calmly at Cadie, who was still fighting her own tears, her hand covering her mouth. "Are you all right, little one?" he asked.

Cadie sniffled and took a deep breath. "Y-yes, I think so," she replied, somewhat nonplussed by the term of endearment, something she hadn't heard from David before. "I don't like to see her hurting." She nodded in Jo's direction. "It gives me a stomachache."

David smiled kindly, his gray eyes twinkling as if he recognized the feeling somewhere deep inside. "I think it's a good thing that we had this conversation, though," he replied. "Don't you?"

"Oh yes," Cadie agreed. "It's been a long time coming."

"That it has," David murmured. He looked at his family. Jo had stopped crying and was leaning wearily against her mother. Maggie looked happier than he could remember seeing her in a long time. *Mothers and their daughters.* He smiled at the picture. For the first time in...well, years...he felt like something was going right. "Who wants another drink?" He grinned as hesitant chuckles broke out from the three women in his life.

"Make mine a double," Jo muttered.

"HOW DOES IT feel?" Cadie whispered, enjoying Jo's warm breath against the skin of her neck.

"Pretty good," Jo rumbled. She let her fingers slide under the sheet and across the silky surface of Cadie's stomach. They were both naked, something they hadn't made a habit of in the three weeks they'd been at Coonyabby. But for some reason, tonight they'd both opted for skin, though they hadn't talked about it at all.

Cadie chuckled. "You know that wasn't what I was talking about, wicked woman," she murmured happily.

"I know," Jo burred close to her ear. "But you didn't really expect me to resist, did you?"

Cadie shivered as Jo's rich alto tingled its way down her spine. They were both a little drunk, but she was rather hoping that might loosen their inhibitions about making love in Jo's childhood bedroom. *Not that we've exactly been abstaining,* she thought with a grin as Jo continued to nuzzle her neck. *We've just indulged Jo's taste for the outdoors a little more than usual.*

"What are you purring about?" Jo slid her leg across Cadie's thighs, relishing the way their bodies melded together.

"I was remembering our little adventure in the barn yesterday," Cadie replied. She turned her head and buried her nose in Jo's hair, breathing deeply of her partner's unique scent. They had enjoyed what could only be described as a laughter-filled roll in the hay, taking advantage of the fact Jo's parents were well out of hearing range.

Jo laughed quietly. That delicious interlude had led into a quite extraordinary evening. *Can't believe it's all out in the open now,* she thought with relief.

"You haven't answered my question," Cadie reminded her.

"It feels kind of surreal," Jo replied after a brief pause to collect her thoughts. She lifted herself up a little and rested her chin on Cadie's chest, looking up into the gentle green eyes trained on her. "I feel a lot lighter," she admitted, smiling back when Cadie's face broke into an unrestrained grin. "Yeah, I know. I should have talked to them a long time ago."

"That's not what I was thinking," Cadie said. "You couldn't tell them until you were ready, and you haven't been. So second-guessing yourself doesn't serve any purpose." Cadie noticed Jo's expression had turned pensive. "Are you angry with Ken?"

Blue eyes swung back into focus. "Yes," Jo answered honestly. "But how can I be, really?" She rolled away from Cadie, onto her back. "He made it so much easier for me...and for them too, I guess." Her eyes returned to Cadie. "Know what I mean?"

Cadie nodded. "He took away your right to tell who you wanted, when you wanted, though," she said softly. "On the other hand, he probably saved your parents five years of worrying. And allowed them to get to a place where they could accept you back into their lives without hesitation."

Jo grinned. "So I guess I owe him another carton of cigarettes and a case of Johnny Walker."

"At least," Cadie agreed.

"They really didn't hesitate, did they?" The wonder of it was still something Jo was coming to terms with.

"Not even for a nanosecond," Cadie confirmed. She pushed herself up on one elbow and looked down at her dark-haired lover. Jo had a childlike look of amazement on her face that was obvious even in the dim glow of the candles that were scattered around the room. "They're a wonderful pair, Jo-Jo," she said.

Jo looked up at her. "Yes, they are." She reached up and pushed a lock of pale hair out of Cadie's eyes. "Thank you for bringing me back to them," she said simply.

"I think you would have made it back to them without me,"

Cadie answered.

Jo shook her head. "Thank God, I never have to do anything without you again." She slid her hand around to the back of Cadie's neck and gently pulled her down into a long, slow kiss full of promise.

Cadie felt a languid tingle begin somewhere south of her waist. It could have been the kissing or it could have been the sensual explorations of Jo's hands as they brushed across the skin of her shoulders and lower back.

"I want to make love to you, Jossandra," Cadie growled softly against her lover's earlobe. She lifted herself up until she had a hand on either side of Jo's torso, and she looked down into the shadowed face below her. "Will you let me?"

Jo was already beyond the point of being able to deny Cadie anything. Her general lightness of being seemed to extend to any inhibitions she'd harbored about being in her childhood bed with her parents a few feet away behind a wall.

"Yes, my love, I will," she whispered.

Chapter Fifteen

"GOOD MORNING," CADIE said, marching into the kitchen.

Jo had already left with her father, allowing Cadie to grab another couple of hours' sleep. *I guess a couple of hours are better than none,* she thought, barely suppressing a well-satisfied grin. *And there are definitely worse reasons for losing sleep.*

Maggie looked up at her daughter-in-law's entrance. She lifted the sizzling frying pan, showing Cadie the bacon and eggs. "Breakfast?"

"Yes, please," Cadie replied.

She accepted the warm plate of food and sat down at the kitchen table, waiting while Maggie assembled her own breakfast and joined her. They ate in companionable silence for a while before Cadie put down her fork.

"Jo and I figured out that we need to start heading back tomorrow," she said as Maggie chewed. "I know we've got another couple of weeks, really, until I need to go, but there are a lot of things we need to get squared away before we can leave again." Maggie raised an eyebrow and Cadie continued. "Hopefully, Jo's going to come as far as Sydney with me."

Maggie smiled. "Putting off the inevitable as long as possible, eh?"

Cadie nodded silently, dropping her eyes against the sudden threat of tears.

The older woman reached over and patted her hand. "It's okay, sweetie, I understand. We've been delighted that you could both stay as long as you have. We've had a great visit."

Cadie broke into a wobbly smile. "We sure have," she agreed. "Thank you for making me feel like part of the family. I've really appreciated that."

"Tch, you are part of the family Cadie," Maggie said firmly. "Even the Neanderthal I'm married to can see that."

"He's been lovely," Cadie defended David. She still felt warm inside after his unexpected affection for her the night before. "And I don't think he's a Neanderthal at all. It's been an awful lot for him to absorb, I think."

Maggie nodded. "That's true. It took him a bit longer than I would have liked, but I think he's with the program now." That provoked a laugh from Cadie. "The Maggie Madison Diversity Acceptance Program." She grinned as Cadie spluttered around a mouthful of bacon. "Try not to choke, sweetie. That would be really hard to explain to Josie."

DAVID GLANCED ACROSS at his silent daughter. They'd barely said a word since grabbing a quick bacon sandwich each and heading out for the back lots of the property. He wasn't too concerned. As far as he could figure out, the silence wasn't about last night's revelations, but more about fatigue. David stifled a yawn. *I like knowing we can be honest with each other from now on, though,* he decided. *It's a good feeling.* Observing Jo's head drooping, he deliberately dipped the ute into a pothole, jolting them both.

"Ow, shit," Jo yelped as her temple hit the metal stanchion of the ute's door none too gently. "What did we hit? And what are you grinning about?" She rubbed at the sore spot.

"You wouldn't have been falling asleep there, would ya now, Josie?" David asked. "Expect you to be looking out for things we need to fix, not taking a nap." He tried to sound severe but was in too good a mood.

"I wasn't asleep," Jo denied. She grinned back at him. "I was resting my eyes for a second."

"Right."

"No, really."

"Resting them pretty well, then. They were snoring."

"I was *not* snoring," Jo yelled. She glared at the older man for a few seconds but neither of them could keep up the pretence. Laughter exploded out of them both and David reached across and shoved his daughter's shoulder playfully. *Wow, he's in a good mood,* she thought. "So what's got you all blissy?" she asked cheekily.

David shrugged. "It's a beautiful morning, we don't have a hell of a lot of work we need to do out here and," he turned his head and looked deliberately into the blue eyes gazing back at him, "I have my daughter back." He smiled, facing the front again as he guided the ute around a fallen tree.

Jo dropped her eyes. "Well, unfortunately, we pretty much figured out that we need to start heading back, probably tomorrow," she said quietly.

"That's not what I meant," David answered.

Jo felt herself blushing. "I know," she muttered. There was

a pregnant pause as she thought about the previous evening. *Such a simple conversation, really, but look at the effect it's already had.* She glanced over at her father again. *Maybe now I can talk to him about money and he might actually listen.*

Her train of thought was interrupted by their arrival at the day's destination, a small, derelict storage shed that was in dire need of rebuilding. Jo sighed, knowing that her father was likely to push pretty hard to get the job done. She mentally rolled up her sleeves.

"Come on, girl," David said gruffly as he opened his door and slid out of the truck. "Work to be done."

NAOMI SLOWLY SWIRLED the bourbon in her glass, watching the ice cubes clink together as the amber liquid washed around them. It was her fourth of the evening, not that she was counting. The alcohol hadn't come close to unraveling the cold knot of fury in her stomach.

A long, tedious day in her DC office had ended with an infuriating conversation with her public relations staff, Jason and Toby. *Ex-staff,* she reminded herself. *Treacherous bastards.* She knocked back the last of her drink in one angry gulp before reaching again for the half-empty bottle balanced precariously on the arm of her chair. She poured another, this time turning a double into a triple.

Naomi cast her eyes around the darkened apartment. The place looked like a bomb had hit it. Over by the front door, the remains of a crystal vase—she vaguely recalled it being a present from Cadie's mother—lay scattered on the carpet, the aftermath of her cutting conversation with Jason and Toby. It had missed them by inches.

"What is it with everyone?" Naomi muttered, tilting her glass and taking another swallow. The harsh heat of the bourbon burned its way down her throat and settled in the pit of her stomach. Instead of the calming effect she had been hoping for, a rolling ball of nausea made her wince. *Everybody's leaving me,* she thought morosely. Self-pity welled up in her momentarily, but was soon replaced by another wave of anger and resentment. *Fuck them. Fuck them all.*

She stood and carried her glass over to the big bay window that looked out on the city streets. *I don't need a goddamn single one of them. New people, that's what I need around me. New people and new plans.* She took another swig. *Except Cadie. She's the only thing I want back.* She smiled grimly as the plan she had been hatching for weeks formed itself in her mind once more.

The details had been lovingly crafted through many sleepless nights and the time was rapidly approaching when she could actually make it happen.

And Cadie will be back here, where she belongs, Naomi thought, a tiny kernel of anticipation warming through the nausea. *That's all it will take. Once she's back here and away from that Australian bitch, she'll see that she made a huge mistake and that she really belongs here with me.* "She'll see." A giggle escaped, its sound hollow and eerie in the empty room. "She'll see."

"CADIE!" MAGGIE LEANED out the back door of the homestead, hoping her voice would carry to the stables. She was in the middle of a marathon baking session and didn't feel inclined to leave her scone mixture to traipse down to the barn. She held still for a moment, listening for a response from Cadie, but none was forthcoming. "Damn it," she muttered.

She picked up the phone again. "I'm sorry, but Cadie's not within shouting range at the moment. Can I take a message?"

The man on the other end of the phone cleared his throat. "Um, yes please," he said, his American accent curling around the words intriguingly. "Could you ask her to call Toby McIntyre at home, please? She has my number, I'm sure."

Maggie wrote the name down. "Is it urgent?" she asked, conscious of the long-distance call and the time difference.

There was a long pause as if the man couldn't quite decide. "No, not urgent exactly," he said finally. "But she needn't worry about waiting until it's morning here. She can call any time."

Sounds pretty urgent to me, Maggie thought. "Okay, well, I'll get her to call you as soon as she gets back to the house," she replied.

"Thanks," Toby said.

"No worries." The line went dead, leaving Maggie to ponder the latest development in her daughters' lives. She returned to her baking and began kneading the ball of dough that was sitting on the wooden countertop. "Maybe I should go and find Cadie," she muttered to herself.

The woman in question was knee-deep in horse manure at that moment. Cadie wielded the shovel enthusiastically as she mucked out the stables. Tilly and the two colts gazed over their stall doors with equine tolerance as she danced to a tune blaring from the small radio sitting on the top of the rail. It was late afternoon and, after a day spent helping Maggie around the house, Cadie had volunteered to do one of Hughie's chores. The young Aborigine was out working on his own today and would appreciate one less thing to do when he got back to the homestead.

"Wide open spaces," she warbled, unconcerned that she was making the Dixie Chicks sound distinctly ordinary. Singing was not one of Cadie's fortes, unlike her more musical partner. But that didn't stop her, usually. Certainly not when there were only three horses to complain. Not that they were. She glanced over at her audience. "Pretty good, huh, guys?"

"Well, I've heard worse," Tilly replied, startling Cadie no end.

She turned and grinned at her mother-in-law, who was leaning on the doorpost of the stable. "You scared me out of about five years' growth," she said, provoking a chuckle from the older woman.

"I guess that's happened to you quite a few times, huh?" Maggie quipped, looking the petite blonde up and down.

Cadie's eyes widened. "Was that a short joke?" she said, affecting mock outrage. "Boy, it's not enough I get it from the younger one, now I have to put up with it from the older version as well?" She threw her hands in the air, breaking into a grin when she heard Maggie laugh.

"Sorry about that, shortie. No wonder you couldn't hear me yelling," Maggie reached for the radio and turned it down.

"Oh, sorry," Cadie said, abashed. "I got a bit carried away."

Maggie smiled kindly, loving the girl's enthusiasm. "You had a phone call from America," she said. "I thought it might be important." Cadie looked startled, as if it was the last thing in the world she expected. *Interesting.*

"My mother?" Cadie asked.

"Nope. A man called Toby McIntyre."

"Ah." Cadie's eyes took on a faraway look for a few seconds and then she refocused on Jo's mother. "Sorry. Um, he's my ex-partner's PR guy," she explained. "And whatever he's calling for, it can't be good news."

"Oh dear," Maggie responded. "He said it wasn't necessarily urgent, but could you call him at home as soon as you can."

Cadie sighed. *This can't be good,* she thought. *If it was a social call he would have waited until we got back to Shute Harbor. And if he wanted to book another holiday he would have gone ahead and done that with Doris. Damn.*

Maggie watched the range of emotions crossing Cadie's expressive face.

"My guess is, Naomi's gone and done something stupid and irrational," Cadie theorized. "And the bad news is, he wouldn't be bothering me with that unless it had some repercussions for

Jo and me."

"Ah," Maggie replied noncommittally. "But she's an awfully long way away, Cadie. What can she really do?"

Cadie leaned her shovel against the wall of the stable and pulled off the rubber work boots she had worn to clean out the stalls. There was no easy answer to that question. She really had no idea anymore how far Naomi would go, or how many strings she would, or could, pull.

"That is the sixty-four million dollar question," she said.

JO HANDED THE hammer back to her father and watched him lovingly wrap it in an old rag and tuck it back into its proper place in the toolbox. He had always been like that, so particular about his tools. She thought about her own habits when she was onboard Seawolf, recognizing for the first time the little traits she'd obviously inherited. *No wonder Cadie keeps smirking at me like she's got some secret,* she realized. *She's seeing where all my quirks come from for the first time.* It was a minor revelation and she took a few seconds to look more closely at her father, who was now wiping off his calloused hands.

They'd worked like demons through the morning, skipping lunch to get the barn back into a usable state. Jo was sore in places she'd forgotten she had muscles. They really could have used Hughie's help with it but she was glad, in the end, that her father had opted to send the young man out on his own. *It'll make it easier for me to talk to Dad,* she decided.

Wearily, she dropped down into the dirt and leaned against the side of the ute, grateful for the meager shade the vehicle provided. It was late afternoon, but the sun was still wickedly hot. Her father eased down beside her and handed her a foil-wrapped package of sandwiches and a cold can he'd retrieved from the foam cooler tucked into a corner of the ute's tray.

"There you go," he said, cracking open the seal on his own soda with a satisfying whoosh of air.

Jo swallowed long, cool draughts of the liquid, the first few mouthfuls barely touching the sides. "The barn looks better," she said.

"We've done well there," David said. "Didn't think we'd be as far along as we've gotten. Thanks for your help."

Jo glanced at him quickly, then went back to her sandwich. "You don't have to thank me, Dad," she said. "It's been fun. The whole visit has been fun, actually."

He nodded silently, preferring to chew rather than talk. Jo hesitated, knowing that now was probably her best, last chance to talk with her father candidly about the state of the property. But she was also acutely aware that she was, in effect, a Johnny-come-lately, and telling her father how to run the farm was akin to teaching her grandmother to suck eggs. Not that she wanted to tell him how to run it, exactly.

"Dad?"

"Hmmm?" David was still looking over the barn between mouthfuls, figuring what, if anything, still needed to be done before they headed back to the homestead.

"Can I ask you something personal?" His eyes flicked back to hers and he paled slightly. Jo raised a hand in quick reassurance. "Not personal, exactly," she said hastily. "I mean, can I ask you about Coonyabby?"

David relaxed visibly. "Sure. Ask away."

"Okay." Jo thought carefully about how to approach this. "I know things have been pretty tough around here the last few years, what with the drought and all."

Her father shrugged. "Nothing much changes out here on the land, Josie, you know that. If it's not a drought, then it's a flood. If it's not a flood, it's the salinity. If it's not salinity, it's erosion. There's always something out here making it tough."

Jo nodded. It was a familiar refrain that she'd heard from her father and his fellow farmers throughout her childhood. "But I mean, it's been tougher than usual, though, hasn't it?"

David looked at his daughter. He had a fair inkling of where she was going with this and he swallowed the urge to let his pride do his talking for him. *Don't get all up on your high horse with her now, mate.*

"Yeah this has been a rough one," he conceded. He could see she was trying to ask him outright what the financial bottom line was, and he decided to put her out of her misery. "We're not making money, that's for sure. Haven't been for a long time." He screwed up the foil that had been wrapped around his sandwiches and flicked it from hand to hand. "Last year I had to refinance to keep the stock in feed through the winter." That had been tough to swallow.

Jo listened in silence. Nothing she was hearing was surprising her any. She only had to look around Coonyabby to know that her parents were barely keeping their heads above water.

"Cadie and I have been talking a lot about this," she started. "We've...um...we've got quite a bit of money put away and...well...basically, Dad," she took a deep breath and ploughed on, "basically, we want to help, any way we can." Jo saw her father open his mouth to respond and she rushed on.

"We can afford it, and it would mean a lot to us both...it would mean a lot to me...if you'd let us."

David smiled. For once, finally, he let his daughter's good intentions override their history. *She's got a lot of her mother in her*, he thought, watching the anxious blue eyes across from him.

"I can't let you do that, Josie," he replied quietly, stilling her response with a touch of his hand on her thigh. "It's not that I don't appreciate the offer. I do. But you'd be throwing good money after bad. And I'm not going to let you do that when you've got your own business and future to look after."

"Dad, it's not going to jeopardize any of that," Jo insisted. "We can afford it. Really." She shifted around so she could face him. "I could understand if you have a lot of questions about where I got that kind of money, and that's okay. I'll answer 'em." She dropped her eyes again, the old shame welling up for a moment. "But I figure it's time that money was put to a good use, instead of burning a hole in my conscience like it's been doing." She met her father's eyes again. "Let me help, Dad. I owe you that much, at least." Long seconds ticked by as they let the truth of that pass between them.

Finally David broke the silence. "That's not the point, love," he said. "The fact is, your mother and I have been doing a lot of thinking, as well." He took a deep breath and expelled it in a long, pensive sigh as he looked around at the harsh, beautiful landscape. "This place has been home for us for a very long time, but we can't make it work anymore. And neither of us is getting any younger."

Jo looked at him quizzically. *Where's he going with this*, she wondered.

"I'm almost 62," he continued. He laughed at the look of surprise on Jo's face. "Come off it," he said. "You can't tell me I don't look a day over 70." He grinned.

She shook her head. "I never really thought about it before. I don't think of you as being..." She hesitated.

"Old, love. The word is old." He patted her thigh again. "Well, that's the truth of it, and at some point I have to start thinking about how your mother and I are going to live when I'm too old to work this place." He looked at Jo. "And the truth of *that* is it's not too far away. And we don't have any savings to speak of. We've poured everything into this place for 40 years."

"That's why Cadie and I want to help," Jo said again.

David shook his head. "That's not going to work, Josie," he said. "There's more debt here than your average third-world nation, and no amount of cash is going to bring rain, or make sure that another drought doesn't come again in 10 years when we're even less able to survive it."

Jo looked puzzled. "So what's the answer?"

David sighed again and turned back to the landscape. *Blood, sweat and tears I've poured into this place,* he thought sadly. *Bugger the cash. Blood, sweat and tears. But that's not enough any more. Maggie deserves better. So do I.*

"It's time to sell up, Josie," he said softly, a faraway look in his eye.

"SELL UP?" CADIE looked at Maggie incredulously. It had never occurred to her, nor Jo either, she suspected, that leaving Coonyabby was an option for the Madisons. Maggie had said it matter-of-factly as they had begun preparing the evening meal. *Almost as if it was as everyday as peeling the potatoes.* Cadie stood dumbstruck, a knife in one hand and a half-denuded potato in the other. She had started this conversation with a view to making the suggestion that she and Jo help the station survive the drought, but Maggie had turned it on its ear. Cadie wondered briefly if David was doing the same to her partner. "Things are that bad?"

Maggie shrugged. "Not yet," she said. "But we're getting too old to fight this battle constantly, year in, year out."

"But that's not true," Cadie protested. "You're both so full of energy. Surely..." She stopped at the tolerant look on her mother-in-law's face. "You guys have been thinking about this for a long time, huh?"

Maggie nodded. "Yes. Since the last time we had some decent rain. David said back then that he didn't know when the next lot would come, and that maybe it was time we started thinking about how we were going to live for the next 30 years." She quartered another peeled potato and added the pieces to those snuggled against the leg of lamb she was roasting for the evening meal. "We're at the point now where, if we sell up, we'll have enough to pay off all the debts and have a bit left over to set ourselves up. Then we can both settle in and do some of the other things we like to do when we get the chance."

Cadie tilted her head to one side, taking in all that Maggie was telling her. "It's not worth hanging on a bit longer?" she asked.

"No," Maggie said with a sigh as she looked out the back window over her beloved garden. "Now's the right time to sell. If we waited another season and no rain came, we'd be beyond the point where we could make any profit at all by selling. It's now or never, really."

Cadie nodded, understanding that Maggie and David had made a considered decision. "It has to feel kind of weird, though," she pondered aloud. "Leaving after all this time."

"More so for David than me," Maggie said, liking Jo's choice of partner more with every minute they spent together. "He was born in that bedroom over there." She nodded in the direction of the room in which she and David slept. "So was his father. So was Josie, for that matter." She tucked the last of the potatoes into the pan and opened the oven door, bending down to slide the roast inside. "It was different for me. I wasn't born to it like he was."

"It's still home, though."

"Yes," Maggie admitted, checking the oven settings. "But I'm not a sentimentalist like David. I'm more the wherever-I-lay-my-hat-that's-my-home kind of person." She crossed to the kitchen sink, filled the kettle with water and placed it on the stovetop. "It was his idea to sell. I never would have suggested it. That's when I knew that it really was time to leave."

Cadie reached up into the cupboard above the counter, pulling down two coffee mugs and handing them to Maggie. "I'm glad I got to come out here and see Coonyabby," she said. It made her sad to think this place would pass out of the family's hands. "I wish it didn't have to be the last time."

"Me too, love," Maggie said. Her voice cracked on the last word and Cadie moved closer, placing a gentle hand on the older woman's shoulder.

Disconcerted, Maggie wiped away her tears. "See, not a sentimental bone in my body," she laughed tearily.

Cadie laughed along with her, knowing that tomorrow's departure was going to be infinitely more emotional than she had expected it to be, for them all. *I wonder how Jo-Jo is doing with all this?*

"WHERE WILL YOU go?" Jo asked. They were all seated around Maggie's dining room table, the family matriarch having decided that Jo and Cadie's last meal at Coonyabby should be a more formal affair. Hughie had joined them too, though he had stayed largely silent through the continuing discussion about selling the property.

It was the question Jo had been avoiding since her father had told her of his decision that afternoon. Asking it meant she had conceded defeat and was accepting her parents' judgment that life on the land was no longer a going concern. *I hate the thought of them leaving, but it's their decision, not mine. I gave up any right to have a say in this a long, long time ago.* She had even, at one point during dinner, offered to buy the property outright, keeping it in the family by hook or by crook. But her father had shaken his head and said no, again.

"Josie, buying the land doesn't solve the problem," he had said. "Keeping the stock fed and healthy, maintaining the equipment, staying ahead of the weather—those are the things that suck the money away. Look, I appreciate the offer, believe me, but all you would be doing is saddling yourselves with a lifetime of debt. For every good year, you'll have three bad ones that will bleed you dry. And I'm not going to let you do that."

Jo was silent for a few seconds, knowing that her next question was the real crux of the matter. She took a deep breath. "Dad, if the property is such a money pit, who the hell is going to buy it?"

Her father smiled at her, but the smile didn't reach his eyes. "Good question. There's a big interest in tourism lately. A group called FarmTrip are buying up properties and turning them into, um..." He struggled to find the right word.

"Dude ranches," Cadie murmured, remembering one memorable childhood summer spent in the wilds of Nevada.

David snorted, but nodded his head. "Yeah, something like that."

Jo lapsed into silence for a while, letting Cadie and Maggie drive the conversation while she sorted through her emotions. In a way, it was weird how she felt so strongly about wanting to keep Coonyabby in the family. *After all, I couldn't wait to leave it when I was 17,* she thought glumly. *And it's not like I gave much thought to ever coming back to it.* But she was willing to admit to herself that those had been bad decisions on her part. *The last three weeks out here have been great. I've really enjoyed rediscovering the place.* A piece of self-realization floated to the front of her consciousness. *Maybe that's it. Maybe I'm pissed off that I don't get to indulge myself with it for any longer.*

That's when she accepted that her parents' decision was made and that it was for the best.

She shook herself back into the conversation. "So, where will you live?"

Maggie took another sip of port and put her glass down. "Well, we haven't really settled on that yet, to be honest," she replied, looking at her husband. They'd talked around a few ideas, to be sure, but having Jo and Cadie in their lives for the last three weeks had got them thinking.

"Sydney?" Jo asked, hoping like hell that wasn't going to be the answer. She loathed the big city and didn't relish the thought of having to visit it on anything like a regular basis.

"No fear," David replied quickly. "Can't stand the place. I'd rather crawl under a rock and die."

Jo sniggered, understanding her father's sentiments exactly, but for completely different reasons. "So, what's the plan, then?"

The two elder Madisons looked at each other for a few seconds, obviously having an unspoken conversation, until finally David shrugged his shoulders. Maggie laughed quietly. "Up to me then, I guess," she murmured. She looked her daughter in the eye. "I want you to answer this question honestly, okay? Because we know that it's only been a few weeks and the last thing we want to do is make you feel...well, crowded, I guess."

Cadie could immediately see where this was going, but Jo was a beat behind. "Crowded?" she asked.

"How would you feel about your dad and me moving up to the Whitsundays?" The words spilled out in a hurry as Maggie's eagerness to see Jo's reaction took over.

Elegant dark brows rose quickly as Jo absorbed that piece of news. "Really?" she blurted, the beginnings of a 1000-watt grin touching the corners of her mouth. *Good girl,* Cadie thought happily. *I knew you'd like this idea.* "Mum, I think that's a fantastic idea." Jo turned to her father, who was smiling behind his cup of coffee. "You're gonna love it up there, Dad, honestly," she enthused.

David took another mouthful of coffee before putting his mug down and grinning at his daughter. "We've had our eye on a five-acre lot somewhere out the back of Airlie Beach. Some place called Cannon Valley."

"Yes!" Jo exclaimed. "It's inland, between Airlie and Proserpine," she replied, naming the small sugar cane-growing community an hour's drive west of her home. "Are you going to farm it?"

Maggie chuckled. "We're not sure yet, sweetheart," she said. "We really only started thinking about it seriously a week ago. When it became obvious that you didn't find your old parental units too obnoxious." She smiled winningly.

"Oh, stop it," Jo scoffed. She turned to Cadie, unsurprised to see green eyes sparkling back at her in obvious happiness. "Good idea, huh?"

"Oh yeah," Cadie affirmed. She looked over at Hughie, who was sitting silently at the opposite corner of the table. He seemed unconcerned about the recent developments going on around him. *But then, he usually does take things in his stride,* she realized. "What about you, Hughie?" Cadie asked. "What are you going to do?"

The others fell silent, realizing that the young Aborigine's life was likely to change as much, if not more, than anyone's. It was the one thing that had troubled Maggie the most about their decision.

"Not sure, Miss," Hughie said, flashing Cadie a sunny smile. "Go where there's work, I reckon."

"You know you can come with us," Maggie said quietly. She had tried to have this very conversation with Hughie a few days earlier, but he'd steadfastly refused to give it much thought, let alone come to any firm decision. It shouldn't have surprised her, as that had always been his nature, to go with the flow, but it hadn't helped ease her anxiety.

"I know," he answered.

Jo's mind was running at about a thousand miles an hour. "Have you ever seen the ocean, Hughie?" she asked, the germ of an idea forming.

He shook his shaggy head slowly from side to side. "No, Miss Josie. Don't reckon I know what that much water could look like."

Jo grinned back at him. "Would you like to see it?" A look of wonder came over Hughie's wide open face. He nodded mutely. "So, why don't you stick with Mum and Dad and come and work for me on the boats, when they don't need you on their land?"

"Oh, Jo-Jo, that's a great idea," Cadie exclaimed. "Hughie, you'll love it up there, I promise."

"I reckon I might like that," he said.

"Sounds like a plan to me," Jo replied firmly. She looked at her father. "So, do you think you might get into cane farming, Dad?" She grinned.

"Oh, I don't think I'll be taking it too seriously, Josie," he answered. "My days of worrying about yields and irrigation and all that are coming to an end, thankfully. It'll be more of a hobby farm, if anything, and I expect Hughie will be able to do a lot of it, eh, mate?" He nodded at Hughie and received a confirming grin in return.

"You don't really hate it that much, do you?" Cadie asked, not believing for one moment that the elder Madison felt anything other than a passion for the land.

"I don't hate it all," he admitted. "I'm just ready to take things easy. I reckon we've earned it." He looked at Maggie and smiled when she tucked her hand into his weather-beaten one under the table. "Don't you think?"

"I think," his wife agreed.

"CADIE." JO NUDGED her deeply-sleeping partner. It was still dark and she wanted to get up and out of the house before the sun came up. "Cadie, darling, wake up." She nudged a little more insistently.

She really is utterly gorgeous, Jo acknowledged. Long, blonde eyelashes fluttered and, even in the gloom, Jo could make out the green of Cadie's irises as she blinked awake. "Good morning, sweetie," she whispered.

"Morning? Jo-Jo, it's still dark," Cadie grumbled sleepily. "Why are we awake?"

"I thought you might like to watch our last sunrise at Coonyabby."

Arcadia, when are you going to learn that this place means more to her than she's ever going to let on, Cadie chastised herself. *She's about to say goodbye to her home. Again.* "Yes, love," she said, pushing herself up on an elbow and leaning in to kiss Jo softly. "I really want to see the sunrise."

Jo grinned up at her. "I love you, y'know."

"I know. So, come on, lazybones, where are we going?"

"Not far," Jo replied as she pulled aside the sheet and clambered out of bed. "In fact..." She grabbed the flashlight from the bedside table and walked over to the desk on the other side of the room. Flicking on the beam, she illuminated the ceiling above the desk, revealing a small panel that obviously led to the roof space.

"Ahah," said Cadie. "Why do I get the feeling we're about to make use of a childhood haunt?"

Jo waggled an eyebrow at her. "Because you know me too well?" She studied Cadie's naked form. "Gorgeous as you are in the flesh, my love, you're gonna need to put something on. It's gonna be cool out there."

"You too."

Together they hastily pulled on some clothes, Cadie opting for a pair of leggings and a sweatshirt, while Jo reached for her sweatpants and a t-shirt.

"Ready?" Jo asked a couple of minutes later.

"You bet."

Jo climbed up onto the desk and reached up, nudging the panel aside. Dust sprinkled down on her and she blinked and shook her head. "Ugh. S'been a while since anyone's shifted this," she muttered. "Hand me the torch, love?" She waited until Cadie placed the flashlight in her hand before she pushed the panel the rest of the way. "Hopefully there's nothing living up here."

"Like what?" Cadie asked as she watched her partner

readying to hoist herself up into the roof.

"Possums, maybe." Jo balanced the flashlight on the edge of the ceiling, the light bouncing eerily off the inside of the roof. "Snakes." Her hands found purchase and she sprang up, using her upper body strength to lever herself through the opening. Cadie watched as Jo's long legs slithered up and disappeared from view momentarily. There was much scrabbling and scraping before Jo's face reappeared. "All clear."

Cadie climbed onto the desk and looked up. "Don't think I'm tall enough to do your trick, sweetheart," she said ruefully.

"That's why the universe provided you with me, darling," Jo replied cheekily. She reached down with one long arm. "Come on, shortie. Between the two of us we should be able to get you up here."

"Brat."

A few dusty, scrambling minutes later they were up on the roof. Jo settled herself on the sloping corrugated iron, feet braced firmly as she drew Cadie down between her long legs.

"Comfortable?" Jo asked, amused by Cadie's squirming.

Cadie snuggled back against her partner and sighed contentedly. "I am now," she said softly, turning her head and kissing Jo under the line of her jaw. "This was a good idea, Jo-Jo. Though I'm not even going to try and understand why your roof has a removable panel in it."

Jo grinned. "When I was about 12, Mum decided she wanted to put a sunroof in the bathroom. They got half the work done and then she changed her mind." She chuckled throatily. "Let's say I saw an opportunity for some fun and found a way to bypass the repairs."

Cadie laughed softly. "I wish I'd known you then. I bet we would have had some fun." She pondered a moment. "Doesn't the roof leak when it rains?"

"Darling, we've been here three weeks. Have you seen one cloud?"

"Good point."

Jo looked away to the east, where a thin line of pinks and oranges was beginning to emerge along the horizon, outlining the stark silhouettes of the trees. Somewhere, a lone, early-rising kookaburra let loose with a string of warbling laughs.

"S'beautiful," Cadie whispered. She placed her hands on Jo's thighs, feeling the warmth through the fabric of her sweatpants. "You're going to miss this place, aren't you?"

There was a pause as Jo took it all in. "Silly, isn't it?" she finally replied. "I didn't miss it enough to come back here for 15 years. Now I've only been here five minutes and I hate the fact

I'm going to lose it again."

Cadie patted her thighs softly. "Not silly at all, love," she answered. "I've only been here five minutes as well, and I'm certainly going to miss it." She tilted her head back and watched Jo's profile, its distinctive angles and unique beauty turned golden by the rising sun. *Gorgeous.* "I like the thought of your parents coming north, though," she said aloud. "It's going to be great to have them close by."

Jo grunted noncommittally, but the tiny smile said plenty.

"Dad said they would bring the horses and dogs with them, so that's good," Jo said. "I didn't like the idea of selling them off with the sheep and cattle."

"I know." The rim of the sun broke above the horizon's haze and both women stared silently at the lightening sky for a few moments of contentment. "Thank you for bringing me here, Jo-Jo," Cadie whispered.

"My pleasure, love."

Chapter Sixteen

"DID YOU EVER call Toby back?"

Cadie's head snapped around at the question, which had come out of the blue. Or rather, out of the damp, drizzling gray. They were onboard the Seawolf, battling their way up Whitsunday Passage against a stiff breeze and a rain squall. Below decks, a small group of Japanese tourists was trying to enjoy Jenny's seafood lunch; a challenge, given the rather rough ride. Jo and Cadie were braving the weather on deck. The women had been back from their Coonyabby adventure for just three days when they had to pick up this group. The tourists were half way through a two-week cruise, but their skipper had fallen on a wet deck and broken his arm.

"Where did that come from?" Cadie asked, her eyebrow rising.

Jo grinned from under the hood of her wet-weather gear and shrugged. "Who knows?" Perched as she was on the port rail, her right foot and hand keeping the wheel on a steady heading, she looked, and felt, like a half-drowned rat. "My mind was wandering all over the place, and for some reason, it stopped on that thought."

"I love the way your mind works," Cadie said with an affectionate smile. She tucked herself under Jo's sheltering arm and they endured the drizzling rain together for a few comfortable minutes. Cadie watched a long, slow drip of cool water hang and then drop from the edge of her raincoat's hood.

"So, did you?" Jo asked eventually.

Cadie sighed. "Too much to ask that you would forget that question, huh?" she said, a little grumpily. The truth was, she had been avoiding any thought of Toby, Naomi, or the United States in general since the senator's PR manager had called, and she didn't really want to think about them now.

"Sorry, love." Jo could hear the note of annoyance in her partner's voice and wished she hadn't raised the topic. But she was curious. With a twist of her wrist, she adjusted the

Seawolf's position as they continued to beat into the wind. Then she glanced down at her shorter lover, and squeezed her shoulder in reassurance.

Tired eyes, more gray than green in the overcast conditions, looked back up at her. "No, it's okay, Jo-Jo," Cadie said. "Take no notice of me. I'm a grumpy bitch today."

Jo kissed her damp forehead softly. "No worries, sweetheart," she said. "It's not like you to not return someone's call, so I guess that's why it was nagging away at the back of my brain."

"I guess I couldn't imagine that he was calling for anything other than bad news," she admitted. "And, to be honest, I don't want to go there." She glanced up at Jo's puzzled look. "In my head I mean, not to the US." She thought about that. "Well, actually, I don't want to go there either, but that's not how I meant it." *Jesus, get to the damn point, Arcadia.*

"I know," Jo said softly. The thought of saying goodbye soon, even if it was only for a few weeks, bothered the hell out of her, too. But she didn't want to make a big deal out of it since she figured that would only make Cadie feel worse.

"And I guess I also decided that if it was urgent, he would call back," Cadie continued. She looked a little sheepish at Jo's slightly amused, if tolerant, look. "Yeah, yeah, I know. I'm making excuses. But it's not like we've been easy to catch lately."

When Jo had decided to fill in for the sick skipper herself, Cadie had opted to come along for the ride, and to help out where needed.

"He could be ringing to say g'day, y'know," Jo said calmly. Inside, she knew that was unlikely. Although Jason and Toby obviously had a lot of affection for Cadie—after all, Jason had even helped Cadie make her getaway from the senator at Sydney Airport all those weeks ago—Jo didn't think Toby would go to the trouble of tracking her down out at Coonyabby just to say hello.

"I doubt it," Cadie muttered, confirming Jo's private opinion. She snuggled closer, and Jo was more than happy to accommodate her. She reached inside Cadie's wet-weather gear and wiggled her fingers under layers of clothing until she found the warm softness of her lover's stomach. Jo let her fingertips slide in comforting circles and was unsurprised to feel the compact body begin to relax.

"Oh, I love you," Cadie purred, resting her head against the tall skipper's solid, if damp, shoulder. "I'm giving you an hour to stop that."

Jo chuckled, appreciating her partner's tactile nature. Before Cadie had sailed into her life Jo had not known what it was like to express her feelings through touch. Sex, she was familiar—more than familiar—with. And violence, absolutely. But affectionate, intimate touch? That hadn't been anything she'd ever had a chance to learn. Cadie's tendency to touch her whenever they were talking privately, and sometimes in public, had been a revelation. She liked it. A lot.

"When will we be home?" Cadie asked.

"Tomorrow morning," Jo replied. "This mob," she tilted her head in the direction of the companionway, where warm, golden light was shining up from the main cabin, "has a plane to catch in the early afternoon. They can stay in Blue Pearl Bay tonight, then head back to Shute Harbor at dawn."

"Sounds good," Cadie murmured. Jo's light touch on her belly was setting off the gentlest of tingles and she was rather looking forward to getting her home. "When we get home, can we spend a few days in bed?" She grinned up into Jo's rain-soaked face and laughed as a damp, but elegant eyebrow disappeared up almost to the skipper's hairline.

"Something on your mind?" Jo drawled, a smile playing across her lips.

"You," Cadie answered bluntly. "And warm, dry sheets...and a boycat."

Jo laughed. "What on earth do you want to do with him?"

"Well," Cadie replied speculatively. "That really loud purr he has could come in really ha— " A long-fingered hand muffled the end of her sentence, and she took the opportunity to lick Jo's palm with the lingering tip of her tongue.

"Oooo, wicked woman," Jo murmured. She took her hand away and ducked her head, taking advantage of their solitude on deck to claim Cadie's lips in a searing kiss that made them both forget the rain, the wind, or Toby's call. They shifted so their bodies were more in contact and deepened the kiss.

Jo felt Cadie begin to pull away when she heard a polite cough from behind her, but a gentle squeeze let her know that they were being interrupted by their deckhand, Jenny, and not a tourist. Cadie relaxed against her once again and Jo reveled in the kiss, bringing it to a long, leisurely and altogether satisfying conclusion.

After a moment, the deckhand moved towards them, shrugging herself deeper into her wet-weather jacket. "You two are the only people on the planet I know who actually would rather stand out here in the rain than be down in the warm."

"Someone's got to drive this thing, Jen," Jo said, tucking

Cadie into the crook of her arm.

"And someone's got to keep the skipper company," Cadie tagged on.

Jenny shook her head in mock exasperation. "You two are something to see, you know that, right?"

"What can I tell you, Jen? It must be love." She felt Cadie snuggle closer. "Either that or the incredibly adorable blonde under my arm is increasing my cute potential exponentially."

"Oh, big words, Jo-Jo," Cadie teased.

"I took my smart pill this morning."

"I see that."

Jenny threw up her hands in surrender. "Oh, stop it, you two, you're going to make me puke."

"What's happening below?" Jo asked.

"Not a lot," replied her crew member. "I think they're pretty much sailed out. Ready to go home."

"They're not the only ones." Cadie stifled a yawn. "I don't feel like I've even had time to unpack since we got back from Coonyabby."

"We haven't," Jo said bluntly.

"And I guess it won't be long before you have to be packing again, huh, Cadie?" Jenny said.

Bummer, Cadie thought. *Thanks, Jen, like I needed reminding.* "Yeah, I guess so," she muttered.

"Sorry," Jen said. "Didn't mean to blow the mood."

"S'okay," Jo said. "We've got to think about it some time."

"When do you have to go back, Cadie?"

Cadie sighed heavily. "Ten days," she replied. *Ten very short days.*

THREE VERY SHORT days. Jo leaned on the top rail of the verandah, gazing out over the lush, green forest that surrounded the house, and beyond to the rich colors of Whitsunday Passage and the islands. *Three very short days. It feels like we've been saying goodbye ever since we left Coonyabby.* She sighed. It left a cold knot in her stomach to think about Cadie being gone for several weeks. *I want to get this over and done with, so we can get on with the rest of our lives.*

It had been a busy time for them both. Jo had been flat-out at the Cheswick Marine office, catching up on all the paperwork that had accumulated during their vacation at Coonyabby. She had discovered that as a company manager, she made a damn good yacht skipper. Then again, she was relishing the challenge of learning new skills, even if that did mean rudimentary accounting.

"Hi," came a soft, familiar, and very welcome voice from behind Jo's right shoulder. Jo smiled in reflex. "You look like you could use this," said Cadie, handing her a tall, icy-cold glass of white wine.

"Thanks." Jo took a sip and purred as the cold liquid slid down her throat. "I don't mind admitting, I'm flogged." *Come to think of it, she doesn't look too perky either,* Jo thought, taking in Cadie's weary expression and the dark circles under her eyes. "I think we've hit the wall the last few days. It was a bit of a shock coming back to...all this after Coonyabby."

Jo brushed her lips across Cadie's, tasting the wine there.

"What brought that on?" Cadie teased.

"Nothing much," Jo replied. "Felt like it, so I did it." She took another mouthful of wine and looked out to sea. The sun was beginning to set behind them and the gorgeous gold and yellow tones of the fading light cast a surreal glow across the water. "Besides, it's hard to look at that," Jo nodded at the view, "without wanting to acknowledge it. Kissing the closest beautiful thing seemed to be a reasonable way to do that." She grinned at the charmed expression on Cadie's face.

"My, my, Jo-Jo, you can be such a romantic." Cadie rested a hand on Jo's upper arm and stood on tiptoes to return the favor, lingering over the delicious contact. "I do adore you."

Blue eyes blinked at her. "And I you, sweetheart."

They pulled apart again and stood in comfortable silence, drinking their wine and watching the ever-changing seascape before them.

Finally, Jo turned back to her lover, smiling at the sun-kissed profile. "Did you get your flights booked?" she asked, quietly acknowledging the undercurrent that had colored their interactions all week long.

"Yes." Cadie sighed. She had hated doing it, and the travel consultant had looked at her somewhat askance when Cadie had expressed irritation over the details. "I'm afraid I pretty much bit Samantha's head off in the process, though."

"Who's Samantha?" Jo asked.

"Travel agent," Cadie replied. "She kept wanting to know if I wanted to go via San Francisco or LA, or what airline, or whatever." She locked eyes with Jo, warmed by the understanding she saw there. "I told her I didn't much care if I went over the North Pole, as long as I got a return ticket."

Jo chuckled and wrapped her arm around the shorter woman's waist. "How long do you think you'll need to be gone?"

"I booked the return flight for three weeks from Wednesday.

I figured that would give me enough time to clean out the rest of my stuff, get it either to Mom and Dad's place in Madison, or ship it here. Plus a little extra time to visit long enough to keep them satisfied. And I have to get a new visa, of course."

Jo grimaced. *This sucks.*

"Sucks, doesn't it?" Cadie said. She looked puzzled when Jo laughed out loud. "What did I say?"

Jo dropped a kiss on the fair hair. "You literally took the words right out of my mouth, sweetheart, that's all." She grinned down at her partner and then sobered again. "And yes, it does suck. Mightily."

The phone rang inside the house and Cadie groaned inwardly. Jo had been at everyone's beck and call all day and she had planned a quiet, romantic evening. *If people would leave her alone for two minutes*, she thought grumpily.

"I'll get it." Jo let go of Cadie and turned back inside before Cadie could object. *One of these days, I'm going to unplug this damn thing*, she thought absently as she picked up the receiver. "Hello, this is Jo."

"Madison. It's Ken Harding." The cop's familiar growl was a surprise and Jo took a moment to adjust. Finding out that Harding had been in contact with her parents almost from the day she had turned herself in had been a shock.

I'm still angry with him, she realized. *Then again, he probably did me a huge favor.* "Hello Ken," she said quietly. His breath, which he had obviously been holding, came out in a rush.

"Thought for a moment you were going to hang up on me," he said gruffly.

"Maybe I should have," Jo answered. A wry smile touched her lips, unseen by the policeman but noticed by Cadie, who had followed her into the living area. "Ken," she mouthed.

"I know you're probably pretty pissed off with me, yeah?" Harding continued. "Bottom line is, I made a judgment call, and I think it was the right one." Jo could almost see his rugged, probably unshaven, jaw sticking stubbornly out.

"Relax, will ya," she said. "Sometimes I think you forget what I used to do for a living. If I was really angry with you, you'd know about it already." She was tweaking him and it probably wasn't fair, but she couldn't let him get off completely scot-free.

On the other end of the line, in his seedy studio apartment in Sydney's inner city, Ken Harding rocked back on his heels. He could never work out when Madison was joking and when she was seriously threatening him, but the memory of what she used to be was still cold and clear in his mind.

"Uh, look, I'm sorry, okay," he said, trying not to sound like his testicles had retracted what felt like several inches.

Her laugh surprised him.

"Harding, for Christ's sake," Jo admonished. "It was a joke." She laughed again, then turned serious. "Look, I'm not going to tell you that I was entirely happy with what you did. But the bottom line is, you saved me from one of the scariest conversations I could imagine. It worked out fine, Ken. Forget it."

There was a pause before the cop finally let it go. "Okay," he said. "It's forgotten."

"Good. Now, is that why you called?" Jo watched as Cadie walked into the kitchen and began making fine adjustments to the dinner she was cooking for them.

"No, actually," Harding said, the business-like tone returning to his voice. "I have good news and bad news."

"Oh, great," Jo growled. "Just what I need. Okay, tell me the bad news first."

Cadie looked up sharply, wondering what was coming next. *Please don't let it be something that hurts her,* she silently begged the universe. The time at Coonyabby had been a healing period for Jo and her parents, but Cadie knew her lover's self-confident outer appearance still cloaked an underlying fragility. If nothing else, the almost desperate way Jo clung to her when they were sleeping was evidence enough. Cadie sliced a couple of tomatoes for the salad as she listened to Jo's half of the conversation.

"Well, the bad news is I need you down here on Thursday," Ken said. "Marco di Santo's court case has come up, and he's fit enough to go through the committal hearing."

Jo felt her skin go cold. Marco di Santo. The right-hand man of her former drug lord boss. The one who had slipped through the fingers of the law when she had turned state's evidence. The one who had come back for her five years later. The one she had practically castrated, and would have killed if it hadn't been for Cadie's intervention.

"He's back on his feet, huh?" she said around the lump in her throat.

Harding chuckled humorlessly. "Yeah, he's walking again. Got a bit of a girlie limp about him, but he's walking. More importantly, he's talking, though he sounds pretty rough."

Jo closed her eyes and winced against the memory of the feeling of the garrote cutting deep into the henchman's neck. Her face only relaxed when she felt Cadie move close and slide under her arm, a reassuring hand on Jo's belly.

"So, what was the good news?" she asked hoarsely.

"I'm probably only going to need you to be available on Thursday and Friday," Harding replied. "God willing and the creeks don't rise, he'll be one step closer to being locked up for good."

"What about Josh?" she asked. The young man, a neighbor who had been house and cat-sitting for Jo while she had been at sea with Cadie's touring group of Americans, had been taken hostage by di Santo in a successful bid to get Jo to come to him. Josh had been beaten and badly shaken by the encounter, and she knew he would have to testify.

"The judge agreed to let him testify by video," she heard Ken say. "It's already done. No worries there at all."

Jo breathed a sigh of relief. "That's great," she murmured. "I'm glad he doesn't have to go through all that." She looked down at Cadie and saw a question there. Quickly she dropped a kiss onto the end of Cadie's pert nose, and held the phone's receiver away from her mouth. "Josh doesn't have to testify in person," she explained.

"But you do?"

Jo nodded. "Sorry, Ken, say that again. I was explaining things to Cadie."

"No worries, mate. I've organized you a plane ticket. Your flight's at four in the afternoon."

Jo thought quickly. "Can I make a change to that?" she asked. "Cadie's flying out to the States that day. I'd like to swap my flight to hers down to Sydney so I can see her off."

Jo heard Harding rustling around with bits of paper. "Yeah, I can do that. What flight's she on?"

"Hang on, I'll let her tell you," Jo replied, handing the phone to her partner with a grim smile.

As the taller woman moved into the kitchen, Cadie greeted Ken.

"G'day," the policeman replied. He had a lot of time for the American, having learned from experience that Cadie was a pistol. She had shown a lot of guts that afternoon he and Cadie and a handful of Airlie Beach coppers had gone after Jo and di Santo.

"How are you?" she asked, amazed, as always, that Harding and her partner seemed to maintain a rapport without ever asking those kinds of social questions.

"Ah, not bad. You know, still plugging on. How about you?"

Cadie smiled, recognizing the man's awkwardness around her. "I'm good, thanks," she replied gently. "You need to know what flight I'm on?"

Jo kept track of the conversation as best she could by listening to Cadie's side of it. Absentmindedly, she stirred the spaghetti sauce that was bubbling away on the stovetop. When Cadie eventually said goodbye and hung up, Jo remarked, "So, I guess we're going to Sydney." Her stomach knotted at the thought. Sydney was the last place on the planet she wanted to go. "At least I get to see you on to the plane for LA." She smiled wanly at Cadie.

"And believe me, I'm happy about that." Cadie walked over and wrapped her arms around Jo's waist from behind. She took a second to drop a kiss on Jo's shoulder before resting her cheek against the strong back. "Well, maybe happy is the wrong word. I don't think I'm 'happy' about any of this." Jo grunted her agreement. "Least of all the fact that I'm going to miss the hearing. I really wanted to be there for you during that."

"Don't worry about that, love. I've been there, done that. I'll survive."

Cadie thought about that. She knew enough about Jo's past to remember she had testified against a lot of big-time crime lords. "Sweetheart?"

Jo shifted slightly, maneuvering slowly around Cadie's embrace as she spooned the pasta and sauce out on to two plates. "Yes?"

"Those times that you've testified before...will this be as bad?"

Jo stilled for a few seconds as she considered her answer and Cadie took the opportunity to slide to her side. Warm, green eyes blinked up at her and she couldn't help but smile back.

"I don't expect so," she replied, bending to brush her lips against the soft ones waiting for her. "God, you taste good." They indulged themselves for a few blissful seconds. "In those cases, I was the only witness," Jo continued. Cadie tipped her head to the side as she listened, a gesture Jo found hopelessly endearing. "All the pressure was on me, and all the risk. I was pretty much the prosecution's entire case." She sprinkled some Parmesan cheese on the plates. "This time it's a bit different, I guess."

"Because of Josh?"

Jo nodded. "Yes. And because the cops saw the last part themselves." Memories of that nightmare afternoon, di Santo's blood on her hands, caused her to blink rapidly.

"I was there for that, as well," Cadie reminded her. "Why haven't I been called as a witness?"

Jo shrugged. "My guess would be Ken is doing us a favor by

having the prosecution keep you out of it. He probably doesn't need to have you involved, anyway. There were other witnesses." Cadie watched the emotions sweeping across Jo's face. The dark-haired woman was usually a closed book to other people. Not hostile-looking so much as hard to read. But whether it was because Cadie had learned to read Jo better, or Jo's trust in her allowed her to reveal herself more, every twitch and flicker was like a neon sign.

She's as wound-up as hell, Cadie realized. "Come on, love. Let's eat." She picked up the two plates and wandered over to the dining table.

Soon they were eating together, enjoying each other's company as quiet music wafted through the house. It wasn't long before Jo was doing more food redistribution than eating however. Cadie watched as the skipper chased a pile of pasta around the plate with her fork. *If it wasn't so worrying, it would be adorable,* she thought.

"So..." she began hesitantly.

"So." Jo nodded, knowing she wasn't being the most communicative of dinner companions but at a loss to know how to unblock whatever was jamming her up inside.

"I could hazard a guess and suggest that Sydney's not your favorite place to spend a few days," Cadie said.

"And you'd be spot on," Jo admitted. "Apart from the bad memories..." She swallowed, surprised by the knot of emotion in her throat. "Apart from those, I know that it's likely I'll, um, revert a little, once I'm there." She turned and looked Cadie in the eye. "And that scares me."

A tiny, cold sliver of *something* trickled through Cadie's gut. Her instinct told her it wasn't fear of Jo, but fear for her. "It's a self-defense mechanism, Jo-Jo," she said. "I'd be worried if you didn't feel that." Blue eyes blinked at her, as Jo tried to understand what Cadie was suggesting. "Do you think you're going to be in any danger down there?" Cadie asked, her mouth suddenly dry.

Jo shrugged. "I don't have any friends in that city, that's for sure."

"Except for Ken," Cadie pointed out. "And he'll be looking out for you, right?"

A flash of something hard and angry flickered in Jo's eyes for a moment. "He doesn't need to look out for me," she snapped, wishing she could take the words—and the tone—back as soon as she let them go. "Damn it." Long fingers pinched at the bridge of her nose. "I-I'm sorry, love. I didn't mean that the way it sounded."

"Sure you did," Cadie said quietly. She touched her lover's arm. "And it's okay. You can look after yourself. That's what Sydney taught you. I don't think you should beat yourself up for self-protection."

Jo snorted. "As long as I don't beat anyone else up in the process, huh?"

There was a silence as Cadie waited for Jo to look at her again. When blue eyes finally met hers, she made sure her gaze didn't waver. "That's not what was I was thinking, Jossandra," she said quietly, but firmly. "I meant that, back then, you had to look after yourself and it became habit. I don't think it's surprising that being back there would kick that habit into gear." She caught Jo's chin as the older woman made to turn away again. Tenderly she urged her focus back. "Don't put words in my mouth, sweetheart."

As quickly as the hardness had appeared, it vanished, replaced by welling tears and a slightly wobbling chin.

"I'm sorry." Jo was confused by her wildly swinging emotions; she felt about two years old.

Cadie smiled again. "It's okay. God knows, neither of us is too happy about the timing of any of this. It couldn't be worse."

Jo leaned forward, resting her forehead on Cadie's shoulder. Cadie slipped her fingers into the long, black hair that cascaded over her chest. It was silky and soft to the touch.

"I wish I could say my piece in court, watch that arsehole get locked up, and then get on the next plane and come after you," Jo said miserably.

"So do I, angel. So do I." Cadie inhaled the scent of Jo's shampoo. "There's no possibility of that, is there?" She sighed. "You'd think after 12 years with a US senator that I could pull a few strings somewhere."

That produced a chuckle from Jo, who finally pushed herself upright again and slumped back in her chair. "Yeah, well. Somehow, I think Naomi is the last person to ask for help in that area, my love."

"Can't think why," Cadie muttered.

"Something to do with me stealing her wife away from her, I think." The women looked at each other, both mentally reviewing the events of the last few months. "I don't think I'm on Naomi's Christmas card list," Jo opined. "Just a wild guess..."

"Perhaps not." Cadie quirked an amused eyebrow at the skipper, happy to see that Jo seemed to have regained some semblance of good humor. "Would you want her to help, even if she had a mind to?"

Jo laughed again, knowing that Cadie had her pegged, well

and truly. "No, and you know it." She drank a mouthful of wine. "I'm going to miss you." Their fingers tangled across the table. "So much."

The last was said so quietly, Cadie almost thought she had imagined it. "And I will miss you horribly too," she said. "Jo-Jo, you know I'm going to try and make this trip as quick as possible, don't you? Because, God knows, I don't want to be away from you any longer than I have to be."

Jo nodded. "I know. I don't want Naomi hassling you. And I wanted to be ther with you to back you up."

I really do need to call Toby back, Cadie reflected, kicking herself for putting off the conversation. "Jo, don't worry about that," she said, pushing aside her annoyance with herself for now. "I handled Naomi for 12 years. I can handle her for another three weeks. Besides, I'm not going to give her much chance. The Senate's in session and she has to be in DC while I'm going to be in Chicago. All I need is a couple of days to clear the rest of my stuff out of the Chicago house then I'll be safely up at Mom and Dad's in Madison. She's not going to come within 50 miles of me."

Jo turned their hands around so she could stroke Cadie's palm with her thumb. "Promise me you'll call if you need to talk things out?" she asked.

"Darling, I'll be calling you a million times a day, if I get the chance." Cadie laughed. "Do you really think I could last more than half a day without talking to you?" Affectionately, she ruffled Jo's hair. "Silly girl."

"HI, TOBY. SORRY to call so late."

"Cadie! That's okay, sweetie. You know we're a couple of night owls anyway. Wow, it's great to hear from you," the former PR man said happily. "I was beginning to think you were never going to return my call. What have you been up to?"

Cadie sank down into the leather armchair, glad Toby didn't seem too put out by the lateness of the call. It was close to midnight in Washington, DC, but she had wanted to wait until Jo had left for the day before calling.

"Sorry about that," she said, hooking one leg over the arm of the chair. "It was difficult to call from Jo's parents' place and since then we've been incredibly busy." It was a lie, and she knew it, but she also knew Toby well enough to know he wouldn't push the point.

"It's okay," Toby replied. "I'm glad to hear your voice. How's Jo?"

Cadie smiled in reflex at the mention of her lover's name. "She's great, actually. Since we last spoke, she inherited the yacht business from her boss and now she's kind of queen of her own country. She's like a kid in a candy store."

"Excellent!" She could hear talking in the background and Toby obviously turned his head away from the receiver. "It's Cadie." More talking. "Jay says hello," he said.

"Say hi back," Cadie said amiably. She waited while Toby passed the message on to his partner. "So what's new with you guys? Or were you calling for a chat," she teased.

There was a momentary pause.

"Well, uh, actually we do have some news," Toby continued quietly. "We've left Naomi."

Wow. Cadie knew better than most how devoted Toby and Jason had been to the senator in the early days. "Seems to be catching," she remarked. "What brought that on?"

Toby sighed. On the one hand, he did want to warn Cadie about how nuts Naomi had been lately. On the other hand, he was well aware that despite their breakup, Cadie was big-hearted enough to still care about her former long-time partner.

"Things have been a little crazy lately," he said carefully.

Cadie felt the beginnings of a headache nagging away behind her eyes. She pinched the bridge of her nose in a bid to keep it at bay. "Crazy busy, or crazy as in insane?" she asked.

"Well, insane would be a little strong, I think," he replied. "But Naomi's certainly been ..." He nibbled on his bottom lip as he tried to think of the right words. "Unstable, I guess."

Great, Cadie thought. *Unstable enough to drive away her two most loyal staff.* She exhaled slowly. *Besides me, of course.* "And my guess is, she's blaming me," she said.

"You did what you had to do," Toby replied. "We know that. God knows, she wasn't exactly giving anyone or anything more than a second's thought towards the end there. We still think you did the right thing. It's just..."

Cadie waited, letting the older man find the words for whatever it was he was trying to say. *Not sure I want to hear it, though.*

"She really fell apart when we got back," he finally said. "And there's a lot of other pressure on her, too. After that whole house-party fiasco on Hamilton Island, the press was merciless when we got home. And of course the GOP went nuts and they've been riding her ever since."

Cadie hated how easily the old, familiar guilt had settled over her. *Damn it, I'm entitled to a happy life,* she told herself. "What else?" she asked hoarsely.

"Lots of little things," he acknowledged. "She threw an ashtray at the housekeeper, who then quit, of course. There was the afternoon she was stand-up drunk in the Senate chamber." Cadie winced. "And...well, there's the threats."

"Threats?" The back of Cadie's neck prickled..

"Yeah." She heard Toby swallowing. "The last thing she asked me to do was to hook her up with a contact in Immigration. That's pretty much when Jason and I decided we didn't want to be working for her anymore."

Cadie couldn't quite see the connection. "Um, maybe I'm dense this morning, Toby, but I don't get it. Why is that a problem?"

"Honey, we're pretty sure she's trying to keep track of you any way she can. She wants to know when you come back into the country."

Cadie shifted in her seat. She gazed out on the glorious view over the Whitsundays and tried to reconnect with the way her former partner's mind worked. "You don't think maybe there was some other reason she wanted to talk to Immigration?" she asked hopefully. "I mean, maybe a constituent had a problem or a question, and she was looking for answers."

Toby snorted. "Not to be too blunt or anything, sweetie, but if it was a constituent thing, we would have heard about it first. And if there were answers to be found, she would have had us find them for her. Personal attention is not the good Senator's style."

Ain't that the truth, Cadie thought ruefully. "Yeah, I know. So, you think she wants to know when I'm back in town, huh?"

There was a pause, and Cadie almost repeated herself, thinking that perhaps they'd been cut off or Toby had somehow not heard the question. Before she could say anything else, though, the ex-PR man spoke up.

"I think it's more than that," he said quietly. "I think she means to do a lot more than keep track of you."

He can't be serious. "Toby, come on, what exactly are you trying to say? You don't honestly think she will do me any harm?"

"Oh, Cadie, I don't really know," Toby replied, a note of frustration evident in his tone. "I know she's been nuts lately. Throwing things, drinking 24/7. And..." He hesitated again. "She's been smoking weed as well. I know that for sure." Cadie said nothing, trying to digest the information. "I know it doesn't sound very dangerous or threatening, but she's pissed, honey. And if she doesn't mean you harm, then I'll bet my last buck she'd do almost anything to hurt Jo."

The light dawned. "Ah. And, of course, the quickest way to hurt Jo is—"

"— to hurt you, yes," Toby finished.

Cadie found herself suddenly short of breath. The possibility that Naomi had actually slipped into a mental state that would allow her to act so irrationally was a new and very uncomfortable thought. *My fault,* she couldn't help thinking. *My goddamned fault.*

"Jesus," she muttered, rubbing again at that pounding spot between her eyes.

"I'm sorry," Toby half-whispered. "I thought you should know."

"It's okay, honestly. I'm glad you told me," she replied, wondering what the hell she was supposed to do with the information now that she had it.

"Are you going to tell Jo?" she heard Toby ask.

Sixty-four thousand dollar question. "I honestly don't know, Tobes," she answered. "I'm going to have to think that one through a little more."

Again, she heard Jason talking in the background. "Hang on, someone else wants to say hello." There was a scrambling sound as the phone changed hands.

"Hey, you," came Jason's cheerful greeting.

"Hey, yourself," Cadie replied, letting the man's good mood push her own grim thoughts down, even if it was for a few seconds. "So, now that you're a free man, what are your plans?"

He laughed. "Free, my ass. Toby's got me roped into some Caribbean cruise next week. If I had my way, we'd be pounding the Senate looking for a new job."

"Somehow, I find that hard to believe," Cadie retorted, knowing damn well that Jason, in particular, had taken to sailing like a duck to water, and was more than likely the instigator of their new vacation plans.

"You know me too well, Miss Jones," Jason replied playfully. "Actually, I don't think we have a clue what we're going to do once we're back from the cruise, but frankly, I could care less right now."

Cadie smiled. "Well, you two have certainly earned a break," she said. "Who knows, maybe I've done you a favor by driving Naomi insane." She meant the words lightheartedly, but there was an edge to them that Jason certainly didn't miss.

"Hey, sweetie, don't do that," he chastised gently. "Remember what I said to you back in Sydney Airport that day?"

She smiled. The chaos of the day when she had left Naomi floundering in the middle of a gaggle of journalists had become a little blurry. "Remind me?"

"I told you that you deserved better. I was right then and it's still right now. If Naomi's brain is dribbling out of her ears because of it, then I can only think that that's her problem to deal with." He paused to let her absorb his words. "You know what, Cadie? Jo was the best damn thing that's happened to you in a very long time."

The headache receded a little. "No argument from me," Cadie agreed.

"So quit beating yourself up for letting that happen. You deserved it." He sounded vehement. "And Naomi, well, she can kiss my rock-hard ass."

That made Cadie laugh out loud and Jason readily joined in.

"Hey don't laugh, it *is* rock-hard."

"I don't doubt it, Jase, honestly," Cadie chortled. "It provoked a mental image that was too priceless for words."

"Ewww, I don't even want to go there," he said. "Hey, Toby's fallen asleep on my shoulder here, so we're gonna call it a night, okay?"

"Okay. Thanks again for the warning."

"Cadie, sweetie. You know that we're here if you need us, right? Any trouble from the Senator, you give us a call and we'll come get you, okay?" She could hear the very real affection in his voice.

"Thanks. You two take care, okay? And I'll call you once I'm back in Madison."

After the goodnights, Cadie hung up the phone and sat for a few minutes, contemplating the clouds scudding across the sky, their shadows sweeping across the islands below her. She glanced down at the approach of Mephisto, and smiled when the big, black feline leapt up into her lap and settled in for a snooze.

"Hi, handsome boy." She ran her fingers through his long fur. "So, what do you think? Do we need to give Jo one more thing to worry about? Or are Toby and Jason making a mountain out of a molehill?"

Sleepy, golden eyes blinked up at her and the cat offered no solution, preferring to knead her thigh with his front paws.

"Thanks. That's a big help."

Chapter Seventeen

JO RESTED HER forehead miserably against the cool glass of the big-paned terminal window. Outside, in front of her, was the gray-domed nose of the 747. She was slightly above the level of the cockpit, and from her vantage point she could easily see the captain and his co-pilot going through their pre-flight checks. Not that that cheered Jo up in the least. Part of her mind was willing there to be some minor technical problem that would delay the flight indefinitely.

I couldn't get that lucky, Jo decided. She and Cadie had already said their goodbyes, Cadie walking backwards slowly down the rampway, her eyes locked on Jo's until she had disappeared around the bend. Jo had been left, feeling very much alone amongst the milling crowd of still-boarding passengers and family members. Eventually, she had made her way to the window.

It's not that much different from the last time I said goodbye to her, she thought morosely. *That day sucked, too.* Memories of standing on the deck of the Seawolf as Cadie's water taxi receded into the distance floated at the front of her mind even as the big plane began moving away from the gate. The plane slid backwards, retreating from the low terminal building before the tug disengaged from its front landing gear and departed. Before long, the big jet was taxiing forward under its own steam, the rumble of its engines felt, more than heard, by Jo as she pressed her forehead against the glass.

She tried to imagine where Cadie was, knowing she had a window seat somewhere forward of the wing. For a moment Jo let herself believe she could see a familiar face in the one of the tiny windows, but the reality was she couldn't see any details at all. She reached up to the patch of condensation her breath had formed on the glass, and absentmindedly drew a tiny heart in the mist. *This time, I know she's coming back.*

A niggling doubt surfaced. *I do know she's coming back, right?* The little voice of insecurity—the same one that had made her so afraid of talking with her parents, the one that had stopped her from telling Cadie the truth about her past right from the word go—piped up again now, like a worn-out old recording spinning around in her mind. *I mean, this isn't just a nice way of telling me it's over, right?* Jo dug her hands deep into her jeans pockets, hunching her shoulders as the plane disappeared behind a line of buildings, its giant tailfin visible above the roofline.

Her fingers came up against a piece of paper at the bottom of her left pocket and she pulled it out, puzzled at its presence. Carefully, she unfolded it and found it covered in an instantly recognizable handwriting.

Darling, I know right now you're feeling at least as miserable as I am. The saving grace for me is that I have a lot of traveling to do before I can sit down and really process the fact that I'm so far away from you. And if I know you – (do I completely, yet? Maybe not.) – you're already in the middle of that, and feeling a bit blue.

Jo smiled. The note was so characteristic of her partner's tendency to dissect her own emotions and those of the ones she loved that it was strangely reassuring.

I want you to know that you are the most important thing in my life. In a few weeks we can laugh and joke about how it wasn't that hard being apart for such a short time, but right now I know that it hurts, and that in some ways it's scary, too.

Listen, Jo-Jo, because this is important. I am coming back and when I do, we can really get started on building this life we both seem to want so much. I love you with all my heart, sweet Jossandra. Don't ever forget that.

Soon I will be home again, I promise. Kisses, your Cadie.

Jo sighed. She felt embarrassed about the doubts she had been wallowing in a few minutes earlier. *That woman can reduce me to mush in the space of a paragraph and a half, I swear. Honest to God, I don't know what I ever did to deserve her,* she thought ruefully.

A deepening rumble intensified from somewhere in the distance and Jo quickly looked up again, in time to see the United Airlines jumbo heave itself upwards as only a 747 can. Jo didn't mind flying herself, and she knew Cadie wasn't bothered by it, but there was still something death-defying about the giant metal creature lurching skywards.

"Get up there, you bastard. Go," Jo muttered, urging the plane on. Finally, after what seemed like forever, the plane broke the shackles of gravity and suddenly became graceful, soaring as its landing gear lifted and tucked away. "Bye, sweetheart," Jo whispered, her eyes stinging. "See you soon."

CADIE CLOSED HER eyes as she felt the kick of the engines at her back. There was always that moment where she wondered if they were going to make it safely into the air. Three hundred-odd people hung in that limbo of doubt for a few seconds before it seemed a collective breath was released and Cadie felt herself relax into her chair.

She glanced around at her fellow travelers, jam-packed into the crowded coach section. She had opted not to use the return section of the business-class ticket she and Naomi had used to get to Australia in the first place. Somehow, it hadn't felt right. Instead she'd bought a brand-new, coach-class ticket.

She was sitting in a window seat on the left-hand side of the plane. The man next to her had already settled in for the 14-hour leg to Los Angeles, turning away from Cadie and tilting his seat back, a sleeping mask over his eyes. *Great. He's going to sleep for 14 hours and I'm going to be trapped in this space.* Cadie sighed. *I should have asked for an aisle seat. Live and learn.*

Cadie decided she was far too awake to try and sleep and instead she reached for the airline's monthly magazine in the seat pocket in front of her. The truth was, she was looking for a distraction. Despite her words in the note she had sneaked into Jo's pocket as they had hugged their goodbyes, Cadie was by no means calm about walking away from her partner, even if it was for a relatively short time.

They had flown down from Hamilton Island that morning, both loaded with enough luggage to see them through their respective journeys. They had transferred from the domestic terminal to Sydney's international terminal and had spent the few hours before Cadie's flight killing time in various passenger lounges and coffee shops.

Cadie had debated the merits of telling Jo about her phone call with Toby and, over a cup of coffee she had finally decided to break the news.

"He thinks what?" Jo had snapped her head around upon hearing Toby's theories about Naomi's latest mind games. "You're kidding, right?"

"Um, no," Cadie muttered, wondering if perhaps keeping quiet might not have been the best option after all. "He thinks she's going to be tracking me, though he's not really sure what she intends to do about it."

"For God's sake, Cadie, what do you think she's going to do about it?" Jo exclaimed, exasperated. "She's nuts. I wouldn't put anything past her." She dropped her spoon onto the table and it clattered against Cadie's mug. "That's it, you're not going. Come on." She made to stand up. "Let's go cancel your ticket and get your luggage back."

If the expression on Jo's face hadn't been so fierce, Cadie would have found her lover's gesture comical. Instead she reached out and gently took Jo's hand, pulling her back down in to her seat. "Jo, sweetheart, let's be rational about this. What exactly is it that you think she can do? It's not like she can kidnap me and sell me into white slavery."

The words were accompanied by a wide smile and Jo had visibly relaxed a little.

"Honey, that bitch is not rational, honestly. I don't think she knows right from wrong anymore."

Cadie had nodded. If what Toby and Jason had told her was accurate, something had happened inside the senator's psyche over the last few months. Even 12 years' experience dealing with Naomi might not help Cadie this time. But she'd thought the better of voicing those doubts to her agitated lover.

"I'm sure she's gonna try and put on a show for the media," she told Jo. "You know, like she did the last couple of days here. I'm almost positive that she may try and force me into playing the dutiful, returning, soon-to-be-pregnant wife."

Jo had snorted, no doubt remembering Naomi's desperate and, to her mind at least, almost hilarious attempt to keep Cadie by her side by announcing to the waiting media that they were planning on becoming parents as soon as they returned to the United States. Cadie had gazumped that idea by telling the journalists that if she was going to spend the rest of the year making babies, then she was going to extend her Australian vacation for a while longer, in preparation.

"The bottom line is, I have to go, sweetheart," Cadie had finally said. "My visa runs out in two days, and I know you'd rather do this whole immigration thing the legal way. Right?"

"Yeah, yeah," Jo grumbled. "But I don't have to goddamn well like it, do I? And I swear, if that lunatic lays a hand on you, Cadie, I'm coming after her. I'll beat the crap out of her."

Jo had, momentarily at least, allowed the angry, dark young woman she used to be to emerge through her eyes and Cadie watched it happen, fascinated. It wasn't anything she hadn't seen before, of course, but it was only her innate trust in Jo's control that allowed her to observe it calmly.

"I love you, Jo," she said quietly.

Immediately the fiery intensity of Jo's expression softened into something much more benign and beloved. "I love you too," Jo responded. "You're going to tell me that you can handle Naomi, and that I shouldn't worry about it, aren't you?"

Cadie nodded, smiling across at her lover. "Yes."

Jo's ensuing sigh sounded resigned. "Okay."

And now here we are, Cadie thought, brought back to the present when the plane banked sharply to head across the Pacific. *I'm getting further and further away from Jo and closer and closer to who knows what.* A knot tightened in her stomach at the thought of whatever she was flying towards. *This is ridiculous,* she decided. *I can't spend the next 24 hours worrying away at this or I'm going to be a wreck.* She called Jo's face to mind once more. *Hang in there, sweetheart, and I'll be home before you know it.*

JO SAT GLUMLY in the back of the taxi. Harding had booked her into a decent hotel in the heart of the city, not far from the criminal court complex. She'd barked the name at the taxi driver and left the route up to him. Right now, the last thing she wanted to do was take in the sights of Sydney, a city that held so many dark and unwanted memories for her. But it was hard not to find herself recognizing landmarks—a nightclub still operating, a restaurant where she'd spent many a night by her former boss's side—and the closer to the center of the city they got, the more familiar the landscape became.

At least Ken had the good sense to find a hotel away from King's Cross, she thought. It would have been too much to find herself in the middle of her old haunts. *Too many nightmares waiting for me there.*

She let her mind wander back to Cadie. A glance down at her watch told her that only a couple of hours had passed since her lover's flight had departed. *Probably drinking a nice glass of champagne and watching a movie,* Jo imagined. *Wish I was with her. Maybe one day we can make that trip together. That might be nice. I'd like to see where she grew up.*

The headline on the front page of the newspaper lying on the seat next to her blared its message. DI SANTO TRIAL BEGINS TOMORROW.

And maybe pigs will fly, too, the ex-assassin thought grimly.

Chapter Eighteen

HELENA JONES STOOD calmly in the arrivals area of Dane County Airport. Despite its small size, Madison's only airport was a busy portal, serving the state capital more than adequately. Even at this hour of the night—Helena glanced down at her watch and noted that it was after 11 p.m.—people were still streaming in and out of the terminal, most of them coming on and off the small commuter flights from Minneapolis, Milwaukee and Chicago. The petite and elegant woman stayed still as passengers milled around her, preferring to keep her eyes fixed on the small door that opened out onto the tarmac.

It had been four months since she had seen her only daughter. That had been a Christmas visit cut short when some urgent business had unexpectedly taken Cadie and Naomi back to Washington. *There's been an awful lot of water under the bridge since then,* Helena thought. She had known for a long time, of course, that all was not entirely well in her daughter's relationship with the senator. Cadie had kept most of it to herself, but a mother could sense when things were not right. Naomi had always been utterly charming whenever she had been in their home here in Madison, but Helena had seen enough of the senator in her own environment to know there was a mean streak there.

Jo, she wasn't yet entirely sure of. She'd had the chance to speak on the phone with the Australian who had stolen Cadie's heart. She sounded pleasant enough, if shy and reluctant to talk about herself. That Cadie was head over heels in love was obvious, but Helena also sensed a calm happiness in her daughter that was reassuring.

Helena moved to one side slightly so she could see around a large farmer-type walking towards her from the tarmac. She was rewarded with the sight of her daughter's compact frame coming through the door, a backpack hanging from one shoulder and a light sweater over her other arm.

Cadie caught sight of her mother and broke into a broad

smile, dropping all her carry-on baggage on the floor and walking into Helena's open-armed embrace.

"Hi, Mom," Cadie said, trying hard to keep the weariness out of her voice. She had forgotten how draining the trip from Sydney was. It felt like about three days since she'd had any kind of decent sleep. Let alone a meal that had any flavor to it at all.

"Hello, darling," her mother replied, happily squeezing Cadie in a gentle hug before they stepped back for a good look at each other. The two women were more or less the same height and resembled each other enough that there was no doubt to anyone walking past that they were related. The only real differences were in hair color—Helena's was a refined silver-gray throughout—and build, Cadie having muscles in all the right places, while her mother tended to be more willowy.

"My, look at you, so tan," Helena said, brushing a lock of sun-bleached hair off Cadie's bronzed face. "You look wonderful, dear."

Cadie grinned at her ever-elegant mother, who didn't have a hair out of place, and was beautifully turned-out in a pale blue pantsuit. "Well, I feel like I've been dragged through a bush backwards. I can't wait to get out of these clothes." She rubbed her face wearily. "You, on the other hand, look fabulous, Mom," she said. "Sorry I'm late. We got held up on the ground in Minneapolis."

"That's okay. I've been having fun watching people."

Cadie smiled. Her mother had always been an observer of people, drawing amusement from the quirks of strangers. She slid her arm around the older woman's waist as they walked towards the baggage claim area, and Helena reciprocated.

"You must be exhausted," she said, smiling at Cadie. The mirror image of her own eyes glinted back at her.

"Actually, I feel kind of discombobulated. It's weird to hear all these American accents again." They reached the baggage carousel and Cadie put down her bag again. "I was getting used to hearing nothing but Australian sounds."

Helena laughed gently, detecting a certain wistfulness in Cadie's manner. "I suspect part of that is because you're already pining for Jo."

"Gee, Mom, nothing like cutting to the chase," Cadie replied.

Helena shrugged. "I think we know each well enough not to beat around the bush, don't you?"

Cadie didn't reply, but squeezed her mother in silent acknowledgement. It felt good to be around someone warm and familiar. A siren sounded somewhere and the red light on the wall above the carousel began flashing. Machinery ground and the belt jolted into motion.

"The good news is, my bag was probably one of the last ones on the plane," Cadie said. "So, in theory it should be one of the first ones off." Several bags pushed through the rubber strips at the start of the beltline, none of them familiar.

"Nice theory," Helena murmured, provoking a snort from Cadie. "What's your plan, Arcadia?" she continued. "How long are you going to be with us?"

Cadie stifled a yawn. She kept one eye on the conveyor belt as she thought about her answer.

"Well, I thought I'd spend a few days with you and Dad, while I get over the jetlag and get my sleeping patterns back to at least functional. And then, I guess, I'd better drive down to the Chicago house and pick up the rest of my stuff." *Can't say I'm looking forward to that,* she thought glumly. "That's mine," she said, grabbing her one piece of luggage as it drifted past.

"Naomi sent up some stuff when she first got back. I left it all in boxes in the basement," Helena said. She grabbed the handle on one side of Cadie's bag. "I thought it best that you go through them, but at a glance it looks like she threw in whatever she could reach easily."

Cadie sighed as they began walking towards the main exit and the car lot. "Why doesn't that surprise me?" she muttered. "I'd be amazed if Naomi even knew what was mine and what was hers."

Helena kept silent, knowing that trashing Naomi was probably not the best idea at the moment. However acrimonious their parting had been, Cadie and the senator had spent a lot of years together, and Helena knew better than most that that added up to a tangle of mixed feelings.

Cadie shivered, surprised by the cool bite to the wind as they walked outside the terminal. "I forgot it can still be a bit cold in April," she said wryly.

They stopped long enough for her to pull on her sweater.

"It was a late winter, remember?" Helena said. "No snow at Christmas and then it all starting coming down in early January."

"That's right," Cadie murmured, recalling the heavy snowfalls before they'd left for Australia. "I guess three months in the sun can make me forget Midwest winters."

"Sounds lovely," Helena said. "I must persuade your father to take me out there one of these winters."

Cadie laughed and picked up her side of the bag again. "Well, now you have the perfect excuse. You know you can always come and stay with Jo and me." She grinned. "And, it looks like her parents are going to move up there as well."

They reached the car and Helena clicked the remote to open the trunk. "This really is what you want, isn't it?" she asked as Cadie lifted her luggage up.

Cadie nodded, finding tears suddenly very close to the surface. Her mother saved her from actually having to string a sentence together by kissing her on the cheek softly.

"It's okay, sweetheart. It's wonderful to see that look in your eyes again. It's been a while."

Cadie smiled wanly. "It has," she finally managed.

"Come on. Let's get you home." Helena glanced knowingly at her daughter. "So you can give Jo a call."

JO RUBBED WEARILY at her eyes. So far she had done nothing but sit on the hard, wooden bench outside Criminal Court 1. She hadn't been needed since the committal proceedings had begun that morning, and she had a sinking feeling the rest of the day was going to be more of the same. From what she could gather from Harding's sporadic updates, the hearing was mired in legal argument, largely over the preliminary decision to allow Josh to testify by video.

"We could've had him testify and be done with it by now, for all this arguing," she'd grumbled the last time they spoke. Harding had shrugged his shoulders and gone back inside the courtroom, leaving Jo to her own devices.

This afternoon doesn't seem much different, Jo pondered. *Same old lawyers in the same old wigs and robes, talking the same old crap.* She sighed and looked at her watch. *Just after three. Can't imagine they're going to go much longer. Judges don't like to be late home for dinner, after all.* She grimaced ruefully as she leaned back against the wall, her arms crossed. *Should've brought a good book.*

She felt a rhythmic vibration on her hip and dug into her trouser pocket to retrieve her cell phone, flipping it open.

"Madison."

"Yep, that's where I am." Cadie's soft, welcome tones were like an instant shot of muscle relaxant.

"Hiya, gorgeous," Jo breathed. She let her head drop back against the wall. "Damn, it's good to hear your voice."

"Likewise. Where are you?"

"Sitting outside court like a shag on rock. Like I have been all day long."

She heard Cadie sigh. "They haven't called you yet, huh?"

"Nope. Don't think they will today, either." Jo glanced left as someone opened the courtroom door from the inside and walked through. But it was only a reporter, notepad and pen in hand, and she turned her attention back to the phone. "Where are you, more to the point?"

Cadie laughed quietly and Jo absorbed every second of it. "Well, I think I'm at Mom and Dad's place, but as my brain dribbled out of my ears about 10 hours ago, I can't be certain."

Jo looked up at the drab ceiling of the corridor, taking comfort in Cadie's weary humor. "I'm glad you got there safely, sweetheart." She remembered what time it was where Cadie was. "And go to bed, for crying out loud."

"I will. I wanted...I just needed to talk to you."

Awww. "I'm glad you did. I needed to hear you talk to me." Jo heard Cadie shifting her position, and tried to imagine her lover's face. "I think I've figured out that I really hate being out of contact with you."

"Oh yeah," Cadie agreed. "I'm ready to get some sleep, hopefully start to feel human again, and get all this housekeeping done so I can come home as soon as possible."

Music to my ears, Jo thought. "Just in time to get jetlagged again, huh?" she said.

"I won't care if it's you I'm using as a pillow, darling," Cadie replied, her smile almost audible through the phone line.

"And who are you using as a pillow tonight?" Jo teased.

There was a pause and a sound of something that could well have been bedclothes being pulled back.

"Winnie the Pooh, actually," Cadie replied, provoking a more solid laugh from her partner.

"Fair enough," Jo conceded. "Call me in your morning?"

"That'll be pretty late in your night, won't it?"

"I don't care," Jo said, her voice suddenly rough with tears. "Please?"

"Of course, okay," Cadie answered, and Jo could hear that her lover wasn't so far from crying herself. "I miss you, Jo-Jo."

"I'm right here, love," Jo replied, trying to be reassuring. Somehow, saying that from a distance of 9000 miles, no matter how good the quality of the phone line, didn't wash. "I miss you, too."

There were a few seconds of silence before Cadie yawned. "I guess everything will be a bit better in the morning, huh?" she finally said, fatigue making her sound somehow much younger to Jo's ears.

"Most things usually are, darling," Jo agreed, charmed. "Wrap me around you, and sleep deep, okay?"

"Always," Cadie murmured sleepily. "'Night."
"G'night, sweetheart."

Chapter Nineteen

JO COULD FEEL the cloak slip over her personality as she stalked into the courtroom and down the center aisle towards the witness box. She had contemplated willing it not to happen, but as soon as she stepped inside and saw the all too familiar faces lined up on both sides, she knew there was no point fighting it.

It was Friday morning and, surprisingly, Jo had been called to the stand almost immediately. A pronounced gasp had greeted her when she entered the room. Even those who knew nothing about her history—and she supposed there were a few of them—were plainly impressed by the figure she cut.

And the weird thing is, I knew that would happen or I wouldn't have chosen this outfit. I wanted it to happen, she thought as she walked forward. She was all in black—leather pants and boots, turtleneck and a mid-thigh length leather jacket added to her usually imposing stature. Black was a color she had avoided since leaving Sydney, but today had been different. Jo knew damn well she was making an impression. With her long hair and startling blue eyes, it wasn't too difficult to live up to the reputation she obviously still had.

A quick glance left and right told her there were many in the room who, if they didn't want her dead, certainly wanted a piece of her. Marco di Santo, of course, sat at the defendant's table, looking sullen and—she half-smiled—twisted. *I guess being castrated will do that to a fella.*

Behind him sat a row of henchmen, most of whom were known to Jo. In her day they had been minor thugs, soldiers on the street. Now, she guessed, with di Santo at the top of the tree, these were the yes-men who kept him safe and supplied him with whatever was his drug of choice these days. He used to be a coke freak. One look at his haggard features told her his time in the prison hospital had been less than friendly to his habit. *They must have kept a 24-hour guard on him.*

Jo stepped up into the wooden witness box and settled herself into the chair. She kept her face cold and closed as she took in the details of the courtroom. She was damned if she was going to give anyone in the room, least of all the rows of hungry reporters she could see behind the prosecutor's desk, anything.

Technically, of course, this wasn't a trial, but a committal hearing. The prosecution would be trying to convince the judge that there was enough evidence to go to trial. That was where Jo came in. The defense would also have its chance to get the whole thing thrown out.

The courtroom made an interesting sight. All the lawyers were bewigged and robed. The judge beside her was even more so, his robes red and draped in silk, unlike the lawyers, who were in plain black. His gray wig hung down below his shoulders, and his tiny half-glasses perched on the end of a rather florid nose. *Too much red wine and gin chasers.* The Clerk of the Court approached.

"Please place your left hand on the Bible," he said, the radio mike attached to his lapel relaying his words to the rest of the room. "Raise your right hand. Do you swear to tell the truth, the whole truth and nothing but the truth, so help you God?"

Oh, I wish Cadie were here, Jo thought. "I do," she said aloud.

"Please state your name for the record." She smiled as he omitted the requirement for stating her address as well.

I'm still getting some protection, then. Good to know. Not that it did me much good when this goose came calling, Jo thought, casting a jaded eye over di Santo.

"Jossandra Cristie Madison," she said quietly, trusting the microphone perched on the edge of the witness box would catch her words.

The clerk moved away and there was a pause in proceedings as the lead prosecutor shuffled his papers and gathered his thoughts.

Jo knew, because she had been well briefed by the lawyer and by Harding, that more hinged on her testimony than the charges stemming from the attack on her home and Josh. Di Santo had been one of the few who had slipped through the net when Jo had first turned state's evidence five years earlier, largely because he had paid off the right people. The police had tried to bring charges against him, but he had evaded them each time. The home invasion against Jo was just what they'd needed to get him into court. And now she would have the opportunity to bear witness to a number of incidents they hoped would help put di Santo away for a long time.

Jo swallowed and moistened her lips as the prosecutor cleared his throat and looked up at her.

"Miss Madison, please tell the court about your association

with Marco di Santo, the defendant. How long have you known him?"

"I've known him about 15 years."

"What was the nature of your relationship?"

"I worked for Tony Martin as his bodyguard. Mr. di Santo was Tony's second in charge. He ran the King's Cross Martial Arts School, the protection rackets associated with it, and the numbers games for Tony."

"Tony Martin, as in the Tony Martin who you helped put in prison five years ago on three counts of murder and..." He shuffled his papers again, finding the right page. "And five counts of dealing in illegal substances?"

The defense counsel, a small, slightly sweaty man with a number of nervous affectations, rose quickly from his chair.

"Objection, Your Honor. Relevance? This witness is speaking to issues that have nothing to do with the matter before this court."

The prosecutor almost snorted his derision. "Miss Madison is a material witness in this case, your Honor. It will be shown that it was her home the defendant invaded, her house-sitter who was held hostage. In fact, it was Miss Madison who detained the defendant long enough for the police to arrive. By detailing her history with the defendant, we intend to establish a pattern to his behavior that will prove he had ample motivation and the methodology for the attack on Miss Madison."

Jo watched the interchange calmly, almost amused by the game-playing. The judge removed his spectacles and gazed sternly at both attorneys. "The objection is over-ruled. But I will remind the prosecution to stay focused on this case. I will not tolerate any straying from the path..." He glanced at the defense brief again. "From either side."

The prosecutor turned back to Jo. "Please continue."

"Yes," Jo replied. "That Tony Martin." She could hear the coldness in her own voice and hardly recognized herself. *I guess that other self is never going to leave me.*

"Are you being paid for your testimony today, Miss Madison?" he asked.

"No, I am not."

"Could you tell us, in your own words, about the events of February 10, this year?"

Jo nodded and shifted slightly in her chair. "I was working as a yacht skipper in the Whitsunday Islands. My next-door neighbor, Josh Matthews, was house-sitting for me, as I was going to be away for about three weeks. On February 10, I received a phone call from Marco di Santo."

The prosecutor stepped out from behind his desk and walked slowly towards her, hooking his thumbs under the edge of his robe in a rather pompous fashion. "And what did Mr. di Santo say to you?" he asked.

Jo watched a thin bead of sweat trickle from under the man's wig, across his temple and down the side of his jaw. "He said he was at my house, that he had Josh, and that if I didn't come to him straight away he would make Josh a lot less pretty," she answered.

"And what did you take to be his meaning?"

Again the defense counsel piped up. "Objection, your Honor. The witness is testifying about the inner workings of my client's mind, which, unless she's some kind of telepath, is impossible for her to know."

"Over-ruled," the judge said curtly.

Jo smiled wryly, and, at a nod from the prosecutor, continued. "He meant that he would, at the very least, cut Josh, if not kill him."

"Did your previous experience with Mr. di Santo suggest that he would carry out his threat?"

Jo almost laughed. "I knew he would," she said.

The lawyer walked over to the far corner of his desk, where an easel stood. It held a large, rectangular card covered with a light cloth.

"Miss Madison, do you recognize this?" Quickly, he whisked the cloth away, revealing a full-color, blown-up photograph.

At first Jo struggled to make out anything recognizable in the mess of reds and blues and flesh tones. In the time it took for her eyes to adjust and for her brain to be able to organize what she was seeing into something that made sense, Jo felt her world telescope in on itself. It took all her famous self-control not to suck in a deep and noisy breath. Instead, she ground her teeth together.

The photo was all too familiar even though it had to be five years old. It showed the girl Marco di Santo had shot and beaten to death in a Sydney back alley after he had king-hit Jo into oblivion—the girl who had changed Jo's life. The girl she had been sent there to kill.

Jo swallowed. "Yes, I recognize it," she said, her voice a deathly calm, cold whisper.

"What is it?" The prosecutor was in his element now, loving the drama of this line of questioning, and he didn't much care what it was doing to the former assassin.

Jo had a moment of dizziness, backed by a wave of nausea

that threatened to double her over. Instead, she folded her hands over each other and gripped tightly until her fingernails dug into the skin. *And now I'm very glad Cadie isn't here to see this.*

"It's the body of a girl called Shannon, who was a drug addict and a casual employee of Tony Martin's," she said. "She had cheated Tony out of a few dollars and he sent me to kill her." The frankness of those words chilled her, and she felt the eyes of the entire courtroom riveted on her. Jo flinched and looked down at her hands, coldly noting the tiny semi-circles of blood where her fingernails had cut. "I couldn't do it, but before I could let her go, di Santo ambushed us both."

The prosecutor walked back towards her, forcing her to look up at him before he continued. "Was this the first time you had witnessed the defendant in such an act of violence?"

Jo smiled wryly. "No. He made a habit of it."

"Objection, your Honor. Once again, relevance." The defense counsel was on his feet once again. "I'm at a loss to know what this has to do with the events of February 10."

The prosecutor sighed dramatically. He'd played tennis with the defense counsel two days earlier and they were, in fact, good friends. But all was fair in love and court and he was enjoying his moment in the sun. "It goes to establishing a pattern of behavior, milord," he said patiently.

The judge chewed the end of the arm of his half-glasses. "I'll allow it," he said, after some moments' impassive contemplation. "But please get to the point, Mr. Roberts. I don't have a lot of patience for these sorts of histrionics."

Old bugger's probably got a late golf game lined up, Jo reasoned. Her hands were still shaking from the shock of the photograph, and she found it hard to tear her eyes away from it. *All those nightmares.* As bad as they were, they never matched the reality, she thought, staring into the lifeless eyes of the girl crumpled on the damp roadway. In the corner of the photograph was a man's shod foot—Harding's. Jo shifted her gaze to the detective, who was sitting two rows behind the prosecution. Sympathetic eyes met her own.

The prosecutor was talking again. "Let's go back, shall we, Miss Madison, to February 10 this year. After you received the call from Mr. di Santo, what did you do?"

Back on relatively safe ground, Jo stuck to the facts of her rescue of Josh and the arrest of di Santo. By mutual agreement between herself, the prosecutor and Harding, the only thing she left out of her account was Cadie's involvement in the events. She was brutally honest about her own part in the tale, right down to the violence she had committed on di Santo as they had waited for the police to arrive.

By the end of the prosecutor's questions, Jo felt drained and sickened by the whole thing. But she knew there was no easy escape. The defense counsel had to have his turn. With a curt, "your witness", the lead prosecutor sat down and left Jo to deal with the cross-examination.

The defense counsel assumed the floor and studied Jo carefully, allowing a few seconds of silence before he began.

"Miss Madison, let's go back to that alley in King's Cross, for a moment, shall we?" He gestured toward the still-exposed photograph on the easel. "Did you actually see my client kill this girl?"

"He had pistol-whipped me and I was unconscious, so, no, I did not," Jo replied, experienced enough at these games to know how to maximize her case even when the defense was making a relevant point.

"So, you assumed that my client had done the deed?"

"Given that he had threatened to before he hit me..."

"A simple yes or no answer is all that is required, Miss Madison."

Jo sighed. "Yes."

"I see," said the lawyer. "Was there anyone else in the alley, anyone who could corroborate your story?"

"No, there was not."

He turned away from her and returned to his desk. "So, we have only your word—the word of a hardened criminal, a killer in your own right, in fact—that it was my client, and not you, who killed that girl?" He pointed at the photograph again.

"Yes, that's all you have," Jo admitted.

He changed tack, this time going on the offence. "When the police arrived at your house in Shute Harbor on February 10, they found my client on his knees and you standing over him with a garrote around his neck. Is that correct?"

Jo nodded. "More or less."

"And once again, we only have your word for it that you were acting in self-defense. Correct?"

"You have Josh Matthews' word that he was held hostage," Jo said.

"Well, I have my own theory about that, Miss Madison," he said, somewhat smugly. "Would you like to hear it?"

"Objection," called the prosecutor. "Are we here to talk about evidence, or my learned friend's—no doubt rich—fantasy life?"

"Get to the point Mr. Barclay," the judge said, impatience

clear in his tone.

"Certainly, milord," replied the defense counsel agreeably. "I put it to you, Miss Madison, that my client is an old acquaintance of yours. He arrived in Shute Harbor to visit you, found you absent, called you, and when you arrived home, you got in to an argument. I put it to you that Josh Matthews got caught up in the middle of it all and hysteria, combined with his youth and loyalty to you, convinced him to give the fanciful testimony we saw yesterday. I put it to you that what the police actually saw on February 10 was you brutalizing a man with whom you'd had a long and antagonistic relationship." He looked at Jo and smiled. "How am I doing?"

Jo shrugged. "This is your fantasy, not mine," she answered. "That's not how it happened."

"So you say," he replied. "Once again, all we have is the word of a woman who has killed many times, and is here today as part of an immunity deal with the prosecution. It's not a lot to go on, really, is it?" Abruptly he sat down, dismissing Jo with a wave of his hand.

"Do you have anything else for this witness, Mr. Roberts?" the judge asked the prosecutor. There was a pause before he replied.

"One question, milord," the prosecutor said, standing. He leant forward, his hands pressing on the table in front of him. "Miss Madison, are you here today as part of the immunity deal you struck with the Department of Public Prosecutions five years ago?"

Jo considered the question carefully. Would she be here if she hadn't had that previous relationship with the police? She thought about what di Santo had done to Josh and, she supposed, to her. *Damn right I would be,* she concluded.

"That deal covered criminal acts I had committed prior to that time. And I believe at the end of the three trials that resulted from me turning state's evidence, that I signed a piece of paper that allowed me and the DPP to go our separate ways," she replied with a half-smile. "There has been no new deal struck. I'm here as someone whose home was invaded by that man..." She pointed at di Santo. "And whose house-sitter was held hostage. That's all."

The prosecutor nodded in satisfaction. "No more questions, milord," he said, flicking the tails of his robe to either side as he sat down.

"The witness is dismissed," the judge instructed.

S'FUNNY HOW SUCH an evil place can look so pretty. Jo leaned against the A/C-cooled glass, gazing out over Darling Harbor and the sights of Sydney. The bridge, the Opera House, all the tall city buildings were lit in various shades and styles. It was a beautiful sight from high in the hotel, but it left Jo cold.

She was naked, having crawled out of bed after a fruitless few hours of attempting to sleep. *I'm sure I'm making somebody's night,* she thought. *They'd need a pretty good set of binoculars, though.* Jo sat on the narrow window ledge, side-on to the window, legs outstretched and slightly bent, her hands wrapped around her knees. She pressed her forehead against the glass as she looked down on the city.

Ken Harding had wanted her to have dinner with him after they were done in court for the day, but Jo had declined, the pounding headache behind her eyes claiming all her focus.

I'll make it up to him over the weekend, she had reasoned on her way back to the hotel. *I can't face company tonight.*

The day had ended on another downer, the prosecution telling Jo that she could be called again on Monday, and to make herself available. Condemned to a whole weekend in the city she loathed, she had spent the early part of the evening half-heartedly picking at her room-service meal and making her way down a bottle of red wine. It hadn't done her headache much good, but it had at least taken the edge off the churning in her guts.

Her mind was another thing, of course. Sleep was out of the question. Her brain was running at a million miles an hour, with the picture of the dead and mutilated girl swirling like some kind of sick, perverted slide show.

Jo sighed, the condensation from her breath forming a misty cloud on the cool glass. Sydney was one of the world's great cities, but right now all she could see were her own bad memories. She swore the damp stench of that alley was still in her nostrils. *Of course, I could be losing my mind.* She slid a fingertip through the condensation, idly drawing a meandering line, her eyes focused on the running lights of a boat out on the harbor. *Wouldn't be the first time.*

The phone rang, its modulated tone harsh against the quiet in the room. Jo knew it could only be one person at this hour, and slid off the window ledge with an enormous sense of relief. She figured her blood pressure had dropped 20 points by the time she reached for the phone.

CADIE CURLED ONTO her side and snuggled deep into the bedclothes as she tucked the phone under her chin and listened to the ring tone. It was still relatively early in Wisconsin, but past midnight in Sydney. She was probably waking her lover up, but something told her Jo wouldn't mind.

"Hello." The voice Cadie had yearned to hear all day. And one word told her so much. *She's really down. Must have been a bad day in court.*

"Hello, gorgeous," she replied. Cadie heard Jo exhale slowly, followed by a low groan, as if the tall woman had relaxed totally. "Did I wake you?"

Jo laughed with gentle irony. "I wish. No. I couldn't sleep and was sitting by the window. Guess I got a little stiff."

Hmmm. "Where are you now?"

"On the bed. How about you?"

"In the bed. Care to join me?" Cadie smiled to herself, knowing Jo would find that hard to resist. She was rewarded by a soft chuckle from the Australian.

"Sure." Cadie could hear Jo rearranging herself and the bedclothes. "Okay, I'm in bed," Jo said redundantly. Her voice now sounded much closer, and a whole bunch more intimate.

Like she's right here with her mouth close to my ear, Cadie thought. The image drew a tingling physical response, distracting her for a moment. But Cadie forced her mind back to her lover's mental state. *She's not saying a lot, which says a lot.*

"What are you wearing?" Jo asked, out of the blue.

Then again, I could be completely wrong, Cadie conceded with surprise. "Um, you wouldn't believe me if I told you," she answered, glancing down at the pajamas she was wearing.

"Tell me," Jo's voice quietly urged.

Cadie laughed. "Okay. An old pair of pajamas I haven't worn since I was sixteen."

"And what impossibly cute motif do they have?"

Cadie felt herself blushing. "Um, would you believe lots of little pink panthers?" Jo's answering laugh rumbled seductively in her ear and Cadie shivered despite the warmth of both the blankets and the sun peeking through the half-drawn curtains of her childhood bedroom. *I'm sure seduction is the last thing on her mind, though.* "Tell me about your day?"

Jo sighed. Cadie waited as the silence lengthened until she thought her partner wasn't going to answer at all. But then a very small voice piped up.

"It sucked."

No kidding, my love. "I thought so," Cadie said. "What happened?"

"Some of my history came back to bite me in the arse," Jo replied.

"But, weren't you expecting that? I mean, the whole reason di Santo came after you in the first place was because of your history with him."

"Yes, but..." Jo hesitated. "I guess I wasn't expecting it to be quite as hard as it was," she said eventually. "They, um..." She sighed again. "Do you remember me telling you about the girl in the alley? The last person I was sent to..." Cadie heard the words stop dead in Jo's throat.

"Yes, of course," she murmured.

"That came up," Jo said hoarsely, and Cadie could hear the tears much closer to the surface now. "Complete with full-color pictures."

"Oh, Jo-Jo, I'm sorry." Cadie wished more than anything in the world that she could wrap her arms around her lover. But all she could do was listen to Jo sniffling.

"S'okay. It was a bit of a surprise, that's all. I guess I should have known all that stuff would come up, especially given the briefing the prosecutor gave me, but..." Jo sniffed again. "But I guess I've been avoiding thinking about it. My own stupid fault, really."

"Shhh. Don't do that to yourself, Jo. I wish I could have been there for you." Cadie ran her hand through her hair, frustrated at feeling so helpless and far away. "God, my timing really sucked on this, didn't it?"

"Not your fault, love," Jo murmured. "S'the way things worked out. And you couldn't have done anything to change how it was today, even if you'd been here." Her voice sounded grim and weary. "I would still have had to have been that...that person that I was back then. And they would still have shown me that picture. I remember the way she felt in my hands...at the end of my gun barrel."

Cadie swallowed around the sudden lump in her throat.

"You're not that person any more, love," she said quietly.

"No?" Jo replied, a trace of bitterness in her tone. "It sure felt like I was today. All the old cronies were there. And the reporters. I was good copy."

Cadie knew, suddenly, exactly why Jo sounded so exhausted. "Jo, don't you see that it's all an act these days? That's why it takes so much out of you and leaves you feeling like a limp dishrag. You have to put on that persona to survive in that environment. But it's an act, darling. And it takes a lot of effort. That's not who you really are inside."

There was a long pause while Jo digested her words. "I used

to be able to push aside everything else I was feeling," she said finally.

"And now you can't."

"And now I can't."

"I'm glad," Cadie whispered.

"I miss you. Wish you were here."

"I'm right here, angel." *Now it's time to distract her,* Cadie decided. "So, what are *you* wearing?" she asked, dropping her own voice to a more intimate pitch.

There was a pause as she suspected Jo was absorbing the abrupt change in subject, not to mention tone. Cadie held her breath, wondering if she had completely misjudged the situation. It wasn't long before she got her answer.

"Naked as the day I was born, darling," Jo burred in the low register that was guaranteed to send tingles up and down the length of Cadie's spine.

"So I guess if I turned around so I was facing you..." Cadie paused as she did turn over onto her opposite side, even though she had no way of knowing, really, which way Jo was positioned. "I guess if I did that, then I could slide my hand up your side until I can cup your breast in the palm of my hand." The catch in Jo's breath was audible and deeply arousing to Cadie. "And of course, once I'm there, I might as well explore a little bit."

"E-explore?"

Cadie smiled, hearing the beginnings of desire and intrigue in Jo's tiny hesitation. "Well, I can brush my thumb across your nipple, for example." A low groan curled through the phone line so close, Cadie almost felt Jo's breath on her skin.

"Arcadia?"

"Yes, Jo?"

"Are you trying to seduce me over the phone?"

"That's the general idea. Is that okay?" There was another pause, and for a moment Cadie thought perhaps she'd hit a sensitive spot in her lover's otherwise robust sexual psyche.

"Um, very much okay, I think," Jo finally replied. "I'm not really sure. I don't think I've ever, um..."

"Had phone sex before?" *Life is full of surprises,* Cadie thought.

"Um, no." Jo cleared her throat. "What do we...I mean, how do we...?"

Cadie chuckled lightly. "Well, for a start, get comfortable." She heard Jo sigh again and tried to imagine the long, naked form of her lover, sprawled across the bed.

"Isn't this going to cost you a fortune?" Jo murmured.

"Nope. It's Mom and Dad's phone," Cadie reminded her. "And trust me, they won't notice, and if they do, they won't mind."

"Oh, God, don't mention parents," Jo groaned, provoking a laugh from Cadie.

"Don't worry, my love, I'm going to distract you with far more interesting thoughts," she said wickedly.

Jo gulped. "Um, okay. So, what do we do?"

"Close your eyes." Cadie shifted slightly so she could tuck the phone between her cheek and the pillow. She closed her own eyes, blocking out the view of her childhood bedroom and toys, not to mention the presence of her parents on the other side of the wall. Instead she focused on the picture of Jo in her head. "Now, really concentrate on my voice," she said, almost whispering. "Jo-Jo, I want you to do something for me."

There was another sharp intake of breath from her partner.

"Anything. You know that," Jo murmured.

"Let your hands be my hands."

"Oh, my."

JO'S ORGASM, WHEN it hit, was not only an intense physical release, but an emotional explosion. As her body shuddered and shivered in response to Cadie's touch and words, all the tensions and worries of the day erupted in a disconcerting flood of feeling. She sobbed, tears flowing freely even as the last throes of the achingly deep climax ebbed away. Jo could hear soothing, calming words from Cadie, but her heart was beating so fast and hard that she thought it was going to burst out of her chest.

"Shhh, sweetheart, it's all right," Cadie murmured, close and tender. "Feel my arms wrapped around you?"

"Y-yes," Jo stammered, almost certain she could feel Cadie's reassuring presence. *Well, damn, that was certainly unique. So intense.* She let out a long, ragged breath as she finally got to the point where she could formulate a rational sentence. "Y-you kn-know that I love you more than I've ever loved anyone, r-right?"

Cadie laughed gently. "Yes, I think I know that, love."

"And you've made me so happy, Cadie. I've never been so happy, ever, in my life." Jo sniffled again and wiped her nose with the back of her free hand. "So, can you explain why it is that I've done more crying since I met you than in my entire decade of being a hard case? Not to mention the five years since then. How is that possible?" She could hear Cadie shifting position, sighing as she got comfortable.

"I think it goes back to what we were talking about before," Cadie said finally. "You built up a lot of layers of self-defense. You needed every damn one of them, from what I can work out."

"S'true," Jo acknowledged. "And I guess I don't need them around you."

"Actually, I think there's a bunch of people you don't need them with. But so far, I'm the first one you've felt safe enough with to let your guard down. And at the moment, I think you're rubbed raw by everything."

Jo nodded silently, realizing belatedly that Cadie couldn't see her response. "You're right. I am a bit."

"And I've been a bit of a, um..." Jo heard Cadie struggling for the right words.

"Lightning rod," Jo suggested.

"Well, that's probably as close as anything, yes. Sorry, sweetpea."

Jo laughed softly. "Don't be sorry. You're the best thing that's ever happened to me." She grunted slightly as a small aftershock reminded her of their love's more physical manifestations. "And if the last half-hour is any indication, I may never let you out of the bedroom." She sighed dreamily. "That was awesome."

"It sounded wonderful, darling," Cadie said, her own voice still a little rough with barely-suppressed desire. "You are the sexiest woman on the planet. You know that, right?"

Somehow Jo found the breath to laugh. "All your doing, my love. My hands were your hands, remember?"

"Not to mention my tongue," Cadie drawled.

"Quite," Jo breathed. "God, woman, I don't think I can move. You've paralyzed me."

"Well, the lovely thing about phone sex is that as long as your voice is audible, you can still work miracles," Cadie replied.

Jo chuckled, relishing the fact that she felt more relaxed and stress-free than she had in days. "Is that a gentle hint, sweetheart?"

"I want your hands all over my body, Jossandra," was Cadie's frank answer, and Jo could hear every ounce of desire in her tone.

"Then close your eyes, and let your hands be my hands."

"Oh."

Chapter Twenty

"ARE YOU SURE you don't want us to come with you?" Stephen Jones asked his daughter as she loaded empty, folded packing cases into the trunk of the rental car. He knew better than most that Cadie was more than capable of handling things, but something about her being alone in the Chicago house bothered him. Maybe it was because he'd spent the last two days hearing about the dissolution of Cadie's relationship with the senator and Naomi's subsequent descent into instability.

Cadie looked up at her father. In the four months since she had last seen him, he seemed to have aged. She angled her head slightly, taking stock of the man standing on the bottom step of the winding pathway up to the front door. His tall, thin frame was more stooped than she remembered. He also looked worried. *Probably with good reason,* she thought grimly, though the last thing she wanted was to admit that there might be real cause for his concern.

"Dad, you've got that fund-raiser to go to tonight, and I'm going to be fine. I just have to do this. All my stuff from the agency is in the house and I can't wind things up properly without it. Try not to worry." She smiled up at him. "Naomi's not going to be there. I'm going to pack everything as fast as I can and get the heck out of that place."

"Are you sure she won't be there?" her father asked.

Cadie mulled that over. She knew the US Senate schedule, and she was certain it was in session. Besides, she hadn't told Naomi she was coming. *But if Toby and Jason were right, she probably does know,* she realized. *If I tell him that, though, I'll be hard-pressed to stop him coming, hunting rifle in tow.*

She had called Toby and Jason once she'd recovered from her jetlag, but they were away on their Caribbean cruise and not due back until the following weekend. Cadie had also called the Chicago house, getting no answer, not even from the housekeeper—a sure sign that Naomi had closed up the house for the duration of the Senate session and headed back to DC.

"I'm sure, Dad. Senate's in session, and she can't afford to miss any votes. Not with the way she damaged her reputation while we were in Australia." She dropped her overnight bag on top of the packing cases and closed the trunk. *Besides, coming to Chicago would entail a little effort on her part, and God knows, that's not Naomi.*

"All right, then," her father conceded. "You know where we are if you need us."

Cadie stepped up to him and placed her hands on his shoulders, standing on tiptoes to kiss him lightly on the cheek. "Thanks, Dad."

"Drive safely," he reminded her. "Have you got enough change for the tolls? Have you got your cell phone?"

Cadie laughed. "Yes, I have enough change. No, I don't have my cell phone. That's at the house, where I left it before we went to Australia."

"Then take mine," he insisted.

"Dad," she answered mock sternly, hands on hips. "Don't worry so much, okay? It's not that long since I did the drive to Chicago." She walked back to the car and opened the driver's side door. "I won't need it on the drive, and the phone is still connected at the house. I'll give you a call once I'm there, okay? Besides, you'll need your cell phone tomorrow."

"All right, but make sure you call," Stephen said gruffly, sticking his hands in his pockets.

Cadie waved as she drove away, the sight of him in her rearview mirror a comforting and familiar one. It was late afternoon on Sunday, and Madison was at its springtime best. The sky was clear and blue and there was a touch of warmth about the sun even though it was making its way down to the horizon. Cadie wound her way through the flowering suburbs and onto the beltline skirting the southern side of the city. Traffic was light, thankfully, and before long she swung the car onto I-90 heading south.

Looks like I'm going to make good time, she thought. *I should make it to the house by 7 p.m. or so. I can probably get a bit done tonight, and then I'll have the whole day tomorrow to do the rest. One more night in the house should do it and I can be back in Madison before lunch on Tuesday. Perfect.*

She hadn't yet sorted through her mixed feelings about the house. She and Naomi had been very proud of the work they had done on it. A red-brick Victorian, it was in an old part of the city. They had spent a lot of time and money renovating it and making it exactly what they both wanted. The prospect of saying goodbye to it, finally and forever, saddened Cadie, vying with her relief over closing this chapter of her life.

I'm losing a lot, she reflected. *A lot of history.* She thought about Naomi's extended family, including nephews and nieces of whom she was really quite fond. *A lot of people.*

She contemplated that as she dodged around a slow-moving car that refused to move out of the middle lane of the highway.

Then again, look at what I'm gaining. A vision of Jo's face filled her mind's eye. *More love than I've ever known, and no strings attached. No game-playing, no politics, no bullshit neediness, and the kind of equality in a relationship I've always craved. All wrapped up in a drop-dead gorgeous package.* Cadie overtook a UPS semi-trailer and ducked back into the slower lane once she had passed. *Not that that's important. A lovely bonus, admittedly.* She grinned to herself. *But it's Jo and that feeling of safety that I get when I'm with her that I love. I never had that with Naomi, not even in the early days. I never quite knew what she was thinking. So I guess I can live with what I'm losing, because what I'm gaining is more important to me. I don't think I really understood that until I got back here.*

Pushing the car over the speed limit, she rested her left elbow on the windowsill and let the wind whip through her hair.

The next few days could not be over fast enough.

JO SAT ACROSS the small table from Ken Harding and tried not to think too much about the big man's eating habits. They were sharing a late breakfast in a café across the road from the court complex, and Jo winced as she watched the detective plowing his way through a plate of bacon and eggs like a man who hadn't eaten in a month. She contemplated starting a conversation, but the thought of him trying to talk with his mouth full almost put her off the croissants and black coffee in front of her.

She had spent most of the weekend inside the hotel, making use of its swimming pool and gymnasium to ward off boredom and lethargy. The thought of being out and about in the city, particularly when her former colleagues knew she was in town, didn't seem all that sensible. The highlight of her weekend had been the twice-daily phone calls with Cadie.

Breakfast with Harding was her concession to turning down his dinner invitation on Friday.

"You not hungry?" he finally said around a mouthful of fried egg, noting her picking at a corner of her croissant.

"Yeah, I'm okay," Jo replied, giving him a half-smile. "Got a lot on my mind, that's all."

Harding eyed her from over the rim of his coffee mug. "Don't worry about it," he said casually before diving in for a noisy slurp. "They'll be done with you today for sure. You'll probably be home by tonight."

"Trouble is, I don't want to be home," Jo muttered, not really intending for him to hear. She glanced up in time to watch Harding drip a glob of egg yolk on to his tie and winced again. He was oblivious, noisily chewing on another forkful of bacon. Jo twirled her coffee cup absentmindedly with the fingers of her right hand. "Ken, can you find something out for me?"

Harding stopped eating long enough to look at his breakfast companion more carefully. *She looks buggered,* he realized, noticing the dark circles under her eyes for the first time. *Missing that little American sheila, I bet.*

"If I can," he said, putting his knife and fork down. "What's up?"

Jo gazed into the depths of her coffee for a few more seconds before she looked up, almost as if she'd made an important decision, just that second.

"You know Cadie's in the US, right?" she asked, continuing on when she saw Harding's answering nod. "If I wanted to go over there to join her, what would it take?" He hesitated, and she rushed on. "I mean, I guess I've kind of assumed that with my criminal record, they won't let me in the country, but, I don't know, I guess I wondered if you knew for sure."

Harding blinked at her, surprised that she was turning to him for the information. "Um. No, I don't know for sure, not off the top of my head," he answered gruffly. "I can find out, though, if you give me a few hours."

Jo brightened considerably. "Can you? That would be fantastic. I want to know for sure. If I can go, then I want to."

Harding cleared his throat, unnerved by the look on Jo's face. Even though he'd seen quite a bit of her since they'd reconnected earlier in the year, he still expected that hard, cold expression that had been so characteristic of her persona during her killing years. Watching her oscillate from lonely depression through to quiet hopefulness in the space of a few seconds was more of a surprise than he cared to admit. *Hard to believe it's the same woman sometimes,* he thought.

"Yeah, well, they probably won't need me for more than a few minutes in court today," he said. "Then I can make some phone calls for you, see what the go is."

"Thanks, Ken." Jo smiled across at him. The day was looking up.

CADIE SLUNG HER overnight bag over her shoulder and

tucked a few packing cases under her other arm. It was well after dark and the large house in front of her was completely unlit. She juggled her house keys in her free hand, using the light from the car's interior to help her find the one that would open the front door. Finally she had it and she made her way up the path to the imposing portal. She was a little disconcerted that the movement-sensitive security lighting hadn't come on when she'd pulled into the driveway.

I guess Naomi disconnected it last time she was here, she thought. *Either that, or something's tripped the circuit off. Maybe a power surge or a blackout or something. God, I hope the power's not still out.* A tiny shiver went through her and she drove the thought to the back of her mind as she inserted the key in the lock and opened the door.

Inside the darkened foyer, she fumbled for the light switch. Her heart sank when no illumination was forthcoming. "Fuck." The hairs on the back of her neck stood up and she fought the urge to back out of the house as quickly as she had come in. "Don't panic," she muttered. "It's just an empty, dark house. You always said you knew it like the back of your hand. Here's your chance to prove it." Her voice sounded hollow and amplified in the large foyer, but somehow she found it reassuring.

She blinked, letting her eyes adjust to the dark. Gradually she began to be able to make out shapes in the gloom. She thought hard about the layout of the foyer and reached out with her right hand. There was the small antique table, just where she had expected it to be. "Okay. Let's see if I know this place well enough to find the emergency supplies in the pantry."

Cadie moved forward slowly, using her hands as advance scouts. She made her way down the corridor, towards the kitchen, pleased to find her eyes adjusting even more as she progressed. The living room opened out on her right, and she was aware of the deep, dark space beyond the open doorway, but didn't care to look too closely. She stubbed her toe on the porcelain cat she had forgotten was sitting at the foot of the stairs, but it wasn't too long before she wrapped her hand around the doorknob of the pantry.

It was even darker inside the spacious cupboard, but Cadie thought she had a pretty good idea where to find what she was looking for. She crouched down, relieved to locate the box of emergency supplies exactly where she expected it to be.

"Okay, flashlight, flashlight, where are you?" she muttered as she dug around in the box. "Goddamn it!" The big, black torch was nowhere within touch. "Shit!" Another wave of panic set Cadie's heart racing and she felt the heavy darkness all around pressing down on her. "Get a grip, Arcadia, for God's sake." She took a deep breath and reached into the box again, forcing her brain to run through the list of what else was supposed to be in there.

"Ah," she breathed, as her hand closed around a smaller box she knew contained candles. "Now we're talking. Matches, matches, matches—yes! Matches. Thank you, Jesus."

Cadie felt almost chirpy as she struck a match and put it to the wick of a brand new candle. For the time being she didn't care about the wax dripping on the floor, or finding something to stand the candle on; she wanted light. The warm, yellow glow flickered, then grew, and Cadie slid down onto the floor, leaning her back against the open pantry door. She forced herself to breathe more evenly.

"Okay. So...this isn't so bad," she said to herself. "It's an empty, dark house. Nothing to be freaked out about." She laughed, but the sound of it echoing off the walls only weirded her out further, so she cut it off mid-chuckle. "Ugh."

A drop of melted wax fell on to the back of her hand and Cadie hissed at the sting. Pushing herself up, she went in search of a saucer to stand the candle on. The kitchen was basically clean, but there was a fine layer of dust over every horizontal surface.

I'm guessing Naomi hasn't been here since she first got back from Australia, she thought as she dripped a pool of wax into the middle of a small plate. *Can't say that surprises me.* Cadie dropped the rest of the candles on the countertop and went about setting a few more onto plates. *Might as well throw a little light on the subject.*

A few minutes later, she had three candles burning cheerily. With a little difficulty, she picked them up and made her way back along the hall to the living room. One she placed on the side table in the corridor. Cadie stood on the threshold of the spacious room, the candlelight penetrating only so far. All the furniture was draped with sheets and all she could make out were lumps and bumps amongst the silhouettes.

Might as well start here as anywhere, she reasoned as she took a step forward.

"Hello, Arcadia."

A cold shaft of fear stopped Cadie in her tracks. Only one person on the planet said her name quite that way.

Chapter Twenty-one

"I FIND THERE is sufficient evidence to commit Mr. Marco di Santo to trial on this matter," intoned the judge. "He will be remanded in custody until his next appearance on," he glanced down at his diary, "September 12. Court dismissed." He banged his gavel down and rose creakily from his chair, the entire room rising with him.

Thank Christ that's over with, Jo thought as she slumped back into her seat once the ageing magistrate had departed the room. *Guess I get to do it all again in September, but at least by then Cadie will be home, and it will be a bit easier to deal with.* She thought about the prospect of her lover seeing more graphic evidence of her own seamy past and fought down the urge to panic. *Come on, get a grip. She knows the worst by now, and she hasn't run from it, so I guess she'll deal with that as well.*

The prosecutor interrupted her thoughts. Leaning over the low wooden railing that separated his desk from the public gallery, he extended a hand, and she shook it obligingly.

"Good job, Miss Madison," he said. "I trust we can count on you again during the trial?"

Jo nodded. "I'd rather like to see him put away, Mr. Roberts, so, yes, I'll be available if you need me."

"We'll be in touch as the time approaches," he replied, dropping his papers into the battered leather briefcase in his other hand. Without another word, he clicked the case shut and exited down the center aisle of the courtroom.

"And goodbye to you, too," Jo murmured. She looked around the rapidly emptying room. Harding was nowhere to be seen, but the spectacle of two policemen flanking di Santo as they handcuffed him and led him away was worth hanging around for. He cast an evil glance in her direction and Jo flashed him the tiniest of waves.

"See you in September, you son of a bitch," she muttered under her breath.

Harding walked into the courtroom and slid into the row

behind Jo. He leaned forward and rested his forearms on the wooden back of the bench before him. Jo shifted to look at him sideways.

"You missed the decision," she said quietly.

"Yeah, well, I assumed they'd come to the right conclusion," he answered.

"They did."

Harding snorted. "Of course they did. Obvious as balls on a dog that di Santo had to go to trial. Sometimes I think we waste too much time on giving these arseholes their so-called rights."

Jo chuckled. "There speaks a man who's always been on the right side of the law," she said, smiling at the big policeman. Harding looked even more disheveled than usual. His tie was askew and sweat trickled down the side of his face. *One of these days, I swear, he's going to drop dead where he stands,* Jo thought affectionately. "What have you been up to, Detective?"

Harding wiped his brow with a rather gray-looking handkerchief he fished out of his breast pocket before he answered. He stuffed it back and looked right at her. "Running around on your behalf," he said. "The bad news is, there's no way you'll get through Immigration at their end on that passport of yours."

Mentally, Jo repeated what she'd just heard. *That passport of yours.* Was Ken Harding—the man—trying to tell her something he couldn't say, as a cop? "Bugger," she said, schooling her features into neutrality.

"I tried," he said.

Jo's pulse was all over the place, her mind working overtime. "I appreciate it, Ken. Sounds like I'm stuck."

"Yep. Nothing for it." He pulled the handkerchief and mopped his face some more.

Jo met his eyes. "I'm sure everything'll work out," she said. Maybe she was just imagining he'd dropped a hint. Harding wasn't the type to suggest anything illegal. "Want a beer, mate?" she asked.

Harding produced a rare grin, an expression that took years off his age. "Is the Pope Catholic?"

"JESUS CHRIST, NAOMI. You scared me half to death." Cadie hurriedly retrieved the sputtering candle she'd dropped. "What the hell kind of bullshit is that to pull?" A deep anger supplanted her initial fright at the thought that her ex-partner had deliberately set out to scare her.

Naomi sat as still as a rock in the sheet-draped chair across the room from the door. In her hand was the flashlight Cadie had been looking for, its light casting her face with an eerie glow that put Cadie in mind of a grotesque Halloween pumpkin lantern.

"I wasn't pulling any bullshit, Arcadia," the senator murmured. "I had the power disconnected once I realized I had no idea when you would be home. I've only been here a couple of hours myself, so I haven't had time to do anything about it."

Cadie put the righted candle on the nearest flat surface and set about lighting a few more, placing them around the room. "You could have said something when I first got here, instead of sitting there like some kind of malevolent toad." Adrenalin still coursing through her system, she slammed a candle down hard, endangering the plate it was balanced on. *Fuck her.*

"I was asleep," Naomi said calmly. "I'm sorry if I startled you."

Asleep, my ass. I made enough noise coming in here to wake the dead. Cadie whirled on her. "Startled me? Jesus, Naomi. How would you have felt if it had been the other way around?" She slumped down into one of the other armchairs and ran her hand through her hair in exasperation. Her heart was still pounding like a son of a bitch. "Jesus."

A low laugh came from across the room. Cadie would have almost described the sound as creepy if she hadn't been trying desperately hard to minimize the panic Naomi's stunt had generated.

"You can't honestly say you weren't expecting me to show up," Naomi said softly. "You're my partner, this is our house, and I knew you would come here eventually."

Cadie looked at her sharply. Naomi had switched the flashlight off, now that the room was at least semi-adequately lit by candles.

"How *did* you know I would be coming here tonight? I mean, I know that you were informed when I landed in the country, but I only really decided this morning that I would be driving down today. Besides, aren't you supposed to be in the Senate?"

Naomi shrugged. "I'm sure the world will keep turning without me for a few days," she replied mildly. "You may find this hard to believe, but I do still have friends in Madison. Friends who know how badly I want to patch things up with you and who did me the favor of letting me know your movements."

Cadie was appalled. "You've had someone watching Mom and Dad's house?" she asked, incredulous. Naomi chose not to reply, but a mean smile creased her face. "Unbelievable," Cadie exclaimed. "I'd heard you were pretty much losing it, Naomi, but now I'm starting to actually believe it."

The senator showed few signs of emotion, but her hands balled into fists on the arms of the chair in which she was sitting. "I don't know what you expected me to do. You don't accept my phone calls, you don't reply to my emails, and you certainly don't initiate any contact with me, let alone have the courtesy to tell me when you intend coming to my home."

Cadie snorted. "*Your* home? A couple of minutes ago it was *our* home."

"What do you want from me, Cadie?" Naomi snarled. "I want to talk to you. I doubted you would meet with me voluntarily, so I made sure that we would cross paths. You can't blame me for that."

"And you left the power disconnected for effect, I suppose?" Cadie snapped back. "Thought it might be amusing?"

"Surprise," Naomi said, letting another wild grin transform the anger on her face to something completely different.

For the second time in a few minutes, Cadie felt a tendril of fear curl its way around her intestines. This was different, though. It wasn't the shock, this time. This time it was the cold, stark knowledge that her ex-partner was not someone with whom she wanted to tangle. *Not now, and not ever again.*

Cadie said nothing, but sat back in her chair and watched the senator warily. *One thing's for sure, she's not going to let me wander around packing up my stuff.* She crossed her legs and folded her arms, preferring to let Naomi make the next move. *Instinct tells me I should walk out now and drive back to Madison, but somehow I don't think she's going to let me go quite that easily.*

"I was thinking that once we sort all this out between us, we should redecorate the house," Naomi said contemplatively, looking around as if seeing the place for the first time. "It's been about five years since we did this room, hasn't it? What do you think, darling?"

I think you're nuts. "Mom and Dad are expecting me to call, or they're going to worry," Cadie said. "Or have you disconnected the phone as well?"

"Feel free." Naomi gestured at the telephone on a nearby coffee table. "But I don't think there's much point in making a fuss, do you? I'm sure you don't want them rushing down the highway for no reason." She smiled again. "After all, you're perfectly safe with me."

THE TWO FORLORN figures leaning on the bar looked like some kind of bizarre comedy double act. Both leaned with their chins on one hand. Both held a half-drunk glass of something smooth and amber in the other hand. Both gazed ahead soulfully, blinking mindlessly at their own reflections in the mirror that ran the length of the hotel bar. And both sighed intermittently between sips. It wasn't late, particularly, but the day's events were catching up with both of them.

"The depressing thing is, I think I'm actually starting to sober up," Jo said mournfully.

Harding sighed loudly. "Me too. So what are you gonna do now? Head back up north?"

Jo gave a noncommittal shrug. "I guess so. Sure don't want to stay here more than I have to."

Harding gestured at the bartender, and the man refilled his shot glass. "You worried about that cute little sheila of yours going back to her girlfriend?"

Piercing blue eyes suddenly regained their focus and pinned him to the closest wall. "No, Harding, m'not worried about that," Jo said coolly. Was she? *Fuck sake, of course not. And quit breaking Ken's balls.*

"You're a big mushball," Ken muttered, a half-smile playing across his lips. "Take it easy, okay? I was only asking."

"Yeah, I know. Sorry. The thought of that bitch makes me want to resurrect that nice little garrote of mine." An evil twinkle winked back at Harding and reminded him who he was sitting next to.

"I'm sorry I didn't get to meet her," he sniggered.

"You didn't miss much. Try to imagine a cane toad, only with less personality."

"*Bleugh.* No thanks."

Jo leaned her elbow back on the bar. "I had a fabulous dream about her the other night," she said.

Harding looked at the beautiful woman out of the corner of his eye. "You're dreaming about your girlfriend's girlfriend? Kinky."

Jo slapped him across the shoulder. "Not that kind of dream, you old pervert," she chided him. "No, we were all on this beach up in the islands. Can't figure out which one. Anyway, Naomi was giving Cadie grief about something and I was walking towards them, and I was dragging an anchor by its chain. Naomi said something that really pissed me off—can't remember what—and I started swinging the anchor round and round above my head." Ken laughed, because he could see where this was going. "Shut up. I let it go and it sailed through the air in slow motion and—splat!—it nailed the bitch on the back of the head and shoved her face down in the sand. Like Wile E. Coyote and that damn rock." She smiled dreamily at the memory. "And the best thing was the sound," she continued. "It was like when you take a swing at a cane toad with a seven-iron."

This time Ken almost choked on a mouthful of scotch, he laughed so hard. "That's the second time you've mentioned cane toads in the last 10 minutes," he said. "Is this some kind of fetish you only develop when you're half-cut?"

"Not a fetish," Jo mumbled. "S'just the image I get when I think of that bitch."

"Fair enough."

"You gonna be all right to get home, mate?" Jo asked as she clambered off her barstool. "I think I'm about done for the night."

"Yeah, I'll be right. I'll whistle up a patrol car. They can drop me off."

She looked at the big man affectionately. "The perks of rank, eh?"

"Yeah, something like that. M'gonna finish my drink first, though."

"Fair enough." Jo felt a wash of gratitude for the older man. Whatever his motivations, Harding had proven himself to be a good friend. On impulse she leaned forward and dropped a kiss on his florid cheek. "Thanks for everything, Ken," she murmured before she turned on her heel and exited the bar, heading for her room.

Harding sat stunned for a few seconds before he lifted a hand and touched the spot she had kissed with nerveless fingers.

"I'll be damned," he muttered. "She kissed me." He looked down at the almost empty glass in front of him. "That calls for a drink."

JO WAS DREAMING again. The images were jumbled and nonsensical but they were pleasant enough, thankfully. Somewhere in the dreamscape a phone was ringing, loudly and persistently. Ringing and ringing and ringing.

Ugh. She reached out blindly and fumbled for the phone. "Yeah, hello," she grumbled.

"Is that Jo Madison?"

Female. American. Not Cadie. Can only be one of two choices and I'd recognize a cane toad if I heard one.

"Hello, Mrs. Jones. Yes, this is Jo." A sliver of fear washed through her. *Why would Cadie's mother be calling me?* "What's wrong? Is Cadie all right?" Panic tasted bad, she remembered.

"Yes, yes, she's fine," Cadie's mother replied hastily. "At least...well, at least, we think she is. I'm actually calling to see what you think."

Confused and still befuddled by sleep, Jo sat on the edge of the bed and rubbed her face with her free hand. *Come on, Madison, get your brain working.* "Okay," she said.

"Cadie called us a few hours ago. She's at the Chicago house."

"Okay."

"So is Naomi."

A wave of adrenalin cut through the residue of fatigue and hangover. "Cadie told you that?"

"Oh yes," Helena said. "She also said everything was fine and that she didn't need us to drive down to be with her."

Jo felt sick. She could imagine the intimidating figure of the senator listening in on that call. *Don't panic her mother, Jo. No matter what you're feeling.* "And you don't believe her?" she asked levelly.

There was a pause on the other end of the phone. "Well, she sounded very tense. I don't think she was happy about things at all."

I bet. Jo's heart sank and the hairs on the back of her neck stood up. On the one hand, her first instinct was to send in the local reinforcements as quickly as possible. *Especially as, even if I could get on a plane right now, I won't be there for another 24 hours.* On the other hand, she knew Cadie would consider that she was perfectly capable of handling Naomi without any interference from her parents. *Or me, for that matter.* She bounced up off the bed and began pacing. *On the third hand, you know damn well that bitch will do almost anything to get Cadie back.*

"I'm not really sure what to tell you, Mrs. Jones," Jo said quietly, forcing her own uneasiness down deep, where she hoped it wouldn't show. "I think if Cadie had needed you there, she would have found a way to tell you exactly that. It could be that this will be a good opportunity for them to finally tie up all the loose ends." *Right. And it could be a good opportunity for Naomi to start getting nasty when she finally realizes Cadie won't be staying.*

The older woman sighed. "Yes, I suppose you're right. I keep thinking of all the stories Cadie has been telling us about Naomi's behavior lately."

Jo had a quick flash of Naomi's hand pulled back to strike Cadie, when they were quarrelling in the Hamilton Island police watch-house. "Yes, I know what you mean," she murmured. "I wish I was there." *M'going. I don't care what it takes anymore. But how?*

"I wish you were, too," Cadie's mother said. "Cadie's told me a lot about...well, about how you make her feel safe." Jo felt herself blush. "Somehow, I don't think Naomi ever made Cadie feel that."

In a cold flash, what had been idle conjecture in Jo's mind suddenly took shape as a plan. An odd calm settled over her instantly, and she sat back down on the bed. "Look, how about this as a compromise," she said. "Give me the address of the Chicago house and I'll get there as soon as I can. I was thinking of flying over to surprise Cadie, anyway. If I come right away, she'll only have to deal with Naomi for another day. Hopefully, she'll be fine." *Hopefully.*

"Thank you, Jo." The relief in Helena Jones' voice was obvious. "It's always a fine line between letting your children make their own mistakes and keeping them too sheltered from the world. Part of me wants to race down that highway right now. But if everything's fine, Cadie won't thank us for interfering. All the same, we're worried for her."

Jo heard a world of pain and memories in that statement, and she remembered the grief in Cadie's eyes as she had told Jo about the death of her older brother, Sebastian. *No wonder her mother's torn about this,* she thought. *Keep it calm and normal.*

"It's okay," she murmured, thinking that perhaps she might get to like Cadie's mother, very much. She took down the address Helena Jones gave.

"Cadie may even be back here by the time you arrive in Chicago," Helena said. "But you'll be on the plane before I can let you know for sure."

"Yeah, I know," Jo replied. "That's okay." *Of course, I still have to run a few gauntlets before I get there, but why burden her with the details?*

"Well, it will be lovely to finally get to meet you," said Helena, oblivious to the dark thoughts running through the mind of her daughter's lover. "I think Cadie's missing you, really quite badly."

Jo smiled to herself. "Well, that's mutual," she replied. "Thanks for calling, Mrs. Jones. And I'll see you in a couple of days, hopefully."

"Yes, hopefully. Goodbye, Jo. Safe travels."

Jo sat for several minutes after she hung up, her head bowed, her hands clasped in front of her, elbows on her knees. She knew there was now only one way of getting herself to the

US in short order. *And that means resurrecting an old friend,* she thought grimly. *And finding one or two others as well. Somewhere in this goddamned city.*

Calmly, she pulled on clothes and gathered together her money and her attitude. By the time the tall, black-clad, icechip-eyed figure strode out of the door, she was, more or less, her old self.

Time to go a-hunting.

Chapter Twenty-two

IT HAD BEEN a very long night. Cadie rubbed her eyes wearily as she tried to focus on the vase she was wrapping in newspaper. She and Naomi had been hammering away at the same issues, all night long, talking around and around the fact that Cadie wasn't coming back to the senator and that was that. Naomi's emotions had ranged from depression to fury and back again, cycling several times through the night. The only constant had been the glass of bourbon Naomi had kept by her side. The alcohol had made her by turns aggressive and blurry, but nothing had seemed to penetrate Naomi's unwavering belief that Jo was the cause of all the world's troubles and that eventually Cadie would see reason and come home for good.

Eventually, the politician had passed out in the same armchair in which Cadie had found her. Cadie's first thought had been to forget about salvaging her belongings and get the hell back to Madison. But then fatigue, combined with a determination not to be intimidated by the senator's antics, had convinced her to stick it out.

Why the hell should I let her bully me out of the things that are rightfully mine, she had thought, setting her chin even as she watched the older woman snoring where she was slumped. *God damn her.*

And so Cadie had spent the few hours since dawn scurrying about the house, collecting personal documents, including the all-important papers relating to her agency. She had managed to get the most important things out and into her car and now was trying to get a second load of things with sentimental value together before Naomi came to.

Cadie felt anxious and exhausted, not least because the one chance she'd had to call Jo, there had been no reply from either her lover's cell phone or the hotel room. It was now well into the wee hours of Tuesday morning, Sydney time, but she resolved to try the numbers again once she had loaded some more of her belongings into the car. *I wonder where she is.*

She finished filling one of the packing boxes and carried it to the front door. Once outside, she breathed in the sweet, crisp spring air of early morning. *Maybe I'm being too stubborn for my own good,* she thought as she began the walk to her car. *Maybe I should get out of here now while I have the chance.* Before she could follow that train of thought to its logical conclusion, she rounded the large bushes that shielded the driveway from the house and came to an abrupt halt.

Leaning against her car were two large men in black suits. One was reading a newspaper, the other was looking directly at her. She recognized the goons as members of the security team Naomi regularly used when she was campaigning.

"Morning, Miss Jones," said the man watching her. His colleague folded his newspaper into neat sections and tucked it under his arm. "Going somewhere?"

Shit. "If I said yes, would you let me?" Cadie asked.

The goon shrugged. "You know how it is, Miss Jones. We're here to make sure you and the senator have all the privacy you need."

Right. "All I want to do right now, Mr., um, Smith, isn't it?" The goon grinned and nodded at her. "All I want to do now, Mr. Smith, is put this box in that car." Cadie nodded in the direction of their seat. "Would that be all right by you, do you think?" The sarcasm fairly oozed from every word, and she knew it probably wasn't the smartest attitude to take, but now she was really pissed—and somewhat intimidated—but Cadie was goddamned if she was going to let them see that.

"Certainly, Miss," Smith said agreeably. He stood upright and watched as Cadie unlocked the trunk and dropped the box inside. She slammed the lid shut and walked back around to where the two bodyguards stood.

"You won't mind if I hang on to these," Cadie said, dangling the car keys in front of them as she began to walk past the men back towards the house.

"Not at all, Miss."

"Fuck you," Cadie muttered as she climbed the driveway. *Well, that's great. A drunken bitch in the house and a pair of hit men in the yard. How much worse can this get?*

She walked back inside, following the trail of loud and destructive sounds into the kitchen. Naomi had come to with a vengeance and was throwing pots and pans around in a fit of temper. The stocky woman was bouncing off the counters and cupboards like an irate pinball, cursing a blue streak.

It just got worse.

THE WIND WHIPPED around the dark figure as she strode silently along the grimy sidewalks of King's Cross. Even though it was after 3 a.m. there were still people on the streets, as the dance clubs and strip joints began spewing their drunken, happy clientele. There was, however, something about the woman that made them all get out of her way. Those that were too inebriated to notice were pulled out of her way by their more sober, aware friends.

Jo's demeanor was every bit that of someone who ruled the streets and knew it. Cold, hard, pale blue eyes took in her environment, old landmarks tweaking her memories and her sense of direction. She glared balefully at anyone unfortunate enough to step across her path. And for the first time in over five years, she felt naked without her weapons.

The eastern end of the nightclub district led into an even seedier part of town. Warehouses and adult entertainment dominated the scene here and the eyes that met hers were less inclined to be intimidated. More than one pair flashed startled recognition, but Jo ignored them all as she continued to search for her target.

Finally, one alleyway in particular caught her attention and she ducked into it, pacing down its length until she came to a darkened doorway. It was the quintessential gangster movie scene, and Jo would have smiled at the irony if she hadn't felt quite so nauseous. Instead she pounded twice on the heavy door, unsurprised when the tiny sliding peephole at eye level snapped open almost instantaneously.

Jo said nothing, but fixed the beady eyes peering out at her with an intense stare.

"Holy fuck!" came the hoarse greeting and the sliding panel slammed shut again.

"Open the door, Vincent," Jo growled, letting her voice take on its most menacing timbre.

"I'm not in that business anymore, okay?" came the muffled and vaguely tremulous response.

Why do I find that hard to believe? Jo wondered. "Open the door, before I break it down and wring your silly neck," she said aloud.

There was a loud groan and another curse from behind the door and an obvious moment of hesitation in which Jo thought she was actually going to have to break down the door. But then she heard a sigh and a series of bolts being thrown.

The door swung open wide enough for her to slide through and it slammed behind her quickly.

"Heard you were in town. Saw you on the telly. Didn't

expect to hear from you, though." The shadowy figure behind the door paused as if weighing up his words. "Not since you turned rat."

Jo's long, strong fingers were around his neck and she had him slammed against the wall almost before the word was out of his mouth. She leaned close, ignoring his bad breath and oily skin, as she squeezed his throat steadily.

"You're a fine one to be calling someone rat," she snarled. "They don't call you Vincent the Weasel for nothing."

The wizened little man ignored her words. It certainly wasn't the first time he'd ever been insulted, or threatened. His hands grappled with hers, trying to break her grip.

"You're crazy for showing up on the streets, Madison," he gasped. "They're out for your hide, you know that, right?" His eyes widened as realization dawned. "Jesus Christ, how did you get here? Tell me you didn't just walk down here like some fucking tourist?" Jo's feral grin answered that question for him. "Fuck, Madison, if they saw you, they'll come right here to find you. Jesus!" Sweat broke out on his forehead.

"Then you'd better get to work, hadn't you?" Jo muttered. "Because the quicker you finish what I want done, the sooner I'll be out of your way." She let go of him. His feet hit the ground and he slumped against the wall, rubbing his neck ruefully.

"I told you, I don't— " He stopped, catching her glare and deciding against any further prevarication. "What do you need?

"Passport, including a visa waiver stamp for the US, driver's license, and a birth certificate just to be sure." Back in her criminal days she'd had a set of fake documents—*hell, more than one set*—but she had given them up when she'd turned herself in to the police. She pointed a finger at him. "And nothing shoddy, Vincent. Your best work."

He grinned, regaining some of his confidence. "S'gonna cost ya, Madison."

"Don't worry about that," she snapped. "Get the work done the way I want it and this is yours." Jo pulled a hefty roll of notes out of an inside pocket in her coat, holding it long enough for him to absorb its size. She tucked it back out of sight and lifted an elegant dark brow at the man. "Fair enough?"

"Fair enough," he agreed. "When do you need them by?"

Jo glanced at her watch. "You've got five hours," she replied grimly.

"You're not serious?"

Jo nailed him with her most intense and intimidating glare. "Do I look like someone who's joking?"

"Okay, okay. Let me get my shit together here."

They moved through to a dingy-looking room at the end of the passage. Yellowed wallpaper peeled from walls stained with damp and the paintwork was a tapestry of greasy fingerprints. Jo sniffed, wrinkling her nose at the dank and slightly rotten smell. Nothing much had changed here, at least. *Still the same grubby little rodent he always was*, she thought.

The man in question came back into the room, carrying a large camera and tripod, as well as a canvas bag, which he dumped on the wooden table in the middle of the room.

"Need to take your picture," he grunted as he carefully set the photographic equipment down. He indicated the far wall, which, although hardly clean, was at least free of dogs playing pool and not so tasteful nude pin-ups.

Jo sat down on a battered wooden chair, trying not to think about her surroundings or what she was doing. *Doesn't pay to think, Jo-Jo. Not too much. Not right now.* She forced down a lump of panic that threatened to send her running out on the streets. *Wish I could think of another way of doing this.*

It wasn't that she was scared of getting caught, Jo realized. She had spent many years traveling all over Australia, and the world, for that matter, as Tony's bodyguard, and she had never done it under her own name. *It would scare Joe Public silly to know how easy it is,* she thought wryly as she watched Vincent setting up his gear.

No, what was freaking her out, first and foremost, was what Cadie was going through. Those possibilities rattled through her brain at a rate of knots. And then there was what she might have to do once she arrived in Chicago. *And what that might do to me. And her. Hell, us.*

"Are you gonna smile for the camera, or are ya gonna sit there scowlin'," Vincent said, chancing his luck now that he was out of arm's reach of the tall woman.

"Take the fucking picture," Jo muttered.

The counterfeiter didn't waste any more time, taking her picture as soon as she turned square-on to the camera. He immediately began pulling blank passport templates, licenses and certificates out of the canvas bag. Jo stayed where she was, content to grab what rest she could for the time being. *God knows, I'm not gonna get much in the way of sleep for a while.*

"You gonna breathe down my neck, or give me some room to move?" Vincent asked testily, throwing a glance her way as he bent over his work.

Jo crossed her legs at the ankles and clasped her hands in her lap. "You've just finished telling me how dangerous it is for me out there on the streets. Why would I go out there if I don't need to?" she replied, letting a small, cold smile play across her lips. "Besides, I think you work better with supervision." It had occurred to her that this particular weasel could easily turn rat for the right price.

Vincent glared at her for a few long seconds, then shrugged, turning back to the long night's work he had ahead of him. "Suit yourself, Madison."

"Thanks. I will."

"IDIOT," CADIE MUTTERED. "What the hell was I thinking?" She watched Naomi warily as the temper tantrum blew over, and the senator finally came to rest, leaning against the countertop. *I should have known better than to think I could get away with coming down here and quietly cleaning my stuff out. I should have come down here with three attorneys, a bodyguard, Mom and Dad, and an attack dog. And Jo, for good measure. Goddamn it.*

"I guess it's pointless, me asking what all that was about?" she said quietly.

Naomi sighed heavily and turned to face her. "I wanted some breakfast, but there's nothing here to eat," she said grumpily.

Cadie folded her arms and leaned against the doorjamb. "You didn't really think this all the way through, did you, Naomi? I guess you figured that by now I'd be happily back in your life and you could leave it to me to work out how to feed you."

Naomi looked unhappy. *Actually, she looks hung over,* Cadie thought.

"You're right, I didn't really think about it," the politician admitted, rather surprisingly. "I thought that once I had you away from that...from Jo...then I could convince you to stay." She paused, running a hand through her closely-cropped salt and pepper hair. "I didn't really know what else to do, to be honest."

Cadie looked at her suspiciously, not quite believing the vulnerable act so hard on the heels of her ex-partner's temper tantrum.

"It's true," Naomi said, seeing the look of disbelief on Cadie's face. "You left me there at Sydney Airport, looking like an idiot in front of the press, and since then you've refused to talk to me. So what choice did I have?" She broke out what Cadie was sure was supposed to be a charming smile, but it felt nothing but chilling. "All I want is a chance to show you that we can fix our relationship, and that it's worth trying."

"Naomi, you have two goons out there stopping me from leaving. You cut off the power to the house and deliberately scared the shit out of me. But somehow you expect me to believe that you didn't really have a plan for this little confinement you've got going here?" Cadie snorted and pushed herself off the doorframe. *Somewhere in here I know there's got to be coffee,* she decided. *And God knows I need one.*

"What exactly do you think is going to happen now?" She opened up the one cupboard Naomi hadn't ransacked and found the coffee. "Let's get real, shall we?" She pulled down two mugs and began putting together beverages for herself and her ex-partner. "You're acting like a stalker, not someone who's trying to win me over. Do you really think you'd get away with hurting me, or kidnapping me, or whatever it is you think is going to happen if I don't agree to come back willingly?"

"I'm not going to do either of those things," Naomi replied quietly.

"Then why the reinforcements out in the driveway?" Cadie asked as she scooped teaspoonfuls of coffee into the cups. The sudden presence of Naomi close behind her made the hairs on the back of her neck stand on end, but before she could move away, the senator had a strong arm wrapped around her waist.

"I wanted some time alone with you, with no interruptions," Naomi whispered, her breath hot and damp on the back of Cadie's neck. "Is that so much to ask after 12 years of marriage? Don't you think that history demands that we at least talk?"

"Let go of me," Cadie answered hoarsely, her hands frozen, wrapped around the coffee mugs.

"Come on, Cadie, give me a break here," Naomi replied, not releasing Cadie for even a second. "Don't you remember how good this used to be between us? I used to be able to do this ..." She leaned forward and kissed the nape of Cadie's neck. "And we'd spend hours in heaven, enjoying each other."

Cadie swallowed. She did indeed remember how it had been, but the shivers of revulsion radiating out from the spot Naomi had kissed signaled those days were long gone. "I'm not that naïve young woman anymore, Naomi, and you're certainly not the same woman I married 12 years ago."

Naomi moved even closer. "Give us a chance. How can you walk away without giving us a chance? Don't you miss this?" She kissed the same spot again and Cadie found herself hard-pressed not to laugh outright.

"Don't flatter yourself," she said, trying to keep her voice steady. "You have a very selective memory, Naomi. Things have been less than ideal between us for a very long time. Including the sex. Don't kid yourself that you can do anything for me sexually that could change my mind about leaving you."

Cadie felt the mood change very quickly as Naomi's grip tightened around her waist. The sudden shift from sweet and vulnerable to menace was breathtaking and palpable. *Damn, she's all over the place. What the hell is coming next?*

"Perhaps that Australian bitch has turned you on to some weird stuff," Naomi growled, her mouth close to Cadie's left ear. Her left hand began roaming down the outside of Cadie's jeans-clad thigh. "Well, don't you worry. I can match anything that whore did to you. I can make you feel better than she ever could."

"Naomi, let go of me," Cadie urged one more time. "Please. I don't want to hurt you."

The senator laughed harshly and pressed Cadie hard up against the edge of the counter. It was the last straw. Cadie grabbed the closest coffee mug and swung it back over her shoulder, slamming it into Naomi's nose and forehead.

"Argh!" Naomi reeled backwards, releasing Cadie to cover her face with her hands. "God damn you! Jesus!"

Cadie swung around and stepped out of arm's reach of the politician. "I asked you to let go of me, Naomi," she said grimly, watching a dribble of blood drip through her ex-partner's fingers. "You lost the right to touch me like that a long time ago."

"Fuck you," Naomi snarled. "I didn't lose anything. You gave it away. To that criminal. You couldn't wait to give yourself to that bitch, could you?"

Cadie's temper, already frayed by being manhandled, bubbled past its boiling point. "No!" she shouted. "You lost that right a long time before that. That's what I've been trying to tell you for months. You lost that right when you stopped treating me like a partner and started treating me like a secretary. You lost that right when you started abusing drugs and alcohol."

With every word and increase in her anger, Cadie stepped forward until she was right up in Naomi's face.

"You lost that right when you started screwing every bimbo that would bat her eyes at you. I'm nothing but a good-luck charm to you. Don't you—" she jabbed Naomi in the chest with an angry finger "—*dare* talk to me about the rights and wrongs of our god*damned* relationship."

Cadie was so blindsided by the strength of her own emotions, she didn't see the blow coming. The back of the senator's hand caught her across the cheek, hard enough to leave a stinging red mark. Hard enough to send her tumbling to the kitchen floor.

Naomi laughed coldly and shook out her hand as she watched Cadie pick herself up. "You're never going to convince me that Jo Madison isn't the cause of all this trouble, Arcadia," she said bluntly. "And there's that slutty little disposition of yours."

Cadie pulled herself up using the kitchen counter. *I can't believe I didn't see that coming. I can't believe I'm still here, putting up with this shit. Well, no more. That's it. Victim impersonation now over.* She turned to face Naomi, who still smirked with self-satisfaction despite the blood oozing from the bridge of her nose.

Cadie walked towards the phone extension on the wall and picked up the receiver, quickly dialing 911. "I should have done this a long time ago."

Chapter Twenty-three

JO SLID HER carry-on bag into the overhead bin and closed the lid. She glanced around the business-class cabin at her fellow passengers. Not surprisingly, the 747 was packed to the rafters and she congratulated herself again for deciding to spend the extra money on an upgrade. *Being packed into coach would not be my idea of fun right now.*

She was in dire need of sleep. After spending the rest of the night watching Vincent do his thing, Jo had cabbed it back to the hotel to pack, check out and undergo a quick change of clothes. The deadly vision in black had been replaced by a typical tourist, dressed in t-shirt, jeans and sneakers. Her hair was pulled back in a loose ponytail and Jo looked a far cry from the intimidating presence she had embodied in Vincent's dingy living room.

Jo eased her long frame into the seat, giving a polite nod to the man next to her. People were still boarding the plane, forming a long and somewhat disgruntled queue down the aisle as flight attendants moved around trying to get everyone seated. Jo was content to let the masses do their thing before she tried to get herself organized for the leg to Los Angeles.

You can always tell the ones who've never been on an international flight before, she mused, as she watched the faces of the boarding passengers. *They always look so stunned to see the amount of room they have to live in for the next 14 hours.* She stifled a grin and pulled out the legrest, stretching out and settling in.

Sticking a pillow behind her head, she closed her eyes, letting the last few hours catch up with her. She had money, false documents that had so far made getting on the plane a piece of cake, and tickets all the way through to Chicago. All she had to do now was survive Customs and Immigration in LA, avoid any law enforcement entanglements and she would soon be wherever Cadie was.

Hopefully in time to help, she thought as a yawn blocked out all other considerations. *Hopefully...*

CADIE FELT SOMETHING cold and hard press against the back of her neck. At the same time, a hand reached over her shoulder and hung up the phone.

"You're not going to do that," came the low snarl by her ear.

Cadie's blood ran cold. There was no mistaking the feel of the gun's muzzle at the base of her skull. She could smell its metallic tang. Nerveless fingers allowed Naomi to take the phone away and replace it on its rocker.

"You can't be serious, Naomi," Cadie muttered, her mouth dry.

"About hurting you? Probably not," Naomi agreed. "But then, you can never be sure, can you?"

"Not anymore, no," Cadie replied. *Stupid, Cadie, real stupid.* Turning down her father's offer to come with her was looking more and more rash as the minutes ticked by. *Then again, maybe she's nuts enough to have pulled a gun on both of us.*

Naomi yanked her backwards and pushed her down the hallway and into the lounge. "Sit down," she said harshly, shoving Cadie into one of the big leather armchairs. She returned to the chair in which Cadie had first found her, resting the gun across her lap.

"So, now what?" Cadie asked. "You've lost your mind, you know that, right?"

"Shut up!" Naomi shouted then rubbed her eyes roughly with the hand that wasn't gripping the pistol. Cadie could see a fine beading of sweat on the senator's upper lip. "Shut up and give me a chance to think."

She doesn't have the faintest clue what she's doing, Cadie realized. *She thought it would be all over by now – that I'd've agreed to come back to her.* It seemed ludicrous to Cadie that a sane adult could even think that was a possibility. *I've had enough of this.* With a decisive movement, Cadie pushed herself up out of the chair and crossed the room cautiously. "Give me the gun, Naomi," she said softly, her hand outstretched. Immediately the barrel swung towards her and she stopped dead in her tracks.

"Get away from me," Naomi said, her voice breaking on the last word. "Get back."

"You're not going to shoot me," Cadie said, her tone calm, confident and firm. She didn't move any closer, however, all too aware of the muzzle of the gun as it trembled in Naomi's shaking hand. "You didn't come here with any intention of shooting me, Naomi. Let's put the gun away and talk some more."

"There isn't any more to say." Naomi's eyes were wild, flicking from side to side. "You've made it clear that nothing's going to change your mind. So sit down and shut *up*! Let me *THINK*!"

Cadie ignored the thundering request and instead took another step forward. She refused to let herself believe that Naomi would pull that trigger. Instead the politician did the unexpected, swinging the gun barrel around and pressing it against her own temple.

"Stop, Cadie," Naomi whispered as she stared at her former lover. "Stop, or I swear, I will do it."

Cadie sucked a breath in so sharply she felt her ribs twinge. "Come on, Naomi. Don't do this."

"Sit. Down."

"Okay, okay." Cadie backed up slowly, her hands raised in a supplicating gesture. When she felt the chair against the back of her knees, she sat down. Naomi pressed the muzzle harder against her temple and Cadie could see the metal digging into her skin. She winced, at a loss as to what to do. This was a side of Naomi she had never seen before, and while her instincts told her it was another bluff, a nagging doubt pounded away in the back of her brain.

I can't risk that she's bluffing. As many times as Cadie had wished Naomi out of her life over the past few months, she didn't want the woman dead. She didn't even want the woman hurt, if she could avoid it. *And if she is going to hurt herself, I really don't want to watch it happen.* Cadie took in the wild-eyed woman in front of her, seeing the first signs of despair, rather than anger, in the older woman's gestures and expressions. *Somehow I get the feeling I'm finally seeing how she really feels about all this.* Her heart sank. How was she ever going to get out of here?

MAYBE I SHOULD have had Vincent make me up a fake US passport while he was at it, Jo thought ruefully as she watched the queue of American citizens moving steadily forward. *Nah, I'd never get away with the accent.*

The line she was in, packed with non-Americans, crawled forward another foot as it snaked through a series of roped-off twists and turns that led to Passport Control.

Half as many Immigration officers were serving twice as many non-citizens, she noted. *Why does this not surprise me? Ah, the privileges of citizenship.* She smiled wryly to herself as tensions continued to climb around her. *Grumbling in three languages—what a waste of energy.* Jo preferred to keep herself quiet and self-contained, knowing that the biggest test of her false documents was about to start. *In fact, has already started,* she realized as she looked around, noting the extra Immigration officers standing at the periphery of the crowd, watching the passengers. *And probably won't stop until we're out of the arrivals hall at least. Stay cool, Madison.*

Finally she found herself in front of an Immigration officer, handing over her passport and smiling at the man's weary greeting. "G'day," she said.

The man flicked through the pages of the passport until he found what he was looking for—the departure and visa waiver stamps that told him Jo was a legitimate visitor. *Like I'd be standing here waiting for him to catch me if I didn't have those.*

"What's the purpose of your visit to the US, Miss, er, Markson?" the officer asked, flicking his eyes from her picture in the front of the passport up to her face.

Jo shrugged. "I've got friends in Chicago. I'm paying them a visit," she answered casually. "Haven't seen them in a couple of years."

"How long will you be staying?"

"About three weeks," Jo replied.

He turned to his computer screen and studied it for a few seconds before he typed in a few characters. He tucked Jo's immigration cards back into the passport and handed them back to her.

"Thanks. Have a good day," he said, his thoughts already turned towards the next person in the queue.

"Thanks. You too," Jo murmured as she took the passport from him and picked her bag up. She moved out into the main corridor and turned right, following the signs to the baggage claim and yet another long line of people.

"One Immigration officer down, seven thousand to go."

SEVEN HOURS LATER, Jo walked along the concourse of Terminal C of Chicago's O'Hare airport, her backpack slung over her right shoulder. She had never been to the Windy City before, though she'd seen her fair share of LA and New York. *Impressive,* she thought as she followed the crowd towards the center of the long, high-ceilinged building. Shops and boutiques, food stores and newsstands lined the walkways and Jo shunned the moving pathways, preferring to make her way under her own steam.

Jo had changed her clothing before landing in Chicago, happy to shrug off the t-shirt she had worn for the past 24 hours. She had swapped it for a long-sleeved cotton shirt that could've used an iron, but she was just grateful to be in something clean. Her stomach growled as she strode along the concourse, and she contemplated the various cuisines on offer. She stopped outside a hamburger joint, smiling wryly at the all too familiar menu and atmosphere.

The faces and accents may be different, but the junk food remains the same, she thought, hesitating about joining the hungry masses queued up in front of the cash registers. She glanced down at her watch and tried to reconcile the time of day with the fatigue gnawing at the edges of her consciousness. *Screw it. I can eat later,* she decided and rejoined the flow of commuters hurrying for the escalators. *I want to get to Cadie.*

Two minutes later, she was leaning on the rail of a moving sidewalk, gazing up at the tendrils of twisted, colored neon lights that spanned the ceiling of the long tunnel between the two terminals. Tinkling music followed the pattern of lights and provided a backdrop to the automated warning messages that piped up as she approached the end of each stretch of moving walkway. It was weirdly soothing, in a tacky, flashy kind of way.

Any other time, I'd find this pretty, Jo contemplated as she waited to reach the end of the long tunnel. *Right now, it's flat-out bizarre.* She shook her head abruptly, trying to disperse a creeping sense of disorientation. It didn't work, but she didn't have a chance to think twice about it before she needed to pick up her carry-on bag and step off the walkway.

Another climb up a long, steep escalator and Jo was confronted by another busy concourse...and a dinosaur skeleton. It caught her flat-footed, and for several seconds she stood, staring. "I've been through some bizarre wormhole and ended up in the British Museum by mistake," she muttered. "This week is getting weirder and weirder, I swear."

She followed the signs to the baggage claim and waited patiently by the carousel. She cast her eyes about, taking in the security staff dotted about the large room. Jo had enough experience to know that she couldn't relax yet. *Not until I'm out of this airport.* It occurred to her that she might not be heading into fair weather, even beyond the limits of the airport precinct. A flash of concern for Cadie knotted her guts. *Worry about that when you get there, Madison.*

Her leather bag appeared from the bowels of wherever the luggage was processed and she quickly hooked it, hefting it clear of the others. She gave the rental car booths a quick glance, but dismissed them without too much thought, reasoning that it was a lot less hassle to find herself a cab.

Easier said than done, she thought as she caught sight of the long line waiting at the taxi stand. "Damn it."

A red-hatted Skycap appeared at her elbow. "Anything I can help you with, ma'am? Maybe carry your bags for you?"

Jo looked at him, noting that he was barely old enough to shave, if he was a day. But he obviously knew what he was doing, as he had spotted her hesitation and decided she was an easy mark.

"Can you find me a cab I don't have to line up for?" she asked, raising a dark eyebrow as he broke into the cheekiest of grins.

"I can probably go one better than that," he said confidently, reaching for a cell phone clipped to his hip. "Give me a minute?"

Jo nodded, aware that she was probably about to be fleeced, but also willing to spend a little more if it meant getting out of the crowds and on the road towards Cadie. The Skycap stepped away from her by a few yards and spoke quietly into the phone. Jo watched as he negotiated with whoever was on the other end of the line and she chuckled quietly to herself. *Private enterprise at work.* Finally he finished and walked back towards her, a smile plastered across his face.

"Follow me, ma'am," he said, beckoning her in the direction of a side door. He picked up her bags, and Jo decided to humor him, a quick look at the taxi stand telling her there was very little progress being made there.

They walked into what was a brilliantly clear and crisp Chicago morning. Jo breathed deeply, happy to be out of air-conditioning for the first time in days. Her young escort put her bags on the curb and stepped out into the roadway, looking left and right.

Jo paused a moment to take in her surroundings, then asked, "What's your name?"

"Geoff," the Skycap replied cheerily. "And this..." He indicated an approaching minivan. "Is Maurice." He waved the vehicle into the curb. The driver in question—an older black man who smiled politely—alighted and picked up her bags, taking them to the rear of the van. "He'll take you anywhere in the city for a pre-arranged flat fee."

Maurice returned, rubbing his hands together against the cool morning air. "Where can I take you, ma'am?"

Jo reached into her jeans pocket and pulled out the crumpled piece of paper upon which she had scribbled Cadie's address. She showed it to the driver and he smiled in recognition.

"No problem. I can take you straight there for $50."

Jo looked at Skycap Geoff and he shrugged, grinning broadly. "I swear you won't do better in a cab, ma'am," he said winningly. "Maurice knows all the shortcuts."

Jo knew he was probably right. "And I'm sure you won't do too badly out of the deal, either," she said wryly, handing the young man a five-dollar bill. He took the money and tipped his cap to her.

"Enjoy your stay, ma'am," he said, before turning on his heel and whistling his way back inside the terminal.

Jo turned to her new escort. "Lead on, Maurice," she murmured and climbed into the back of the minivan.

"THAT'S THE PLACE, ma'am," Maurice said as they approached an impressive Victorian home at the top of the steeply inclined driveway. The driver glanced over his shoulder at the brooding Australian in the seat behind him.

Jo had said very little on the trip out from O'Hare, preferring the solitude of her own thoughts. She didn't know quite what she was driving into and wanted to be ready for any and all possibilities. About 10 minutes into the drive, she had called the number of the senator's Chicago house, but it had gone unanswered. *So, either Cadie has been and gone and is on her way back to Madison, or...*Jo didn't much like where that thought process led.

For a brief, dark moment she had entertained a tiny doubt about Cadie's intentions. But the thought of the feisty little blonde going back to Naomi after everything the senator had put her through... *Not to mention the fact that I trust her, and she's given no indication that she's not happy with me,* Jo reminded herself. Well, it was too ludicrous a thought to give any credence to for more than about a nanosecond.

Jo had her share of insecurities... *And God knows, Cadie's seen most of them by now,* she allowed. But her faith in Cadie's ability to know what was best for herself was damn near unshakable. *If she's gone back to Naomi, I'll eat my hat, coat and that old, scabby pair of ugg boots hiding in the back of my closet,* Jo decided. *Jesus, I must be tired.* She looked out at the senator's house sitting high at the top end of the cul-de-sac. *None of that makes me feel any better about what might be going on in there, however.*

"Maurice, do me a favor?" she said. "Drive past slowly and then take a turn around the block." *No sense rushing in where an armed police escort would fear to tread.*

Maurice did as he was told, swinging the mini-van in a wide arc around the top of the dead-end street. Jo didn't move from her spot, but turned her head and calmly cast an experienced eye over the landscape. What she saw did not please her. Perched on the bonnet of a late-model sedan was a black-suited goon in animated conversation with someone who could pass as his twin brother, if clothing and attitude were the only criteria.

Hired muscle, Jo assessed. She turned away as Maurice straightened the mini-van up and headed back out to the main road. *And not very attentive muscle at that. They didn't give us a second glance.*

"Okay, Maurice, pull over," Jo said when they were back around the corner and out of sight of the senator's house. Once they had come to a halt, she fished inside her jacket pocket and pulled out fifty dollars. "Thanks for everything you've done so far," she said, handing Maurice his fare. "And this," She waved an additional one hundred dollar bill, "is up for grabs if you're willing to go the extra mile for me." Jo smiled at him winningly, a grin few on the planet could resist.

"You bet," he answered immediately. "Name it."

"Piece of cake, really," she said casually. "Wait here with my bags for an hour, and then come up to that house we drove past, and the hundred is yours. Fair enough?"

Maurice nodded. "Fair enough."

"Good on you." Jo patted his shoulder and moved for the door. "See you in an hour."

She turned into the cul-de-sac and began the walk back to the bottom of Naomi's driveway. *Okay, Madison. No weapons, other than your fists. And since you're here illegally, let's try like hell not to draw any attention to the situation, eh? Last thing we want is anyone calling the police when they see a fight in their neighbor's drive. Let's play it cool.*

Chapter Twenty-four

"NOT SURE I like this, Jim," Mr. Smith said to his colleague. He reached up and loosened his tie as his partner refolded his newspaper.

"Yeah, I know," Not-Smith replied. "I was talking to Rod Makersley—you know, that guy we met after that Stone Temple Pilots concert? The tour manager?" Smith nodded in recognition. "They're looking for more roadies for the tour they're starting next month. I was thinking of applying."

Smith shrugged. "S'gotta be better than this." He jerked his head in the direction of the house behind them. "We got us a virtual hostage situation. What if something happens to her? Guess who goes down for accessory."

"Yeah," Not-Smith muttered. "Who needs this shit?"

"Gentlemen," Jo called out as she climbed the steep, concrete drive. The two men immediately stopped their conversation. Smith slid off the bonnet and together they began to walk towards her, shoulder to shoulder.

"Can we help you, miss?" said Smith, who was on the right.

"You certainly can," Jo drawled. "Would this happen to be Naomi Silverberg's house?"

"Who wants to know?" said Not-Smith.

Okay, play it that way, then. "Nobody, really," Jo said, smiling politely at the two goons. "I'm a friend of Cadie's, come to pay a visit. I heard she was back in town."

"They're not seeing visitors today," said Smith. He had his hand buried in his coat pocket, a stance that had Jo up on the balls of her feet.

Don't make a scene, you bastard. Jo reached into her own pocket, where she felt the large roll of cash she had brought with her. *Could it be that simple?*

Both men had stiffened when she had gone for the pocket and Jo quickly raised both hands to show she was unarmed. Her right fist now held the bankroll. "Look, fellas, this doesn't have to be complicated," she said. "We all know what's going on here. The senator is in there trying to talk Miss Jones into coming back to her. I'm here to make sure that all that happens is talking, and you," she pointed at the two big men, "are being paid a lot of money to stop me. Is that a reasonably accurate assessment of the situation?" She grinned at them amiably and was pleased when Smith took the bait and grinned back.

"I'd say so, yes," he replied, folding his arms across his chest and leaning back against the rental car's trunk. His partner noticeably relaxed as well, and Jo decided it was time to take the plunge.

"Whatever she's paying you, I'll double it," she said quickly, suddenly becoming very serious indeed. It caught the two bodyguards by surprise and they both gaped at her for a few seconds. Finally Smith regained the power of speech.

"You're Jo Madison aren't you?" he asked. Jo looked him squarely in the eye and nodded solemnly. "Thought so. You don't seriously think we're going to walk away from this gig because you wave a lot of cash in front of us, do you?"

Jo looked down at her feet and nudged a small stone away with the toe of her sneaker. "How long have you worked for the senator?" she asked, looking up at him again.

"We don't work for her full-time," Smith replied, sharing a glance with his colleague. "She uses us on and off."

"So, on a job-by-job basis?"

"When she's in Chicago, yes," said Smith. "We've been doing it for about five years now."

In for a penny, in for a pound, Jo thought, taking a deep breath. "Ah, so you've gotten to know her pretty well, then," she said. Both men suddenly seemed a little uncomfortable, she thought, as she watched them exchanging looks. "I mean, you'll have noticed the changes in her personality the last few years."

Smith hedged his bets one more time. "Don't know what you're talking about."

Jo snorted. "Come on, fellas. If you're anything like her other employees, you're beginning to wonder whether it's worth working for the big-shot senator any more. She's losing it, and you know it. Or did you think Toby and Jason left because they got a better offer?"

Smith and Not-Smith shuffled their feet and looked at each other again. Despite the money the senator had given them for this particular job, neither of them was comfortable with the idea of keeping Cadie as an unwilling resident. It was the latest in a series of weird briefs from the politician.

Jo waited, sensing that she was on the brink of an unlikely victory. She began counting bills off the roll in her hand, making sure the men could see exactly how much she was offering.

"Double, eh?"

"That's what I said."

There was another pause before the duo made their decision. "Done," said Smith, sounding relieved.

"Good," Jo replied. "Name your price."

Smith did and Jo didn't even blink as she handed over the cash. *Mission accomplished, no blood spilled, and no authorities alerted.* The two ex-bodyguards pocketed the money and sauntered down the driveway towards their own vehicle.

"Pleasure doing business with you, Miss Madison," Smith said, giving her a mock salute as he walked past Jo.

"And you." She watched them as they reached the bottom of the drive and climbed into their black sedan. They drove off without a backward look. "Hurdle number 17 successfully negotiated. Now for the really..."

A gunshot split the crisp air with shocking clarity. For a stunned millisecond, Jo was motionless, caught like a butterfly on the sharp end of a pin as her brain tried to process what she had heard. A small flock of starlings rippled out of a nearby tree, seemingly in slow motion. The time splinter passed and Jo jerked into movement, head snapping around and legs powering her up the remaining incline of the driveway. Before she could even gather her thoughts into a coherent sentence, she was through the heavy front door and heading towards the unmistakable sounds of struggle from somewhere to her right.

Jo rounded the corner of the entrance to the living room and barely slowed down at the sight of the tableau before her. All she could see was the trail of blood down the side of Cadie's face as she grappled with Naomi. Cadie's hands gripped the senator's left wrist which held a smoking gun high above their heads. The two women were at close quarters, nose to nose, struggling in a do-or-die wrestle for control. Naomi was screaming like a banshee, her eyes wild and manic.

Jo launched herself at the pair. Slamming into the stocky senator's side, she shoved Cadie out of the way. The gun spun from Naomi's hand and clattered into the stone fireplace on the far side of the room. Jo's momentum took her down onto the carpet with the senator, who fought like a whirling dervish to free herself.

Winded, Cadie stared at the brawling pair, hardly believing that it was really Jo wrestling with Naomi. She could feel something warm and wet trickling down the side of her face and somehow knew she was bleeding. Her ears were still ringing from the gunshot.

"Jesus," she breathed hoarsely. "Jesus, Jo, what are you

doing here?"

There was no time for Jo to answer. Despite being taller than the senator, and despite ending up on top of her, she had her hands full as Naomi squirmed and fought.

"You goddamned bitch," Naomi screamed, the spittle flying from the corners of her mouth. "Fuck you! Goddamn and fuck *you!*"

"Owww, fuck!" Jo exclaimed as Naomi's flailing arm caught her across the bridge of her nose. The senator yelled and squealed like a stuck pig as Jo tried to pin her arms to the carpet.

Cadie came to her senses and scrambled to her feet, intending to retrieve the gun.

"No!" Jo yelled. "Don't touch it!" *Don't want anyone's fingerprints but Naomi's on that thing,* she thought. She grunted with renewed effort as Naomi twisted under her in an attempt to gain purchase.

Cadie stopped mid-step, her brain still several miles behind the events of the last few minutes. *Jo's here. How the hell can she be here?* "I'll call the police," she said, changing direction and heading for the phone.

Jo finally managed to get a grip on Naomi's pummeling fists and pinned them to the carpet with her full body weight. *Goddamn, she's strong. Then again, being totally fucked in the head will do that for someone.* As Cadie's words sank in, Jo whipped her head around in alarm.

"No!" she shouted again. "Don't call them. Don't call anyone. Let me get her under control and then I can think." Naomi's screams had turned to sobs and Jo realized the anger was dissolving into a full-blown, emotional meltdown. *Jesus.*

"Why not?" Cadie couldn't see why Jo wouldn't want to call the authorities. The situation was way beyond anything they could handle alone, surely.

Jo looked up at her lover and their eyes locked for the first time. She felt the flow of warmth between them, unmistakable, even under these bizarre circumstances. "I can't explain right now," Jo said, indicating Naomi with a tilt of her head. "Trust me. Okay?" She held Cadie's gaze for a moment longer and her partner nodded with a small, tight smile.

Naomi was almost completely still now, but she was sobbing helplessly. Cadie sat down heavily in the armchair, the shock of the situation finally hitting her. *I could have been killed, or seriously hurt.* With a tentative hand, she touched the blood that trailed from her cheek. *Holy crap.*

Eyes on Cadie's paling face, Jo shifted position so she could more easily control Naomi should the senator get rambunctious again. "Sweetheart, you're hurt," she said, the urge to rush to her lover warring with the necessity of keeping the slippery senator subdued.

"I'm o-okay," Cadie mumbled. "It's just a scratch. She's been holding that gun on me ever since I tried to call 911."

Jo felt a sudden wave of nausea sweep through her. *That was close. So close. And I was too late to stop it. Jesus.* She sent out a silent thank you to the universe for keeping Cadie safe.

"N-now what?" Cadie stammered. She was full of questions, not the least of which was how the hell Jo had managed to get herself here at the right moment. But the warning look on her lover's face made her bite her tongue.

"I don't know," Jo muttered. "I'm thinking about it." She was still half-reclined over Naomi's back, pinning the stocky senator face down on the carpet. Despite the woman's relative stillness, Jo didn't trust her to stay that way if she let her go.

As if to prove the point, Naomi erupted in a renewed burst of manic energy. Jo yelped and almost bit her tongue as the back of senator's head impacted the point of her chin. Naomi snarled and arched her back, attempting to tip Jo off. The Australian, who wasn't as heavy as the senator, but outdid her in the power and reach departments, clung on tenaciously.

Jo could feel her own temper fraying and she had to consciously resist the urge to knock the senator into next week. "For Christ's sake, Cadie, what the hell were you thinking?" A sharp elbow jabbed up at her and Jo ruthlessly pinned Naomi's hands, muttering, "Lie *still*, you maniac. I don't want to hurt you, but I swear to God..."

"What do you mean, what was I thinking?" Cadie asked, bristling at the question, even though it was one she'd asked herself several times in the past two days.

"Coming down here on your own, is what I mean," Jo snapped. She'd had about enough of the wriggling ball of poison under her, and although she was aware she was probably taking out her irritation on her partner, she couldn't seem to help it. "I mean, Jesus, your parents offered."

"How do you know that?" Cadie responded sharply, feeling the sting of Jo's words. "In fact, how did you know to come at all?"

"Look, can we talk about this later?" Jo answered. "I don't know if you've noticed but I've got a bit of a handful, right now."

The handful in question renewed her struggle. "You mother*fucker*!" Naomi screamed.

"Jo, if the gunshot doesn't bring police running in this neighborhood, then her screaming will."

"I know, I know." Jo grunted as Naomi's elbow caught her in the midriff. An idea occurred to her. "Does she have a therapist? Here in town, I mean?"

Cadie's eyes widened. "Yes. Yes, she does. Dr Salinger. And she's on this side of the city as well."

"Call her," Jo said bluntly. "Explain what's happened...more or less. And get her over here."

Cadie nodded and reached for the phone.

"Wait, Cadie," Jo said suddenly. "The gun. If this woman thinks you've been shot, isn't she required by law to report it?"

Cadie hesitated. "I don't know for sure. But I would guess so, yes."

"Okay. You need to hide that gun. There's a handkerchief in my back pocket. Use it to pick up the gun so you don't leave any prints." Concerned about covering their tracks, Jo craned around, scanning the room for the bullet that had grazed her lover. Finally, she spotted it, buried high in the opposite wall. *No need to worry about that right now,* she decided. *I'll pull it out later, when this is all sorted.*

Cadie extracted the piece of fabric from Jo's pocket, careful not to stand within reach of Naomi's feet. She walked over to the fireplace, gingerly wrapped the firearm in the handkerchief and picked it up. It shocked her that the barrel was still warm and she swallowed, knowing how lucky she was. She didn't want to think about that right now. Nor did she want to think about how low Naomi had sunk. Instead, she stuffed the gun under the cushion of the chair she had been sitting in and reached for the telephone.

FIFTEEN MINUTES AND a few more bruises for Jo later, there was a knock at the door. Cadie ran for it, opening the heavy portal to reveal a willowy redhead carrying a medical bag.

"Dr Salinger."

"Arcadia." The psychiatrist frowned. "I didn't know you were back in town. What's going on? Your phone call didn't make a lot of sense."

"I came back to clean out my stuff and Naomi was here." Cadie led the tall doctor down the corridor to the entrance to the living room. "She's been violent towards me, and then she threatened to kill herself." She nodded in the direction of Jo and Naomi, who were still sprawled together on the floor. Jo was breathing heavily from the effort of keeping the senator subdued. "I was lucky," Cadie murmured. "My friend turned up at the right moment."

The doctor reached out and took Cadie's chin in her hand, turning the smaller woman's head slightly so she could get a better look at the scrape on her cheek. "What happened here?"

Cadie swallowed. "She scratched me."

Roxanne Salinger looked her patient's ex-partner in the eye for a few seconds, finding nothing in the determined green stare to make her doubt Cadie's story. Satisfied, she told Cadie to go sit down then turned back to the bizarre scene on the floor. "Okay, let's see what we've got here." The psychiatrist walked over to Naomi and dropped to her knees by the senator's head, carefully placing her bag down, out of reach. "Hello," she greeted Jo, who nodded, preferring not to let her accent identify her.

Roxanne looked carefully at her patient. They hadn't seen each other since just after the politician had arrived back from Australia without Cadie. Naomi had been livid and spitting venom during the two-hour session they'd had together at that time. But that didn't prepare Roxanne for the physical changes in the senator.

Naomi's face was florid, partly, Roxanne was sure, from the weight of the tall and thoroughly gorgeous woman who was practically sitting on the senator's back. But there was spittle in the corners of the senator's mouth, and her eyes were wild and bloodshot. She had been clenching her fists so hard that her fingernails had gouged her palms.

"Hello, Naomi," Roxanne ventured.

"What the fuck are you doing here?" Naomi hissed, more drool dripping from her mouth.

"Cadie called me and said you needed some help," Roxanne said calmly. "Why don't we talk about that?"

"Why don't you go fuck yourself?"

Jo found herself suppressing a wry smile. Frankly, she almost agreed with Naomi. *There's a first,* she thought solemnly. *Quit talking, Doc, and dope her up with something so I can get off her.*

"Naomi. Do you remember what happened here this morning?" The doctor persisted, attempting to assess the woman's mental state.

"I know that everyone's screwing me over. As fucking usual," Naomi snarled. "I wanted to talk to her. Just talk. Put it right. Go back...go back to the way it was." Suddenly, Jo felt all the fight go out of the woman she had pinned down. Naomi started sobbing, her breath coming in huge, wracking gasps.

Cadie dropped her head, feeling like a big pile of horse crap. *I did everything wrong here. This whole trip was a mistake.*

"I think you can get off her now," Roxanne said, looking at

Jo. Crystal blue eyes blinked back at her, hesitating. "Really," the psychiatrist reiterated.

Jo backed off. Releasing Naomi, she stood up and twisted a little to work the kinks out of her back. There was no way she was going to relax, though. *I don't think this doctor has a vague clue what this nutcase is capable of.*

But Naomi was past the point of violence. Instead, she curled into fetal position on her side, crying. Not small, contained crying, either. Big, loud, hysterical tears.

The psychiatrist sat back on her heels, watching her patient. There wouldn't be any talking to the senator while she was in this state. She reached for her bag and, opening it, withdrew a syringe.

"What are you going to do?" Cadie asked hoarsely. The tone of her voice caught Jo's attention and she looked across at her lover. Cadie looked haggard, close to exhaustion and Jo cursed herself. *You were hard on her before, you idiot,* she thought. *She's been through enough the last couple of days without you coming down on her.*

"I'm going to sedate her, then I'll take her to a rehabilitation clinic," Roxanne replied as she filled the syringe with a clear fluid from a small vial.

"Rehabilitation clinic?" Cadie asked. "She's been taking drugs." A statement, not a question.

The psychiatrist finished filling the syringe and reached over to the senator, lifting the sleeve of her polo shirt. Carefully, she inserted the needle, smoothly and steadily injecting the fluid into Naomi's bloodstream. Almost immediately, the older woman's sounds abated, though she continued to cry.

"You know that under doctor/patient confidentiality, I can't discuss the details of Naomi's case with anyone, not even you," she said. "But I will say that I think a rehab clinic is the best place for her to be right now."

"Fair enough. Doesn't she have to agree to it, first?" Cadie queried.

"Yes. But I don't think that's going to be much of a problem." Roxanne reached out and stroked Naomi's hair away from her forehead. "Naomi." Tear-filled brown eyes blinked at her. "I want to take you to clinic where we can get you some rest and some treatment. Do you think you're ready to do that?"

There was a pause and Cadie swallowed as Naomi's eyes tracked to her, as if she was seeking Cadie's advice. She nodded, hoping that, one last time, Naomi would listen.

"Yes, I'm ready," Naomi whispered hoarsely.

"Good." The psychiatrist touched Naomi's shoulder gently.

"I'll make the arrangements." She got to her feet and pulled out a cell phone, talking as she walked out of the room, leaving Jo and Cadie looking at each other over the prone and now almost unconscious Naomi.

"I'm sorry," Jo said quietly.

Cadie shook her head. "Let's not talk about it," she said. "Not now."

Roxanne Salinger stepped back into the room. "The paramedics will be here shortly." Out of her pocket she pulled a business card and handed it to Cadie. "That's where we're taking her. I know that you're probably not going to come visit, but perhaps you could let her people know where she is."

Cadie took the card and looked up at the redhead. "Thanks for coming over."

Roxanne sighed. "You did the right thing calling me. To be honest, I've been half-expecting this. Your coming back was the trigger."

"It was a mistake," Cadie said quietly.

"Don't beat yourself up for it," the psychiatrist answered. "You didn't have any way of knowing how far she would go."

"Thought you couldn't discuss the details with anyone," Jo growled from across the room. *Accent be damned.*

"You're Jo Madison?" Naomi's therapist suddenly put the pieces together. Jo was silent. "You're right. I did say that. But that doesn't mean I have to be a complete asshole, Miss Madison."

The conversation was brought to a halt by the arrival of the paramedics. Cadie watched forlornly as the two men and the psychiatrist talked together in low voices before they knelt by Naomi's side again. For a few moments, all she could see of the senator was her left hand, complete with the wedding ring Cadie had slipped onto it almost 13 years earlier. *Where did she go, that woman?*

IT HAD BEEN a perfect fall day, Cadie remembered. Not a cloud in the sky and she had decided to seize the moment by skipping classes to take in a rally down in the quadrangle. The student elections were only a couple of weeks away and the campaigning had reached a fever pitch. Cadie had decided it was time to get more involved, at least as much as it took to inform herself about the issues, and she had happily settled on the grass to take in the speeches.

She remembered clearly her first sight of Naomi Silverberg. The brunette had been thinner then, still stocky of build, but it was stockiness borne of a muscular athleticism that had only turned to fat after years of campaigning. Naomi was wearing tattered jeans, a simple white t-shirt and a tweed jacket. The notes for her speech were rolled up in her right hand. It was the grin on her face that had first caught Cadie's eye, however.

The moment she stepped onto the stage, Naomi had the complete attention of the crowd. Conversations stilled and Cadie was aware of an intense sense of anticipation all around her. Naomi's grin spoke of a self-knowledge and confidence in her ability to control the crowd's emotions. And it was a gorgeous smile.

The speech itself was nothing special in terms of content. Standard Republican-slanted fare. But Naomi delivered it with more than a dash of panache. Either she's been doing this for years, or she's a born leader, *Cadie thought. Naomi read the audience perfectly, injecting light notes into her speech where they were needed, but looking the crowd in the eye and nailing them with the serious issues when they were most open to hearing them.*

She was brilliant, Cadie thought, and just like that she'd made the decision to volunteer for Silverberg's campaign. Once the speeches were done, she'd walked up to the podium and waited until Naomi worked her way free of a small crowd of students wanting her attention.

"Ms Silverberg?" Cadie called out, and immediately the student politician turned, training intelligent, open brown eyes on her.

"Please, call me Naomi," she said with a smile as she took Cadie's smaller hand in her own and squeezed it gently.

Cadie was struck anew by the woman's charisma. It had been obvious onstage, but that could have been a performance, she'd reasoned. Up close and personal, it was obvious Naomi was naturally magnetic. "I'm Cadie." A quick breath. "I enjoyed your speech."

Naomi held Cadie's gaze and smiled at her, clearly interested in the young blonde with the sparkling green eyes. "I'm glad," she said. "But did it make you think?"

Cadie grinned back, wondering if now was the time to be totally honest. "You didn't surprise me any," she said. "But you obviously know how to make a crowd see things your way."

That had provoked a laugh from the student politician and Cadie decided she liked to hear that laugh. It was warm and totally unforced.

"Well, I guess that's half the battle," Naomi replied. She hadn't let go of Cadie's hand yet either. "Though, the real question is, did I leave you wanting more?" The irrepressible smile widened and it dawned on Cadie that she was being flirted with.

At 18, Cadie was inexperienced, but she knew enough to know her attraction to other women made her different from her classmates. And the wash of Naomi's warm and appraising gaze was a very pleasant surprise. "Um, yes, I guess you did," she replied, disconcerted by how flustered she felt. "Actually, I was thinking of volunteering for your campaign."

Naomi placed her other hand over the top of Cadie's, effectively keeping her firmly at close quarters. "That's fantastic," she said gently, and Cadie was struck by how much she believed that Naomi meant it with every ounce of her being. "Tell you what; me and a bunch of friends are going for pizza right about now – sort of a post-mortem, if you will." She grinned again. "We could use some feedback from a member of the audience. Why don't you come along, and you can figure out if we're your kind of people."

Cadie remembered feeling that she already had no doubt about that. "And keeping me close would be an added bonus," she'd said cheekily, correctly interpreting that there was at least some ulterior motive in Naomi's suggestion.

"There is that," Naomi had readily agreed, taking Cadie's hand more firmly and drawing her away towards her circle of friends. "Come on, we'll have some fun."

THE SOUND OF the two paramedics grunting as they lifted Naomi onto a gurney brought Cadie sharply back to the present. She was surprised to feel tears on her cheeks, and the sight of Naomi's older, wearier, but so familiar features did nothing to stem the flow.

Where did she go?

The paramedics wheeled the gurney out, Dr. Salinger walking behind. Within minutes, Jo and Cadie were watching the ambulance driving away, the psychiatrist's Mercedes following.

"Well, that's that," Cadie muttered absently, as she turned from the front door and walked back into the living room.

Jo waited a while longer, hardly believing that Senator Naomi Silverberg had disappeared out of their lives. *Hopefully for good.* She felt a pang of what could have been guilt, but it only lasted for a fleeting second. *Couldn't have happened to a bigger bitch,* she finally decided.

She found Cadie sitting in the chair in the living room, looking very small and lost. Cadie was sniffling, a sound that immediately tugged at Jo's heartstrings. *Awww shit.* She walked over and knelt down between Cadie's legs, placing her hands gently on her thighs. "Hi," she said softly.

"Hi back," Cadie said huskily.

"Talk to me."

Cadie shook her head, scattering tears. "It's nothing you want to hear," she whispered.

"I might surprise you," Jo replied, angling her head to try and catch Cadie's eye.

Cadie struggled to find the words. "I feel so sorry for her," she finally said, knowing that it would be hard for anyone else to understand that perspective.

Jo pulled her into a hug and Cadie nestled in, adoring the feel of the Australian's long, strong arms around her. Keeping her safe.

"Unless I'm totally misinterpreting what I saw, she tried to kill you, love," Jo pointed out carefully. She knew that no matter how hard she tried, she would never see Naomi the same way Cadie did.

"That's what's throwing me. She...Jo, I loved her once. And she loved me. I know she did. I still care about her."

"I know," Jo replied. "I'm guessing you've been swamped with memories the last few days, right?" She felt Cadie nod. "Were you tempted?" The last came out in a hoarse whisper.

Cadie pushed herself back and looked Jo in the eye. "Tempted? To go back to her, you mean?" Jo nodded and Cadie's eyebrows shot up. "You're kidding, right? Jo, I was remembering how it used to be, but having a gun held to my head was a pretty strong reminder of how much Naomi's changed."

Jo breathed out slowly and caught herself blushing at her own show of insecurity. "Okay, I can see that," she said wryly.

"Good." Cadie returned to her position, nestled under Jo's chin. "She's sick, Jo."

"Yes, she is." *No argument there.*

"I guess I'm finding it hard to believe that the two Naomis I know are the same woman. I almost wish I couldn't remember how it used to be."

Jo kissed the top of Cadie's head. "Don't do that," she said. "It would be good to give her credit for being human once."

Cadie closed her eyes and let Jo cradle her.

"I'm sorry I yelled at you," Jo murmured.

"No, you were right," Cadie said, her voice cracking. "I was an idiot to come alone. Dad even offered me his cell phone and I turned that down. What the hell was I thinking?"

"Sweetheart, you thought Naomi was on the other side of the country. And I'm the last person on the planet to criticize you for trying not to rely too much on your parents." She smiled at the irony. "I wish I could have gotten here earlier. It might have saved you this." She brushed a tentative fingertip across Cadie's cheek, tracing the edge of the scrape the bullet had left.

Cadie reached up and took Jo's hand. For the first time since Jo had appeared less than an hour ago—like magic, she thought wonderingly—she fully absorbed the fact that her lover was actually here. *In the flesh.* With a surge of relief she cupped Jo's now-smiling face in her hands. "You're here. You're really here," she whispered.

"Yes, I'm here," Jo replied. "God, it feels good to hold you."

"I feel like I haven't seen you in weeks...and it hasn't even been one."

"Me too."

Cadie gazed at Jo, a tentative smile creeping on to her face. "How did you manage it? Did Ken help you?"

Jo's eyes dropped and she felt uncertain and more than a little sheepish. "I'm, um, not exactly here legally." She glanced up and saw nothing but love in Cadie's sea-green eyes. "That's why I didn't want to say too much while Naomi and the doctor were around. And why I didn't want the police involved. I've got to keep a very low profile. I'm not here on my real passport."

Cadie brushed her lips across Jo's. "I adore you," she said. "You risked that for me?"

Jo felt a lump the size of Coonyabby in her throat. "I'd do anything for you."

Cadie's heart melted and she went back for a second kiss. This one was slower and delicious as they reacquainted themselves with each other. By the time it was done, both were breathing raggedly and their faces were flushed.

"You do say the most wonderful things sometimes, Jo-Jo," Cadie sighed.

"And sometimes I say the stupidest things in the world," Jo said gruffly.

"Shhh," Cadie replied, putting a gentle finger on Jo's lips, which were impossibly soft. "It's okay. Naomi's gone now." *Really gone.*

"So what would you like to do now?" Jo asked. Cadie sat back in the chair and squeezed her lover with her knees. She exhaled soft and low as she thought about the possibilities the day held. "Well, I guess we can pack up the rest of my stuff."

"Sounds like a plan, Stan."

"And then we could head north and you can meet my parents."

Jo's eyes widened, her face a picture of shock and consternation. "Oh my God."

Chapter Twenty-five

JO DUG THE long-nosed pliers carefully into the small hole high up in the wall of the living room. She was balanced on a stepladder, one hand pressed against the wall and the other manipulating the pliers. Her tongue poked, rather endearingly, Cadie thought, from the corner of her mouth as she concentrated on her task.

"You found it, then?" Cadie asked, chuckling when Jo jumped. Cadie had been outside, loading some more of her things into the rental car and Jo had obviously not heard her come back in. Cadie stepped forward quickly to steady the ladder as her partner recovered.

"Jesus, woman, you startled me," Jo exclaimed. "I nearly had the damn thing, too."

"Sorry, love," Cadie replied. She watched as Jo carefully extracted the crumpled bullet fragment from the hole. "Out of curiosity," she said. "Why do we need it? I mean, Naomi shot it, Naomi loaded the gun, presumably, and I don't think she's going to announce either of those things to the police. So why are we worrying about pulling it out of the wall?"

Jo climbed back down the ladder and they both took a few moments to study the crushed bullet sitting in the palm of her hand. Jo shrugged. "I don't know, really," she finally said. "I'd suggest keeping it as a souvenir, but the last thing we'd want is for it to set off some damn metal detector between here and Sydney." She grinned at Cadie. "Maybe we should put it down to me being a neat freak?"

Cadie smiled but her mind was working overtime. "Let's leave it with Mom and Dad," she suggested, explaining when Jo raised an inquiring eyebrow. "The bottom line is, we don't really know how she's going to be feeling about you and me, even if this rehab clinic does her some good. There weren't any witnesses today. If she wanted to say I'd shot at her, she could. But, if we've got the bullet—which, presumably, she loaded into the gun—at least we have a chance of proving it was the other way around." Her uncertainty turned the last part of the sentence into a question.

Jo nodded and smiled at her. "Spot on," she murmured. "Okay, then. We'll leave it with your parents." She looked at her partner again. "You realize that means telling them pretty much what happened?"

"Yeah, I know. They're not going to be happy."

Jo wrapped an arm around Cadie's shoulder and pulled her in for a quick hug. "They'll be okay. You're safe, and Naomi's in the nuthouse. That's all they need to know." Cadie squeezed her back and both women enjoyed the contact for a few seconds before they separated with a quick smile.

Jo bent down and extracted Naomi's pistol from where Cadie had hidden it under a seat cushion. She unwrapped it from the handkerchief and studied it carefully. It was similar to a million other guns she had seen and handled in her former life. "Does Naomi usually keep a gun in the house?" she asked casually. "Or did she bring this with her just for this trip?"

Cadie looked more closely at the gun. Unlike Jo, she'd never had more than a passing interest in firearms. She had no idea if this was Naomi's only gun. "There's only one way to find out," she concluded. "Come on."

She led Jo across the hallway and into a spacious study lined with dark wood panels. It was cluttered with books and papers, but like everything else in the house, there was a thin layer of dust covering all. Cadie walked over to the large oak desk and sat down in the leather chair. She reached under the desktop. "I know Naomi kept a gun here somewhere," she said as she fumbled around. "Ah." There was a satisfying click and a panel slid out. Inside was a felt-lined shelf, empty except for the faint outline of a handgun on the material, and a box of bullets. "Bingo."

"Well, that answers that question," Jo remarked. Before she could think about what to do next, however, the front door bell rang.

"What if that's the police?" Cadie whispered, her face a picture of alarm.

Jo's eyes widened. Then she slapped her forehead. "Jesus, that'll be Maurice. I completely forgot about him."

Blonde eyebrows rose. "Who is Maurice?"

Jo grinned at her. "My driver. I promised him a hundred dollars to show up in an hour with my luggage. I guess the hour's up."

"That's a hell of a tip, Jo-Jo. Want me to go pay him?"

Jo shook her head. "No, I'll do it." She handed the gun, still wrapped in the handkerchief, back to Cadie. "Slide that back into its place in the drawer—but don't touch the metal at all, okay?" she said. "Then wrap this," she tipped the crushed bullet out of her palm and on to the desktop, "in the handkerchief and hang onto it."

Cadie handled the gun gingerly. "You're sure?"

Jo leaned down and kissed her softly on the forehead. "Cheer up, sweetheart. It's almost all over, and then we can go home."

Cadie leaned against her for a few moments. "I do love you, you know."

Jo kissed her again. "I know. Be back in a minute." With one last pat of Cadie's shoulder, she headed for the front door.

Cadie watched her go then turned back to the task at hand. Sliding the gun onto the felt, she nudged it into place with the handkerchief. Then she picked up the spent shell, again using the fabric to keep her fingerprints off the metal. She tucked the little package into her jeans pocket.

She was about to go find Jo when a thought occurred to her that made her sit back down. A stack of Naomi's personalized stationery caught her attention and she drew a blank page towards her. *After all, my fingerprints should be all over this house,* she reasoned. *I lived here for seven years, God knows.* Cadie lifted Naomi's fountain pen out of the desk set—*I gave that to her three Christmases ago*—and began writing.

Naomi,

I hope the time in the rehabilitation clinic does you good. Believe it or not, I do actually care about you. Enough to wish you well in the future, at least.

In case you're wondering, nobody has touched the gun – yours are the only fingerprints on it. And, yes, I have the remains of the bullet you fired at me. Yours are the only prints on that as well, along with a few scraps of my DNA, I'm sure.

We had a lot of good times together over the years, but those times are long gone. They were gone well before I ever met Jo. Maybe one day you'll see that for the truth it is, and accept your share of the responsibility for it.

But I don't want to hear from you again, Naomi. I hope you'll understand that the bullet is my guarantee of that. Look after yourself, and your career. Those are things that make you happy, and I do want you to be happy. But leave me, and Jo, out of it.

Take care, and goodbye.

Arcadia

JO PEEKED THROUGH the peephole, relieved to see that it was indeed Maurice who had rung the front door bell. She opened the door and grinned at him. "Hello, Maurice."

"Oh, thank goodness, ma'am. I was beginning to think something was seriously wrong," said the driver, relief written on his face. "I saw an ambulance leaving and didn't know what to do."

Jo stepped outside, picking up one of her bags as she walked past him. "No worries, mate, you did exactly the right thing." Indicating the other bag, she said, "Give me a hand, will you?" Together they loaded the gear into Cadie's car, and Jo handed him the promised cash.

"You sure everything's all right, ma'am?" Maurice said, more than happy with his profit on the day, but eager to be of whatever further service was needed.

"Everything's great," Jo answered, and for the first time since she had arrived in the country, she actually felt like that was the truth. "A friend of ours had a bit of a nasty turn, that's all. She'll be fine."

"Well, that's good to hear, that's for sure," he said, enthusiastically pumping the hand Jo extended. He reached into his pocket and gave her a business card that had seen better days. "Next time you're in Chicago and need someone to drive you around, you call my number."

Jo took it happily. "I'll certainly do that, Maurice. If I ever get out of this country and back again without being arrested or shot at, it will be you I call." She grinned at the uncertain look on his face. "I'm joking, mate, honestly."

"Uh, yes, ma'am," he muttered, suddenly not so sure that she was joking at all. "Well, safe travels to you."

"And you."

IN THE END, it had been easier to pile everything in the car and drive up to Madison as quickly as they could. Cadie found she loved showing Jo all the sights—not that that particular stretch of I-90 provided much in the way of picturesque scenery. But Jo seemed interested and plied her with questions. By the time they pulled in to the driveway of Cadie's childhood home three hours later, both of them were happy and relaxed despite the events of the day.

Or maybe because of them, Jo thought. *It's such a relief to be out from under Naomi's dark cloud.*

Stephen and Helena came down the driveway to meet them and Jo hung back a little, knowing that their primary concern would be making sure Cadie was all right.

"And who is this?" Stephen Jones asked finally, turning with a smile to the woman waiting on the car's passenger side. He had an inkling, from the descriptions his daughter had given him, that this tall, dark-haired and attractive stranger was Jo Madison. But he didn't want to assume.

Cadie grinned over her shoulder at her lover and stepped back from Helena's hug. "Mom, Dad, this is Jo," she said simply, pride and love shining from her eyes. "She arrived out of the blue, at the right moment. As usual."

"Well, you can thank your mother for that," Jo drawled as she stepped forward and grasped Stephen's offered hand in a firm grip. En route, she had explained to Cadie that it was Helena's phone call that had finally kick-started her journey to the US. "It's nice to meet you, Mr. Jones," she said, looking the tall man in the eye.

"Please, call me Stephen," Cadie's father replied, already impressed by the cool calm of his daughter's friend. "And thank you. If Cadie says you arrived at the right moment, I can only assume that you saved her from considerable amounts of trouble."

Jo glanced Cadie's way and smiled slightly. "She was doing pretty well on her own, I think."

Cadie snorted. "You are such a liar." She turned to her mother. "The truth is, Naomi was being difficult and Jo stopped her."

Helena reached up and brushed a finger along the scrape on Cadie's jaw. "I want to hear all the details," she said. "But first..." She walked over to Jo and wrapped the slightly surprised woman in a warm hug. "I want to welcome you to the family, Jo."

Jo found herself confronted by a very familiar pair of eyes and was charmed. "Um, thank you," she replied. "I'm very glad to be here."

Chapter Twenty-six

THE THREE LONG sleek yachts were moored together, side by side, pontoon-style in the middle of the lagoon. On the portside was the Beowulf, in the middle was Cheswick Marine's flagship, the Seawolf, and on the starboard side, resplendent in a fresh coat of paint, was the newly-christened Lobo, the latest addition to the fleet.

The sea was calm, and the sun had dipped below the mountains on the mainland away to the west. The clear blue sky of a summer's day was giving way to a glorious speckling of starlight, and the scene was a picture of paradise. If it hadn't been for the raucous music booming from the Seawolf's sound system, and the tantalizing smell of barbecuing meat, not to mention the sights and sounds of a party in full swing, it could have been mistaken for a painting.

It was a Saturday night eight months after Jo and Cadie's return from the US, the first evening of the traditional Australia Day long weekend. Revelers were spread across the decks of the three yachts. Others walked on the nearby coral reef, its wonders almost exposed by the low tide. The air was muggy, though as the sun descended, a gentle sea breeze came off the breaking waves to the east of the atoll, where the open ocean lapped up against the edge of the Great Barrier Reef.

Away from the yachts, but tethered to the Seawolf by a 100 feet or so of floating rope, bobbed an aluminum dinghy. Its two occupants lay along its towel-covered bottom in a contented tangle of suntanned arms and legs. Both women were scantily clad: Jo in a lightning-blue one-piece swimsuit that emphasized the length of her lean, muscular legs, and Cadie in a sea-green bikini that brought out the color of her eyes.

Not that either woman was particularly concerned with clothing at that moment. In fact they were more engaged in removing it, or at least, getting inside it.

Jo's hand slid under Cadie's bikini top, cupping her breast gently. The move elicited a low moan from Cadie as she kissed

Jo deeply, their tongues teasing. She arched up against her lover and her own hand found purchase under the high-cut leg of Jo's swimsuit.

"God, you feel fantastic," Jo murmured huskily, her alto deepened further by desire. The sound and feel of her breath, brushing against Cadie's ear, sent tremors down the smaller woman's spine and she buried her face against the soft skin of Jo's neck, trembling slightly. "Are you cold, sweetheart?" Jo asked, wrapping her arm more tightly around Cadie.

"Not even slightly," Cadie replied softly, brushing her lips against Jo's pulse-point, loving the fluttering response she felt there. "You're just doing very wicked things to my nervous system, darling."

Jo smiled and ducked her face, pressing her nose into the silky, blonde locks tucked up against her. She let her lover's unique scent—apricot shampoo, mingled with sunscreen and ocean—wash through her senses. *Happiness smells like this,* she thought.

"I want to make love to you," she whispered, adoring the little gasp her suggestion drew from Cadie.

"I can tell," Cadie responded, brushing the palm of her hand across Jo's lycra-covered and attentive breasts. "Can we be seen from the boats?" she asked. *Not that I really care at this point. The way she makes me feel, Steve Irwin and his film crew could be turning us into a documentary and I wouldn't care enough to say 'crikey'.*

Jo pushed herself up on one elbow and lifted her head so she could see over the gunwale of the dinghy. "No, we've drifted quite a way away," she said. She turned back and looked down at Cadie. The setting sun was turning Cadie's hair red-gold, and her deeply-tanned skin almost glowed in the low light. "You are so beautiful," she whispered.

Cadie felt the heat of a blush rising up her neck and across her cheeks, on top of the flush of desire Jo had already provoked. Even now, almost a year into their relationship, it never failed to floor her when Jo said something romantic out of the blue like that. She reached up and drew a gentle finger across the high plane of Jo's cheekbone. Sparkling blue eyes, darkened by the fading light, blinked at her. "Back at you, Aussie," she murmured.

Jo's left hand, already wrapped around Cadie's back, deftly unhooked the bikini top, releasing her breasts to the warm, tropical air. Jo groaned softly at the sight and lowered her head, gently enfolding a waiting nipple in a warm, wet mouth.

"Oh, Jo." Cadie's hand slipped into the dark hair and pulled Jo closer still. There was something nurturing in the action.

Quite apart from how completely turned on she felt, she wanted to hold Jo in her arms like this forever.

Jo didn't give her much time to savor the moment, however, as her lips continued to tease and tug relentlessly at Cadie's breasts. Cadie didn't mind in the least. She sighed happily and arched against Jo's solid frame, rewarded when a firm hand strayed down the length of her prickling torso.

"Yes, angel," she urged in a whisper.

Jo needed little in the way of encouragement. Her fingers found the waistband of Cadie's bikini bottom and dipped beneath it, finding soft curls already damp with anticipation.

Somehow Cadie had the presence of mind to reach up and slide the straps of Jo's swimsuit down, off her shoulders, exposing breasts ripe for some teasing of her own.

They knew each other well enough now for their timing and rhythm to be almost automatic and Cadie's fingers found the sensitive nubs of Jo's nipples as her lover's honed unerringly in on Cadie's center. The effect was a simultaneous meltdown as both women gave in to their instincts, letting their bodies take over. The rest of the world faded out as they lost themselves and found each other in the gently rocking motions of love on the ocean.

MAGGIE MADISON FROWNED slightly as she watched the dinghy bobbing suspiciously, away in the distance. A few minutes earlier she had noticed her daughter's distinctive head pop up for a couple of seconds, and it didn't take much imagination to draw an accurate conclusion about what was going on in that little boat. Maggie turned away and tapped Helena Jones lightly on the shoulder.

"Don't look now, but I think I've found Jo and Cadie," she said. The Joneses had arrived for their first Australian holiday two weeks earlier and had been staying with Maggie and David in their new home inland from Shute Harbor. The two couples had gotten on like a house on fire from the word go, and Maggie and Helen were already the best of friends.

"Oh, good. Where are they? I want to ask Cadie about the arrangements for tomorrow." Helena swung around to look at Maggie, who cocked her head over her shoulder in the general direction of the dinghy.

"I wouldn't look too closely," Maggie gave a light-hearted warning.

"Oh dear." Helena seemed a little nonplussed as Maggie's meaning became perfectly clear, the dinghy rocking more emphatically than the calm surface of the surrounding ocean could possibly cause. "Don't tell the men," she said. "I believe it would be too much for Stephen's blood pressure."

Maggie smiled, knowing that David would have a similar reaction if he thought about it too much. "Don't think there's too much danger of that," she said, nodding towards the two elders of the family, who were standing on either side of a portable barbeque set up in the main cockpit of the Seawolf. The men were obviously engaged in an animated discussion about something. "They look like they're talking about politics."

"Or football," Helena agreed.

The two women made their way towards their husbands, out of earshot of their daughters, by silent, mutual agreement. Helena wished she could be as laidback as her Australian counterpart about the easy sensuality that was apparent between Jo and Cadie. *They're so right,* she conceded to herself. *I could never say that about Cadie and Naomi. I would never have been able to think about them doing...* She glanced out at the dinghy, which seemed to have stilled, thankfully. *They're a perfect couple.*

Maggie watched Helena surreptitiously. *Taking it pretty well, considering,* she thought. "Why do I get the feeling that you never had to deal with this kind of thing when Naomi was around?"

Helena took a sip of her champagne and turned to lean back against the Beowulf's rail, shoulder to shoulder with Maggie. She shook her head. "The more distance we all have from that woman, the more I can see that Cadie was really kept in her shell by that relationship. I like the way Jo brings out Cadie's..." She paused, looking for the right words.

"Sexier side?" Maggie prompted, mischievously.

"That, too," Helena agreed, smiling despite herself.

"Whatever happened to the senator?"

Helena sighed. It really had been rather sad in the end. However much she had come to dislike Naomi, she had been rather fond of her once. "Well, it turns out the nervous breakdown was the best thing that could have happened to her," she said. "The way she was behaving, from what I can gather, she probably was heading for censure, which would have been the end of any political career for her. As it was, she resigned from the Senate on medical grounds."

"What's she doing now?" Maggie asked.

"Not much of anything, I think," Helena replied. "Hard to believe she's not planning something, though."

"Ah well. From what Jo was telling me, it's not likely she'll ever bother Cadie again."

Helena smiled, thinking of the spent shell that was safely locked in her husband's safety deposit box back in Madison. "No, I don't think we'll be hearing from her," she said quietly. "Those daughters of ours are pretty smart."

"They certainly make a good team," Maggie agreed. "They've both come a long way."

Helena looked quizzically at her companion. *There's definitely more to the Jo Madison story than I know about yet,* she decided. "You must tell me how far one day," she said.

Maggie looked at her with a coolly assessing gaze. "One day," she promised.

"OH MY." JO breathed as she sagged down, resting her weight, as gently as she could, on Cadie. "You are something else, you know that, right?"

Cadie's breath came in ragged gasps. "I...I didn't do anything." She wrapped her arms around Jo, pulling her close until the dark head was tucked securely under her chin. Their hearts tripped along rapidly, strongly enough that she could feel them both pounding as they lay, chest to chest.

"You did plenty," Jo replied between kisses against Cadie's collarbone.

It was completely dark now, but for the half-moon climbing above the horizon and the myriad of bright stars sprinkled across the wide, black sky. Cadie felt more alive than she could ever remember. The sounds of the party drifted across the water and she sighed deeply.

"I wish we could stay out here all night," she sighed.

Jo chuckled. "Honey, this party was our idea, remember? We like these people."

Cadie laughed. "I know. I just love being out here with you." She felt the warm breeze against her sweat-dampened skin and trailed her fingers down Jo's back. "I especially love being out here naked with you." Jo grinned against her neck, tickling slightly.

"You love being naked with me wherever we are."

Hard to argue with that. "True."

Jo licked up a drop of sweat from between Cadie's breasts with the tip of her tongue. "I suppose we do have to get back to the party," she murmured.

How does she do that, Cadie wondered, appreciating the ripple of tingles Jo's tiniest touch produced. "I suppose we must," she replied. "I mean, we are the hosts, after all."

Jo's mouth traveled further south, following an imaginary

trail down the center of Cadie's belly. Cadie groaned and shifted her position slightly, giving Jo more room to do...*whatever it is she's going...to...do...oh...*

Jo kissed the inside of Cadie's thigh, her lips trailing across the tanned, soft skin. "Not that another half an hour or so would matter, I guess," she whispered.

"N-no...ohhh..."

"LET'S SWIM BACK," Jo said.

Cadie chuckled. "Swim? Honey, I can barely lift my head off the bottom of the boat, let alone swim. You've worn me out." She grinned up at her lover, whose eyes glittered like the stars she was now silhouetted against.

"Well, okay," Jo said casually. "But as soon as everyone sees me dragging us back in, they're gonna know what we've been up to."

"What's the matter? Can't handle a little teasing from a boatload of people who would love to catch us in the act?"

Jo snorted. "Okay, okay, you got me." She nibbled Cadie's chin delicately. "Swim back with me?" she persisted. "It'll cool us off and maybe we can sneak back onboard, take 'em all by surprise. It might be fun."

Cadie patted Jo's upper arm affectionately. "Okay, love." She pushed herself up into a sitting position, surprised to see how far away from the yachts they had drifted. One look over the side of the dinghy and she had second thoughts.

"Um, Jo?"

"Yes?" came the low rumble from the bottom of the boat.

"The water's pitch black. I'm not sure I've got the nerve to swim back."

Jo sat up.

"You know this water, Cades," she said calmly. "We've swum here a thousand times. It's only about 30 feet deep, clear and safe. No bities, other than the hermit crabs running along the bottom. And they're not gonna come out tonight, even at the sight of your loveliness swimming above them."

Cadie bit her lip uncertainly. "It's just...I don't like not being able to see what's coming at me."

"Tell you what. You hold on to the rope with one hand and my hand with the other and we'll be back on the Seawolf before you know it." She took Cadie's smaller hand in her own and squeezed reassuringly.

Cadie hesitated a second longer but then nodded. "Okay."

Jo grinned and slipped over the side of the dinghy. Cadie

took a deep breath and followed her, surprised to feel how warm the water still was.

"Come on," Jo whispered, pulling her around to the tethering rope. Once she could feel its roughness against her palm, Cadie felt better and was able to think rather than panic about the dark water around her. She felt Jo's arm snake around her waist, her partner's solid frame warm and safe against her.

"See, it's not so scary," Jo burred, close to Cadie's ear. "Take a look down below, it might surprise you."

Cadie looked at her and Jo nodded, urging her to give it a try. "Okay, what the hell." She sucked in a breath and ducked her head under the water. They hadn't brought any masks with them, so when she opened her eyes she had to blink several times against the stinging saltwater. All around her phosphorescence shimmered and danced, catching the moving edges of silver fish, the tethering rope and coral outcrops.

Cadie popped up, gasping for air, a grin from ear to ear.

"It's beautiful," she exclaimed. "Why haven't we done this before?"

Jo laughed, a low, sexy growl that Cadie adored. "We never got around to it before. Come on, let's follow the rope."

Together they made their way hand-over-hand along the line, back to three boatloads of friends and family.

"HOW MUCH LONGER do you think you can stay out there, Jo Madison?" Maggie muttered.

"Out where, Mum?"

Maggie jumped six inches in the air and clutched a hand to her heart. "Damn you, girl, you scared me out of 10 years' growth," she yelped, spinning around and facing Jo. Two pairs of blue eyes glared at each other, Jo's holding a touch of innocent inquiry that was irritating in the extreme to her mother. "Oh, don't give me that look. I know exactly what you've been up to," she said with mock severity, planting her hands on her hips.

"Why, Mother, whatever do you mean?" Jo said archly, raising an eyebrow as she handed her parental unit a fresh glass of champagne. "I've been down below, helping Jenny with the food and drinks."

"Right," said Maggie. "And taking a shower and changing clothes as well." She pointed at Jo's wet hair and freshly pressed shorts and polo shirt.

"S'been a long day. I felt like putting something clean on." Jo shrugged. The women eyed each other for a few more seconds then both burst out laughing.

"You are so busted," Maggie said, wiping away a tear.

"I am so happy," Jo murmured, surprising even herself with the comment.

"Oh, Josie." Her mother stepped forward and took her daughter's face in her hands. "I can see that you are," she said, tears welling up in her eyes again. "And I am so happy *for* you, darling."

Jo rested her hands on her mother's forearms, and grinned through her own tears. "Thanks," she husked. A familiar warm presence made itself known behind her and Jo felt, rather than heard, Cadie's approach.

"Hello, you two," Cadie said softly. Maggie removed her left hand from Jo's cheek long enough to place it against the side of Cadie's face instead.

"Hello, sweetheart," Maggie said, smiling tearily at the woman she'd come to think of as her other daughter. She patted both warm cheeks one last time and moved back a little.

"I, um, thought we might get this show on the road," Cadie said, looking from Jo to her mother and back again. *I missed something here, but I don't think it was a bad thing,* she decided.

Jo cleared her throat and looked up at Cadie through lowered eyelashes. "Good idea," she agreed. "Want to do the honors?"

"Your boats, skipper. Your show."

Jo shook her head and wrapped an arm around Cadie's shoulders. "Nope. Our show," she said, planting a kiss on Cadie's temple. "Come on."

Together they climbed up onto the roof of the Seawolf's cockpit. Jo bent down and banged on the fiberglass with the flat of her hand, trying to attract the attention of whoever was below decks. "Hey! Turn it down, will ya?" she shouted.

Almost immediately, the pounding rhythms of the rock music ceased. It also had the effect of drawing the attention of everyone spread across the decks of the three yachts. All faces turned towards Jo and Cadie. Jo straightened up and looked at all her friends.

Paul and Jenny were here, of course. They were still living with Jo and Cadie, the two couples finding that they enjoyed each other's company. Paul was now skipper of the Lobo. The four of them were often at sea at different times, an ideal way not to get sick of the sight of each other.

The Palmieri clan was also present. Rosa and Roberto had their hands full keeping track of the now not so little Sophie, who was growing into a quite gorgeous young lady. Even Tony had managed to find time off from his duties on Hayman Island to come party.

Toby and Jason, now working as PR consultants for a gay advocacy group in San Francisco, had made the trip across and were deep in conversation with Hughie and Josh. The Americans were trying to talk the two young Australians into taking them sailing before they had to fly home.

All the Cheswick employees were onboard, of course, including the newest members of the team, who would be Paul's crew on board the Lobo. Doris was sitting in the stern of the Seawolf, and she raised her glass to Jo, even as her boss waited for the conversations to still around her.

Jo searched the happy crowd for one face in particular, and finally found it. Ken Harding, dressed in an outrageously loud Hawaiian-style shirt and, of all things, purple board-shorts, stood, beer in hand, with her father and the Joneses. Jo grinned at the big cop, delighted that he had been able to get the time off, and had made the trip north for the weekend's celebrations.

Cadie tucked herself under Jo's arm and watched her lover's face avidly. There was such happiness there, and the sight of it made Cadie feel wonderful. *Look at her,* she thought. *Surrounded by everyone she loves. And letting them love her. I'm so proud of her.* Cadie stood on tiptoe and kissed Jo's cheek softly. It caught the taller woman by surprise and she looked down enquiringly.

"Just felt like doing that," Cadie answered the non-verbal question.

"Cut it out, you two," came a raucous voice from somewhere on the Beowulf. "You've already been at it all afternoon!"

Laughter rippled around the yachts and Cadie buried her blushing face against Jo's shoulder.

"Wouldn't you, if you had the chance?" Jo quipped, regaining control of the situation.

"Too right!" That from several voices.

Jo laughed. "All right, all right. Settle down, you lot. We've got some announcements to make."

"Well, hurry up, can't you? It's a pretty dry argument down this end." That voice floated up from the bow of the Lobo. More laughter.

"Hang on," piped up Jen. "I can solve that problem." The brunette vanished below but quickly reappeared hefting a carton of what Jo guessed was ice-cold beer. "Here you go." The carton was soon being passed overhead to the poor, parched souls who had gone almost an hour without a fresh drink.

"Is everybody happy now?" Jo called out wryly.

"Thanks, mate," came the reply.

"Right, then. Finally." Jo felt Cadie shaking with laughter

and she took another moment to look down at her partner. *Everyone's going to know exactly how you feel about her in a few minutes, Jo-Jo,* she thought. *As if they can't already tell.* Cadie looked up at her and Jo kissed her softly on the lips, for good measure. *I'm so damn proud she chose me.*

"Okay," Jo murmured, taking one last look into those sea-green eyes and getting all the confirmation she needed before she turned back to the crowd. "Welcome to the annual Cheswick Marine Australia Day Party Weekend." She grinned as the cheers answered her. "We do this every year, as you know, but this year, we've got a few bonus celebrations for you."

"Great, another excuse for a party," yelled one reveler.

"Exactly right," Jo replied. "I want to welcome all the new crew members. As you can see, the Lobo's had a new coat of paint and she'll be ferrying her first boatload of tourists around next week. That's one extra reason to celebrate." Applause.

"The second reason to celebrate is a little more personal to Cadie and me." Jo looked at Cadie and reached out a hand. "As of 11 a.m. yesterday, when the mail arrived, Cadie is now a permanent resident of Australia." No matter how hard they tried, neither woman could keep the grins off their faces as a resounding cheer went up from the assembled masses. Somewhere, someone started a chorus of "Waltzing Matilda," and soon everyone was singing along.

"Welcome to the country, Cades!" Paul yelled once the song was done, raising his half-empty stubby of beer in her direction.

"Thanks, mate," Cadie replied, trying on her best Aussie accent for the first time in public. Jo winced.

"Ah, let's work on that one later, shall we sweetheart?" she said, softening the sting with a 1000-watt grin.

"Oooo, personal tutoring," Cadie replied cheekily, eliciting another roar of approval from the crowd.

"While we're on the subject, I want to introduce you all to someone." Jo pointed in Harding's direction. "The big fella over there in the incredibly ugly shirt." She waited until Ken waved a reluctant hand at all the partygoers. "That's Ken. He's the one who pulled a few strings so we could get all the paperwork done in eight months. Thanks, mate."

Harding lifted his beer and acknowledged the cheers around him.

"One more announcement, folks, and then you can get back to some serious partying," Jo called out. Her stomach did a double back-flip and she caught her mother's eye for a moment, receiving a nod of encouragement. "You all have until 3 p.m. tomorrow to sober up," she said, grinning at the puzzled looks on the faces of her friends. "Because at 3 p.m. tomorrow, Cadie and I are going to get married."

Chapter Twenty-seven

JO SMOOTHED HER hands across her belly and thighs, settling the cool white linen pants into some sort of order. She looked at herself in the cabin's mirror and frowned critically. Tucked into the pants was a white tank top. A linen Asian-style jacket lay across the bed, waiting for her to put it on. Jo's long, black hair was loose and she pulled it back with one hand, debating whether or not to put it into a ponytail.

"What do you think, Mephy?" she asked of the big black cat, who was curled contentedly on a corner of the bed, his tail flicking from side to side.

"Leave it down. It looks beautiful."

Jo turned to see Helena Jones leaning on the doorjamb. Cadie's mother was looking elegant as always, in neatly pressed khaki shorts and polo shirt. Jo smiled and let her hair down.

"Can I come in?" Helena asked.

"Of course." Jo picked up the jacket and slipped it on, pulling her hair up and out so it spilled across the white material.

"See what I mean? Gorgeous," Helena observed, entering the small cabin, her eyes riveted on Jo.

Blushing beneath this scrutiny, Jo smiled shyly at Cadie's mother in the mirror. "Should I leave this open or do it up?" she asked, fiddling with the jacket buttons.

"Oh, open, definitely." Helena stood up and walked over to Jo. She reached up and adjusted the collar of the jacket, which had caught and folded over when Jo pulled it on. "There you go."

Jo waited patiently as Helena continued to fuss with her clothes. *She has something she wants to say,* she reasoned. *I hope it's not 'Keep your hands off my daughter.' Nah.*

Helena met patient blue eyes that held more than a touch of tolerant laughter in their twinkle. She laughed at herself and patted Jo's shoulder before backing off a little. "What am I fussing about?" she said wryly. "You look great, and you don't need me to tell you so."

"It's okay," Jo said quietly.

Helena looked up at her and Jo recognized the look, not the least because Cadie had very much inherited her mother's eyes.

"We haven't had a chance to really get to know each other, Jo," Helena said. "You were only in Madison a few days and, even though we've talked a lot on the phone, nothing beats getting to know someone in person."

Oh boy, where's she going with this, Jo wondered, her stomach tightening suddenly.

Helena saw the slightly panicked look on Jo's face and rushed to reassure her. "Oh, Jo, don't worry." She made a placatory gesture. "I was about to tell you that even though we haven't had a lot of time together, I knew the minute I met you that you and Cadie were perfectly matched."

Jo grinned. "Really?"

"Oh yes. I've never seen Cadie so relaxed...and contented. She doesn't have to be anything other than herself when she's with you, Jo. And that's more than Naomi could ever do for her."

Jo felt the last vestiges of insecurity over Cadie's ex-partner falling away. "I think I've always known that we had something she and Naomi never did," she said softly. "And of course, Cadie has said so. But thank you for confirming it."

Helena moved forward again and touched her palm gently to Jo's cheek. "Don't you ever worry about that, Jo," she said, equally quietly. "She adores you. And, truth be told, so do Stephen and I." She smiled at Jo's renewed blush. "We have no doubts at all that the two of you will make each other very happy."

Jo exhaled slowly. She had been strangely calm about meeting Cadie's parents, she remembered. Mainly, she suspected, because that day had been so bizarre, meeting her future in-laws had seemed like a doddle in comparison.

"We know you haven't planned a honeymoon," Helena said. "So, Stephen and I thought we'd...well, hopefully we haven't been too presumptuous." Helena held out an envelope. "We checked with your office manager...Doris, right?" Jo nodded and took the envelope. "To make sure you had enough time to take a week off. Go on, open it up."

Jo started to, lifting the flap and peering inside. It looked like an accommodation voucher and when she saw the name on the letterhead her eyebrows lifted. "Wow, Helena, that's very generous. Thank you."

Helena patted her hand gently. "Don't mention it. Now, we spoke to your friend Bill, and he's going to fly you both up there in his helicopter tonight." She grinned at her soon to be daughter-in-law. "After some celebrations, of course."

Jo laughed. "That'll kill Bill. Having to stay sober until he gets back here." She clutched the envelope to her chest and smiled at Helena. "Thank you. This means a lot."

Helena nodded. "It means a lot to us to be able to do it for you, Jo. Naomi never allowed us to make this kind of gesture." She paused, then added in a reflective tone, "It's odd. I feel more involved in Cadie's life now, even though she's on the other side of the world, than I ever did when she was with the senator. Thank you for not shutting us out."

Jo didn't say anything, just pulled the older woman into a hug, a move that surprised Helena, but pleased her more than she could say.

ACROSS THE COMPANIONWAY, in the other double berth, Cadie was also dressing. Her outfit matched Jo's except, instead of pants and a tank top, she wore a long sundress under her jacket. She was putting the finishing touches on her makeup when the knock came at the door.

"Come in," she said, not looking away from the mirror as she applied her mascara. Cadie heard someone enter. "I won't be a minute," she called.

"No worries," came the surprisingly deep response. Cadie smiled at herself as she screwed the lid back on the mascara tube. She had been waiting for a visit from one of the four parental units on board, but David Madison was probably the one she had least expected to come through the door.

Cadie rounded the corner and found the elder Madison standing uncomfortably in front of the bed, his hands buried deep in the pockets of his shorts. Cadie grinned. *He's so cute when he's flustered.* "Hello," she said.

David looked up at Cadie's approach and he found himself even more tongue-tied than usual. "G'day," he said, finally. "Gosh, Cadie you look terrific...just...you look terrific."

Cadie beamed at him. "Thank you." She waited while David obviously tried to gather his thoughts together into cogent sentences. Finally he sighed and sat down on the edge of the bed.

"I had a whole bunch of stuff I wanted to say to you," he said. "But, you know me. I'm not too good when it gets down to talking."

Cadie smiled and sat down next to him, taking his calloused right hand between her own and chafing it gently. "You do fine," she said. "Besides there's some stuff I wanted to say to you too."

"Yeah?"

"I wanted to say thank you for making me part of your family. For making me feel like I have a second set of parents. It's made leaving home a lot easier, knowing that I have another family here to welcome me."

In the five months since he and Maggie had sold Coonyabby and moved up here, David had had the chance to get to know his daughter's partner a lot better. But she never failed to surprise him with her open and warm personality. He cleared his throat. "You're always welcome, Cadie," he said gruffly, placing his other hand on top of hers. "That's one of the things I wanted to say." He felt Cadie bump him with her shoulder, encouraging him to continue. Sea-green eyes met his. "You gave me my daughter back."

Cadie felt tears stinging her eyes and she saw a hint of the same in David's. She shook her head slowly. "I think she would have come back to you anyway," she said. "She wanted to so badly."

"You made her feel like she could do it, though," David insisted.

Cadie conceded the point, shrugging slightly and smiling. "I love her," she said softly. "That makes everything possible. For both of us."

David nodded. After a few seconds' silence, he dug into his pocket and pulled out a small jewelry case. "We, uh, we wanted to give you both something to mark the day," he said. "We know you picked out your wedding bands, but these..." He opened the case carefully, exposing two rings. One was a woman's engagement ring, an emerald slightly darker than Cadie's eyes, set on a simple rose-gold band. The other was a man's signet ring, though it was slender enough to look good on a woman. "These we thought you could wear as well as the wedding rings," David continued. "My father gave them to us when we were married."

"Oh, David."

"If they don't fit, we can always get them resized," he said hastily, aware he was filling air in an effort not to be embarrassed.

"They're beautiful." Cadie picked out the signet ring and looked more closely at it. Inscribed on the gold shield was one word—Madison. She glanced up at David, who was watching her closely. "Do you mind if I choose this one?" she asked.

David was surprised, but he could suddenly see the symmetry of her choice. "Of course not," he replied. *Part of the family. Nice.*

Cadie put the ring back in its case next to its partner and closed the lid carefully. "Please thank Maggie for me," she said, and she reached up and kissed her father-in-law on the cheek.

"No worries," David said hoarsely.

PERFECT DAY. JO stood with her hands on her hips, gazing out across the glassy surface of the sea. The sky was cloudlessly blue, and the light breeze took the sting out of the sun's heat. *Just perfect.*

She felt about 50 pairs of eyes boring into her. Which wasn't surprising, considering she was currently the center of attention. All the partygoers had crowded around the cockpit of the Seawolf, though some, by necessity, had spilled onto the other boats. Jo stood with Paul and the marriage celebrant, Marilyn, as they waited for Cadie.

"Nervous?" Paul asked, a grin splitting his face from side to side.

Jo was about to answer him when she spotted the look on his face. "Oh, you're loving this, aren't you?" She slapped his shoulder affectionately.

"You bet," the tall man agreed. "How often do we get to see Jo Madison, monarch of the seas, flustered?"

"I am not flustered," Jo objected, pushing a lock of her hair back behind her ear. "I want to get started, that's all."

"Well, here's your chance, skipper," Paul said, nodding in the direction of the companionway. Cadie emerged into the sunshine and Jo immediately forgot about every other person onboard.

Perfect. She looks perfect, Jo thought, as she reached out and took Cadie's offered hand. Gently she pulled her closer and Cadie smiled up at Jo.

"Hello," she said softly.

"Hello," Jo replied. "You are beautiful."

The low voice curled around Cadie's senses and magically settled her nerves. She felt herself blushing under Jo's frank appraisal. "Likewise, darling," she whispered back. "Are you ready for this?"

"Oh yes," came Jo's reply, with no hesitation. "Marry me?"

"Happily," Cadie answered.

They turned together to face Marilyn, who had watched the quiet exchange with a knowing smile. The murmuring around the central group settled into an expectant silence that spread rapidly through the rest of the partygoers. Jo felt Cadie's hand squeeze hers and she changed her grip, entwining their fingers as they waited for the celebrant to begin.

"Welcome everyone, to this very special occasion for our friends, Jo and Cadie," Marilyn began. "They have chosen a variation on the traditional hand-fasting ceremony to express their love and commitment to each other. It is very much a ceremony of their own design, but incorporates symbols which have been passed down through centuries of similar rituals."

Between Marilyn and the happy couple was a small round table. On it were two candles, each one lit, and one larger, much taller candle, which was still unlit. In front of the candles was a long, wide, purple ribbon, on which sat the two wedding rings.

"Jo, Cadie, please take the wedding rings." The women reached forward and took their own gold bands, holding them in the palms of their upturned hands. "We have come together here in celebration of the joining together of Jo and Cadie," Marilyn continued, lifting her voice so all on board could hear. "There are many things to say about marriage. Much wisdom concerning the joining together of two souls has come our way through all paths of belief, and from many cultures. With each union, more knowledge is gained and more wisdom gathered. Though we are unable to give all of this knowledge to these two who stand before us, we can hope to leave with them the knowledge of love's strengths and the anticipation of the wisdom that comes with time. The law of life is love unto all beings. Without love, life is nothing; without love, death has no redemption."

The celebrant paused for breath and Jo felt the quiet peace around her. She glanced at Cadie and found an expression of utter contentment on her partner's face. *Like an angel*, Jo thought, drinking in the love that shone from Cadie. At that moment Cadie looked her way and smiled.

Cadie let the happiness well up inside her. She and Jo had spent many hours searching for the right words for their marriage ceremony, and when they had finally found a combination they both loved, all their nerves had dropped away. Instead there was nothing but anticipation. Now, feeling their friends and family becoming absorbed in the words and the meanings behind them, it felt perfect to Cadie.

"Marriage is a bond to be entered into only after considerable thought and reflection," Marilyn continued. She looked up and beyond the immediate circle of Jo, Cadie and their parents. "Jo tells me that she had known Cadie about three weeks when she asked her to marry her." There were grins all around the yacht. "But after watching these two over the past 10 months or so, I think I can safely theorize that they have done most of their reflection over the course of many lifetimes together."

There were agreeing murmurs and "hear, hears" from the watching crowd and both Cadie and Jo blushed.

"As with any aspect of life, marriage has its cycles, its ups and its downs, its trials and its triumphs. With full understanding of this, Jo and Cadie have come here today to be joined as one. Others would ask, at this time, who gives the bride in marriage, but, as a woman is not property to be bought and sold, given and taken, I ask simply if they come of their own will and if they have their families' blessing."

Marilyn turned to Cadie. "Cadie, is it true that you come of your own free will and accord?"

"Yes, it is true," Cadie replied, with a quick smile at Jo.

"With whom do you come and whose blessings accompany you?" the celebrant asked.

Stephen and Helena stepped forward slightly and stood behind Cadie's left shoulder.

"She comes with us, her parents," said Stephen.

"And she is accompanied by all of her family's blessings," said Helena.

Marilyn turned to Jo. "And you, Jossandra, is it true that you come of your own free will and accord?"

Jo tried to speak but emotion clogged her voice, suddenly. She cleared her throat and replied, "Yes, it is true."

"And with whom do you come and whose blessings accompany you?"

This time it was David and Maggie who stepped forward to stand behind their daughter's right shoulder. Jo held her breath for a moment, realizing that this was the ultimate acceptance back into the family she had abandoned so long ago. Cadie squeezed her hand gently.

"She comes with us, her parents," said David, in a clear, strong voice.

"And she is accompanied by all of her family's blessings." Maggie's voice wavered with emotion, but there was no mistaking her happiness.

"Jo, Cadie, please face each other and join your left hands." Marilyn waited as the two women did so, their eyes locked on each other. "Above you are the stars, below you is the water, and below that again are the stones. As time passes, remember ... Like a stone should your love be firm. Like a star should your love be constant. Like water should your love be fluid and adaptable. Let the powers of the mind and of the intellect guide you in your marriage. Let the strength of your wills bind you together. Let the power of love and desire make you happy, and the strength of your dedication make you inseparable.

"Be close, but not too close. Possess one another, yet be understanding. Have patience with one another, for storms will come, but they will pass quickly. Be free in giving affection and warmth. Have no fear and let not the ways of the unenlightened give you unease, for your gods are with you always."

Jo heard a small sniffle from somewhere behind her and a quick glance told her that Helena was dabbing at her eyes as Stephen wrapped an arm around her shoulders.

"We're making your mother cry," she whispered conspiratorially.

A twinkling green gaze smiled back at her. "Yours too," came the answering whisper.

"Jo," Marilyn continued. "I have not the right to bind you to Cadie. Only you have this right. If it is your wish, say so at this time and place your ring in her hand."

Jo's voice was steadier this time. "It is my wish." She gave Cadie the ring they had selected.

"Cadie, if it is your wish for Jo to be bound to you, place the ring on her finger."

Cadie changed her grip on Jo's left hand and gently slid the gold band into place on her lover's ring finger. She bent slightly and kissed it.

"Cadie, I have not the right to bind you to Jo. Only you have this right. If it is your wish, say so at this time and place your ring in her hand."

"Oh, it's my wish."

A soft chuckle broke out among the crowd at Cadie's tone and Jo grinned as she took the ring.

"Jo, if it is your wish for Cadie to be bound to you, place the ring on her finger."

Jo did so, doing as Cadie had done and kissing the band softly once it was in place.

"Jo and Cadie have written their own vows, which they will now exchange," Marilyn said, stepping back a little and letting the two women have the floor.

They had decided earlier that Jo would go first, but now that the moment had come, she was completely tongue-tied. Their left hands were still clasped and Cadie pulled them closer until she could kiss Jo's knuckles.

"Want me to go first?" she whispered.

Jo cleared her throat and then shook her head. "No. I'm okay."

"Time to 'fess up, Jo-Jo," came a playful call from the back of the crowd, breaking the tension.

"Quiet in the cheap seats," Jo retorted, grinning at her friends.

"Aye, aye, skipper."

"Oh, shut up." It was a welcome relief and reminded Jo that she was surrounded by people who loved her. She took a deep breath and turned back to Cadie, drawn in once more by the warmth shining from those sea-green eyes.

"There are an awful lot of things I've done in my life that I'm not proud of," she said quietly. Immediately, the murmuring and laughter around them settled back into attentive silence. "I never felt like I deserved to be loved the way you love me. But when you arrived in my life, it was like you laid me bare. I couldn't resist you." She smiled at the slowly rising blush that colored Cadie's cheeks. "You have taught me so much about trusting again. About recognizing true love. About letting myself be loved." A tear slipped from Cadie's right eye and Jo reached up and gently caught it with the pad of her thumb. "I have some promises to make to you.

"You already know that I will love you forever." They smiled at each other. "But there is more to this than that, isn't there?" Cadie nodded. "I promise to listen to you closely, and speak to you honestly. I promise not to expect perfection from you, nor to demean you, or take you for granted. I will hold your welfare equal to or greater than my own, and I vow to put our relationship first, above all things. And I will thank you in my heart every day, for giving me back my life."

Cadie couldn't speak for several seconds after Jo finished. They hadn't shared their vows with each other before the ceremony and Jo's had come as a revelation. *She knows exactly what's important to me,* Cadie thought. She reached up and touched Jo's cheek, smiling tearily.

"You're welcome, my love," she said softly. "My turn, I guess." Jo nodded.

Cadie took a deep breath. "When I met you I was in a very bad place," she began. "I had lost sight of so many things in my life, I didn't really know who I was anymore, or where I was meant to be going. And then you appeared, like magic." She smiled, the joy radiating out from her. "You are my beacon, Jo. You led me home." Now it was Cadie's turn to brush a tear from Jo's cheek. "I have promises to make to you, too. I promise to treat you, always, with loving respect. I promise to mend my own mistakes, and forgive easily. I promise to defend and support you. I will walk beside you on our path, but I will not try to choose for you, nor ask you to make my decisions for me. And I will also thank you in my heart every day, for giving me back my freedom." Her voice cracked on the last word, and her own tears spilled over once again.

There was hardly a dry eye on board the three yachts, and the sound of quiet sniffling came from every direction. Basking in their connection, Jo and Cadie leaned towards each other until their foreheads touched.

Even Marilyn, a veteran of touching moments, was forced to wipe her eyes before continuing. She leaned forward and picked up the purple ribbon. Jo and Cadie turned back towards the celebrant. Marilyn draped the ribbon over their hands.

"I bind Jo and Cadie to the vows that they each have made." She wrapped the ribbon around their hands three times. "However, this binding is not tied, so that neither is restricted by the other, and the binding is only enforced by both their wills."

With their free hands, Cadie and Jo picked up a lit candle each.

"Your separate lives are symbolized by the separate candles you now bear," Marilyn said. "As you join their flames to make one flame, know that at that moment you are willingly joining your lives forever. Is this what you wish?"

"It is," Jo and Cadie said together.

"Then so be it."

They tipped their individual candles together until the flames merged and then lowered it down to light the big candle in the middle of the table. As the wick flickered into life, they both spoke.

"Heart to thee, soul to thee, body to thee." They replaced their individual candles and turned to each other. "Now and forever."

As they kissed, finally, their hands still bound, applause and cheers broke out around them. But Jo and Cadie were largely oblivious, lost in each other. Not even the meowing of a large black cat as he wove between their feet and bumped against their shins, could distract them from their own, private, celebration.

JO CLOSED HER eyes and let her head fall back as the heat of the newly-risen sun began to sink into her bones. Behind her, at the top of wooden steps she was sprawled across, was a luxurious bungalow. It was raised on stilts above the still, clear waters of a large lagoon, which lapped, tantalizingly, at the bottom step. In front of Jo there was nothing but empty sea and the shimmering sun.

Jo felt wickedly contented. *Tired, but contented,* she thought. She and Cadie had arrived at the resort late the night before and by mutual consent they had done little more than collapse into bed and fall asleep in each other's arms. *Plenty of time for exploring our little world here,* Jo had decided as she drifted off.

She leaned back on her elbows, which rested on the deck. With one hand she pushed her sunglasses back up her nose, the sunlight glinting on the ring her parents had given her. Jo gazed at it. *That was a pleasant surprise,* she thought. *I've always loved this ring.* Cadie had produced the small jewelry box as they were climbing into bed and Jo had thought it absolutely fitting that Cadie had chosen the signet ring. She fingered the emerald setting of her mother's ring absently. *And now I have a constant reminder of Cadie's eyes, even when she's not with me.* Jo smiled.

CADIE EMERGED FROM sleep slowly and rolled towards Jo's expected warmth. The realization that there was an empty space in the bed brought her fully awake. It took a few seconds of blinking at the unfamiliar surroundings for her to remember where she was. The thought brought a small smile to her face.

Cadie sat up in bed and looked around the small but luxurious apartment. Everything was open plan, the large bed dominating this part of the space, the walls lined with bookshelves filled with classic literature. To her right was the living area, comfortable seats sitting on a glass panel in the floor that allowed the occupants to watch the wildlife swimming under the bungalow. A large plasma screen television nestled against the far wall, and beyond that was a well-appointed bathroom that included a huge bath that overlooked the lagoon.

My parents rock, Cadie decided as she took in her surroundings. *I'd heard about this place, but I never thought we'd get the chance to come up here.* It had taken over an hour in Bill's chopper to reach the exclusive resort which was north of the Whitsundays and priced to exclude all but the world's rich and famous.

Cadie stretched and caught sight of a familiar dark head and torso poking up above the level of the decking outside. The bedroom and its decking were shielded from the other bungalows sprinkled around the lagoon by two large rattan dividers, affording this side of the bungalow complete privacy. Cadie therefore had no qualms about slipping out of bed and padding, naked, out onto the deck.

She slid in behind Jo, spreading her legs on either side of her partner's long torso. Jo's hair was up in a loose bun and Cadie took the opportunity to kiss the nape of her neck softly.

"Hello, wife," Jo purred, dropping her head back until it rested on Cadie's shoulder.

"I like how that sounds," Cadie whispered, kissing any exposed skin she could find.

"Me too," Jo agreed.

Cadie's arms wrapped around Jo's waist and her hands traveled north, cupping Jo's breasts playfully. "Aren't you rather overdressed, wife?" she murmured close to her partner's ear, even as one hand slid under the strap of Jo's swimsuit and slipped it off her shoulder.

Jo shivered involuntarily. "Probably," she answered. "I didn't really think about it, to be honest. I just got up and put the suit on." She reached up and kissed Cadie's cheek. "I'm more than happy to take it off for you, though," she burred.

Cadie chuckled, recognizing the tone of Jo's voice for what it was, a blatant come-on. Grinning, she decided a little more playing was in order. "Oh, I don't know, I could go for some breakfast," she said playfully, as her fingers continued to tease Jo. "By the way, how do we get food?" she asked. "We don't seem to have a kitchen."

Jo was finding Cadie's wandering fingers incredibly distracting and she groaned. "Um, we call room service, and a little man comes out in a boat from the main island," she finally said, trying to ignore the wide grin on Cadie's face. "You are a wicked, wicked woman."

"And you love it," Cadie confirmed.

"No question." Jo wriggled out of Cadie's grip and stood up. She turned to face her partner and Cadie was treated to a silhouetted vision as the rising sun formed a halo around Jo's lean and shapely figure.

Cadie leaned back on her elbows. "You are beautiful," she said breathlessly, gazing up at Jo, whose features were in shadow, though her smile was evident.

"You're biased."

"And you're still beautiful," Cadie retorted, long used to Jo's strategies for deflecting compliments.

Jo continued to smile as she reached up and let her hair down, allowing it to spill across her shoulders. Cadie sucked in a long, slow breath, loving every minute of the show her lover was putting on. Jo slipped the other strap off her shoulder and wriggled seductively out of her swimsuit, letting it pool around her feet. Cadie groaned.

"You know," Jo said casually as she dropped to her knees between Cadie's legs. "That privacy thing could come in very handy." She leaned forward, sliding her body over Cadie's torso. "If we wanted to, we could make love, right here, on the deck."

Cadie felt the tingles from the tips of her toes to the top of her head as Jo ducked down and began dropping slow, sensuous kisses across her neck and breasts. "We could do that," she murmured, wrapping her legs around Jo's hips and pulling her closer. "But I know for a fact that that big bed in there is a lot softer and easier on the bones than this."

Jo's mouth claimed hers in a searing kiss that made Cadie forget everything but the heat they were generating, quite apart from the sunshine beating down on them both. Her hand slid up into Jo's hair, tangling in the long, silky locks. Jo moved against her and soon they were rocking and sliding together in a sweaty, sensual tangle of limbs.

"Then again," Cadie gasped once Jo's lips found another target. "We do have a week. I guess...oh...uh, I guess we could make love on every square inch of this place if we w-wanted to." She arched as Jo teased a particularly sensitive spot. "God, woman."

A throaty chuckle came from somewhere south of Cadie's navel.

"Jo, darling, we're going to get sunburned in the most wicked...p-places," Cadie reasoned dreamily. Not that she was feeling in the least bit rational at that moment. Far from it. *In fact...* A surge of passion claimed her and Cadie felt herself slipping into blissful oblivion.

Jo made a decision and took a firmer grip on Cadie's body, using her powerful legs to push them both upright. She paused for a few seconds to regain her balance as they threatened to topple backwards into the ocean, then surged up and forward, walking them across the deck and through the open sliding glass door, into the cool shade of the bedroom.

Kissing Cadie deeply, Jo carried her inside. Her wife's skin felt like it was on fire and all she wanted was to fall into bed and ravish this gloriously sexy woman until they had exhausted themselves. She turned so her back was to the bed and then dropped slowly.

Cadie had a vague sense of how strong her new wife was and then suddenly she was astride those slim hips and gazing down into impossibly blue eyes. They were both breathing heavily and for a few seconds they gazed at each other.

"I don't ever want to stop feeling like this," Jo whispered.

"We don't ever have to stop, Jo-Jo," Cadie replied. Jo's hair spilled across the pillow and Cadie didn't think she had ever seen anything as entrancing. "We can do this forever. I'm yours forever."

Nothing will ever beat this feeling, Jo thought, mesmerized by the deep love shining out of Cadie's eyes. *Nothing.* "And I'm yours, my love. Now and forever."

The End

Also available by
Cate Swannell

Heart's Passage

Jo Madison is a yacht skipper in the Whitsunday Islands of Australia's Great Barrier Reef. She has a dark and violent past she is trying to leave far behind her, and the last thing on her mind is love. But when Cadie Jones, long-time partner of a US senator, sails in to her life, her priorities change.

There's no rest for the formerly wicked, however and Jo's past comes back to haunt her, throwing herself and Cadie into mortal danger. Jo is forced to rely on skills and weapons she had thought long-buried, while Cadie struggles to balance her Midwest life against her attraction to the mysterious woman.

Set in the splendor of Australia's tropics, *Heart's Passage* traces Jo and Cadie's rocky path to an uncertain future.

ISBN 1-932300-09-0

Cate Swannell is a journalist and writer living on the east coast of Australia with her boycat Siggy and her Dell. She was born in Birmingham, UK, before moving to Australia with her parents when she was six. Her home on the web can be found at www.kotb.net. *No Ocean Deep* is her second novel. Her third novel is currently residing halfway between her brain and her hard drive.

Printed in the United States
53822LVS00003B/52-69